I0636144

The Luckless Prince

Rie Sheridan Rose

THE LUCKLESS PRINCE

Copyright © 2011 by Rie Sheridan Rose

All Rights Reserved. No part of this book
may be reproduced or transmitted in any form
or by any means, electronic or mechanical,
including photocopying, recording, or by any
information storage and retrieval system, without
permission in writing from the publisher.

Names, characters, and incidents depicted
in this book are products of the author's
imagination or are used fictitiously.

Any resemblance to actual events, locales,
organizations, or persons, living or dead,
is entirely coincidental and beyond the
intent of the author or the publisher.

ISBN 978-1-77400-033-5

Look for us online at
http://www.DragonMoonPress.com

To all those friends *** forced to give me feedback on the original (especially Darcy, Wyndie, Tam, James, and Atlanta, Pher, and Susie G.) – see it worked!

And to Newell, as always, for everything.

Acknowledgments

Thanks to my parents, Bill and Kathalee, for never telling me I couldn't do it; to Patricia Gibson for her wonderful pre-submission edit of the original; to Ariana Overton for polishing the original. Thanks to Ginjer and Debra for waiting on us all those nights working on changes. Huge thanks to Dorris Beaird for her patience with my forcing her husband to read and reread those changes while she waited to drive him home. Thanks to my beta readers: Summer Wilbur and Frank and Julia Bielowicz. Thanks to Zumaya Publications for giving the book a new home, and especially Elizabeth Burton for showing me how powerful an edit can be.

And a huge thank you with sugar on top to my critique partner, Jim Reader, for catching all those things the ladies and I missed in the first incarnation and forcing me to think of new ways to say things. This version is much better.

Chapter 1

"If you look here, Your Highness..." High Chancellor Marcell Tolkot pointed one thin finger at the large vellum map spread on the oak conference table. "...you will see how the face of the continent altered when your grandfather united the provinces of Bellesaria and Fellstone in the year fourteen-twenty-one and settled his capital here at Crown Keep.

"He chose this castle as his stronghold because of its long history as a seat of power and culture. This final action effectively created the consolidated kingdom of Irthlan on the mainland with your uncle, Duke Roderick, as your father's representative in the south. Of course, since the duke's untimely death, his son has assumed those duties, acting as viceroy in the lower provinces."

Stefan craned his neck, trying to see the map from his position at the back of the room. As a mere squire, his presence in the class was no more recognized than that of a prize hound, but he was much more interested in the subject than his master.

Prince Roland Frederickson had no head for history or politics, preferring to spend his time with sword in hand or a book of romantic tales. The only lessons to capture his attention were those of tactics and strategy—earning him consistent praise from his fencing master and General Teodore Gunderson, but headshakes from Tolkot.

The high chancellor shook the sleeves of his robe into place with a self-important sniff, continuing his lecture.

"Of course, there are still the island chieftains, who claim sovereignty, but they are of little consequence."

Roland leaned back in his chair, eyes on his quill as he slowly riffled the spines against the grain. He murmured a response with a cool, matter-of-fact calm that made Stefan uneasy.

"My mother was the daughter of one of those chieftains, if you recall. I believe my father considers the island kingdoms important allies."

Tolkot's equine features bloomed scarlet, and he tugged at the thin wisp of beard dirtying his chin.

"I meant no disrespect to her late majesty, Your Highness. Of course the king holds *all* his allies dear. Shall I continue?" He fussed with the map and books on the table. "We were to cover the history of the last war this afternoon."

The prince rose to his feet with a yawn. "Not today, Marcell. I have had enough politics for the moment."

"But, Your Highness—"

The prince waved his hand at the chancellor in dismissal; the heavy ruby ring on his finger flashed in the sunlight slanting through the narrow windows.

"It is too lovely an afternoon to sit tied to a classroom. Coming, Stefan?" Without waiting to see if his squire followed, the prince strode out of the chamber.

Stefan flashed an apologetic smile at the chancellor and slipped out after his master.

"Fetch your lute and meet me on the roof," Roland called over his shoulder, bounding up the winding staircase leading to the top of the tower.

Stefan shook his head indulgently and hurried to follow his master's orders. By the time he had retrieved the instrument from their rooms and slipped through one of the many secret shortcuts scattered through the ancient castle to join Roland on the flat roof, the older boy was leaning over the battlements with a book in hand.

Stefan heaved himself up onto the crenellations, settled back with his lute, and began to play one of Roland's favorite ballads.

Roland read silently, and Stefan hid a smile. How like the prince to demand his presence and then ignore him.

"Listen to this, Stefan. 'And thus Angvarad slew the last of the interlopers and, turning to his bride, promised undying fealty with a kiss.'" Roland closed the book with a snap and laid it on the wall beside him with a heavy sigh. "Now, that's an adventure," he murmured, tucking a stray lock of russet hair behind his ear. "Much more interesting than Marcell's boring history lessons."

He gazed out over the shimmering Golden Heath surrounding the castle at Crown Keep. "Somewhere out there is a quest where I will be the hero, Stefan. When I am here on the battlements, I can almost feel it calling to me. Can you feel it too?"

"Aye, my lord." Stefan stared out over the plain as well, noting the depth of gold that spoke of ripened grain. Perched atop the weathered wall of the castle, his right leg tucked beneath him as he leaned against a merlon, he strummed the lute. Music rippled from his fingers like the restless breeze as he hummed the melody under his breath.

A breath of wind ruffled his hair, and he shivered at the touch.

"The air is chill. Do you smell the frost on the breeze? Soon it will be too cold to linger up here."

"I suppose you're right...another boring winter cooped in this drafty old prison." Roland leaned his elbows on the wall, his emerald eyes focused dreamily on the distant horizon as he rested his chin on his cupped hands. The lock of hair swept forward against his cheek once more, and the prince tucked it back behind his ear impatiently, the sun drawing another flash of crimson fire from his heavy ring.

"I would give my soul to travel to those mountains there!" Roland gestured toward the distant horizon. "Or *anywhere*, for that matter. Just look down there!" He pointed at the bustling docks nestled along the riverbanks. "All those boats will be heading downriver to the sea. And then...who knows where?" He hopped up on the wall beside Stefan. "I think that is Jarome's raft over against the far bank. See there?"

Stefan looked where Roland indicated. The raft was large, and appeared well-kept to his sharp eyes. Several men swarmed about the deck, one brawny figure in particular catching his eye as a spark of light reflected off some ornament about the trader's neck.

A shiver ran of premonition ran through him. Something strange was in the air.

"I grow tired of eternal cosseting." Roland picked up his book and jumped down from the wall, spinning like a child on the broad flat battlements. "I want to see the world! History and etiquette bore me to tears. I want adventure, like Angvarad and Gilthesand had!" He shook the heavy volume of legends for emphasis. "At my age, my grandfather had built his kingdom from a single duchy to half the continent. By Father's age, he ruled the entire land."

"And was dead soon after. Patience, my prince. You are young yet."

"And you're a bearded ancient? Don't forget you're younger than I am."

Stefan grinned.

"We should go down soon." He heaved a reluctant sigh. "The king expects you at table this evening."

"Always the conscience." Roland chuckled. "All right. Coming?"

Stefan hopped off the wall, staggering as his left leg took more of his weight than anticipated. He regained his balance with a frown of frustration. Even after all this time, he sometimes forgot his limitations.

They descended the broad tower stairs toward the throne room. One hand lightly tracing the cool polished stone of the wall, Roland rounded the corner leading to the Great Hall. He pulled up short at the sound of voices and held up a hand. Stefan halted behind him, covering the strings of the lute so they wouldn't accidentally sound and give them away. Roland leaned against the wall, eavesdropping. Stefan bent to whisper protest, but the prince glared him into acceptance.

"The shipment of furs is ready to leave for Stormhaven, My Liege." The voice belonged to Captain Jarome Boatman, leader of the river traders.

"What a life they must lead," Stefan murmured with a touch of envy.

"Just think," the prince whispered back. "Nights under the stars, days spent journeying the river between Crown Keep and the sea..." His eyes shone with excitement.

"When will you depart?" Stefan recognized the gravelly voice of the king.

"We'll set out early, my lord, with your permission."

"Very good."

He could picture the king's measured nod, having seen it so many times.

Roland turned to him, face aglow.

"This is my chance, Stefan!" he whispered, breathless with eagerness. "If I can convince Father to let me go with the traders on this run to Stormhaven..."

Before Stefan could answer, he heard Jarome coming their way, the sailor's measured, rolling gait as distinctive as his voice. Not wanting the man to catch them eavesdropping on the king, he dragged Roland up the stair until they were out of sight

The prince nodded his thanks then broke free from Stefan's hand. With an air of perfect innocence, he bounded down the stairs again.

"What ho, Captain? How fare you?"

Jarome laughed. "Well enough, scoundrel. Listening at keyholes again, are you?"

Stefan saw Roland's back stiffen at the tone, and then relax. As the king's oldest and dearest friend, Jarome held the right to a few liberties.

"Aye, sir," the prince admitted with a rueful grin.

"Learn anything of interest?"

"How long is the journey to Stormhaven?"

"Depends on many factors, my lad. If you spent as much time on your maps as your swordplay, you might know." Jarome chuckled. "It takes five days or thereabouts for a normal run. Sometimes the river favors us, sometimes she throws a tantrum."

"You speak as if the river lives," Roland scoffed.

"Aye. That she does. She is my lady, boy, and more alive than some of the skirts I've known." The trader winked. "Now, run along, lad. I know your father waits for you. You mustn't keep the king idling while you chatter in the hallway." He reached out a bear-paw hand and ruffled Roland's hair.

The prince ducked away, face stained crimson with embarrassment.

"Good day to you, sir. Come, Stefan!"

Stefan followed as quickly as he could, greeting the sailor with a nod as they continued into the throne room. Swallowing against a sudden nervous lump in his throat, he slid into his place in the shadows beside Roland's throne.

The prince bowed to his father.

The king sat at ease in his scarlet robes of office, a vivid splash of color that brightened the pale-stone room. Frederick Benedickson was still a handsome man, although his chestnut hair now glittered with strands of silver, and lines of care framed a stern mouth once quick to laugh.

At eighteen, he had met his queen, Catianya, and fallen instantly in love—an impulse to passion Roland had inherited from them both. Only their lack of an heir marred their happiness as the young king struggled to rule with honor.

Then Roland's birth blessed their union, and the land flourished as the child grew. Frederick's praises were sung throughout the kingdom.

When Queen Catianya lived, the castle rang with laughter, Stefan remembered wistfully.

When he had been found wandering in the wilderness by a royal hunting party, the golden-haired queen took the foundling waif to her heart, and he had adored her. He had understood nothing they said to him—whether as a result of trauma or foreign birth, none could say—and the queen had spent many an hour teaching him to communicate.

Then she succumbed to a fever two years later, and he felt twice bereft, although he remembered no other mother. Yet during long nights spent comforting the mourning prince came teasing wisps of memory too fragile for him to catch hold of.

Since the queen's death, Frederick seemed to have lost any emotion save for the fiercely protective love he felt for his son. The heart of the realm had turned to ash.

"Roland, my son." A faint smile flitted across the king's rugged features, and Roland's face lit up.

"Hello, Father."

"Where were you hiding this morning? You missed your lesson with Master Fortenbraes. He is pleased with your fencing skills. He cannot stop talking about your prowess with the broadsword, although skipping today's rapier lesson will not win you his favor."

Roland sighed, slowly mounting to his smaller throne, and sinking down on it. Stefan could feel disappointment radiating from the prince.

"What troubles you, Roland?" the king asked.

"My lord, I am nigh twenty years old, and I've rarely left Crown Keep. My time is spent in lessons and meaningless practice. It has no grounding in reality. How can I rule cities I've never even seen? My journeys have been few, and always I am escorted by a squadron of guards, at the very least. That is no way to learn of my people."

"Where do you wish to go? Rushing headlong about the countryside with no plan of action is no way to learn, either. You are my only child, Roland. If anything happens to you..."

Stefan heard the catch in the king's voice. It revealed so much Frederick could never say aloud.

"...the throne passes from our House to your cousin Norfulk," the king continued. "I would not willingly subject my people to his rule, even if he is my brother's son. Although Chancellor Tolkot reports that his regency goes well in the southern regions, I do not feel comfortable with the notion of him ascending to the throne. There is something...unnatural about him."

Stefan had seen Roland's older cousin only twice, and both occasions had left him with a sense of dread so strong the feeling took weeks to fade. The tall, dark-haired Norfulk radiated a malevolence that abraded Stefan's soul, though no one else seemed to sense it. He felt as if the duke's strange copper eyes stared straight through him. He had made a point to stay out of the man's sight as much as possible.

Rumors abounded that Norfulk dabbled in sorcery. Although not unheard-of, magic was a rare gift and those who wielded it considered less than human... or more. For a member of the royal line to hold such powers was looked at as cause for suspicion, especially as it was said villagers sometimes disappeared from Crypticia Keep without a trace. Whispers said Duke Roderick himself had died under mysterious circumstances, after a swift and painful illness.

With a start, Stefan pulled his concentration back to the conversation. Whatever resulted from this discussion would affect him as well, so he really should pay attention.

"I planned for you to take the crown when you come of age next spring," Frederick continued. "I would much rather pass it to you of my own volition, and offer you counsel for a time, than leave it as my father did."

Roland sighed, his head falling back against soft golden cushions. He let the book fall from his hand to the floor.

King Benedick had fallen in a minor uprising during Frederick's sixteenth summer, leaving a frightened boy to be thrust unprepared onto the throne. He sympathized with the king's position, but Stefan also knew Roland's spirit needed an outlet for its restlessness.

"Of course, I will honor your wishes, Father." The prince's voice was flat and lifeless. "You are my king as well as parent. It's simply—"

"Would you care to represent me in a fur deal?"

Stefan caught the ghost of a smile flitting across the king's lips. Roland sat upright, and he could almost feel the prince's heart racing.

"Sire?"

"Captain Jarome goes at dawn to Stormhaven. Would you care to travel with him and negotiate with the fur merchants for me? You know something of furs and their quality. It will give you a chance to see some of the kingdom without the constraint of the Guard but under the guardianship of one I trust. Perhaps we can arrange a trip across the Heath to the sea in the spring."

"Do you mean it?"

"I *am* the king—some consider my word good," Frederick replied in dry amusement.

"But why now, Father?"

Frederick smiled, his eyes focused on a far-away memory.

"Because I remember a boyhood spent without ever seeing my kingdom unless a state escort traveled with me, not even on my wedding trip." He shook his head. "Sometimes I tend to forget how it felt. Go with Jarome, but come back in one piece. I command you," he finished sternly, but his gaze held a fond softness.

"Thank you, sire!" Roland leapt to his feet. "You won't regret it."

"Just take care, Roland. And keep that temper of yours under control. I shall be very displeased if you get thrown overboard for brawling."

Roland flushed at the deserved rebuke.

Stefan sighed inwardly. The prince's gravest fault lay in his quickness to anger. The fire of his temper matched the red-gold of his hair. Stefan had honed his diplomacy skills keeping that temper from flaring and, when he failed, polished them more by making amends.

"Yes, my liege," mumbled the prince.

"And, as for you, Stefan," the king called, "come out of the shadows, lad."

He stepped forward, kneeling awkwardly at the foot of the throne.

"My liege."

Frederick's hand rested on his head.

"Take good care of Roland, my boy. I'll rest easier knowing you travel with him. Despite your youth, you have a wisdom my son needs. You are the conscience he tries to ignore."

Stefan flushed at hearing his own thoughts put into words.

"I will do my best, milord."

"I know you will, lad, though I do not envy you the duty."

Stefan glanced sideways at Roland.

"I will take pleasure in the task."

"Go along with you both. You've much to prepare before dawn."

Roland started forward, as if to embrace his father, but halted before he completed the gesture. Instead, he bowed then ran from the room.

Stefan saw longing in the king's eyes, and wished Roland had seen it, too. Lurching to his feet, he stepped forward and laid a tentative hand on the arm of the king's throne.

"He loves you, my lord. More than he knows how to say."

Frederick looked down at him with a grateful smile. He patted the boy's hand.

"I know, lad. I just wish we both had the strength to tell each other so. Go on, now. The brunt of preparation will fall on your head if I know Roland."

Stefan laughed.

"'Tis true, my lord." He bowed, scooped up the abandoned book, and started for the door.

"Stefan." The king's voice halted him.

"Yes, my lord?" He turned, curious what other task the king might set.

"Keep him safe."

"I'll do my best. You have my word on it."

Chapter 2

Roland trotted through the halls, excitement surging through him like fine wine. He could hardly contain his joy. He wanted to shout to the world, "Finally, I leave this prison of a castle!"

Reaching the kitchen, he scanned the large stone chamber impatiently. Three huge fireplaces ranged along one wall, spits turning under the less than watchful eyes of the kitchen boys. Tantalizing scents of roasting meats and fresh bread mingled in the warm air. Smoke from the cook fires tickled the throat and added its woodsy tang.

He snatched a cooling roll off a tray as he passed, breaking it in two and savoring the taste. Even plain bread seemed sweeter in light of his father's decision. On the far side of the room, he peered through a yawning archway down the wide stair leading to the root and wine cellars. Nothing stirred in that direction.

Hearing a clash of pans in the scullery, he called loudly, "Sara, news! Are you there?"

A buxom girl with coiled blond braids appeared, wiping her hands on a cloth.

"Aye, milord. What brings you to the kitchens when you'll be at table in scarce an hour?"

"Can you fix provisions for a week's travel? And, perhaps, a skin of red wine from the south vineyards?"

"Are you going away, milord, and without a word of farewell?" she replied with a flirtatious pout.

"Don't tease me, girl!" Roland laughed, slipping an

arm around her waist. "You know I would never leave you unprovided for. You warm my bed too well." An arrangement that was satisfactory to both and placed no ties on either—as long as it remained a secret, which, so far, it had.

He spun her in a circle until she squealed in protest then leaned over to whisper in her ear, "Can you keep a secret?"

"Don't I always?" she answered with a hint of throaty chuckle.

"I travel downriver tomorrow with Jarome. Can you believe it? Finally, to get out of this blasted town without the Guard breathing down my neck!"

"Then why do you need provisions? Don't the rafters feed their crews?"

"Some secrets I keep, my girl." He kissed her with a resounding smack. "Remember, not a word to anyone."

"As you command, my prince."

Whistling off-key, Roland hurried back to his chambers. As he passed the room assigned to Master Fortenbraes, someone called his name. Turning, he found the slender swordmaster standing in his open doorway.

"What occupies your thoughts, young master?" the man asked with a chuckle. "You seem in an awful hurry for someone who was indisposed just this morning."

Roland felt his face heat under the veiled rebuke.

"I apologize for missing my lesson, Master Fortenbraes. It was foolish of me."

"Everyone needs a missed lesson now and then, my lord." The silver-haired fencer stepped back from the doorway and gestured. "Come in a moment. I have something to give you."

Curiosity welling, Roland followed his teacher inside. He glanced about the sparely appointed room with interest—he'd never been invited into the sanctum before. One wall was covered with mounted weapons, from a conventional foil and rapier to an elaborate jagged-edged short sword with a sharply curved blade that was like nothing the prince had ever seen.

Fortenbraes crossed the room to a locked chest and opened it with a key worn about his neck.

"Your father and I have discussed it, and we think it is time you received this portion of your inheritance."

The swordsman lifted a tooled-leather scabbard from the chest. He turned back to the prince and held it out. There was a sword in it, a richly detailed hilt visible beyond the leather.

"You have gifted hands with a sword, Your Highness, though you need to realize that the tactics and history Teodore and Chancellor Tolkot strive to teach you go together. You may learn all the techniques of the blade and still fall to an enemy who understands the strategies of ambush and espionage. But take this to keep you safe upon your travels."

Roland lifted the sword from his teacher's hands, drawing it out of the scabbard. It was a beautifully wrought blade, with protective runes etched into the gleaming surface.

"It's exquisite," he breathed.

"It was your grandfather's sword. It was in his hand as he battled the lords of Bellesaria and Fellstone in Fangspur Cove. It has a tradition of honor and courage. May it continue that tradition."

Roland felt a roil of emotions rush through him—

hope that he did not dishonor his grandfather's memory, desire to wield the sword in the field, guilt that the gentle gibes about his studies were true.

"I will do my best," he whispered.

"That is all anyone can do." Fortenbraes gave a measured nod.

Re-sheathing the blade, Roland returned the nod.

"Thank you, Master Fortenbraes."

Carrying the sword in thoughtful reverie, he continued to his own chambers, nodding greetings to guards and servants as he passed. He knew he was well liked by the inhabitants of the keep, despite the tendency of his temper to flare. Stefan had told him it was because they recognized the good heart behind the fiery demeanor...he hoped it was true.

Arriving at his suite, he leaned the sword against the wall just inside the door and hurried to the wardrobe, dragging out clothing at random. Shimmering silks and heavy velvet glowed like jewels in the torchlight illuminating the cozy chamber. The smell of freshening herbs wafted from the interior of the cabinet as Roland glanced at each item. What did not suit his fancy he discarded, and soon a welter of garments littered the flagstones to supplement the soft fur rugs.

"Stefan!" he called over his shoulder. "Come! I need you. We have much to do before morning."

Stefan appeared in the inner doorway. He tossed raven hair out of his eyes like a restless colt and leaned against the door frame with the unconscious grace of a statue. A playful smile curled his lips as his dark eyes regarded the clothing scattered about the room.

Roland made a little face and tried to fold the tunic

he held instead of tossing it among the rest.

"Here, now, let me do that, my lord. You'll bollix it beyond all help." Stefan's voice had a curious lilt, bringing to mind the song of birds. The younger boy smiled to show he merely teased then began to gather the scattered clothing.

The illusion of grace shattered.

Roland watched Stefan move about the room, left leg hampered by an awkward limp. His face warmed with shame as he shied away from the memory of how that old injury had occurred. But guilt couldn't be allowed to change his mind.

Stefan halted with an expression of dismay.

Roland gulped. He could never hide anything from the younger boy.

"You're thinking of going alone," Stefan stated flatly.

"If I wish to move swiftly, I must." Roland fumbled open a smaller chest, pretending to examine a hunter green tunic for flaws. "I have to go alone. You would only slow me down. You couldn't possibly keep up."

"But I promised your father! If we are rafting downriver with the fur shipment, I won't..."

Stefan's face grew still, all emotion locked away behind an ivory mask. His eyes seemed like two bottomless black reflecting pools, the pupil indistinguishable from the iris. Those fathomless eyes unsettled many people, chilling even Roland at times. The more superstitious townsfolk went so far as to make a ward against evil whenever the boy limped by.

The twin pools of darkness slowly lost their sharp focus and blurred into solid ebony orbs as Stefan's sight slipped into the world only he could enter.

"I see," he said, coming back to himself, his voice hushed. "You're not planning to stay with the river traders, are you?"

Roland's own eyes narrowed to slits.

"Another vision?" he murmured, temper tightening his throat.

Stefan's gift of precognition often proved more a curse than a blessing.

The squire bowed his dark head.

"It doesn't take a vision to guess your mind in this, my lord," he murmured.

Roland's heart softened at the sight of Stefan's misery. He knew how much the younger boy looked up to him, and it would be unnecessarily cruel to leave him behind.

Spending so much time at his master's side, Stefan had no friends among the castle boys. The rest of the servants treated him like an outsider rather than an equal. And, at fifteen, a sensitive boy like Stefan noticed slights more than he had as a child.

"I can hide nothing from you as long as you are plagued with those infernal visions." Roland relented, his quicksilver smile glowing. "And if I can't hide my secrets from you, I'd better take you with me. It's the only way to protect them."

Stefan's face lit with joy. "You won't regret it, my lord. I swear it."

"I will take you at your word, Stefan. And you must promise not to whisper a word of my plans to my father. If you do, I swear to you I *will* go without you."

Roland watched duty and desire warring in the squire's face, but finally the boy nodded reluctantly.

"I will keep your secrets, my lord."

"Can you make some order from this chaos?" the prince asked, waving a hand at the scattered clothing. "I still have a few more details to take care of."

"Aye, my lord."

"I *will* make this work, Stefan. Father *will* be proud of me. If we leave the traders at Woodwatch Ferry and cut straight through the Forest of Night, we can save at least a day's travel and have the bargain for the furs sealed before the raft even arrives. We'll meet the traders in Stormhaven with the deal signed for them."

"Do you think it wise to venture into the Forest? There must be a way to avoid that wicked place."

"Not and save the time. Don't tell me you believe all those hearth tales of elves and changelings?"

Stefan shivered. "Not all hearth tales are false. Did you hear nothing of Chancellor Marcell's account regarding the War for Golden Heath? Yes, it was many years ago, but if elves fought humans without mercy in the days of your ancestors, who knows whether or not they still lurk in those dark trees, like the stories say. "Much evil walks beyond these walls, the likes of which you've never seen."

"I'm not afraid of some silly children's story, or the bugaboos of the past," Roland boasted. "If you come with me, you come through the Forest."

"As you wish, my lord." Stefan sighed and nodded, prying the now-crumpled tunic from the prince's excited grasp with gentle fingers. He folded it with practiced ease. "I'll pack lightly so we may travel fast."

"And I'll ask Alexendar to see our horses are waiting for us at Woodwatch Ferry."

Roland hurried from the room, head filled with plans for the journey.

***

The sweet smile remained on Sara's lips until Prince Roland stepped out of sight, then twisted into a snarl. She drew the back of her hand across her mouth as if to remove all trace of his kiss.

"Idiot! May he rot in the Flames," she spat, her blue eyes flashing.

A flicker of movement in her peripheral vision drew her attention upward. Soaring in through the high kitchen window with a beat of powerful black-satin wings, a raven settled on the pot rack. It uttered a hoarse croak to acknowledge her.

Sara shivered. The winged messenger always seemed to anticipate her need to pass information to its master.

She glanced around the kitchen. The pot boys and spit turners wrestled in the courtyard, taking advantage of the fact their dinner tasks were done. She could hear their shouts through the open window. Cook had gone to the cellar to retrieve wine for the king. She had only a moment.

"I have a message for your master," she told the raven, her tone imperious. "Something your lord will pay me well for, but I cannot discuss this information here in the castle. Have him meet me in an hour in the usual place."

Nodding understanding of the message, the raven rose into the air. It circled the kitchen once then darted out into the late-afternoon sunlight.

Sara stepped to the window and watched it speed southward. Soon she would be free of Roland and this servitude. She would be a fine lady with sparkling jewels and elegant clothes.

"Sara! Stop your daydreaming and get those apples washed. 'Tis time to set the table and your chores not near done. Quit your lollygagging, miss!" the cook ordered, tone harsh with exasperation.

Sara stole a final glance at the raven's path then turned back to her duties with a sigh.

***

Dinner and its aftermath took longer than she'd anticipated, and she could not slip out of the castle before full dark. Making sure no one saw her departure, she opened a secret door out of the cellar and stepped out into the night. Roland had shown her the exit as a way to meet him in the orchards without being caught. She hurried into town, heartsick over the lateness of the hour.

"What if he is angry?" she murmured to herself. "Or worse, did not bother to stay? I must deliver this message tonight!"

The creak of a swinging signboard from somewhere down an alley caught her attention, and she realized with a start she had almost overshot her destination. She squinted into the gloom. Yes, little illumination fell into this shadowy cut between buildings, but she could see the sign well enough—a flaking white cloud blowing the ornately painted words *The Wayward Wind* from pudgy lips. She drew her threadbare cloak closer about her and pushed open the door, jostled by patrons with missions of their own.

Pipe smoke and the mouth-watering scent of roasting meat filled the tavern. She swallowed hard. Food might be plentiful in the castle, but not for a lowly kitchen wench. She did not starve, but neither did she dine on spiced mutton. She would make a mug of beer and a plate of food a condition of her news.

She shoved through the crowded common room toward the scarred counter, looking for the raven's master.

"You're late," said a low, musical voice at her shoulder.

Sara whirled. "My chores took longer than expected," she replied, dropping into a curtsey. "I beg pardon."

"Stand up, girl," he ordered, glancing from side to side to see if anyone had noticed her bow. No one paid them any attention.

Sara looked the other up and down, intrigued as always by the raven's handsome master. His dark hair lay smooth as silk, although he wore it a little longer than fashion dictated. The man towered nearly a foot above her. Tan and lean, he habitually dressed in black and white silk. And his eyes were the most beautiful sea-blue.

The other quirked an eyebrow, a sardonic smile playing about his sensual lips.

"See anything you like?"

Sara flushed. "Forgive me. I shouldn't stare, my lord." She bowed her head.

"You claimed your news was urgent...and private. We cannot stand here and discuss it. Come and sit down."

Sara shuddered. "'Tis unnatural, the way the raven and his master seem to read each others thoughts," she muttered, "but fear is easily brushed aside with the glitter of gold."

The man cocked his head. "Did you say something?"

"Just agreeing with you, milord." She followed the graceful figure through the eddying waves of sound and smell to a back corner of the tavern.

"Sit." The man gestured, long hands elegant as he indicated an empty place at the table. A trencher of mutton and a flagon of ale sat before it.

How can he know my very thoughts? Sara made the sign against evil under the shelter of her cloak. She sank onto the bench, plucking restlessly at the cuff of her sleeve.

"Well?" prompted her companion.

She leaned forward, her voice low and urgent.

"The puppet prince is to travel to Stormhaven with only the river traders as guard. It is the perfect opportunity for the Master to rid himself of Roland the Vain."

"That decision does not rest with you," the man replied coldly, his voice like steel.

Sara felt her face go hot then cold. "I-I am sorry, my lord. Forgive my presumption."

Her companion pulled out a heavy purse and opened it. He shook a spill of gold coins from the bag and weighed them in one hand thoughtfully.

"What is in this for you, Sara? Surely, there is more to life than gold?"

"You have never been poor," she replied with a scornful laugh. "If you had, you would know nothing has more worth than gold. Love, duty, honor—all words. Gold is real. Something you can hold in your hand."

"So cynical for one so young."

"I was never young. By my fifth name-day, I mended nets for my father until my fingers bled, but I'll be a lady someday. I have the word of—"

"Do not speak of him here!" the man warned, glancing again from side to side.

Sara pouted.

The man leaned over the table until he loomed scarce inches from her. His strange blue-green eyes dominated his tan face.

"Do not presume you know anything, girl. You fancy the master has need of you. He does not. He can find treachery anywhere. You are merely...convenient." He slammed down the handful of gold between them.

Sara gulped and drew her cloak closer, suddenly chilled. She had cast her nets with a black-hearted crew, but there was no other route to her dreams. By the Flames, she would stay the course through this storm and reach her final port with a full haul.

She snatched the coins from the table.

Chapter 3

"Haul in that line. Look alive, look alive!"

"Watch the stern!"

"Shove off there."

The bustling dock rang with shouted commands in the crystalline dawn, ordered chaos reigning as men and boys swarmed the wharf. The reds and blues of the king's uniformed sailors contrasted with the gaudy silks of the privateers and the sturdy serge of the rafters and merchantmen. The acrid tang of boiling pitch mingled with the odors of fish and river decay while a haze of smoke drifted lazily from cauldrons set over fire pits along the riverbank. Bright flames crackled in the still air, and each pit they passed radiated a pocket of warmth in the chill morning.

Stefan wrinkled his nose, threading his way in Roland's wake through the press of workmen.

"Look at it all, Stefan! Have you ever seen the docks so busy?"

"No, my lord," he replied, a trifle short of breath as he concentrated on keeping up with the excited prince.

Roland wove through the jostling crowd of dockworkers, sailors, and the occasional rare passenger. "And today we are part of the reason it is so busy!"

Stefan nodded, shifting the luggage to a more comfortable position. He carried one of Roland's bags slung over his shoulder in addition to his own, and his precious lute knocked against his back.

"Hurry, Stefan. They wait for us."

"Coming, my lord." Stefan pushed his pace to the limit but darted stolen glances at the activity around him.

Dockworkers loaded cargo onto the boats and rafts moored along the river, punctuating their work with rousing bursts of song and snatches of raucous laughter. Casks thundered up makeshift ramps to thump into place on decks. Sailors efficiently stowed crates and sacks in the holds of the larger craft and wound lines for castoff. Sunlight danced on blue-green water, adding its own siren call, promising adventure beyond the bend. The exotic perfume of spices brought upriver from the sea wafted from a trim skiff tied to the far bank.

Stefan inhaled deeply as they passed the spicer. The sweet scent of cinnamon provided a welcome relief from the acrid bite of pitch, and he thought he caught a whiff of sandalwood, as delicate as air.

The prince's excitement proved contagious. Scurrying men and shouted orders just added to a sense of adventure waiting to begin.

Roland spun on his heel, arms thrown wide, eyes shining as he tried to drink it all in at once. His grandfather's sword hung at his belt, threatening to trip either prince or passerby as he whirled.

"We're here, Stefan. We are actually here! Today the docks seem bigger, somehow. Do you feel it?" Roland backpedaled away from the squire, adjusting the sword as he continued his enthusiastic monologue. "The world is so full of sound, and smell—"

"Here, you! Watch where yer goin'!" growled a rough workman when the prince bumped squarely into him.

"Sorry, sir," Roland apologized absently, sweeping off his cap and bobbing his head.

The workman accepted the apology with ill grace, muttering as he continued about his work.

Stefan felt a twinge of misgiving at the man's reaction, but Roland's face looked so comically indignant at the slight he had to laugh.

"I never thought I'd see the proud Prince Roland humble himself to a dockman," he teased.

Then, his apprehension grew as Roland's green eyes narrowed, and his jaw set.

Did I go too far? Roland has uncertain control of his temper at the best of times.

He had endured it on enough occasions to know. Although the prince was just as quick to regret his hasty actions and apologize, Stefan had learned to keep out of Roland's way if his mood turned foul.

Then the prince's lips twitched, and he grinned. He jammed his cap back onto his russet curls with a shake of his head.

"I know, I know. If I intend to play the dock boy, I must act the part. I do so want to make Father proud of me."

"You do well, my lord. Though I suggest you might want to hide that sword."

"Good advice, as always." Roland unbuckled it and hastily wrapped it in his cloak. He slipped the bundle through the strap of his rucksack. "Thank you, Stefan." Slinging the bag back over his shoulder, he pointed at a large raft berthed nearby. "There! That's Jarome's raft. Come on."

He broke into an impetuous run then skidded to an abrupt halt, waiting for his companion.

"I shouldn't have...I'm sorry. I got so excited I forgot for a moment," he muttered when Stefan limped to his side.

The squire grinned up at his prince. "Do not concern yourself, Lord Roland. You have every right to your excitement. Go on. I will catch up with you."

"Are you sure?" The prince's glance darted to the craft then back.

"Go on!"

Stefan shooed him in the direction of the raft. Roland nodded thanks and raced onward.

Stefan watched him sprint off and bit his lip with a touch of envy. Once, he, too, could run like the wind, but those days belonged to the past.

Shaking his head to dismiss what he could not change, he resettled the lute and followed his master, left leg dragging behind him with each step. Although he had regained more control over the limb than anyone had expected, it still proved untrustworthy under stress.

By the time he reached the raft, Roland was deep in consultation with Captain Jarome.

"As I say, my lord," Jarome continued, blue eyes twinkling in his weatherbeaten face, "we have plenty of work to do, if you are willing."

Stefan had always liked the gregarious trader, and he felt safer about the journey knowing Jarome would be their pilot. A bluff, hearty man with sandy hair beginning to blur to gray at the temples, the captain habitually stood with feet planted wide. It appeared to Stefan he endlessly stabilized himself on a moving deck, even when on dry land.

Now, Jarome raised a hand to his mouth and bellowed, "Collyn! Collyn Silverbrook!"

At the far end of the raft, a burly blond sailor straightened from his task and glanced toward them. Jarome waved the other to him and threw an arm across his shoulder. He introduced the sailor to the boys.

"Lads, meet my second, Collyn Silverbrook. I trust him with my life. More important, I trust him with my raft!"

The newcomer's strapping size struck Stefan first; second, the calm steadiness in his gray eyes. His linen shirt hung open to the waist, revealing muscles bulging beneath a deep tan. A crystal arrowhead hung about his neck on a leather thong. The crystal refracted the sunlight when he nodded a greeting.

Stefan realized this must be the man he had spotted from the battlements. The same tremor of premonition shivered through him, and he frowned. What was it about the man?

The arrowhead winked in the sun again, and Stefan's eye was drawn to the object. The unusual keepsake aroused his curiosity. All the arrows he had seen at Crown Keep had tips of iron, and he wondered where it came from but felt too shy to ask.

"Collyn," Jarome continued in his amiable roar, "as I told you earlier, His Royal Highness Prince Roland and his squire, Master Stefan here, will journey with us to Stormhaven this trip. I promised King Frederick nothing would happen to these pups along the way, and I charge you with their keeping. Don't make me a liar." He wagged a playful finger at the sailor. "Now, go along with you, lads."

The captain gave Roland a hearty clap on the back, and the prince staggered to keep his balance. Jarome chuckled affectionately and returned to other duties. From anyone else, such familiarity might have proved dangerous, but Jarome had bounced Roland on his knee before the prince could walk and had earned these small liberties.

Stefan followed Roland as Collyn led them on a quick tour of the broad, flat raft. By the time they had paced the length of the huge craft—fifty feet wide and twice as long—he felt the strain, but he bit his lip and kept up as best he could.

A small square cabin near the stern served as Jarome's quarters, and several lean-tos provided shelter for the crew on stormy nights. A fire pit smoldered in the bow, safe within a sand-lined metal box sitting on the deck, a spit suspended above it. The cook sat beside the firebox, having no duties beyond preparing meals and tending the flames. He nodded at the trio as they passed then returned to his study of the coals, peeling potatoes as he watched.

Stefan noticed a padded crutch on the deck, and was startled to realize the man was missing his right leg below the knee. So, there is a place for a cripple on a crew such as this, he thought in wonder.

A company of twenty hearty traders manned the oars in shifts. The trim, well-kept craft impressed both youths.

"Stash your gear in here," Collyn told them, pointing to one of the lean-tos. "There is much to do before we cast off. If you're willing to make yourselves useful, the help would be greatly appreciated, Your Royal Highness."

Stefan sighed to himself. He felt so tired of being overlooked—or worse, treated as less than human. He knew the big trader didn't intend to slight him, but it rankled just the same, and the resentment made him felt guilty as well.

"You can hang your instrument here, lad," Collyn continued, turning to Stefan, and indicating a hook on the support post of the lean-to. "It will stay safe there while you work."

He felt gratitude well up inside him, all out of proportion to the suggestion, simply because Collyn had included him. He slipped the strap of the lute over his head and hung it on the hook. Stacking their other belongings in a neat pile against the wall, he followed Roland and Collyn back into the strengthening sunlight.

"These ropes need to be coiled and stowed, Your Royal Highness, and the tarps need oiling. The season is unpredictable, and it could ruin the furs if we are caught in a sudden storm without any protection."

Roland nodded and caught up a length of rope. He began to bundle it into a ball.

Collyn caught his hand. "No, my lord. Let me show you."

As the raftsman showed Roland how to create uniform loops between hand and elbow, Stefan coiled the other lengths into orderly rings and stacked them away against the outer wall of the captain's cabin. Then Collyn brought out a cask of drying oil and showed the boys how to work it into the canvas of the tarps to provide waterproofing. He left them to the task and moved on to oversee his mates elsewhere on the raft.

Roland ran the back of a grimy hand across his sweating brow, leaving a streak of oil behind.

"I didn't expect to find myself playing servant," he complained.

He doesn't realize what he's saying. Roland never thinks before he speaks. It is just his way. And, irritating as it may be, pointing out the slight will not correct it, Stefan thought. Glancing sidelong at the prince, he said softly, "You are not 'playing' at anything, my lord, you are working as a riverman—and it is at your own request."

Roland's face flushed. "You are right. As usual."

"Cast off!"

The cry echoed the length of the raft as the traders moved to obey. The raft began to slip with majestic dignity down the broad expanse of the river. As the current took them, and the craft began to gather some speed, they passed Crown Keep castle. Stefan felt a thrill race through him as the pale towers dwindled slowly behind them.

Roland glanced at him, and he could see excitement bubbling up inside his master as well.

"We are actually leaving the castle, Stefan. We have been sheltered too long! Somehow, until this moment, I still feared this adventure only a dream."

Stefan laughed. "Then you'd better wake up. You almost stepped off the raft."

Roland moved away from the edge with exaggerated care and returned to his task. Stefan stifled his laughter. The studied nonchalance with which Roland avoided his eye told him how foolish the prince felt, and he decided to forgo any further teasing.

A sudden shadow drifted over Stefan's heart, and he frowned, glancing about him with wary suspicion. He saw nothing out of place along the river or its banks, but something made him uneasy.

"What is it?" asked Roland, always quick to read his squire's mood.

"I don't know. Something odd, I..." Stefan shaded his eyes to peer upward and noticed a bird wheeling high above them. The sight sent a chill through him. He shivered.

"Stefan...?"

"It's nothing, just a stray breeze. Come, we have work to do."

Despite his light words, he found his eyes drawn again and again to the bird, which continued to circle high above the raft. He felt curiously defenseless under its gaze.

Sometime later, finished with his allotted tasks and granted an hour's respite, Stefan retrieved his lute. It had become so much a part of him, he felt incomplete without it. Roland vaulted onto the flat roof of the captain's cabin with unconscious ease, one of his beloved adventure books in his hand. Stefan, glad of the chance to rest, clambered awkwardly after him. He gritted his teeth against a twinge of pain from his leg.

As soon as they were settled in their places, Stefan began to tune the strings. The artfully crafted lute, a present from the king, was his most precious possession. He listened anxiously to the tone of the instrument. The flimsy walls of the lean-to were not much protection from the damp air of the river. Perhaps he should ask the captain if there were somewhere more secure, he could store it.

When he was satisfied with the tuning, he began

to play the instrument as he watched the riverbanks glide past. Music rippled from his deft fingers while he hummed under his breath. He coaxed forth the sound of a tumbling brook dancing in the sunlight; the image brought a faint smile to his lips. Then the music shifted of its own accord, the gurgling brook deepening to the more sober sweep of the river. Stefan closed his eyes and began to sing, his clear tenor voice soaring sweetly.

> Down to the sea
> Flows the river,
> There I must go—
> Parted from thee
> By the river,
> Loathing to go.
> Wait thou for me
> At the river,
> When I must go—
> I'll come to thee
> On the river,
> Or rest below.

When the final haunting notes died into silence, scattered applause sounded around him. Stefan's eyes flew open with a start. He had lost himself in the music, letting it take him where it wanted, forgetting his surroundings. Now, as he glanced around the raft, he saw the entire crew standing idle, all eyes upon him. More than one rough trader dabbed the corner of an eye with a hasty swipe of a sleeve.

"Beautiful, lad," Jarome called. "Now give us something lively so I can get the value of my money from these ne'er-do-wells of mine."

Ducking his head to hide his scalding cheeks, Stefan played a rousing tune that soon had the men whistling about their work. One of the traders called out a request, and from that point on, the calls came thick and fast as the raftsmen asked for their favorites. Even after Roland had put away his reading and reluctantly returned to helping Collyn, Stefan remained perched atop the cabin. He played until his fingers ached as the riverbanks slowly glided past under the warm afternoon sun.

Chapter 4

At sundown, the men poled to shore and anchored close to the bank. Roland sought out Jarome, who was working on his accounts in his cabin.

"Why are we stopping?"

Jarome threw back his head and roared with laughter.

"You really are untraveled, aren't you, my prince? We've come thirty leagues today—that's not a record day, but it isn't bad. Hopefully, we will make up some time tomorrow. It's fifty more to Woodwatch Ferry, which is the halfway point.

"I told you, four or five days constitute a good run to Stormhaven. Six or seven is not unheard-of. Plus, there's an arm of the cursed Forest between here and the ford—and I am without my best pilot till morning. No wise man ventures under those trees in the dark, and certainly not without a skilled hand at the tiller. There is witchery beneath those boughs.

"Besides, my crew needs rest, my lord, so we tie up at night. Don't fret. With luck, we'll dock at Woodwatch Ferry early enough tomorrow for you to sleep in a bed—with company, if you like." The trader winked at him.

Roland felt himself flush. "I see," he murmured.

He gave Jarome a curt nod of farewell, holding the reins of his temper in a tight fist until he quit the cabin. He stalked toward the lean-to where he and Stefan were to sleep—he needed to cool off before seeking the fireside.

He had just thrown himself down on his belly atop his bedroll when Stefan entered.

"Are you all right?" the squire asked quietly.

Roland sighed, turning over to lean on an elbow and smile up at Stefan.

"I've been too sheltered in the castle, Stefan. I know nothing of my kingdom. I should've paid more attention to the maps and charts. Though parchment scrolls don't teach me how to deal with her people." He sat up and slammed a fist into the palm of his other hand, wincing at the results. "I guess I'm not cut out for manual labor, either," he muttered, glancing down at his blisters.

"Let me see."

Roland held out his hands. Stefan's hiss of reaction revealed his sharp eyes could see them even in the dim light of the lean-to.

"Why didn't you say something earlier?" the boy clucked, shaking his head as he dug in his bag for ointment.

"Quite honestly, I didn't notice. I've been too excited to think about it."

Stefan spread a cool, soothing salve on the prince's palms. Roland's hands felt better at once as the unguent numbed the pain. The mixture smelled of herbs and flowers, and the scent lightened his heart.

"I realize things aren't going as you planned," Stefan murmured, "but don't take it out on the traders. They will be valuable allies to you when you are king. Learn from them while you can. Woodwatch Ferry will come soon enough."

"Right—as always. My impatience will prove my undoing."

"You're learning, my lord."

Roland stretched, looking around the cramped space.

"Wasn't this a glorious day, Stefan? The free air, the changing scenery...what would it be like to stay on the river and pursue the trader's life? Or, better yet, venture across the sea!" He imagined standing at the prow of a sailing ship, the wind ruffling his hair as he braced against the roll of the sea. "Wouldn't it be wonderful to sail the globe in a ship all our own, like Vartesh the Mariner, winning treasure for the glory of Irthlan? All the world would know of my kingdom." He sighed happily.

"'Tis a lovely dream."

"Aye...but only a dream." Roland bounded to his feet. "I owe it to Father to be the best king I can be, even if it does mean remaining trapped inside castle walls. But I will cherish every drop of this freedom for as long as I possibly can!" he vowed with a wink. "Shall we go and see about supper? I'm starved."

Stefan teased, "You're feeling better."

"I'm a growing boy." Roland drew himself up and peered down his nose at Stefan in mock disapproval before heading to the cook fire.

The crew was already gathered around the cheery flames. A large brisket turning on the spit sent the aroma of home into the night. Hearty calls of greeting came from the men, who shifted to give them room.

The circle around the firepit formed an island of shifting color in the blue-gray twilight when sleeve or cap caught the light. Red-gold flames lent a ruddy glow to Stefan's pale cheeks.

Roland found himself seated beside Collyn and took the plate the big trader handed him, nodding his thanks. It felt good to be accepted as workmate, rather than prince. His spirits soared.

After dinner, the traders fell to boasting and telling ribald tales. Even Roland managed to spin a few, mixing bits of the truth with the exploits of his fictional heroes.

"Go fetch that lute of yours, Stefan lad, before these mountebanks sink my raft with the load of manure they're spreading," Jarome roared, shaking his head.

The men denied the charge but added their entreaties to the request. Stefan ducked out of the firelight and faded into the night, soon returning with his precious instrument. Then, a sly smile on his face as he glanced sidelong at the prince, he strummed a rousing martial tempo and sang:

> I'm off to be a sailor,
> And sail upon the sea,
> Or raft upon the river,
> It matters not to me.

As he moved into the chorus, he glanced at the prince once more. Roland began to suspect something lay behind the choice of song.

> Let's give a cheer for danger,
> A rousing one, two, three-
> I'm off to be a sailor,
> Yes, that's the life for me!
>
> I long for an adventure,
>
> No stay-at-home I'll be
> Just give me stars to steer by,
> And that's enough for me.

When the chorus was reached again, Collyn began to clap and sing along in a pleasing baritone, nodding to the others to join him.

> I weary of the hearthside,
> The world I wish to see
> With a sturdy deck beneath me
> And jolly company.

When the chorus next came around, several of the others began to clap along.

> I'll return with golden treasure,
> And bales of silk for thee.
> Jewels of fiery splendor,
> And other mysteries.

By the final chorus, the entire group roared out the song, and even Roland clapped his hands in time.

> Yes, sailing on the ocean,
> How splendid it will be!
> I'm off to be a sailor
> Till my mother catches me!

Stefan finished the air with a rousing flourish, and the last line was greeted with raucous laughter and thumping applause. Roland took the ribbing with good grace, laughing as hard as the rest.

The crew began to call for their favorite songs, and Stefan obliged until Roland could see he was having difficulty forcing his cramped fingers to play. He fought the urge to say something and was spared the necessity as Jarome called a halt to the music.

"All right, lads, let's all to bed except the watch. We

must get an early start tomorrow."

***

Collyn Silverbrook stood to go man his watch. The prince cleared his throat, and Collyn glanced at him.

"May I watch with you for a while?" Roland asked, as if not quite ready for the day to end.

The trader eyed him in the flickering light of the fire. He remembered his first venture from home and hearth and recognized the excitement radiating from the young man.

"Aye, my lord," he replied. "Glad to have you."

The prince's squire hid a yawn behind his hand with limited success.

"Go to bed, lad," Collyn told him kindly. "I'll keep an eye on your master."

Stefan glanced at Roland. His shoulders relaxed at the prince's nod.

"The boy's so tired he can barely stand," Collyn murmured, watching Stefan lurch to the lean-to.

A muffled sigh brought his attention back to the prince. Roland's green eyes were shadowed in the firelight.

"What is it?"

"Nothing," the prince replied with a shrug, but Collyn sensed more to the story.

"Come. My post is at the rudder."

He led the way astern. They were all alone with the moonlit water and the sleepy cries of night birds. Roland sank down on the smooth planks of the deck, his back against the rudder housing. Collyn leaned on the great oar.

The prince stared out over the shimmering water and sighed again.

"Do you want to talk about it?"

Roland glanced up at him. "I should never have let Stefan come along. This life is hard enough for a whole man."

"Was he born lame?"

Roland blinked in surprise. "You don't—oh, yes...I forgot. What is common knowledge around Crown Keep township might not be so well known elsewhere."

"True, my lord. I joined Jarome's crew this season, and don't know much of local affairs."

"No, he wasn't born...that way. He used to run like the wind. I could never catch him when we played."

"What happened to him?"

Roland bit his lip, shoulders hunched as he brushed at bits of dirt on the deck. "An accident."

"I see." Collyn realized pressing for the details would not get them, merely alienate the prince. Roland would tell it in his own good time if he wished to share.

They watched the peaceful river in companionable silence for several minutes, and then Roland began to talk in a low monotone. Collyn had to strain to hear the mumbled words.

"I was eleven and Stefan eight. It was a hot midsummer afternoon. We were playing at swords in one of the courtyards, using short staffs for foils." Roland stared up at the stars. "The day was sweltering! Across the courtyard, a fruit tree shaded a section of the wall, and a pair of my father's prize staghounds dozed in that relative coolness."

Collyn sat down beside the prince. "Sounds like a

perfect day."

"Oh, it was. Aside from the heat, it was glorious. And Stefan trounced me soundly," Roland admitted with a rueful chuckle. "Although he was smaller and lighter than me, he moved so much faster I found myself trailing in the match, and I...began to lose my temper." He looked down at the hands clasped around his knee.

"We all have our breaking points, my lord, and you were very young."

"It's just—it felt like Stefan always had to best me. And I know he never set out to do so. He was just a better natural athlete than I."

Roland sighed—the memories were obviously painful to him. Collyn waited, sure it was better for the prince to get this out than to keep it pent up inside.

"My anger exploded. I threw my staff across the courtyard, and it hit the castle wall. It ricocheted off the stone and struck the male hound."

"Ah, I believe I can guess what happened next."

"The dog sprang up instantly, snapping and snarling. Its mouth seemed nothing but razor-sharp teeth. I froze, just staring in horror as it rushed toward us. But Stefan didn't. He grabbed my arm and dragged me toward a nearby tree. I still don't know where he found the strength, but he shoved me up into its lower branches."

"We find wells of strength inside us when we must," Collyn observed.

"True," Roland acknowledged. "Coming to my senses at last, I clambered up in the tree until I was safe then reached for Stefan's hand. My heart was pounding so hard I could feel the beat in my ears." He reached out his hand, as if he were once more in that hot courtyard. Then he snatched it back, and continued raggedly, "I was in too great a hurry to be careful. The first time I pulled, my hand was slick with sweat, and I lost my grip. Before I could catch Stefan's hand a second time, the dog seized his left leg in its jaws."

Roland buried his face in his hands.

"The dog's fangs ripped through flesh and muscle and snapped a bone. Stefan almost died of a fever after the attack. When it finally broke, his grace was gone, leaving him with the limp." He let his head fall back against the rudder housing. "Bloodstains still tinge the flagstones of that courtyard. Even after all this time. I...I avoid it unless absolutely necessary."

"You shouldn't claim fault. As you say, it was an accident—a trick of Fate."

"Perhaps, but I still feel ashamed when I see how calmly he accepts the results of my childish temper."

"Did you learn anything from the incident?"

"I've tried."

"Then, perhaps, it was a lesson worth the price in Stefan's mind."

Roland shuddered. "A fearsome price indeed." He stifled a yawn.

Collyn laid a hand on the prince's shoulder then removed it swiftly, thinking better of the liberty.

"Go to bed, my lord. You've had a long day, and tomorrow will prove the same."

"You're right," Roland agreed with another yawn. "I think I could sleep until noon."

Collyn chuckled. "Not aboard the raft of Captain Jarome you won't. Get what sleep you can."

The prince stood and bowed slightly.

"Thank you for listening, Master Silverbrook. Now and again, a man needs to unburden himself."

"Aye. And you will always find me a willing listener."

Roland strode off to find his sleeping pallet, and Collyn sat watching the river until the end of his watch, lost in thought.

Chapter 5

When Stefan woke the next morning, Roland still slept. The squire stole out of the lean-to and drifted toward the stern, soundless from long practice. He nodded a greeting to the man on the rudder and stepped to the edge of the raft.

The pearl-gray of dawn glimmered all around him. Rising mists mingled with an early fog to give the appearance they were drifting within the clouds. A damp chill in the air warned him again of summer's waning, but it wasn't unpleasant.

Stefan's nostrils flared as he caught the ripe perfume of the river, a fragrance comprised of bottom mud, fish, and decaying reeds mixed with the heavy scent of flowering trees blooming on shore. Stefan studied the trees and their huge white blossoms with interest. The type of bloom they bore seemed unusual for the season. He had never seen their like—and yet, they seemed so familiar.

He sat on the edge of the raft, bad leg trailing in the water. Chin resting on bent knee, one hand toying with a silver disk that dangled about his neck on a thong, he studied the shimmering opalescent river. He couldn't recall where he had gotten the medallion, try as he might, but it provided a source of comfort for him, and was his dearest treasure—after his lute.

Stefan smiled down at the water, feeling a rare tranquility as the current slipped past his dangling leg. *I could sit here all day and never be bored. It is so peaceful.*

"Stefan! Where are you?"

He stifled a sigh of regret.

"I'm coming, my lord." Climbing awkwardly to his feet, he limped back to help Roland make ready for the day.

"Now, pack our things as small as you can," Roland whispered as soon as he was dressed. "We must be prepared to leave when the raft arrives in Woodwatch Ferry."

"You're still determined to do this?"

"Just think, Stefan! If we can reach Stormhaven before the traders, I can negotiate the trade agreement before the furs arrive and make Father proud of me. I'll show him my lessons haven't all been for nothing. I have a plan, but we've got to slip away without Jarome noticing until it's too late."

"My lord," Stefan began, choosing his words carefully, "I must advise against this course. Your father is not likely to be pleased that you disobeyed his order to stay with the traders, no matter what the results."

"What do you know about the ways of the world?" scoffed Roland. "I say Father will be impressed by my initiative. He has always praised forward thinkers. Come with me, or stay behind—your choice—but what need do I have for a squire who doesn't obey me?"

Stefan bowed his head, knowing better than to say anything more. He was bound by oath to obey Roland's wishes, no matter how foolhardy. Still, he had also promised the king to protect Roland, and he would do his best to make sure he obeyed that command as well. He could only do so if he remained at Roland's side. He sighed and nodded.

They joined the crew at the cook fire for a hot drink and a meat pie. They laughed and joked with the men as if they had been on the raft their whole lives.

Jarome sauntered up to Roland.

"Your Highness, I have a task for you today. We need to make a quick stop at the next village for fruit and grain. I'd like for you boys to go into town with Collyn and get the supplies."

Roland opened his mouth as if to protest, and Stefan tensed, ready to intervene if necessary. Then, visibly controlling himself, Roland nodded.

"As you deem best, Captain."

"Good, good!" The trader beamed his approval.

Stephan felt a surge of pride to see Roland's restraint. It might be vain to think so, but he felt like his advice might finally be having the desired effect.

***

A league downriver, the raft slipped as close as possible to shore. Stefan followed Roland and Collyn through knee-deep water to the squelching mud of the river-bank. The thick ooze let off an odor of rot and decay, and he wrinkled his nose in distaste.

Roland didn't seem to notice as he scanned the shore. There was little to see—stands of reeds and dying marsh grass. None of the flowering trees grew on this section of the bank, and Stefan was vaguely disappointed.

The village was a poor one. Homes that were little more than hovels leaned slightly, as if in a high wind. Most of the dozen or so dwellings clustered tightly around a dusty square with a ramshackle well in its center. The thatched roofs showed need of repair—as Stefan watched, a raven tugged a piece of straw from one and flew into the trees.

A handful of villagers peeked at the party as they went about their chores—here a woman sweeping her yard, there a cobbler with his last. They were dressed in worn but clean clothing that appeared almost more patches than fabric.

Chasing a fleeing goat, a tow-haired boy stopped dead in his tracks and stared at them, mouth agape. When Stefan smiled at him, the child's eyes widened, and he darted off, calling for his mother.

There was the stench of sewage in the air, mixed with cook smoke and animal dung. A skinny pig wallowed in the mud beside one hovel, a frayed bit of rope around its back leg to stop it from wandering.

Roland sniffed. "Why don't these people take more pride in their homes? These buildings are a disgrace."

Stefan winced at the disgust in the prince's tone.

Collyn shrugged. "Not every home is built of strong stone, Your Highness. When you are poor, you do as you can and pray to the Power you don't find your walls blown down about your ears."

Roland had the grace to look abashed.

"I'm sorry, Master Silverbrook. I meant no offense."

"These are hard-working people, my lord. They do the best they can, but times are hard. The signs point to a light harvest this year, and the villagers have nothing to spare on improvements."

He led the way to a slightly larger dwelling that leaned in one direction rather than three at once. A colorless woman with stooped shoulders answered his knock, a toddler balanced on her hip and another clutching her skirts. Her face lit up at the sight of him, and she smiled.

"Collyn! I did not expect the raft back so soon."

Collyn swept her into a hug.

"It's good to see you, Anie. How is your ne'er-do-well husband? Ready to do some honest work? We have need of a good helmsman again, and only Ethen can navigate that spell-witched section through the Forest."

Anie's face fell.

"So soon? I had hoped..." She sighed, turning toward the interior of the house. "So be it. I'll bring him along."

"Anie..."

She stopped and looked back over her shoulder, adjusting the toddler in her arms.

"How is he, really?"

"The coughing has nearly stopped and he's able to be up and about. I think the worst of this bout is over...but he'll never again be the man he was, Collyn. I hope the captain realizes that." Her face was pinched with worry.

"He knows, Anie. He knows. But a good helmsman needs keen eyes and a steady hand, not the brawn of an oarsman. Ethen will do fine." He reached into his shirt and pulled out a small purse. "The captain sends this for the winter," he continued, handing her the purse, which clinked as he passed it. "This is our next-to-last trip for the season, so Ethen should be home to you soon."

Stefan watched her face clear, and a tremulous smile started to curve her lips.

"There is no finer master than Captain Jarome,

bless him," she breathed. "Ethen is lucky to have so good a berth. I'll fetch him now."

She hurried off into the gloom of the house.

"What ails her man?" Roland asked.

"He has the wasting sickness. Sometimes the symptoms worsen, sometimes they ease. Whenever he feels well enough, Jarome takes him on the river— the fresh air does him good. But there won't be many more trips for Ethen, regardless." Collyn's expression was grave. "He is a good friend. It will be a great loss."

Before Roland could ask any further questions, Anie returned, followed by a gaunt, hollow-eyed man.

"Collyn! Is the raft back already?" Ethen coughed into the folds of a stained cloth. "I lost track of time."

"We're on our way to Stormhaven, and we really need you to get us through that stretch of Forest, Ethen. No one knows the river better than you." Collyn rested his hand on the man's shoulder. "Jarome is counting on you."

The sick man straightened at the praise, like a flower responding to the sun. Collyn is a born leader, Stefan thought, filled with admiration for the big trader.

"Marden promised us a bushel of apples and three sacks of grain," Collyn continued. "With any luck, we'll still make Woodwatch Ferry by nightfall."

Roland shot Stefan a glance, and he tried to pretend he hadn't seen. Perhaps if he didn't encourage him, the prince would change his mind...but it was unlikely.

All four said goodbye to Anie and her children then headed across town to the most prosperous building they had seen yet. Its stout walls were of huge oak logs, and it boasted a front porch of split planks. Collyn knocked on the door, and a portly man opened it at once, as if he'd been waiting for them.

"Master Silverbrook! Always a pleasure."

Stefan was struck immediately with a sense of unease he could not explain. The man seemed friendly enough, but something lurked in his eyes.

"Have you the supplies Captain Jarome ordered, Master Marden?" asked Collyn, his voice clipped and cool.

"About that." The man frowned. "There's been a bit of trouble."

Collyn raised an eyebrow.

"It seems the crops fell short of what I was led to expect," continued Marden. "A considerable shortfall. And you know how greedy the throne is about its taxes."

Roland's fists balled at his sides, and Stefan feared the prince would explode any instant.

Casually, Collyn turned to the prince.

"I am sorry, Your Royal Highness. I neglected to introduce our host."

Marden's face paled to the pasty white of unbaked dough.

"Y-Your Highness?" he squeaked.

"Yes, this is His Royal Highness, Prince Roland Frederickson. You were saying?"

Marden sputtered, "What would the prince be doing with the likes of you? You're merely trying to trick me."

Roland arched an eyebrow. "I assure you I wouldn't bother." His tone was a perfect match for his fathers at his most regal. The stare he favored the merchant with could have frozen the river.

"A thousand pardons, my lord," the man panted,

bowing so low Stefan wondered if he would prostrate himself on the floor. "I meant no disrespect."

"Do you have the captain's supplies or not?"

He sounds so like the king it is eerie, Stefan thought.

"Most of them, my lord. W-we are a bit short on the grain, however."

"I am sure it will be acceptable—if you refund the difference in his purchasing price."

"Of course!"

"Bring what you have," Collyn ordered, impatience evident in his voice. "We are wasting daylight and have far to go before nightfall."

"Of course. At once." Marden disappeared into the building.

"Won't he cheat us?" Stefan asked, confused by the exchange.

Collyn caught his eye and winked.

"It's all a game. He's expected to cheat, and Jarome accepts it—to some degree. But Marden has proved greedy one too many times."

"It seems Roland and I both have lots to learn." Stefan shook his head.

Collyn shepherded his crew around to the side door.

"Well done, by the way, Your Highness. You may have bested the best con man in the borough."

Roland's face was flushed.

"What did he mean about the throne and taxes, Collyn? Father is not a tyrant."

"No, but he trusts more and more of his business to ministers of late. He takes little interest in the day-to-day operations of the kingdom—and the tax rate has risen often these last few months. There is much the king does not realize, I fear."

Before Roland could reply, Marden and two servants brought out a small basket half-filled with wizened apples and two thin sacks of grain. The merchant had recovered his aplomb.

"Here are the goods I promised," he said with a smirk.

"Not by half," Collyn grunted, fingering one of the fruits. "These apples are nearly rotten, and you've only two-thirds of the grain—at a stretch."

Marden's tone sharpened to a whine. "'Tis all I have. To give Jarome more would starve my children."

Stefan thought of Anie's stick-thin offspring and doubted this man's children were in any danger.

Collyn slung both bags of grain to one shoulder.

"We'll remember your burden next time the captain seeks supplies."

Roland stepped forward, hand out-thrust.

"I believe Captain Jarome overpaid you?" His tone brooked no dissent. Sullenly, Marden counted out two gold wheels and a sliver of silver from his purse.

"He looks like he's been eating raw bitterroot," Stefan whispered to Roland behind his hand.

Roland hid his smile with a cough as he took one handle of the basket of apples. Stefan leaned down for the other.

"Let me do that," Ethen murmured.

Stefan met the man's eye and saw his need to be useful. He nodded, and Ethen lifted the other side of the basket.

They returned to the raft and got back on the river with only an hour's delay. Jarome met the news of Marden's shortcomings with a philosophical shrug.

"'Tis his loss. I won't deal with him again, and he

can be sure my fellows will know of this 'shortfall' of his as well." He turned to Ethen and clapped him gently on the shoulder. "Glad to have you back, lad. We need your sure touch as we pass under the Forest. I trust no one but you to steer me through that cursed place."

"I won't fail you, Captain," the helmsman promised.

***

At midday, the raft passed under the edge of the Forest of Night. Stefan had heard tales of this place all his life. The name came from the darkness beneath the trees and the fact that those who crossed its borders were rarely seen again—men did not travel there willingly.

Only the river provided a path from one side to the other, and even that was fraught with peril, as the riverbed was seldom the same from one voyage to the next.

A hush fell over the crew, and they unconsciously edged toward the center of the deck. The trees leaned almost to the surface, as if reaching for the those who dared trespass. The air grew heavy and still, with a musty scent that caught at the throat. Stefan saw many surreptitious wards being signed.

Ethen the helmsman kept to the exact center of the current, careful to avoid the bending trees. His eyes never left the water as he continuously adjusted the course of the raft.

The feeling of watchful silence under the great trees dampened the crew's spirits, yet Stefan moved as close to the edge as he dared, searching the darkness as if it might hold some indefinable secret. The call of a bird rang out in the stillness, and his attention swiveled to find it. For an instant, he thought he saw a grim face peering down at him from within the interlaced branches, but it disappeared before he could be sure.

"Just your imagination," he chided himself, too softly for anyone else to hear.

His companions did not share his fascination with the forest, and a collective sigh of relief rose when the vessel drifted out into sunlight. The raft came back to life as the trees fell away behind them.

The sun had just begun a noticeable descent when Collyn called his new recruits over for another lesson. He threw back the tarp on a pile of furs and hunkered down beside it, lifting a heavy pelt from the stack.

"Do you know what this is, Your Highness?" he asked Roland, holding up the fur.

Roland fingered the pelt.

"Good quality, from the feel of it."

"Aye, the coat is good enough for this animal. Do you know the type of fur?"

"It's soft enough for trim. We've always called it 'Queen's Choice'—I don't know the common name for it." Roland frowned.

"Well, then, we should give you a quick lesson. Since you'll be in charge of the negotiations, you should know what you bargain with." Collyn rose to his feet. "This is a common-grade leaper pelt. They're good for medium quality garments. The well-to-do tradesfolk prize them highly, but they're not very rare or expensive."

"Really?" the prince replied. "I'd have considered it fine indeed."

"One this good might bring two wheels." Collyn bent and picked up another fur, this one larger and coarser, but with a beautiful striation to the color of the individual hairs. "This is a mountain tunnel cat. They hide in the rocks and are extremely hard to trap. Although the fur is not as soft, it's much more precious. A fur this size is worth between ten and twenty wheels."

Roland nodded, stroking the cat pelt.

"Ah, yes. I have a winter coat of this. We've always called it 'Fire-tip.'" The prince loved to dress well—which had led to the nickname of "Roland the Vain" being bandied in the streets.

"That coat is probably worth more than one of these traders is paid for a season on the river, and Jarome is known as an extravagant master," Collyn said with a grin. "But the fur merchants in Stormhaven are more likely to use the name of the animal in their negotiations than some fanciful designation."

"I have much to learn..." Roland sounded thoughtful.

Collyn chuckled. "You have a quick mind, my lord. You will learn it in time."

As he bent to pick up another fur, a jolt shuddered through the raft, nearly throwing Stefan to the deck.

"What happened?" Roland cried.

"I fear we have run aground, Your Highness." Collyn scanned the raft, searching for his captain. "Please, excuse me." He strode off toward the prow, where Jarome stood berating one of the crew.

"Come on!" Roland followed Collyn, and Stefan hurried after the prince at his best pace. As they joined the others, they caught the end of Jarome's diatribe.

"How could you be so careless? Did you fall asleep at your post? We've traveled this course four times this season. I've never seen such incompetent wastrels!"

"But there have been heavy storms these past three weeks, Captain. The sands shifted. See the new lay of the river?" The man pointed to the sparse reeds along the shore.

Jarome looked where he indicated, studying the bank carefully.

"I suppose you're right," the captain conceded with a thoughtful frown. "It *has* changed since our last trip south." He sighed. "Well, nothing for it but to dig her off. Come on, men. Let's get to it."

"What can we do to help?" Roland asked, stripping off his shirt in imitation of Collyn and rolling up his leggings.

Stefan watched the prince's preparations with trepidation. He didn't mind the work but disliked the thought of baring his scars to the world.

As if reading his mind, Jarome laid a hand on his shoulder and leaned to whisper, "I think you could be of immeasurable help, lad, if you take that magical lute of yours and sit yonder to keep our spirits up. Would you play for me?"

"Certainly, sir." Stefan gave him a grateful smile.

Jarome winked at him. "Go on with you, Stefan. You're a good lad." He turned his attention to one of his men. "Here, you! Where'd you learn to handle a shovel, you layabout oaf?"

Stefan retrieved his instrument from the lean-to then slogged through the shallow water to the bank and sat on a stump to play. From this vantage point, he could watch the digging. He noted with a mixture of pride and envy Roland kept pace with the best of them.

He played his most stirring airs to inspire the men,

singing until his voice was a hoarse croak, but by the time the heavy raft floated free, the sun had sunk midway below the horizon. The bright autumn day was descending into twilight.

"We're stuck here for the night, lads," Jarome announced, dusting his hands together. "Let's see about some dinner."

"But, Captain," Roland protested, "the moon is nearly full tonight, and it can't be much farther to Woodwatch Ferry. The furs—"

"Will keep, lad. They aren't going anywhere. Neither is Stormhaven. I'm not risking another grounding tonight. A day or two either way will not matter to the king, but if I lose my raft, I lose my only livelihood. I'll not jeopardize her for any man, prince or no."

Stefan read Roland well enough to know what flashed through his mind. He watched uneasily as the prince spared Jarome a cool nod.

"Very well. I think I will retire early tonight. Coming, Stefan?"

The squire rose from his perch and waded back to the raft.

"Aye, my lord." He paused before Jarome. "Good night, Captain. Thank you...for everything."

Ignoring the puzzled look on Jarome's face, Stefan followed Roland into the lean-to. Roland already wore his light pack under his cloak, and his grandfather's sword buckled about his waist. The prince held out Stefan's bag, giving it an impatient shake.

"Come on. We're going. We will leave the rest of our things behind and retrieve them when the raft reaches Stormhaven."

"But how can we slip away, Roland? The watch will be posted."

"Not until after supper. This is our best chance."

"But it is not yet full dark—someone will see—"

"Not if we keep the lean-tos between us and the cook fire. I'm going, Stefan. I would prefer to have your company, but I am going—with or without you. What is your choice?"

Stefan drew his pack over his slender shoulders and slung the lute on his back.

"I'm coming," he murmured, "but this can only end badly."

They crept toward the stern. Luck favored them. The raft was tied to the west bank, so they didn't have to cross the river as well as the open plain between them and Woodwatch Ferry.

A sudden chill brushed Stefan, and he cocked his head, searching the darkening sky. High overhead, a lone bird wheeled, sending a shiver up his spine. He heard it give one piercing call.

Stefan laid a hand on Roland's arm.

"Master—" he began softly.

Before he could finish the warning, harsh yells shattered the evening calm as black-clad horsemen thundered towards the raft from a narrow band of trees separating the river from the wide plain beyond. Stefan instinctively flattened against the wall of the captain's quarters, mind racing as he searched for an escape route.

In the deepest recesses of his memory, something hideous stirred and slithered. His head reeled with the sense that all of this had happened before.

Ululating cries echoed through the twilight as the horsemen swung out of their saddles and swarmed the raft. The traders dashed for weapons stowed among their belongings, shouting encouragement to their fellows.

An arrow hissed through the air to bury its head in the planks at Roland's feet. Flame licked from the burning tip toward a nearby heap of furs.

Without conscious thought, Stefan bent to beat at the flames.

"Leave that!" shouted Roland, drawing his sword with a sharp singing of steel.

"But the furs—"

"Are worth less than our lives. Don't be a fool! Damn the luck. Five minutes more, and we would have been gone!" The prince grabbed Stefan's arm, thrusting him toward the interior of the cabin. "Get out of sight. You're no use without a weapon."

Stefan knew it was only the truth. While he still bested Roland quite often at fencing practice, despite his limp, he never wore a sword outside of those practice sessions. He had come away from Crown Keep without so much as a dagger. Even the thought of shedding blood made him physically ill. He could not stand the sight of it.

Steel rang against steel all around him in counterpoint to the less musical thud of club on flesh and bone. He hesitated a moment, torn between Roland's order and his concern for his master's safety. Then he turned and ducked into the cabin, only to find a burly man in black bending over Jarome's bunk.

Heart in his throat, the squire stumbled back

the way he had come. In his haste, he bumped into a wooden chest, which slid across the planks with grating protest.

The man in black jerked upright. A thick club dangled from one hand. Stefan's heart hammered in his chest as if trying to break free of his ribcage.

He surveyed the room in panic—nothing in the cabin could serve as a weapon. He stepped back and hit the doorframe; his lute connected with the wood with a resounding twang. Heart pounding, Stefan grabbed behind him for the neck.

Swinging the lute with all his strength, he smashed it into the attacker's face. The delicate wood splintered into a thousand pieces, and the man went down with a satisfying groan. Tears blurring his sight, Stefan turned and staggered out of the cabin...into hell.

Everywhere, piles of fur burned out of control, filling the night with the horrendous stench of scorched hair.

Men swarmed to snatch up their weapons and scramble to the rocky cliffs. He began to run, weaving through the hurrying men surging about him, calling fearfully for his mother.

"Roland!" he shouted, panic surging. "Where are you?"

Hideous, shrieking war cries mingled with the clash of swords and screams of agony, creating a symphony of death. Firelight silhouetted crumpled bodies and revealed shattered bows. Air tainted with the heavy metallic stench of blood also carried the sickly-sweet aroma of a body fallen too near the flames.

Stefan shook his head to clear it of the flashing images. *Where is the prince? Why have I been abandoned?*

He clutched the silver disk around his neck and felt its comfort wash over him.

With an overwhelming relief that left him weak in the knees, he spotted the prince, a shadow against a burning mound. Roland's sword flashed, and the firelight gleamed off his bright hair.

"Roland! Behind you!"

Stefan dropped his hand from the amulet as an attacker loomed up behind the prince. Roland spun and planted his foot in the raider's stomach, kicking him backward into the river with a splash.

"Stefan, look out!" he yelled in turn, running forward.

Stefan whirled—the man he had clubbed leered down at him, blood streaming from several cuts. He flinched, stumbled back a step. The brigand seized the leather thong around his neck and jerked it loose.

"No! Give that back!"

He grabbed for his medallion as a heavy cudgel slammed into his temple with an ominous crack. There was an explosion of stars, and then the world went black.

Chapter 6

Collyn Silverbrook snatched up a timber from a broken lean-to and waded in to protect the raft. Fires burned everywhere.

"These are no common raiders, lads!" he yelled to his crewmates. "They would not fire the raft if robbery were their motive. They come for other cargo, I wager."

Raiders in black inundated the craft, and the traders found themselves hard-pressed to defend it. Some of the marauders moved in ways no normal man could, and glimpses of evil, twisted faces in the firelight revealed less than human ancestry.

Collyn laid about him with his makeshift bludgeon. The traders fought valiantly, those who hadn't thought to bring arms snatching up whatever was at hand, as he had done. He glimpsed individual duels in the flickering firelight, and his heart ached to see several of his fellows fall and not rise—one of them Ethen.

Poor Anie, he thought. Her greatest fear come true...but at least he died a man, not wasting away from the sickness.

The big man spared a silent word of prayer for his fallen companion then darted from one end of the craft to the other, lending a hand wherever he found an opening. Glancing up from a fallen opponent, he saw Jarome locked in a grim sword battle with a hulking invader who fought with a speed and skill belying his size.

Jarome's sword flashed red in the firelight. Even in the shifting light of the burning furs, Collyn could see blood soaking the captain's right side. He struggled toward them, hampered by fallen bodies and pulsing mounds of flame. Before he could come to Jarome's aid, the raider plunged his sword into the captain's chest.

"Soulless bastard!" roared Collyn, hurtling over a burning pile and slamming his makeshift club down on the invader's head. The thug crashed to the deck, and Collyn fell to his knees beside Jarome's body.

He pillowed the captain's head on his knee, and Jarome chuckled weakly, a thin trickle of blood dribbling from the corner of his mouth.

"Some mess I've gotten myself into, Collyn."

He gasped in pain. Collyn felt his own heart contract in empathy.

"Tell Frederick I tried my best." Jarome coughed up another gout of blood. He shuddered, and his eyes closed.

Collyn bowed his head then leaned forward as the captain made a final effort to speak, his voice barely audible amid the chaos. Collyn strained to catch his final words.

"Save the boys, Collyn. You must save—"

With a sigh, Jarome fell limp in Collyn's arms. He eased the dead man to the deck of his beloved raft.

"It will become your pyre now," he murmured. Then the big trader straightened, searching the raft for the prince and his companion. He spotted Stefan just as the boy fell.

He leapt up and sprinted toward the lad as Stefan's attacker raised his club for a second strike. Launching himself at the man in a flying tackle, he knocked the raider away. The man's head impacted the oak deck with a satisfying thunk, and Collyn noted with grim satisfaction that necks were not intended to bend at that irregular angle.

"You've hurt your last child," he growled.

Roland skidded to a stop before him. The prince took one look at Stefan and his eyes locked on Collyn.

"I'll need your help!" Roland went down on one knee beside his squire. "Please, Collyn!"

Collyn scooped Stefan up in his arms—a sluggish trail of blood caught the firelight, black against the boy's pale skin.

"Come, let's get him out of here. Once we clear the raft, we'll be better able to assess his wound."

Roland nodded, his expression grim in the firelight, as he scrambled to his feet and followed the trader to the edge of the craft farthest from the bank. They slipped into the waist-deep water without a sound, wading toward a spot on the grassy riverbank beyond reach of the fitful firelight. Collyn could hear the prince's teeth chattering as they stumbled out of the cooling water.

"Are you all right, Your Highness?"

"I–it's just cold, that's all."

From the riverbank, the stench of burning furs did not claw at the throat quite as badly, but the air hung thick with wood smoke as the raft itself now began to burn. Sounds of battle still carried through the night behind them.

Collyn was torn. His friends were dying—but he had a duty to the boys as well, a duty given him with his captain's dying breath. He decided which duty meant more to him and put the fight behind him.

The trader knelt on the muddy riverbank, studying Stefan's wound. The cut ran from the crown of the boy's head to his brow.

"No, my lord, the water is still quite warm for the season," he murmured absently in belated response to Roland. "You're in shock—which is to be expected under the circumstances." He probed the jagged gash with gentle fingers. Blood matted Stefan's raven hair, and the flow showed no signs of stopping. "The first time I saw a man die in combat, I cried like a child. It happens to everyone going into battle the first time, if they are a decent man—and you are. It never gets easy, but in time it becomes...bearable."

"I've been fencing since I could walk. I know how to handle a sword."

"Knowing the moves and actually seeing the blood are two entirely different things, Your Highness." He felt dangerously exposed where they were. He glanced back over his shoulder. The fire raged mere yards away. "We can't stay here, Your Highness. If we cannot get under some type of cover, our escape from the raft will be only a respite—a brief one, at best." He jerked his chin at a stand of trees smudging the horizon. "Those trees are our best defense."

"What about Captain Jarome, Collyn? Shouldn't we try to help?"

"Jarome is dead, my lord. There is nothing left to save."

Roland gasped, and Collyn could sense the prince's misery. After all, the lad had known the captain all his life.

"I am sorry, Your Highness."

"He was a good man." The prince's voice was thick, as if struggling to hold back tears.

"Yes, he was. His last thoughts were for your safety, and I promised him I would get you away from here. It's no coincidence they attacked while you were aboard, my lord. They were after you. They will look for you among the slain. We must hurry before they realize you aren't there."

The near-full moon Roland had predicted had risen, limning the level, grassy verge sweeping to the reed-lined bank. The brilliant moonlight coaxed a trace of color from the darkness, its strong rays illuminating everything on the plain with woodcut clarity. The grass provided no cover.

Collyn stood and lifted Stefan in his arms once more. "Head for the trees, Your Highness."

Roland began to pick his way carefully over the moonlit grass, stumbling now and again as an animal burrow or uneven tussock of grass caught at his feet. Their progress was far too slow for Collyn's taste. The open plain was too exposed. All it would take would be for one of the marauders to glance their way, and they were discovered.

Borne on the wind came the sound of a horse's nervous whinny. Collyn cocked his head at the sound.

"Can you carry him?" he breathed in Roland's ear as they struggled up a slight rise.

The prince nodded.

"I think so."

"I'll be back as soon as I can." Collyn carefully settled the unconscious squire in Roland's arms; the lad stumbled under the unexpected weight. The riverman steadied him. "Wait in that clump of bushes over there." He pointed at a small thicket several yards away. "If I am not back by dawn, you must get him to Woodwatch on your own."

Moonlight glittered in Roland's eyes, reflected by tears Collyn pretended not to notice.

"Will he be all right?" asked the prince, his voice barely audible.

"I can't promise you. I wish I could, but it would be a lie. Now, please, get out of sight."

Roland took a deep breath and staggered into the bushes.

When he saw them safely hidden, Collyn circled cautiously back to the muddy riverbank. Flames from the burning raft licked skyward and reflected on the water. Their ruddy oranges and golds competed with the silver of the moon, giving the scene a lurid, nightmarish quality.

He could see none of his companions. The fighting appeared to be over—the figures silhouetted against the bright flames like paper cutouts now seemed more intent on wanton destruction than anything else.

"Look at this one," chortled a harsh, guttural voice. "He thought he were a gentleman, this one did. All in silk and leather. Didn't stop a sword in the gullet, now, did it?"

Coarse laughter followed, and Collyn seethed, knowing they spoke of Jarome.

"The Flames are too good for him! Dump him over," suggested one of the raiders, and a chorus of agreement echoed him.

Men scurried in the firelight, surging toward the edge of the raft. A loud splash followed as a heavy object hit the surface of the water, and Collyn forced himself to remember his errand. He longed to exact revenge for Jarome—and, indeed, the whole company—but the captain's final command rang in his ears.

He would die before breaking that vow.

He made a wide arc to come in close to the raiders' horses without being seen—he remembered they had scattered when their riders dismounted. Obviously, someone had collected them, which argued some of the brigands remained behind when the group attacked.

Collyn crept through the reeds, bent almost double to take best advantage of their inadequate screen.

The animals were tied to a picket line hastily thrown up beside the river. The destruction on the raft continued, the shouts and coarse laughter covering any slight noises he might make. He could smell the sweat of the restless beasts. The horses danced nervously, frightened by the odor of smoke and the metallic stench of blood that spiced it.

Collyn picked his way carefully, the soft mud squelching beneath his boots threatening to send him sliding. He cursed himself for not having a weapon with him but had spent his hard-won coin on greater necessities. He hadn't expected to need sword or dagger on this trip; he wore only a belt knife, more suited to slicing bread than throats, but he drew it from its sheath.

Luck favored him. When he reached the horses, only two men stood guard.

"It ain't fair, Leam!" whined the smaller of the two. "Why do I always have to stay to the back? I never get to have no fun."

His companion grunted.

"Just like a boy, to think of killing as play. You'll get your chance soon enough."

"Admit it—you wish you was over there, too, don't you?" The boy gestured toward the conflagration. "Slicing throats and winning treasure, 'stead of watching those foreign bastards do it for you."

"I'll collect my share just as well from here, Jakoby. And I don't have to risk life and limb to do it."

"Coward!" taunted Jakoby, squaring off against Leam with his hand on the hilt of his sword.

Leam took a step toward his companion.

Collyn felt tempted to let them fight it out, but the outcome was too uncertain. Crouching, he picked up a fist-sized rock then threw it as far as he could.

The two men instantly forgot their differences and went on the alert. Leam drew his sword.

"Guard the horses," he ordered, sprinting off in the direction of the noise.

Jakoby unsheathed his own weapon and peered about him nervously. Collyn lunged, one brawny arm snaking around the sentry's throat as he covered the man's mouth with his free hand. He kept pressure on the guard's throat until he went limp then lowered the small body to the ground. He looked down at a boy barely older than Stefan.

"You're lucky. I won't kill you," he whispered, sweeping up the boy's sword and sheathing his belt knife in favor of the better weapon. "Your friends didn't have the same respect for youth. Perhaps this second chance will change your life the way one changed mine."

Wasting no more time, Collyn ran to the horses. They whickered anxiously as he approached, jerking against their reins. He caught the bridle of a large black stallion, but before he could lose the animal, he heard someone behind him and spun, sword flashing in the moonlight.

Leam rushed him, sword set to attack. Collyn neatly sidestepped when he lunged. His sword grazed the riverman's hand, but the muddy bank betrayed him and the villain sprawled flat. As he struggled to regain his feet, shouts rang out from the raft.

Collyn spun back to the horses. A quick slash with his blade severed the stallion's reins, and he swung into the saddle. Reaching down, he seized the reins of the next horse, freeing it as well. Then he cut the rope tethering the remaining mounts.

Turning the stallion, he galloped back toward the waiting prince and unconscious Stefan with the second horse in tow. The shouts of approaching marauders spooked their milling mounts into skittering flight.

He yelled the horse to greater speed, no longer having anything to gain from stealth. He could only trust to swiftness and luck.

***

Roland studied Stefan in the moonlight, desperate for a sign of returning consciousness. The squire remained as still as death. The analogy made him shudder, and he looked out over the plain, searching in vain for Collyn. In time, his search brought him back to the dying flames of the raft.

Without conscious thought, he began to pray.

"Stefan must live. Please let him be all right. He has to be all right. Nothing else will do. I want to share a pint over the memory of this night while he shows his scars to the tavern wenches.

"Stefan is the healer, not me. By the Flames, why couldn't our positions be reversed? He'd know what to do if I were injured. I should never have taken for granted all the skills he has learned instead of paying attention and learning myself. If only I knew what he would do..."

And suddenly he did know.

"He'd stop the bleeding somehow—that would be the first thing!" He ripped the bottom of his shirt free with the point of his dagger and tied a makeshift bandage about the squire's wound. It still bled heavily.

Collyn had been gone for some time, and the prince grew increasingly anxious. Brilliant moonlight bathed the plain around them with its mysterious radiance, but within the shadows of the thicket all was dark. He felt as if something crawled toward them in that darkness, and his gaze darted from side to side.

"Where is Collyn?" he whispered. "Why does he not come? What will I do if he doesn't come back? How can I help Stefan when I don't even know how to help myself?"

Smoke from the raft penetrated their hiding place, and Roland fought the urge to cough as it tickled the back of his throat. Other odors rode the wind, many of them unfamiliar to him. However, he recognized the damp scent of decay wafting from the nearby river, and fancied he could smell the blood that must fill the river by now.

Roland gulped. Alone, for all practical purposes, he

admitted to himself what he would have hidden even from Stefan.

He was terrified.

Despite the chill air, he could feel sweat pasting his shirt to his body, and he shivered. His fencing lessons and tales of chivalry had not prepared him for the reality of squatting in hiding while men died not five hundred yards away.

Hoofbeats thundered toward him—at least two horses, by the sound of it. Roland's heart leapt into his throat. His hand tightened on the hilt of his dagger. He would make any attacker work for victory.

The horses slowed to a walk, and he heard a rider dismount. He rose to his haunches, ready to spring to Stefan's defense.

"My lord," came a soft whisper, "are you there?"

"Collyn?"

"Aye." The big riverman moved forward, leading two mounts. "I have horses. We will get him to safety."

Roland sighed.

"Thank the Power. Is it far to town?"

"Too far to move him in the dark. We'll make do with that stand of trees yonder—it's far enough from the raft to be safe for the night. Come. Help me get him on a horse. You'll have to support him for the ride."

"As you deem best."

Roland nodded, grateful to have someone else in charge. He swung into the saddle of the smaller horse, and Collyn lifted Stefan into his arms. The squire moaned softly but showed no other signs of consciousness.

Roland's heart lurched.

"We must hurry, Collyn," he murmured. "He needs

warmth and medicine."

"We will try for the first, but I don't know if he'll get the second tonight. I saved nothing from the raft."

Roland thought guiltily of the medicines in Stefan's pack. *Who could have known we would have need of them so soon?*

His arms tightened around Stefan as Collyn clucked and the horses moved forward.

Chapter 7

An acrid stench assaulted Stefan's nostrils, making his eyes tear and his throat constrict with coughing. Flames danced with lurid flickers upon inky water. He searched frantically for someone he had lost, but he was alone.

Suddenly, he spotted Roland. The prince stood, feet braced for action, eyes narrowed against the smoke. Soot smeared his determined expression as his lips twisted in a snarl. His sword gleamed like a snake's fang in the firelight.

Stefan's heart leapt. "Roland!" he cried, stumbling forward.

The prince started to turn.

An arrow hissed through the night in a fiery arc, thudding home between his shoulder blades. He collapsed in a broken heap.

"No!" Stefan cried, jerking upright.

"Easy, lad."

He swiveled toward the source of the gentle command. His aching head reeled, and he moaned, falling back on his unfamiliar bed. Raising shaky hand to whirling head, he lowered fingers damp with blood.

Confused by the unaccountable weakness, the boy rolled onto one elbow and levered himself up with more care. He frowned as he gazed around the sheltered campsite

"Be still, Stefan. You've taken a nasty crack on the head. You must rest." Collyn Silverbrook laid a firm hand on his shoulder and eased him back onto the blankets.

"Where is this place?" Stefan's voice trembled as he fought a surge of panic. "Where is the raft? Where is my master?"

"You're safe here."

"But the raft, and Roland—"

"The raft is gone, lad, but the prince sleeps yonder. He's fine. A good deal better off than you are."

"How did we come here?"

"We were attacked. Do you remember anything at all?"

Confused images of swooping, screeching riders in black flitted through his mind. His hand flew to his throat, seeking a comfort no longer there

"My amulet. It's gone," he whispered, voice catching. "And my lute..." The dim predawn light blurred as his eyes misted at the memory.

A lopsided smile quirked Collyn's lips. "You'll live," he teased softly. "Rest now."

Then the enormity of what the man had said sank in.

"The raft is gone? Captain Jarome...?"

"We will talk of it later. You must lie still and rest." Collyn's tone brooked no argument.

Listening to the sounds of Collyn moving about the camp, Stefan clutched at his chest, searching out of habit for the stolen charm. He smelled the clean, fresh scent of growing things borne on the breeze, but an unpleasant hint of decay underlay the fragrance. His stomach clenched in response. Something about the wood saddened his heart with an almost physical weight.

By the time Roland awoke, Stefan felt well enough to sit up and drink the draught Collyn had concocted for his headache. The bitter potion dulled the pain, but he heaved most of it up again when the trader probed the wound on his scalp.

"I'm sorry," he murmured as he dragged a trembling hand across his mouth.

He looked up to find Collyn's gray eyes studying him with a grave expression that chilled the boy's heart.

"You're in need of greater healing than I can manage, lad. We must get you to Woodwatch Ferry as soon as possible."

"I'm fine," Stefan protested and attempted to stand. The slightest change in position made the ground swoop and dive around him, and he swayed on his feet.

"Sit down until we strike camp," Roland ordered, slipping an arm about his squire's waist, and settling him on an old fallen tree nearby. A broken branch curved out from the downed trunk, and Stefan leaned back against it, grateful for the support. His head started spinning again, and the temptation to just let everything slip away from him was overwhelming. He gave in with a sigh.

***

Roland glanced up from rolling his bedding and bounded over just in time to prevent Stefan's limp form from sliding to the ground.

"Collyn!" he shouted, struggling to control the squire's dead-weight.

The big riverman hurried over to help lay Stefan on the soft grass beside the fallen tree

As Collyn studied the boy's pale face, a thoughtful frown creased his brow.

"He's lost too much blood to be moved, but we

really have no choice." He gave the prince a sharp look over the unconscious boy between them. "I say again, Your Highness, last night's raid was no random attack. The raiders who survived will be hard on our trail. Let's hope there are few of them." He scanned the visible horizon through the screening trees, mouth set in a grim line.

Roland swallowed hard and nodded. His impetuous plea for permission to raft with the traders had nearly killed them all. He felt a renewed tightness in his throat at the thought of Jarome's hearty welcome and the captain's pride in his fine craft. His heart ached with grief and guilt.

"What of the traders?" he asked, his tone hushed

"They fought to the end, but they were outnumbered." Collyn's words were matter-of-fact, but his hands, knotted into white-knuckled fists, betrayed rage at his helplessness.

Roland busied himself collecting their few belongings in order to avoid thinking about the merry companions he had joked with around the cook fire. His father would be devastated to lose Jarome

Father!

"Collyn, I must get back to Crown Keep at once." His words tumbled over each other as he began pacing the camp, picking things up and dropping them again, unable to follow an action through to a conclusion in his agitation. "My father will be beside himself when he hears of this attack. I must let him know we're all right."

Collyn grabbed his shoulders, forcing him to stand still. Roland felt a cold upsurge of fury at the man's temerity. He tried to jerk free, but Collyn was too strong.

"Your Highness," Collyn pleaded, "please, listen to reason! Stefan is badly hurt. If he doesn't get a healer's attention soon, he'll join the others killed in the raid. It may already be too late, but we must try.

"You'll never beat the news of the raid to your father's ear, not even if your horse could fly. Help me get the boy to a doctor—you can send a message from Woodwatch quicker than you could return. The hour or so delay will not make much difference to your errand."

The sense of Collyn's words began to sink in, despite Roland's anger. Stefan was hurt. He owed the boy this much at least. He drew a deep breath then exhaled gustily.

"You're right," he murmured with a tense nod. "At least we can try to salvage what may be saved. But please, let's hurry."

***

Stefan regained consciousness before they finished breaking camp. He drank some weak tea, but the effort sent another wave of nausea through him. He could not remember what Collyn had told him earlier about getting to this place, and he dared not ask again.

Teeth gritted, he made it to his knees, panting with the effort. The world spun. Taking a deep breath, he rose shakily to his feet and limped to the black stallion. He leaned against the horse's warm neck, fingers twined in its mane for both comfort and support. He locked eyes with the horse

"I cannot think," he whispered in its ear. "My thoughts are spinning like leaves in a dust storm. By the Flames, you must help me stay on your back as Roland commands, my friend…he'll leave me behind if I cannot keep up." He stroked the soft muzzle with a trembling hand. "I can't be left alone again!"

The stallion whickered, turning its head to nuzzle his shoulder

"That's a good fellow. We'll get along fine."

He laid his cheek against the warm neck. The stallion tossed its head and nudged him again

Stefan laughed. "Don't worry, my friend. I'll be all right."

As if to prove him wrong, the world suddenly grayed, and he felt his knees buckle. The stallion neighed loudly as he slid down its side.

He looked up to find Roland beside him

"Are you all right?" asked the prince anxiously.

Stefan fought to focus. "I–I'll be fine. Just help me on the horse."

"I'll have to ride with him, Collyn. He can't sit a horse alone in this condition."

"I'll be fine, Master Roland," Stefan protested, trying to push up from the ground. His shaking arms would not support him, and he fell back.

"We only have two horses anyway," Roland pointed out with cool logic. "Someone will have to ride with you in any case."

"I can walk then," Stefan declared stoutly. "It is my place." He tried again to stand.

"Collyn!" Roland ordered.

Collyn lifted Stefan from the ground and set him on the horse's back. He felt the blood rush to his cheeks

"I'm no baby," he muttered, feeling like a child

despite the grumbled protest.

"Then stop acting like one," Roland commented as he swung up behind him

The squire turned to reason with the prince, and the motion sent his head reeling. He would have fallen had Roland not steadied him.

"Sit still, you little fool. You'll only wind up killing yourself. Then where will I be?"

Stefan resigned himself to the inevitable.

***

By the time they rode into Woodwatch Ferry an hour later, Stefan had passed out again. The rough bandage circling his forehead bore fresh traces of blood seeping from the wound

Roland cradled the squire in his arms. He studied Stefan's still features, and his heart sank. *I brought this hurt upon Stefan, too. Will I ever stop causing him pain?*

"We must get him to the doctor as quickly as possible, Collyn. This isn't right. He should be conscious by now."

"'Tis a grave wound, my prince."

"I...He...He can't die, Collyn. He would follow me into the Flames without protest to protect me, and yet he is always the one who suffers."

"He's not dead yet. I know of an inn where we can stop for the night. A town this large is sure to have a competent healer. Stefan will be fine."

Roland said nothing further, but his arms tightened protectively about the squire.

Woodwatch Ferry was a large township butting up to the very skirts of the Forest of Night. As the horses' hooves clopped over the hard-packed streets, Roland's glance roved from side to side.

These buildings were large and airy, most of them sturdy stone constructions. The streets were free of debris and bordered by storm gutters. Compared to Ethen and Anie's village, it was a thriving city. He could not help but be impressed, despite his worry for Stefan.

The citizens observed the newcomers with obvious curiosity but continued on about their business. Well-dressed matrons herded plump children. Men stood beside a corral stocked with fine horses; the sound of their dickering punctuated the morning air. The entire town radiated a sense of stability.

He felt a bit more hope there would be a doctor of skill available when he saw the town's prosperity.

It was here his original plan had called for them to desert the raft. He devoutly wished the trip had gone as intended.

"The inn is just there."

Collyn pointed to a two-story structure set into a wide lawn. Roland nodded and pulled the horse to a stop outside the large inn. Collyn dismounted and tied both sets of reins to the rail. Far overhead, a bird wheeled—a mere speck against the blue sky—then swept down to perch on the signpost of the inn. Roland glanced up with a frown.

The sleek black raven tilted its head, watching them. The intensity of its scrutiny made Roland uneasy. He bent from the saddle and eased Stefan into Collyn's strong arms, holding his breath until the transfer was completed safely. Rolling stiff shoulders, he swung his leg over the stallion's back and dismounted.

"Come," he ordered, turning toward the inn, and trusting Collyn would follow. He strode inside confidently with Collyn at his heels. The raven flew in behind them and soared up to the rafters.

"Innkeeper, I need a room at once, and summon the town physician to attend me."

The grizzled innkeeper eyed Roland with a sneer

"And just who do you think you are, Sir High and Mighty? The prince?"

Roland felt an iron band cinch about his head. His volatile temper ignited at the man's insolent tone. Leaning over the counter, he bit his words short

"Yes, I *am* the prince. Shall I show you my portrait on this coin?" He slammed a golden wheel onto the surface of the bar. "This boy is seriously hurt, and if he worsens, you will be very, very sorry."

The innkeeper's face paled.

"I—I am sorry, Your Highness. Of course, you shall have a room at once. Best in the house. Straight up the stairs and first door on your left. I'll send for a doctor immediately."

Roland nodded curtly. He quirked a finger at Collyn.

As he turned to lead the other up the stairs, he vaguely registered the raven swooping out into the sunlight as the innkeeper hurried to fetch the healer but spared it little thought. He fought to rein in his anger, every breath forced between gritted teeth.

Inside the chamber, he gave in to his fury. He threw his cap across the room. Blood racing, he paced the breadth of the space

"How dare he speak to a paying customer with such insolence? Any paying customer!"

Collyn laid Stefan gently on the bed and checked the bandage.

"He's bleeding again. I hope the healer arrives soon."

"You didn't answer my question." Roland turned, fists balled into knots on his hips.

Straightening, Collyn met Roland's eye calmly.

"Perhaps he took exception to your tone. Were you any less insolent to him? This is his establishment, not yours. Forgive my bluntness, my lord, but it's the truth. You're not in Crown Keep now. Few people outside the castle township have ever seen you. Why should they instantly grovel at your feet? It's better to earn respect than demand it. You've earned mine."

Roland felt his face flush under the gentle rebuke. Striding to the window, he leaned forehead against arm, staring out into the street

"Am I really so arrogant?"

"You're young, my prince. You have much to learn."

A brisk knock sounded at the door; Roland nodded, and Collyn opened it. A stooped old man with long, gnarled fingers bustled in, took one look at Stefan, and hurried to his side with a *tsk* of disapproval. Turning a birdlike eye on Roland, he shook his head.

"Why didn't you attend to this boy earlier? He burns with fever and has lost a great deal of blood."

Roland moved to the foot of the bed

"We've just arrived in town, sir. We called for you as soon as we did so."

"You're lucky it was me here to call." The doctor swept off his long black cape; it swirled like silken wings as he hung it on a peg behind the door.

"Who are you?" Roland asked.

"My name is Ravenwing, Prince Roland. Remember it well. That's all you need know." The elderly doctor clucked his tongue again. "Irresponsibility, that's what it is. Complete irresponsibility." He carefully unwound the makeshift bandage and examined the wound. "How'd he get a thing like this anyway, fall off a horse?"

"No," Collyn answered, "he was struck with a club."

"Powerful arm behind that stroke."

"We were attacked on the river," Roland added.

The doctor shook his head once more

"And the little one here gets the worst of it. 'Tis a fine state of affairs we are coming to, I warrant you." He continued to mutter under his breath as he deftly cleaned Stefan's wound and packed it with a poultice. The squire moaned, and the old man whispered over him, too softly for the others to hear. "He should sleep now. Give him some barley soup and a good strong cup of tea when he wakens. No matter what he says, do not let him out of bed for three days."

He fixed a piercing eye on Roland once more. "What kind of royalty brawls with brigands on the river?"

The prince scowled.

"How do you know so much?"

The strange little doctor ignored him and turned to Collyn

"Let me see your wound, Master Silverbrook."

Reluctantly, Collyn held out his right hand, with its grimy strip of bandage

"I didn't even know you were hurt, Collyn," Roland scolded.

The riverman shrugged

"Just a scratch, Your Highness. Nothing to worry about."

Ravenwing undid the rag and cleaned the jagged cut with an expert's efficient economy of motion.

"You will live. Keep it clean, and change the dressing daily." Replacing his instruments and ointments in his bag, the doctor continued, "Now, remember, Stefan must be kept abed for the next three days, no matter how he protests. I leave that unenviable task to you, Master Silverbrook, for I believe the prince plans on riding on before sundown. See you take the task to heart."

He brushed the hair from Stefan's forehead with a curiously gentle gesture.

"I would hate to see him lost...again." Picking up his bag, Ravenwing scuttled out of the chamber without a backward glance.

Chapter 8

"What do you make of that?" Roland muttered, sinking onto the end of the bed. "I suppose the innkeeper told him he was to attend my servant, and Stefan's name is not unknown, but how did he know yours? And how could he know my plans when I'm not sure of them myself?"

"I don't like it. It isn't natural." The trader's hand clasped the crystal arrowhead about his neck, as if to ward off evil. The gesture reminded Roland of Stefan and his amulet.

"What are you suggesting?" the prince scoffed. "Sorcery?"

Collyn shrugged.

"There are dark things in this world, though not all magic is black."

A sigh from Stefan ended the conversation; Roland moved to the boy's side.

Stefan raised shaking hand to bandaged head.

"What is this place?" he whispered.

"Don't worry," Roland soothed. "You're safe here. Rest. We'll get you something to eat. Would you like that?"

"I–I think I could manage a little."

"Good. Collyn, go down and request the barley soup and tea the doctor ordered."

"Aye, my lord." The big riverman bowed and left the room.

Stefan tried to sit up, and Roland gently pushed him back onto the pillows.

"Save your strength until your food arrives. Then, you'll eat and go back to sleep."

"I'm fine, honestly."

"You're to rest for three days. Doctor's orders."

"But that's impossible! We must return home. Your father will be frantic. News of the attack will not take long to reach him."

"Hush now. We'll get word to the King. Don't you worry your head about it. Your health is more important at the moment, and you *will* follow the doctor's commands."

A timid knock sounded on the door, and a serving girl peeked around the jamb.

"T-the man said ye wanted soup, Yer Highness. I brung it to ye."

"Thank you, my lady." Roland flashed the girl his most winsome smile. "Bring it over here."

She did as she was bid, but her hands trembled so badly she almost upset the dishes. The prince rescued the laden tray from her grasp before disaster struck. Along with Stefan's soup, Collyn had sent up a bowl of thick mutton stew and a chunk of fresh bread. A flagon of ale stood beside the mug of tea.

"Thoughtful fellow," the prince commented to the girl. "Where is the man who ordered the meal?"

"He be eatin' in the kitchen, milord. Said 'twere more his place."

"I see. Thank him for me, please." He fished a coin from his purse. "This is for you."

"Oh, 'tweren't no trouble, milord," she murmured in a husky voice. Then her cheeks bloomed scarlet, and she bobbed a hasty curtsy. "Thank ye, milord."

"You're quite welcome, my dear. Now, go and ask Master Silverbrook to attend me when he finishes his meal. Can you do that?"

"Aye, milord. At once, milord."

"Good girl. Off you go."

She backed across the room, bobbing curtsies as she went, and ran solidly into the doorframe. With a little squeak of dismay, she slid around it and scampered out down the hall.

Roland chuckled. "At least I command a positive response from some of my subjects." Helping Stefan to prop against the headboard, he handed the squire the bowl of soup. "Eat up. You need to build your strength."

"But—"

"We'll talk after lunch. Eat your soup."

Roland found he was hungrier than he'd realized, and the mutton stew disappeared rapidly. He refused to let Stefan talk until the they had eaten. As soon as the squire finished his tea, a stubborn scowl warned Stefan would not be put off any longer.

"Where is this place, Master Roland?"

"This is the finest inn Woodwatch Ferry can boast. Nothing but the best for you, my lad."

"How did we get here? The last thing I remember is the clearing in the woods."

"We rode into town about an hour ago, Stefan. The innkeeper called for a doctor to tend your wound, and here we are."

"But—"

"No more for now. You must rest. The doctor left specific orders. Lie back now and sleep."

"I'm fine, Master Roland. I should be up and about

my duties." Stefan moved to rise, and Roland shook his head.

"You're going to lie right there and take a nap, my boy. That's your duty for today. Consider it an order."

Stefan smiled faintly.

"As you command, my lord," he sighed, eyes drifting shut.

As soon as he was sure Stefan was asleep, Roland decided to go look for Collyn, too restless to wait for his return. He found the riverman in the inn's common room.

They selected a secluded table in a corner of the nearly empty room, and the prince called for beer. They sat silently while the little serving girl set the steins before them.

Once she was gone, the prince took a long pull on his beer then set it down with a thump.

"You know the doctor was right about my decision to leave, don't you?" he blurted.

"I suspected," Collyn replied. "It isn't in your nature to let anything stand in the way of your wishes. Not even disaster."

"That sounds so callous, Collyn."

"Not necessarily. It's a good trait for a ruler to have, as long as those wishes are reasoned ones."

"Many stalwart men were killed because of me. I must return home at once and explain what happened—I owe Captain Jarome that much. His raft was destroyed, and a valuable cargo lost. The merchants in Stormhaven will think Jarome cheated them out of their furs. My father must send word of the truth. That's why I have to go home."

"Wouldn't it save time to hire a messenger to take a letter to those merchants from here? We're two days closer to Stormhaven, at least, and that's not considering the extra time to return to Castle Keep first."

"But—"

"So that's not the only reason you want to return home, is it?" Collyn asked, his voice soft.

"I'm not ashamed to admit I'm also worried about my father. He's not as young as he once was, and he's not been well of late. He'll hear of the disaster and think the worst. I must put those fears to rest as quickly as possible for the sake of his health."

"Something worth considering. But what of Stefan?"

"I need you to wait with him until he can travel, then take him somewhere safe. Maybe Overlake would be big enough to get lost in. I can't swear who ordered this attack, but I can guess. If my cousin Norfulk *is* behind this, he's a ruthless man who will stop at nothing to achieve his ends.

"Stefan will be a liability if it comes down to a fight— he's safer in hiding. I'll can return home secretly and reassure my father, but Norfulk must think his plan has succeeded so we can flush him into the open. After Stefan is safe, come to the castle. I may need you. But we must first make sure Stefan is hidden somewhere."

"Why should a boy squire cause any anxiety to someone willing to murder kings? Surely he would have required some proof of your demise, and if the raiders could not provide it, he would hardly take their word."

"The entire kingdom knows of Stefan's loyalty. He would never leave me, not even to save his own hide. If

I am to play dead, he will have to be dead as well."

"My lord, do you seriously think Norfulk still believes you dead? The way you spoke to the innkeeper earlier, the entire town knows the prince is here in the inn—I've heard three whispered conversations about the subject since I sat down. And Woodwatch Ferry is one of the busiest hamlets in the kingdom. By nightfall, the news will have spread far beyond its borders. If Norfulk has the network of spies I suspect he must, he'll have word by tomorrow morning at the latest."

Roland stared at him.

"By the Flames," he whispered, "you're right. I never thought—but Stefan can't be moved yet. And that doctor's last comment made me uneasy." Frowning, he studied the rings left on the table by his stein. He felt like he had missed some sign he should understand, but didn't. It made him nervous.

He swiped a hand across the surface of the table, obliterating the neat rings into a single puddle of water.

"Will you leave immediately?" Collyn asked.

"I should, but I think it'll be safer to travel at night with the moon full. Besides, you're right—I know nothing of my people. I think it's time I walked among them a little. I want to explore the town a bit before I go. I am seldom alone. Stefan is like my shadow, constantly at my heels. Today, I can forget the throne for a time and just be me." He rose to his feet.

Collyn took a slow sip of his beer.

"If you leave him behind, it will break his heart."

Roland felt his chest tighten and his face harden as his temper rose.

"I don't need criticism from you, Master Silverbrook.

Better a broken heart than dead. Where I go, he's too ill to follow."

"You're the prince," Collyn replied with a shrug. "But at least you owe him the courtesy of telling him you're abandoning him."

"I am not 'abandoning' him. I am trying to save his life! How can I tell him? Stefan has the heart of a lion, but it's as fragile as a soap bubble. Telling him will only hurt him further. He'll forgive me in time." Roland stalked out of the common room and up the stairs, grinding his teeth in frustrated anger.

When he reached their room, he found the decision postponed. Stefan slept, his dark hair a sharp contrast to the snowy linen of the pillow. He appeared at peace, but Roland noted his face bore the same pallor as the pillow. He didn't have the heart to waken him.

He decided to slip away and explore the town instead—he would leave the inevitable for a later time and try to screw up his courage to tell Stefan as Collyn had advised. Quickly changing his doublet for a rough hunting jerkin, he pulled his cap down low over his bright hair. He hesitated over his sword belt. He already felt rather defenseless just thinking about being without it, but it was too fine a blade for a villager. In the end, he left the sword leaning in the corner.

Stealing out of the room, he bounded downstairs and into the sunlight. He paused on the porch, taking a deep breath of the crisp autumn air.

"It is so wonderful to be free!" he breathed.

Strolling down the wide lane in front of the inn, he followed the smell of baking bread and cries of merchants to the marketplace in the heart of the town. The day had warmed as the sun rose, and the marketplace bustled with color and sound. Roland tried to take everything in at once.

"I could become used to this." He chuckled softly. "Freedom tastes like wine."

As he sauntered through the bustle, the calls of the vendors rose all about him.

"Fresh fruit! Sweet as summer. Taste the springtime. Get your fresh fruit!"

"Silks like a baby's skin. Soft as a mother's touch. Dress like a king!"

"Knives sharpened. Grindstones, whetstones, flint and steel."

The calls cascaded around him in an eddying stream, overlapping each other, rising to the surface then slipping back into the general bedlam. Roland examined the soft silks laid in inviting display across a counter and complimented the owner. The thought he could buy whatever he could afford, and no one stood at his shoulder to moderate his decisions, made him giddy.

As he made his way through the crowd, the prince absently fingered the coins in his pouch. He didn't have much money—he had never needed to carry any—but what he did have should suffice to enjoy himself a little. He bought a ripe globefruit and bit into it, laughing with delight as its sweet juice ran down his chin. He swiped it away with the back of his hand and walked on. Savoring the taste, he continued his wanderings.

He drifted to a stall specializing in leather-bound books. The offered wares proved as good as any he'd seen in the shops of Crown Keep township—it drove home the prosperity of Woodwatch Ferry yet again.

As he browsed through them, he picked up a beautiful old volume of illumined ballads covered in soft forest-green chamois. This could be a sort of consolation present for Stefan, he thought. It will not ease the parting, but perhaps it will speed the recovery.

He glanced up at the bookseller, a stocky young man scarcely older than he was.

"How much for this?"

The shopkeeper glanced at the prince.

"More than you can afford by half, I wager," he replied with a sniff.

Roland felt his cheeks heat up but forced himself to take a deep breath.

"I won't know until you quote me the price."

"It's hand-tooled, that leather is, and them illustrations were done by the Brothers of the Flames."

Roland was beginning to wonder about the shopkeeper's choice of wares—he seemed no connoisseur of his own stock.

"Lovely. How much does it cost?"

"Three wheels and a talon."

"I'll take it." As he reached for his purse, his hand brushed another's, and he jerked back, staring down open-mouthed into a pair of eyes as green as his own.

The little cutpurse was short and slender, a tress of pale-blond hair falling over one eye from under his cap. He recovered with more speed than Roland, giving the prince's pouch a hard yank as he slashed the strings with his dagger. He took off at a full sprint before Roland could gather his wits.

"Here! Stop, thief!" Roland shouted, chasing after the villain.

A burly tradesman stepped in front of the fleeing boy, making a grab for him. The thief dove and somersaulted between the man's legs before scrambling back to his feet. Roland danced around the man, who still stood in the center of the path, staring after the boy with mouth agape.

The cutpurse darted into an alley, and Roland skidded around the side of the building after him. The stench of refuse bins billowed around him, and he gagged. The thief upended a barrel of garbage in front of him, but the prince vaulted over the rolling cask. He stumbled as he came down on the other side.

"Stop, you little wretch!" he bellowed. His temper flared as he began to tire. He was unused to such exertion, and the realization fueled his anger.

The boy didn't waste breath in reply. He looked back over his shoulder, but his flying feet didn't slow as he took another corner. They raced out of the alley and back onto a broader thoroughfare. Roland smelled the sharp, rich scent of horses, and guessed they were at the corral he had glimpsed on their way into town.

The boy slipped through the fence and dodged the milling animals. Roland leapt over the gate and followed, barely keeping his feet when his boot hit a clump of freshly deposited manure.

"Damn you!" he roared. "Stop! I order you!"

The little thief cared no more for his orders than the innkeeper had done. If anything, he ran faster than before. Roland felt a stitch in his side and had to stop. Head hanging, he panted, trying to catch his breath.

"If I ever catch you, so help me, I'll—"

As if the prince's sincerity at last registered on him,

the culprit dropped Roland's purse and disappeared into the crowded marketplace.

At the same instant, Roland sensed a flare of heat singe his finger. It felt like someone had dropped a live coal on his hand. With a startled oath of pain, he shook his hand reflexively then glanced down, catching his breath with a sharp hiss.

The ruby in his heavy signet ring glowed with an inner fire—the gold ring was so much a part of him he often forgot he wore it. Another inheritance from his grandfather, he'd never heard of such a phenomenon associated with it.

He stared wide-eyed at the glowing ruby then felt himself tugged forward; it seemed as if the ring propelled him. Curious, yet wary, he followed the urge, scooping up his purse as he passed it.

The compulsion led him to a sheltered corner where a jewelry peddler had set up his stall. His hand reached forward of its own volition, drawn to a pendant dangling from a length of gold chain. It swung in gentle arcs as the breeze teased it.

Suddenly, he realized he still clutched the book he had admired. Roland shook his head ruefully.

"I must be more careful with my cries of 'Thief!'" he murmured to himself.

The prince shrugged—he would pay for the book on his way back to the inn.

Catching at the chain, he stopped the pendant's swing. His ring flared crimson, the pulse mirrored by the buttery stone set in the amulet. He studied the piece more closely. It bore the likeness of a gryphon, worked in heavy gold, carrying a large topaz-like stone on its back. The stone glowed like the sun when it touched his grandfather's ring.

"Find something you like?" a man asked at his elbow.

Roland dropped his hand so the other would not see the unusual glow.

"Maybe." He shrugged, turning to the shopkeeper. "It's a quaint enough piece."

"Oh, aye, that it is."

The middle-aged peddler was tall and tanned. His coal-black hair sported a prominent streak of silver, and his eyes were an unusual blue-green. He cocked his head, and Roland frowned. The gesture seemed somehow familiar.

"There are rumors it came from the elves," the merchant whispered confidentially. "An ancient myth about a gryphon carrying the sun across the sky or some such rot. But o' course, 'tis merely an old wives' tale. The elves were conquered long ago."

"What do you want for it?" Roland asked, falsely casual. In truth, the mere mention of that legendary race excited him beyond measure. The elves had vanished from the world when Crown Keep was still an empty hillside in an unclaimed land.

The merchant pretended to weigh the matter.

"I think five gold wheels might do. 'Tis an incredibly old and valuable piece."

"I'll give you three," Roland countered. He longed to have the talisman, but the man asked more than he carried in his purse. Heart hammering, he waited to see if the peddler would accept his offer.

"'Tis worth seven, young sir. I'm already giving you a more than fair deal."

"It's probably a cheap bauble you won at cards," Roland scoffed, his voice tight with suppressed emotion, "but it's a pretty thing. I'll give you three and a half." It would take nearly every coin in his purse, and was the highest he could possibly go.

The shopkeeper sighed.

"You drive a hard bargain, young master. Many customers like you, and I would be beggared for sure. Take it. It's yours."

Heaving an inner sigh of relief, Roland handed the merchant the proper coins and slipped the chain around his neck. He walked on, turning the pendant this way and that to watch the play of sunlight on the stone's faceted surface. Then he settled the amulet inside his jerkin, deciding it was safer to secure the piece with thieves running so rampant.

As he headed back toward the inn, thinking about what he would say to Stefan, he saw the slim blond cutpurse lift a heavy pouch from a fat merchant leaning over a competitor's stall. The thief casually strolled off between two lanes of booths, glancing back over his shoulder and catching Roland's eye.

The boy started when he realized he'd been seen and began to run, weaving easily through the crowd. Roland started to follow him then glimpsed the volume in his hand.

I'm no one to judge. Mine may have been a theft of absent-mindedness, but theft it was, nonetheless.

The boy glanced back over his shoulder once more, obviously expecting Roland to raise a cry; but the prince shrugged and winked at him then continued toward the inn, lost in thought.

Did I make the right decision? Should I have intervened? He sighed, shaking his head. *Let the boy go. He's merely trying to survive. I wish him well, despite the ill nature of his business.*

As he passed the bookstall, Roland stopped, laying the volume on the counter. The dealer grabbed his wrist with a grip of iron.

"Here now, you! What do you think you're playin' at?"

"I am sorry, sir. I was distracted, and I carried the book away with me by mistake."

"You ain't paid fer it yet."

"I realize as much, my good man, so I am returning it to you." Roland sketched a bow.

"Here, now! Do you mean you ain't going to buy it?"

"I'm sorry. I'm afraid I can't afford it."

"So you lied to me as well, you thief!"

Roland twisted his hand free of the man's grip before rubbing the feeling back into his wrist.

"If I were a thief, I wouldn't have brought back your property."

"You owe me three wheels and a talon!"

"I'm sorry I cannot complete our original agreement, but I can no longer afford it," Roland repeated patiently. "Here's a talon for your trouble." He handed the dealer a small gold coin. "You make a bit of profit, you're not out anything, and you can still sell the book to someone else."

"But you owe me three wheels!"

Before Roland could protest further, an elegantly robed man with a scholar's stooped shoulders stepped into the stall.

"What seems to be the trouble here, Tamos? I could hear you bellowing halfway to the inn."

"This young wastrel is trying to cheat us, Master Newel. He took off without paying for that book, and now he says he ain't got the money. All he give me was this." He held out the talon.

"Tamos, sometimes I think you care for my business with more passion than I do myself."

"I'll call the watch, Master." The clerk turned to leave.

The scholar peered more closely at Roland, and then laid a hand on Tamos's arm.

"Hold a moment," he ordered, hiding a smile behind the stroking of his snowy beard. "Take down that book there, Tamos." He gestured to a high shelf behind the counter. "The big black one. Yes, that's the one. Now, open it to the chapter on the Battle of Fangspur Cove. I know you like that story." He winked at the prince.

Tamos laid the book on the counter with a suspicious look at his master. Opening the thick volume to a page with a detailed woodcut of the final battle for unification, he peered at the illustration. Suddenly, his eyes widened to the size of globefruits, and he gasped. He stared up at Roland, his face blanched.

"You bear a great resemblance to your grandfather, Your Highness," said the old scholar, bowing to Roland. "I saw him once as a boy. He was a fine king."

"Thank you, sir," Roland replied. "I am sorry about the book. I did wish to buy it, but I was drawn away by a thief, and when I realized I still carried it, I no longer could afford it."

"Please, Your Highness, accept it as a gift." The scholar laid hand to breast and bowed again.

"Thank you, sir," Roland replied sincerely. "It's a present for a friend."

"May he or she have joy of it."

Roland bowed in turn and left the stall. He could hear Tamos continuing to grumble behind him but paid it no mind. As soon as the clerk realized he still had the talon, all would be well.

No longer charmed by the marketplace, the prince returned to the inn with all possible speed. As he climbed the steps, a chill raced down his spine, and the hint of a shadow fell over him. Squinting upward against the glare of the sun, he caught sight of a single bird wheeling high overhead. The soaring bird made him feel very vulnerable. He hurried inside.

Chapter 9

The dark-haired jewelry peddler watched Roland start back toward the market proper then stepped into the shadows of the stall and vanished. Moments later, the little blond thief ran into the stall out of breath and swept aside the curtain separating the counter from the rear of the booth.

"Master?"

Finding the stand empty, the slender cutpurse sank to the ground with a shrug, dumped the contents of the fat merchant's purse, and began to count the take.

"Did the prince make it back to the inn, Daerci?" the peddler asked, appearing from nowhere. He brushed the silver out of his raven hair with a careless sweep of his hand.

The little pickpocket appeared unfazed by the abrupt arrival.

"I think so, Master. I didn't see him go in. He saw me, so I ran."

The peddler rubbed a damp linen cloth across his face, and the wrinkles of middle-age disappeared.

"I see. And how did he come to notice you?"

The thief flushed.

"I got careless and weren't watchin'. I was nickin' this at the time. We needed money." Defiance tinged the words punctuated with a handful of coins held up for his inspection.

"Will you never learn?" the man sighed, his transformation complete. Sara would have recognized him at once as the raven's master, but he had many guises in his repertoire. Lifting a full black cape from its peg, he swung it over one shoulder and fastened it with a flourish. "That is no behavior for a well-bred lad."

Thief looked daggers at master.

"Hold your fire, Flame-Cat," laughed the peddler. "I meant nothing by it—though it's a good thing I *was* watching him. He has, indeed, reached the inn, and it's time for phase three. You pack up here while I check on our prince."

"Aye, Master."

The thief stuffed the purse in his shirt and began to dismantle the stall with an efficiency bespeaking long practice. The peddler strode off into the marketplace.

There was much to do.

***

Far away, in the midst of a desolate plain, a lanky young man lounged on an ebony throne in a castle of pitted black stone. He stared at the cowering brigand before him with eyes of copper frost.

"Well? Have you the proof I require?"

"W–we destroyed the raft, my lord, as you commanded. All hands were lost or captured."

"Did you count the bodies personally?" asked Norfulk Roderickson with false casualness.

"No, my lord."

"Then how do you know all hands were lost?"

"The raft burned to the waterline. My men slaughtered anything moving."

"And did you see the bodies of the prince and his

brat of a squire?"

"No, my lord. But one of my lieutenants reported seeing the squire dispatched with his own eyes. He brought me this." The man held out Stefan's amulet.

Norfulk's eyes narrowed to slits as he snatched the silver disk from the man's hand.

"Most unusual. Why would a squire have a thing like this?"

"I–I don't know, my lord."

"It was a rhetorical question, idiot." He flipped the amulet between restless fingers. "You didn't see the body yourself?"

"No, my lord—but that lieutenant's one of my best men. Said the man what did it were done in turn, but he plucked that out of the dead man's hand and brought it straight on."

Norfulk thrust out his hand...then drew it back, the small black dagger concealed in his sleeve dripping with the villain's blood.

"I'm sorry," he replied, smiling almost sadly, "that answer just isn't good enough."

With a curious gleam in his cold copper eyes, he leaned back on his throne and watched the man bleed to death.

***

The shadowy throne room of Castle Keep was silent; King Frederick brooded in his great chair, chin in hand.

"My Lord," murmured Sara tentatively, bobbing a curtsy as she held out a tray of food. "They sent up your dinner. You must eat. You need to keep up your strength."

The thick cut of roast beef sent up an appetizing aroma that made her mouth water, but Frederick seemed unmoved. She set the tray down on a small table beside the throne, arranging the items as slowly as possible. She had seen High Chancellor Tolkot heading this way, and she wanted to hear what he had to report. Confident in the invisibility afforded her as a servant, she melted into the shadows behind the throne.

Marcell entered with an open scroll in his hands. He shook his head as he scanned it.

"My King, there's nothing untoward in the day's dispatches. Some minor bother about the taxes from Overlake, but I'll see to that personally. Your nephew writes of record harvests from Fellstone and Bellesaria. All in all, an excellent report. Set your mind at ease."

Frederick sighed. "I don't know what it is...but my heart tells me that something is dreadfully wrong." He turned to the plate of food, picking at the fruit arranged there. Shaking his head restlessly, he pushed the plate away.

Sara stepped forward, set a goblet of wine closer to his hand and faded back again, willing him to drink. It's already begun to work, she mused. Just as the Master said it would. He weakens daily—soon, I will be queen.

Marcell opened his mouth to speak, but he was interrupted by a noise outside the door. A man stumbled into the chamber, dressed in charred clothing. One arm was caught up in a bloody sling, and a filthy bandage was knotted around his head.

"Your Majesty," the stranger croaked, falling to his knees before the king.

Instantly alert, Frederick leaned forward. "What is it?"

"I crewed for Captain Jarome, my lord. We were attacked—less than a day out of Woodwatch Ferry. The raft was lost. I–I found no trace of other survivors, although I hunted most of the night. I couldn't account for all the men among the dead, Sire, but I fear the prince is among those missing."

Sara bit her lip to hide a smile. *The Master's plan is working beautifully. That brat of a prince has received his comeuppance at last, it seems.*

"No." Frederick whispered hoarsely, collapsing into the depths of his throne. "It cannot be."

"I wish the news were otherwise, Your Majesty. I dare not hold out hope."

"Roland..." murmured Frederick in a daze.

"Is there anything I can do, my lord?" Marcell asked anxiously, stepping forward, dispatches falling from his hand, forgotten.

The king made as if to stand but slumped back onto the seat.

"Call my physician. I feel most strange."

"You!" the chancellor ordered, snapping his fingers at the riverman

"My lord?" he stammered in bewildered dismay.

"Go at once and fetch the king's doctor to his chambers. You should find him in the dining hall at this time of day."

"Aye, my lord."

The man hurried out. Slipping an arm about Frederick's waist, Marcell chided him gently as he helped the king to his feet.

"You must rest, my lord. You'll need your strength to face what further news may come. Don't give up hope so easily. We may yet hear that the prince is safe."

"You're a good man, Marcell," The king's voice was a mere whisper as he leaned heavily on the minister as they exited the chamber.

Left alone in the throne room, Sara laughed aloud.

"Oh, yes, as big a fool as his son the father is," she told the empty room, sweeping the tray off the table and practically dancing from the chamber. "The Master will have his throne before the week is out at this rate—and when he is king, I shall be queen!" With a little skip of happiness, she headed back to her place in the kitchen...for now.

***

Stefan tossed restlessly among the coarse pillows. Although his fever had broken, his sleep was filled with dreams he dared not ignore.

The throne room of Crown Keep filled with silent shadows...Frederick brooding in his great chair...A man stumbling into the chamber—Stefan vaguely recognized one of the men from the raft.

"Your Majesty," the stranger croaked, falling to his knees before the king.

Frederick leaned forward. "What is it?"

"We were attacked, my lord...out of Woodwatch Ferry... the raft was lost."

"No." Frederick whispered, collapsing into his throne. "Call my physician. I feel most strange."

The man hastened to obey.

The image faded as Stefan jerked into wakefulness, drenched with sweat, to find himself alone. He feared for the king more than ever.

We must go straight home! Where is Roland? He had only the dimmest recollection of his earlier conversation with the prince.

An attempt to rise from bed sent his head reeling, but he saw the prince's pack still lay slung beside his sword in the corner. Roland would never go anywhere without that sword. Just the same, he was beginning to worry.

A soft knock sounded on the door, and he murmured, "Come in."

Collyn Silverbrook regarded him from the doorway.

"Would you rather I didn't disturb you?"

Stefan lay back, propping himself against the headboard as he fought the wave of dizziness crashing over him.

"No, it's all right. Please, come in."

Collyn approached, light-footed despite his size. The crystal arrowhead swung forward as the trader laid a gentle hand on Stefan's shoulder.

"How are you feeling, lad?"

"Better. I'll be ready to travel by morning."

Pity clouded Collyn's clear gray eyes.

"Don't push yourself, Stefan. It's a grave wound." He checked the bandage with practiced ease. "The poultice seems to have stopped the bleeding. That's a good sign. I'll leave you to rest."

Stefan's lips quirked in a rueful smile.

"I am tired," he admitted. "But I must speak to the prince. It can't wait. I must tell him something of utmost importance."

"I'll see if I can find him," Collyn promised, but Stefan heard evasion in the big man's voice.

"Where is he?"

"I believe he went to explore the marketplace. I'll see if I can find him," the riverman repeated.

Collyn left, and Stefan eased back into the sanctuary of the pillows with a heavy sigh. When he told the prince about his dream, they would go straight home. He was certain of it.

Even the slight exertion of the conversation had left his head spinning, but he must be fit to ride when the time came. Frederick's life might depend on it.

Chapter 10

Roland had come to the decision that Collyn was right—he must tell Stefan face-to-face that he was leaving. He met the riverman on the stair as he climbed toward their room. Collyn paused, leaning against the wall.

"How is he?"

"Awake and alert, but still quite pale. He's in great pain, but he'll never admit it. He's most anxious to speak to you."

The prince nodded and continued up the stair.

"Roland..."

The quiet hail halted him. It was the first time Collyn had called him by name instead of a title. He turned, curious as to what might make the trader forget formalities.

"I'm glad you're going to tell him yourself. It takes a brave man to face his responsibilities squarely."

A wry smile tugging his lips, Roland replied, "It took a wise man to convince me I should do so. I owe Stefan that much. Though I don't relish telling him."

"I'll order another round of stout."

Roland's grin widened.

"I'll join you soon."

Reaching the doorway, he rapped softly upon it. The answer came at once.

"Come in."

Stefan's voice sounded weak but steady. Taking a deep breath, Roland went inside.

"Hello, laze-a-bed," he teased, closing the door behind him.

Stefan attempted to sit up straighter, wincing as he jarred his wound. Roland was at his side in two steps.

"Lie still!" he commanded, settling the boy back among the pillows. "What are you thinking of? You'll kill yourself for sure without me here to fuss over you..." His voice trailed off as he realized what he was saying. He turned away, unable to face Stefan's dark eyes.

"I'm fine, my prince, I swear to you. My fever is broken. I can ride whenever you say. We must return to Crown Keep as soon as we possibly can. Your father..."

Roland sat in the chair beside the bed, slipping the book of ballads beneath it.

"What about my father?"

"He is ill. I had a dream."

"Merely the fever, Stefan."

"No, Roland. There's trouble. Please, we must return at once. I can travel, I swear to you."

Stefan's fever-brightened eyes and face paler than alabaster belied his words. Taking another deep breath, Roland plowed ahead.

"Stefan, you know I trust you, and I know I can count on you when I need a loyal man—"

"You're planning to go without me!" the squire cried, once more struggling to rise.

Roland forced him back, leaving his hands on the boy's shoulders.

"Listen to me, you little fool. You're seriously hurt and under doctor's orders to stay abed at least two days more. I can't wait. This dream of yours should convince you I need to move quickly. You *must* stay behind. I can't afford to move at the pace having you along would force."

"B–but you can't leave me." Stefan's voice was pleading.

Roland felt the helpless anger welling inside him—his instinctive reaction to circumstances he could not control. He knew he should fight his temper, but time was pressing.

"Be still!" he snapped. "I order you to remain behind. If you refuse to obey me, I'll have Collyn physically restrain you until I'm well gone. It's your choice. You've been given a direct command." He strode across the floor and swept up his pack, slinging it over his shoulder, then buckled on his sword.

Stefan's eyes were huge pools of night in his white face. Roland could not bear the hurt accusation on his squire's wan features, though Stefan tried to hide it.

"Rest," he ordered curtly, then turned on his heel and left the room.

Shutting the door with a firm click, he let his head fall back against the heavy oak plank. Only then did he remember the peace offering under the chair.

"Damn," he swore under his breath.

He hated himself for causing Stefan pain, but the main reason he didn't want the boy with him was the possibility he might be leading the squire into further danger. With a heavy sigh, he trudged down the stairs to join Collyn in the common room.

Collyn stood as he approached, but the prince waved him back into his chair. Roland plopped down onto an empty stool and drained half the mug the trader pushed to him.

"You told him, I see," remarked the big man dryly.

"Aye. 'Twas one of the hardest tasks I've ever faced." He took another pull on his pint.

"I don't doubt it, my lord. But there're harder days to come."

"You speak truth there, my friend." Roland emptied the mug and stood, pushing back his stool with a sigh. "It's time for me to go. It will ease my heart to have my own horse beneath me on the race north."

"And how did he come to wander so far from home, my lord?"

Roland flushed, tracing circles on the wet surface of the table with an idle finger. "My friend Alexendar arranged for Noble and Astreal to wait for us here."

"You never intended to raft the remainder of the journey."

"No," Roland admitted, his voice soft with shame.

"It's too bad you ever started with us, then. Good men died needlessly for your whim." Collyn's voice was grave.

The sadness in the riverman's gray eyes brought another surge of helplessness to Roland's breast.

"I know, Collyn, and I must live with it, but I can't change it. I must do what I can to see no further harm comes of this. Guard Stefan well, Collyn Silverbrook."

"I shall."

The big man rose also, and Roland clasped his hand

"I'll see you one day in Crown Keep, my friend. We'll lift a pint again."

"I look forward to it."

Roland nodded and left the inn, seeking out the town stables. He soon located the stall holding his bay gelding Noble and saddled the horse quickly—after giving the animal a fond pat on the withers.

"Ready to ride, boy?" he murmured, and Noble's

big head bobbed in reply, nudging the prince's cheek with a velvety nose. Roland laughed, swinging easily into the saddle.

Turning the gelding's head, he headed north-northwest out of town in the afternoon sunlight, cutting toward the edge of the Forest of Night. As he rode toward the dense line of trees, he debated his next course of action.

The quickest way back to Crown Keep would be through the arm of the forest the raft had traversed the morning before, but even that short time beneath those dark trees had left him feeling oppressed and uneasy

Don't be a baby. This time you'll be riding, and Noble is a match for any woodland beasties.

The gelding tossed his head and chuffed, as if agreeing.

Roland laughed.

"Brave heart," he crooned, giving the horse's neck an affectionate slap. "Nothing daunts you, does it, my beauty?" He scanned the line of trees ahead. "They are, after all, merely trees. Rumors and hearsay shouldn't dissuade a prince of the blood. Such foolishness isn't for heroes!

"And think of the time we'll save. With every moment so precious, how can I waste a one? There couldn't be more than ten miles of Forest at this point, but if we go around, we'll be at least a day's ride out of our way. Besides, if we enter here, we can skirt the area where the raft was attacked without risking any straggling raider catching sight of us."

Still, his hand strayed to the hilt of his sword, toying nervously with the peace guard. He couldn't help but remember all the whispered tales that had haunted his dreams as a child. Stories of wicked creatures that walked like men but ensnared the unwary in their woodland lairs. Beautiful beings like ivory statues that could slay a trespasser with a single word.

"No. Father's life may be in danger. I have no choice. I'm not a witless fool or a helpless child. I can take care of myself, and the time I save may make all the difference." He slipped the sword free of its peace cord and felt a great deal safer.

When he reached the trees, he discovered one slight miscalculation in his plan. There appeared to be no entrance to the formidable forest. Trunks as thick as an ale cask had slender saplings standing between and, filling the gaps, thick shrubs with sharp thorns

He dismounted and explored the verge of the wood. Some distance from town, he at last found a break in the solid wall—a barely discernible path heavily overshadowed. He could tell it had little traffic—if indeed anything beyond a small animal ever had used it. Roots protruded above ground, while vines tangled into a matted mass, hiding any unevenness of the pathway.

Roland bit the inside of his lip.

"I hate to risk taking you along that faint track, boy," he told the horse, stroking Noble's soft nose, "but if animals created it, then it must be possible for them to travel along it. If we go slowly and carefully, we'll be alright. It's either go forward or go around the forest. If I lead you, we should be fine."

Taking a firm hold of the reins, he stepped into the fringes of the forest. Noble started forward willingly enough, but as soon as his nose broke the plane of the trees, he reared back, almost jerking Roland's arm from its socket. The horse gave a trumpeting neigh, his eyes rolling in his head. His hooves beat the air as he strained against Roland's hold.

Roland quickly moved out of the wood, crooning softly to the terrified animal. He could smell the fear on the high-strung horse.

"What's wrong with you, boy? It's just some silly trees. Come on now!"

He started back into the trees, and once again, Noble went mad. The horse absolutely refused to set foot into the forest.

Roland swallowed hard as he weighed the options. The time he would save still tempted him, but if he were afoot, would it really be so great a gain? And, on the other hand, could *all* the tales be false? Some of his bravado leached away.

"No! I refuse to change my mind now it's made up," he told the horse. "I'll simply have to find another mount on the other side of the wood. It won't be you, perhaps, but it'll see me home. It's foolish to waste time circling the wood simply because I'm frightened by children's ghost stories. That's not the hero's way. Go back to the stable where you'll be safe with Astreal."

Lifting his saddlebags from the horse, he slapped the gelding on the rump, knowing he would return to the stables where Stefan's little gray mare Astreal waited. Shouldering the saddlebags, Roland began to whistle tunelessly as he plunged into the forest.

Chapter 11

Stefan lay back, hands clenched as he willed the tears not to fall.

"You are too old to cry! Roland is only doing what he feels is best. It's the practical thing to do. Besides, he is the prince. You've no choice but to obey or face the consequences!"

Even so, a single tear slipped down his drawn cheek before he dashed it away.

"No! I will *not* lie here like a baby while Roland heads off into who knows what danger." And an oath to a king superseded the orders of a prince.

He eased out of bed, catching the edge of the headboard as another wave of dizziness broke over him. There was a slight thud, and he glanced over at the door, heart pounding with anxiety—he was almost certain Collyn stood watch in the hallway outside.

Exhaling against the pain, he tucked his shirttail into the waist of his leggings to keep it from catching on anything. He noticed the book lying under the chair, and stuffed it into the top of his pack without really examining it. Carefully settling the pack on his back, he limped to the window and looked out.

The room in the back of the inn; directly below, a small, steeply pitched roof covered a service porch. It was an eight-foot drop, and seven more to the ground. Even looking down sent waves of nausea crashing over him.

Gulping back the queasiness, Stefan eased open

the window and threw his good leg over the sill. He dragged his left leg after it and turned, lowering himself until he hung by his fingertips. With a prayer for luck, he let go.

His feet hit the roof of the porch and continued to slide—his knees connecting with a solid jolt. Fighting to stay conscious, he slipped off the edge of the roof. Fingers scrabbling in panic, he managed to find finger-holds in the shingles and somewhat control how he hit the ground.

Facedown in the dirt, he gasped for air then struggled to hands and knees and rested for a moment, head hanging.

"Here, let me help."

A strong hand lifted him to his feet, and then remained on his arm to steady him. Stefan peered up, vision blurred and doubling, to find Collyn gazing down at him with calm gray eyes that—thankfully—held no laughter. He blinked until the twin images resolved into one.

"How did you...?"

"I heard you through the door."

"I wouldn't make a very good thief, would I?" Stefan chuckled then winced. His head felt ready to float off into the sunset without him.

"You should be in bed," Collyn scolded.

"No. I must follow Roland."

"Then I suppose *I'll* have to follow *you*—or better yet, come with you. The prince told me he arranged for your horses to be here. We'll see if he managed that, at least. You'll feel more secure on your own mount, I warrant, and it will care more for your safety. Come along, then."

Stefan attempted to nod, and Collyn caught him when he started to fall.

"My boy, you're setting out to kill yourself."

Stefan drew himself up, his carriage proud.

"No one is asking you to come with me, Master Silverbrook. I'll go alone if I must."

"He left you in my charge, and I'm no more eager to fail him than you. Therefore, you're stuck with me, and I with you."

"Then let us be off."

Stefan started for the stables, his bad leg more of a burden than usual. Collyn followed, taking great care to remain a step behind despite the slow pace he set. Stefan noticed and felt a rush of gratitude.

As they approached the stables, Noble flew into the innyard with a thunder of hooves.

Riderless.

With a wordless cry, Stefan hurried to the horse's side, catching his bridle, and whispering, "There, there, boy. You're safe. Calm yourself."

Noble tossed his head and pawed at the ground then stood quiet under Stefan's hand.

"I've never seen a horse return to a stable he's unused to rather than head for hearth and home."

"He must have sensed Astreal—they've been stablemates for years. He must have been trying to get back to her...and he would have had to traverse the Forest to return to Crown Keep."

"His saddlebags are gone," Collyn observed. "Either the prince set out on foot, or he's been robbed, maybe taken."

Stefan studied the horse's saddle and bridle. "There is no sign of damage. Except for the missing saddlebags, the tack is in good shape. It would be like Roland to venture off through the trees. He would never let rumors and superstitions stand in the way of what he wants—and he wants to return home as soon as he is able."

"I don't much like the sound of that, my lad." Shaking his head, Collyn exhaled gustily.

"Noble will have to show us where he's gone." Stefan put a foot in the stirrup and hauled himself into the saddle. He swayed before gaining his balance. "There's no time to go for the other horses. Besides, if Roland did send him back of his own free will, it's pointless to take them where a horse cannot go. The prince and I have ridden Noble double in the past. You're heavier than Roland, but we have no choice. Frankly, I doubt I can sit him alone."

With a nod, Collyn mounted behind him.

Mentally wishing godspeed to the dainty gray mare who had been one of his few friends, Stefan turned Noble and headed for the forest. The big gelding went easily enough until he saw the trees; then he began to fight the bit, and Stefan had all he could do to control him.

Collyn slipped from the gelding's back and took the reins, leading the big horse to the very edge of the trees. Noble rolled his eyes and planted his feet but was no match for the riverman. Inch by inch, it seemed, they drew nearer to the fringe of the forest.

Stefan feared his master had taken on more than he dreamed and hoped they were not to late to rescue him.

***

Collyn began studying the ground. Little question remained. The bruised undergrowth still sent its sharp odor into the cool evening air. His heart sank. The headstrong prince really had cut through the forest.

He sighed.

"There is a path, or at least a trace of one, with footprints leading up to it, and the marks of churning hooves," he told Stefan. "I'm sure the prince came this way. The horse was released here."

Taking a deep breath, Stefan slid off the horse. He grabbed the saddle for support in time to prevent a fall.

"Thank you for finding the way, Collyn. Take Noble back to the inn and wait."

"Oh, no, you don't get rid of me so easily, my young friend. The prince may be free to order me about, but you don't have that privilege. What if you get lost? It's getting colder by the night. Can you build a fire with your music? No, you're stuck with me still, my lad. Besides, the prince is young and untried. He can't imagine the perils of these woods. I can't let him go into those dangers alone, either."

"He will not be alone. I will be with him."

"There's no doubt in my mind that you *will* follow him, foolish child—you're loyal beyond the bounds of sense. Since you will go after the prince, with or without my help—and likely kill yourself in the process—I'll ignore old promises and come along. You need me, whether you believe that or not. Did you even think to bring along any provisions?"

He shifted his own pack, hoping he had thought of everything they would require.

Stefan smiled.

"Very well. I admit I'll not mind the company. Shall we go?"

The branches met overhead in intricately woven knots, with the slanting rays of the setting sun barely penetrating the darkness beneath. The air felt damp, and was redolent with the scent of decaying bracken and the sweet, sudden aroma of a night-blooming vine as it opened to the growing shadows. The combination cloyed, sticking in the throat, and brought to mind things better not said aloud. An ominous aura pervaded the area, and Stefan shivered.

Collyn's sharp eyes caught the faint shudder.

"It will soon be nightfall. Wouldn't it be wiser to wait until morning?"

"No, I must go now. The prince may be in danger. My eyes are good—"

"How do you feel, Stefan?"

"Better. I promise you, I'll be fine, but I'm worried about the prince. He's so headstrong."

"He's not the only one." Collyn grinned, placing a gentle hand on the boy's shoulder. "Let me lead the way. It'll be rough going, and the prince may veer from the path."

Moreover, if trouble rears its head, I'll be better able to protect the foolish child.

In the direct rays of the late sunlight, Stefan's face had a waxen sheen, and beads of perspiration dotted his upper lip as he fought to hide his pain. Faintly crimson sweat stained his neat linen bandage.

I hope this venture will not prove more than the boy bargains for.

As they started into the forest, Stefan's head jerked

up, and he staggered. Collyn steadied him.

"Collyn, do you see anything there?" He pointed at the sky.

"Aye, lad." Collyn raised a hand to shade his sight. "I think it's a raven."

Chapter 12

It was slow going as Roland pushed through the tangled undergrowth. He had assumed crossing the Forest would be like moving through the well-tended orchards at home with their neatly planted rows and mowed undergrowth. Instead, these trees grew mere inches apart in some places, and he had to detour around clumps of dense—and usually thorny—brush.

He kept an eye to the ground, searching for an easier path, ducking under low-hanging limbs, sweeping away whip-thin branches that snapped back to lash at his face and hands. The vines and creepers carpeting the ground twisted about his boots, and kept him stumbling and off-balance.

The air seemed heavy, an acrid stench of decay lying thick and hot in the lungs. Sharp flares of odor heralded fetid pools or wild, strangely beautiful blooms on barbed stalks that ripped at his unprotected flesh.

I should have taken the long way after all. This is much harder work than I thought it would be. At this rate, it'll take me as long to get through as riding around would have, perhaps longer! A good thing for me to remember—the most direct route may not be the best path to travel.

He dragged forearm across face, mopping at the sweat. He could never have imagined such dense growth, which hedged him in on all sides as if trying to force him back the way he had come. His scabbard caught in the underbrush, and he jerked it free with an impatient tug.

He was tempted to draw the blade and slash the vines out of his way, but two things prevented him. He knew it would damage the carefully honed edge, of course, but more important, something about the forest itself stayed his hand—he felt as if eyes were watching him from unseen vantage points.

He spun to look behind him, as if—were he quick enough—he might catch the spies. No birds sang, and the usual quiet scrabblings of small creatures in brush were missing; only a soft breath of the wind high above him broke the stillness.

The silence was eerie.

The farther into the forest he went, the fainter the traces of the path he followed. After only a few hundred yards, he was fighting through completely untraveled territory. Cursing himself for a fool, he broke through a final screen of brush into a small clearing and sank down onto a fallen tree with a grateful sigh. The cool breeze whispering among the treetops deigned to ruffle his sweat-soaked hair.

"Where did I lose my cap? It surely didn't take me long," he scolded himself aloud, comforted by the sound of his own voice in the strange stillness.

He pushed the heavy waves of hair from his face, doubly regretting the loss of the cap as he disengaged a fallen twig tangled in his curls. "By the Flames, it's hot work slogging through this lot!"

He took a deep breath, and his attention was caught by the pungent scent of mint. Glancing around the clearing, he found a clump of the plant peeking from the broken base of the tree he sat upon and snapped off a piece, chewing thoughtfully on the juicy stem as he weighed his options.

"Well, now, this is a fine mess you've gotten yourself into, Roland Frederickson! You can keep on the way you're going, forcing a path through the woods until you finally get through to the other side, or you can go back the way you've come. It's only a half-mile at most from here to the edge of the trees if you backtrack."

He stepped to the point where he thought he had emerged into the clearing and searched for signs of the path. The brush had sprung back into place, and all traces of his passage had vanished.

"On the other hand, the forest is at least ten miles wide at this point, if those vague memories of your geography lessons are any true indication." He balled his hands on his hips, disgusted with himself. "Why couldn't you have paid attention to your tutors like Stefan did?" He tossed the stem of mint aside. "No, my lad," he sighed. "Your way lies forward. I won't give the others an opportunity for sport."

He yawned. "But no sense being a fool, either. It's been a long, eventful day. Now that I've seen the way these trees grow, I can tell that even the full moon won't penetrate those branches enough to risk further travel tonight. I guess tomorrow is soon enough to go on. I hate to waste the time, but a broken leg won't help my speed. This is as good a site as any to camp. I'll rest here for now and start on my way first thing in the morning."

Gathering a pile of dried branches and kindling, he built a small fire near the fallen tree, as much for comfort as warmth. The forest pressed in around him, and he moved a little closer to the flames. Reaching into his saddlebag, he pulled out his cloak and fastened it round his shoulders.

The mutton stew he had eaten at noon had long since worn away—forcing his way through the undergrowth had been hungry work. He dug in the bag for one of Sara's journey cakes and the flask of wine. Munching on the cake, he examined the clearing. Now that he thought about it, it seemed unnaturally circular in shape. The only defect in its circumference lay in the large boulder behind his log.

"Who could ask for more?" he grinned, placing his back firmly against the stone.

The warmth stored by the rock during the day radiated through his clothing and soon combined with the wine to make his eyes heavy. Settling his sword across his knees, he pulled his cloak about him and let his eyes drift closed.

***

Collyn pushed aside tangles of vine and threw fallen branches out of the path, but their progress through the trees was hard-won. His broad shoulders broke through the screening branches, and he helped Stefan over the worst outcroppings of roots.

Even with Collyn easing the way, though, Stefan fought to keep up. Vines clutched at his bad leg as if with conscious intent, and his head spun. He was repeatedly on the verge of falling, and his breath came in ragged gasps.

As they struggled through the heavy growth, the silence struck him. Only their clumsy footsteps, trampling down living matter that gasped out dying scents of crushed herbs and bruised foliage, broke the stillness. Underlying the fresh odors lay a stench of decaying leaves and stagnant water.

He forced himself on with grim determination. When they caught up with the prince, he must be able to pull his own weight, or Roland would simply send him back to the inn.

After what seemed an eternity forging through undergrowth, Collyn halted, holding up a hand for silence. Peering around the riverman's broad back, Stefan felt his heart lift.

Scant yards away, on the far edge of a circular clearing, lounged the prince, leaning back against a rock. His soft snores revealed he was fast asleep.

A roguish grin split Collyn's rugged features, sloughing years from his face. He motioned Stefan to stay hidden and slipped his pack from his back. Reaching inside and withdrawing a waterskin, he stole across the clearing.

Stefan's eyes sparkled as he waited for the inevitable explosion, but as the trader crossed the clearing, he glimpsed a wisp of movement behind Roland. He started forward, ready to cry a warning, but ducked back behind a tree trunk at a sign from Collyn.

Sweeping up a thick branch, the big man slipped ahead soundlessly. When he drew even with Roland, he clapped a hand over the prince's mouth, startling him awake. Before he could warn the prince, however, the face of the boulder split in two, and a party of tall, lithe archers armed with longbows poured from the crevice in a deadly flood.

Stefan watched in helpless horror as the others

were surrounded. One of the newcomers removed Roland's sword from its scabbard and slipped it through his own belt. The prince made a move as if to protest, but Collyn stayed him with a hand on his shoulder. Roland glared at the trader, shaking loose the hand, and turning back to the archers.

They were all pale, with long, dark hair streaming about their shoulders. Dressed in greens and browns, they appeared to merge with the forest, slipping in and out of focus. One, whose cloak was fastened with a leaf-shaped brooch edged in gold at one shoulder, stepped forward and spoke, his words carrying with crystal clarity to Stefan's hiding place. His voice rang like silver bells chiming in the wind.

"Roland, son of Frederick, we greet thee, and thy companions—seen and unseen—and trust you have valid reason for trespassing within our borders." He bowed fluidly from the waist.

Stefan frowned. What could the stranger mean? He was puzzling over the choice of words when he glanced across the clearing and saw the cloaked figure staring directly at him. Heart pounding in his throat, he shrank back farther into the shadows, praying he was wrong and that he remained undetected; but he feared he was only fooling himself.

Stefan could see the anger swelling up in Roland like a flood tide—his temper was about to flare into fire before he thought. His heart twisted within him. He must restrain Roland for the prince's own good. These strangers would not care that he was of royal blood. Even the thought of what could become of the mercurial prince brought the warning to the verge of

Stefan's lips—too late.

Roland exploded.

"*Your* borders?" he shouted, his reddened face twisted into a scowl as he again shook off the warning hand Collyn laid on his arm. "I am heir to the throne of Irthlan. My borders extend from Block Wind Cove to Dangerous Harbor, from Dark Wood to Stormhaven. I have the right to roam wherever I please!"

The tall figure spoke again, the bells of his voice frozen with formality.

"This land has been the holding of *my* people for countless ages. Your ancestors wrested the Silver Plain from us, but my lord's father's father decreed the insult should go unanswered as long as our forest remained inviolate. Now you have penetrated Starlit Wood. You have one last chance. Turn back and take your own road or proceed as captives of Andundal, King of the Starlit Elves."

***

Although tall, Roland had to look up to meet the other's eyes. So, these were the legendary elves.

The leader of the elven patrol was pale, with silver highlights scattered through ebony hair. Eyes like pools of jet ink dominated his grave face. Suddenly, the prince realized he could be looking thirty years into Stefan's future.

"I cannot turn back, but let this man go. He's here against direct orders, abandoning a solemn charge. Escort him from the forest."

"My Lord Prince, let me come with you," Collyn murmured, falling to one knee. "My charge is safely fulfilled, and I crave permission to attend you. It is the least I can do for the one I leave behind."

The elven leader murmured, "You are very brave, Collyn Silverbrook, but very foolish. The outcome of the meeting between your prince and King Andundal is uncertain. As for you—the warders know well your name. You know the cost of returning here."

"Aye, sir, but I must serve my prince. I have pledged him my arm," replied Collyn, his own voice steady.

"You could well be going to your death."

"I will discharge the old debt without quarrel, if necessary."

"As you wish. You have chosen your path. May it prove wise."

"Just a moment!" Roland exploded, confused by the cryptic conversation. "I refuse to have him come with me! Collyn, I order you to return to the inn."

Collyn stood his ground.

"I cannot obey, my lord—it's out of my hands. It's my destiny to follow here, and I owe it to the one who cannot follow. If it is without permission, it will be by stealth, which is much more likely to get me killed."

Roland ground his teeth in frustration. The situation had gone beyond him, and he felt a helpless fool.

***

Stefan's breath came in ragged gasps as he struggled to keep from shuddering. The whispered rumors of elves he had heard were no longer merely legends. He could not simply stand by and watch...but his legs betrayed him. He could not force himself forward, and only his grip upon the tree trunk kept him from collapsing in a nerveless ball.

Nevertheless, he steeled himself to try.

Then, as if by chance, Collyn glanced idly around the clearing. He locked eyes with Stefan, shaking his head in a nearly imperceptible gesture. The squire retreated farther behind his tree. Logically, the big trader was right. Only if he remained free could he help the others.

"You speak truth, it is certain death to all who proceed farther without our consent," commented the elven leader casually.

Stefan's heart turned to ice when the tall figure again turned and looked directly across the clearing into his eyes. There could no longer be any doubt—the elves knew of his presence and were telling him to do the one thing he could not bring himself to do.

An indefinable sense of loss surged within his breast, as if he had seen something he wanted very badly only to have it taken away, deemed unworthy. The feeling frightened and confused him.

"What makes me feel this way?" he breathed.

Whatever his unease, Roland was the only family he knew, and Collyn was fast becoming a valued friend. He could not let them go into danger alone. No matter how many of the terrible old tales proved true, he could not abandon them. If death followed, then he would die—if he must.

The tall elf gave a trilling call, and his companions converged on the captives, arrows nocked but bows lowered.

"Bind them loosely," ordered the captain.

One of the company stepped forward to obey.

***

Roland studied the newcomers curiously. These elves might all be brothers, and Stefan would blend into their band without a ripple. Was this the secret of his birth?

He brought his attention back to the present predicament to find his hands ingeniously tied behind him. He felt no discomfort but could not bring them forward, despite his best efforts. He glanced over at Collyn, still angry but glad of the company. Collyn stood impassively while the elves bound his hands. He wondered what the elf's cryptic words to the riverman had meant.

The captain made a sweeping gesture, and his archers fell in around them. He led the way at a quick march, the undergrowth melting away as they moved then closing again behind them. From the corner of his eye, Roland caught a flicker of movement on the far side of the clearing, and his heart fell. He prayed it did not mean what he feared.

They walked for hours, and Roland began to tire. He felt as if he were forcing every step but knew he dared not falter. He glanced at Collyn's stoic expression. The big man strode ahead with no indication of weariness, so Roland steeled himself to continue. He must not show any weakness.

The elves showed no sign of fatigue, either, as they talked quietly in their birdlike language. The beautiful, twittering music of the conversation struck his heart. It soothed his soul, despite its strangeness, and he found some of his exhaustion slipped from him as he focused his attention away from the march.

The captain glanced behind him, and Roland stumbled. He remembered the movement he had seen, and prayed once more he had mistaken its cause. He forced his concentration back to moving along the path, determined not to give anything away.

They marched on for another hour then came to a second circular clearing identical to the one where they had been captured. The captain of the warders stepped up to another of the large boulders and passed his hand over the face of the rock, caroling in his flutelike voice, "*Andundal stimariali.*" With a harsh, grating rumble, the rock opened to reveal the top steps of a descending stairway.

Roland felt a thrill of fear at a prod in the small of his back. As he set one boot on the top step, his foot slipped, and he lost his balance. Startled, he overcompensated and fell backward, unable to stop himself. A strong shoulder broke his fall and steadied him.

"Careful, my prince," cautioned Collyn as Roland regained his balance. "'Tis a dark way ahead."

"Aye," Roland murmured, his voice grim as he carefully edged down into the stairwell.

Another wisp of movement on the far side of the clearing. The captain gestured, and one of the scouts dropped back into the trees beside the faint path and faded from view. The prince felt his heart sink to his boots.

If what he feared was true, the consequences could be disastrous for them all.

***

Sheer strength of will kept Stefan's feet beneath him as he stumbled after the elves. His head reeled, and ghostly shapes flickered in and out of his sight, vanishing if he tried to focus. Finally, he ignored the illusive movements, forcing his feet to keep moving. At least the footing was better—the vines no longer clutched at his ankles.

When he thought he could go no farther, the warders stopped inside another circular clearing. Stefan caught himself just before following them into the open, sinking to his knees in exhaustion. As he watched, the captain opened the rock, and the band of elves passed inside with their captives. Roland's slip brought him to his feet, and he nearly swooned from the resulting vertigo.

By the time he recovered full control of his senses, the entire party had entered the rockbound doorway, and the face of the rock grated slowly closed. Stefan dashed across the clearing as fast as his bad leg would allow, ignoring the swirling of the ground as his vision faded in and out. He reached the boulder just as the gap slammed together with crashing finality.

"No!" He banged his fists on the rock until his flesh was bloody. "Master Roland, do not leave me behind!" The plea was almost a sob, his control at the breaking point. Tears of pain and frustration coursed down his cheeks.

Stop acting like a child! he cursed himself. *Think. You have to do something. You can't let them go into danger alone.*

Swiping the tears from his cheeks with the back of his hand, he straightened his shoulders.

"Concentrate!" he whispered.

Passing his hand over the face of the rock, Stefan struggled to remember the words the captain had spoken to open the portal. His lilting voice found it easy to recreate the trilling sounds, and he felt a faint stir deep in his memory.

"*Andundal...sti...sti...*" The final word eluded him. Try as he might, he could not remember how the command ended.

Closing his eyes to think, he wracked his brains.

"*Stimariali,*" spoke a cool voice behind him, and the rock began to slide apart.

Stefan's eyes flew open, and he found himself facing a stern elf with an arrow trained on his heart. Terrified, the boy stepped back, his heel striking thin air as he overshot the top step. Arms pinwheeling for balance, Stefan uttered one wordless cry as he crashed backwards into darkness.

Chapter 13

Roland's head snapped up.

"What is it?" Collyn asked.

"I thought I heard—I am sure it was nothing."

He studied the dimly lit corridor; the faint illumination came from delicate crystalline lamps spaced at wide intervals along the rough-hewn walls. The soft light, in pastel hues of green, blue, and gold, did not extend far into the passage. The floor of the corridor ran smooth, which Roland considered lucky, as it proved difficult to see.

The air had a dry, dusty scent, overlaid by the fragrance of flowers rising from braziers of smoking incense standing between the lamps. The elves' footsteps whispered, their progress nearly silent in their soft leather boots, but those of the humans echoed faintly as their boot heels rang on the stone floor. Roland found the quiet eerie.

Finally, the captain raised a hand and called out, "*Aithmi.*" The column halted, and he turned to Roland.

"Wait here until you are called." He nodded to his men, and they melted into the shadows, one remaining behind to guard the prisoners.

"*Opieviami.*" A doorway opened, and the captain entered; the door slid closed behind him.

"It doesn't look good, my prince," Collyn muttered.

"Does it ever?" The attempt at levity fell flat, even to his own ears.

"Life has many pinnacles and valleys to offer. In the

world outside Crown Keep, there are often more valleys than peaks. A hard lesson...but best learned early."

"Considering recent events, I'm beginning to regret leaving my old schoolroom for this one," Roland replied with a rueful shake of his head. He glanced at Collyn. "You are quite the philosopher for a riverman, Master Silverbrook."

Collyn shrugged his massive shoulders

"I haven't always been a riverman."

The door slid aside, and the captain reappeared, trilling a command to the guard. Roland was urged forward into a carved rock chamber larger than the Great Hall at Crown Keep. Imposing pillars of the same illuminated crystal supported the roof. Here, torches in wrought gold sconces augmented the softer light. Scattered throughout the room lay silk and velvet pillows, glowing in the torchlight like soft jewels of amethyst, emerald, and ruby.

More dark-haired elves reclined on the cushions, some talking softly, others listening to the strains of a harpist playing on the far side of the chamber. A couple sitting before a low table played a complicated board game, reminding Roland vaguely of his father's chess matches with Jarome. The thought sent a spear of remorse through him.

In the center of the room stood two ornate golden thrones, bases fashioned like tumbled rocks. The arms were designed to simulate waves suspended in gentle curves for all time. Backrests of intricate filigree rose as tall as Roland's head—elaborate creatures chased each other around gilded tree trunks.

The center back of each throne featured a billowing

gilt cloud. From the larger rose a carved gryphon, wings spread and mouth open in an endless roar. On the smaller, a full moon peeked from behind a delicate veil of spun-filament cloud.

A handsome elf with a streak of silver in his raven hair and a wide circlet of gold about his brow sat on the larger seat, but the lesser throne drew Roland's eye. Upon the smaller chair sat a beautiful girl with long ebony braids entwined with golden chains.

Unlike the other elves, her eyes were an unusual sea-green. She appeared no older than he was, but an air of ancient wisdom enveloped her like a cloak. On her head sat a circlet of silver, and a warm smile played about her lips. She radiated the confidence born of royal breeding.

"Who is she?" Roland breathed, unaware he spoke aloud.

The guard who had waited with them in the hallway, a lively elf who seemed younger than his fellows, bent down to whisper, "That is the Princess Mendana, King Andundal's daughter."

"She is beautiful."

"Aye, she is," agreed the young elf. His twinkling eyes sparkled the same clear sea-green as hers

King Andundal was deep in conversation with Mendana when they arrived. Roland used the time to steel his courage. The king was stern of visage; his commanding features seemed hewn from living rock. Yet in the bottomless depths of his black eyes danced a spark of laughter—which died when he turned his attention from his daughter to the prisoners.

Roland faced the king with chin held high, although

his heart sat heavy with the realization of all Andundal held in his power. Despite his hot words to the warder captain, he knew he had chosen a dangerous path of his own free will and must accept the consequences.

Andundal gave a curt nod in acknowledgment of the captain's salute. The warder stepped forward.

"These are the men apprehended in Starlit Wood. We offered them a chance to retrace their steps but they refused and now await your judgment."

Collyn fell to one knee, head bowed, the crystal arrowhead around his neck reflecting the illuminated crystals. Roland remained standing, his bearing proud as he met Andundal's eye.

Andundal's voice rang out, deep yet musical, the heavy tolling of watch bells.

"Thank you, Captain Aerlann."

The captain bowed and stepped back.

The king turned his attention to the prisoners once more.

"Greetings to thee, Roland Frederickson. In ages past, we might have met as comrades, equals in rank and honor, but your ancestors grew discontented with what was freely given and declared a war, which raged with inestimable bloodshed. When the massacre was over, only tiny pockets of elves remained, with the Starlit Wood our only fortress.

"It is all we have. Only in secret may we stray beyond its borders, and all men fear us. Against our better judgment, we allow men safe passage through the heart of our dominion if they stay to the river. You should have taken the river path, which we do not claim. Instead, you struck through the center of our lands. We cannot permit the least invasion of this sanctuary. For this, there must be reckoning."

"If our positions stood reversed, and I found myself ruler instead of trespasser, I would show no leniency to one who willfully ignored a warning such as I received," Roland replied, his voice hushed and grave. "You hold my life in your hands, my lord, and you would be well within your rights to claim its forfeit."

"It is well that you recognize that fact. As for you, Collyn Silverbrook, you knew the price for breaking your vow. I hereby decree—"

A flurry of movement at the rear of the throne room interrupted him in mid-sentence, and an elven scout strode forward, cradling a motionless body in his arms.

"My lord King, I crave pardon for this intrusion—"

"Stefan!" Roland cried, leaping forward. "What have you done to him?"

The elf laid the boy at Andundal's feet

"He fell, Majesty. I could not catch him."

Roland went to his knees beside his squire.

"Stefan! Stefan, please..."

He felt a light touch on his shoulder and turned to find himself staring into the blue-green eyes of the princess.

"Let me see if I can help. I am considered skilled in the healing arts."

Even in the midst of this crisis, Roland could not help but note her voice was rich and deep for a woman, with the sound of a sparkling stream. He could listen to it for hours, given half a chance, but now he moved away to let her near Stefan.

Mendana took one good look at the unconscious boy, and her ivory skin paled to the white of new-fallen snow. She turned to her father and spoke rapidly in the musical tones of the elven tongue.

"*Noile, astami Steavil!*" Father, it is Steavil!

"*Twuia steami, Mendana?*" Are you sure?

"*Reve,*" she whispered, sinking down onto the dais, and lifting Stefan's head into her lap. "Yes, *Noile*, I am sure."

"What is it?" asked Roland, a note of anxiety creeping into his voice.

She looked up at him, her beautiful eyes luminescent with unshed tears.

"He is my brother."

Roland blinked in shock.

"He is your...?"

"He is my brother," she repeated with a hint of impatience. She unwrapped the now-filthy bandage with skilled care, gasping aloud at the jagged wound. "What happened here?"

Collyn remained kneeling, his voice hushed as he answered, "The raft upon which we sailed to Stormhaven was attacked. Stefan was hurt in the fighting. We took him into Woodwatch Ferry, and the doctor who treated him there counseled he stay abed for three days. The boy refused to listen, and I gave in to his desire to follow his prince, despite my better judgment and the old pledge. I take full responsibility."

Andundal rose from his throne to tower above the assembly. Although all the elves were tall, the king stood more than seven feet in height, topping his nearest subject by inches. His face grew granite cold with fury, as he turned his wrath on the riverman.

"I thought you a man of honor, Collyn Silverbrook. I see I was mistaken. You shall die for this, as promised."

"I expect no less, Lord King," murmured the trader. His tone was resigned, and his shoulders slumped.

"No!" Roland cried, stumbling to his feet, and standing up to Andundal. "Collyn could not force Stefan to listen to reason. The boy has always been stubborn when his mind is set. If not for this man, Stefan would have died before we ever reached the doctor."

Collyn turned to him.

"Please stay out of this, my lord. The debt I owe the king is an old one."

"I don't care!" Roland turned back to the elf. "Collyn is a good and loyal man. I vouch for him with my life!"

Andundal stared down at him, his eyes bottomless pits of darkness.

"So you shall, my young prince. Take them to the dungeons!"

"*Neve, Noile!*" Mendana protested, easing Stefan gently to the dais and rising to her feet. "Father, no! You can't send them to the dungeons. You mustn't!"

Roland noticed the girl stood as tall as he did. At six feet, that was remarkable for a woman. Her shining braids swung to her knees. He was glad his hands remained bound because he longed to touch her, despite the warnings of common sense.

"Please, Father. Is this the hospitality we show our neighbors? Is it any wonder the elven race is held in fear and hatred by our human counterparts?"

"I cannot forgive this, Mendana. I cannot. If my son dies—"

"Father." The princess laid her hand on the king's arm. "Please. What else has he been to you for these past fifteen years but dead? Now these men have returned him to us. We have been given another chance. They brought Steavil back to us. I will tend his wound, and by the grace of Andailia, he will be saved. Give these men the honor they are due."

Emotions warred across Andundal's face. Obviously, the princess's words swayed him. Then his eyes fell once more upon Collyn. He shook his head.

"No, Mendana. I cannot revoke my order. Take them to the dungeon, Dèodar. *Threami ruaen oth thyesti!*"

Their young guard stepped forward to take the prince's arm and lead him from the dais. Collyn stood to follow.

"*Noile!*"

"*Yrethsti,* Mendana. Enough! Dèodar, take them."

***

Stefan fought back to consciousness, like swimming upward through a sea of congealing mud, one breath shy of drowning. With a shuddering gasp, he broke the surface and opened his eyes.

Raising a shaking hand to his splitting head, he experienced the all-too-familiar disorientation he had been cursed with of late, and when he blinked his eyes into focus, the feeling shifted to fear.

He did not recognize this chamber and had no memory of how he came to be in it. Bright tapestries wrought in vibrant silks warmed the cold austerity of the hewn-rock walls. Rich green grass seemed to wave in an unseen breeze, while scarlet birds—no,

150

dragons!—circled in azure skies. A sleeping dragon lay in the foreground, wisps of smoke drifting from each nostril. He almost expected to see a tongue of flame erupt from the powerful jaws.

The room smelled faintly musty, although a bowl of fragrant autumn roses lent their perfume to the air. A sharp, pungent odor, vaguely medicinal, overlaid the roses, and the silken cushions pillowing his head gave off the scent of lavender. He buried his face in their softness for a moment, comforted by the fragrance.

The silks of the cushions mirrored the tapestries, and he marveled at the bright, sharp hues—he had never seen such brilliance in a fabric. The colors seemed almost alive in the muted light of the delicate lamps on either side of the doorway.

The lamps seemed spun of spider silk and fossilized into stone. Fretwork of open stone enclosed a glowing orb of pastel light—blue with the faintest tinge of green, reminding him of the river at twilight back home in Crown Keep.

The reminder of home made him remember his master.

I must find out where the elves took Roland and Collyn.

He moved to sit up and bit back a cry of pain. Every muscle ached, but his left leg felt as if pinioned on a rack. The dull flickering throb he had learned to live with now had been supplanted by a roaring inferno.

"By the Flames," he swore fervently, "must it always be the left?"

"Lie still," commanded an unfamiliar voice, and a face from his dreams edged into sight.

Stefan shrank back against the bed. "Where am I?"

"You are safe, Steavil. Rest easy."

"My name is Stefan," he replied automatically, but her words stirred the porridge of his memories. He pushed up onto his elbows.

"If you are determined to jostle your brains, let me help you," scolded the lady, slipping a slender arm behind his shoulders. With her aid, he managed to sit up.

"Where is my lord Roland?"

The lady frowned, and his heart rose into his throat. She hurried to reassure him.

"Do not worry, Stea—Stefan. The prince is safe." She laid a cool hand on his forehead, soothing away some of the pain.

"And Collyn?"

"He is safe as well. For now."

"Where are they? I must go to the prince."

Stefan forgot the new injury in the depths of his anxiety for Roland and struggled to stand. This time he could not stifle the cry torn from him when his ruined knee sent a knife of pain up his leg. He rocked back and forth, biting the side of his hand to stay the screams.

The girl tightened her hold about his shoulders.

"Lie still. Please. It will only make the pain worse."

A torch burned directly beside the couch; Stefan took a closer look at his companion. She was older than he—nearer to the prince in age. Long black hair hung like ribbons of braided coal to below her waist, and her eyes reflected the green of her soft dress. A warm smile played about perfect lips and danced in her eyes.

"Mendi...?" he whispered, the name springing forth unbidden and unrecognized.

"*Ithneimi endi, inithi thiuveia.*"

He frowned in confusion. A memory stirred deep in his soul, but it danced away as if on a wayward breath of wind.

"Where are the others? For that matter, where am I? The last thing I remember is the rock in the forest grating closed before me. Then the elf appeared...and the ground disappeared like smoke beneath my feet. I don't understand any of this."

"You will. When you are stronger. For now, let me translate my words." A dimple graced her cheek. "Rest easy, little brother."

Stefan felt his mouth drop open. "What...?"

"Enough for now." She bent and hugged him. "I'm so glad you are home. We'll talk more later. I've put you here in your old chamber so you would feel more at home. Here—perhaps this will keep you occupied. It fell out of your pack." Smiling, she handed him the slim volume of ballads. "I'll return this evening. Till then, lie still!" she commanded, playfully shaking her finger at him. With a swish of skirts, she was gone, leaving him more troubled than before.

He sank back against the cushions.

"If only I could think!" he whispered.

Restless, he tried to leave the couch, hissing at the flare of agony. Someone had slit his leggings to the thigh on the left side, and his leg lay bare, the knee tightly splinted. Once the agony faded to its usual dull throb, he studied the limb with dispassionate detachment.

From ankle to knee, scar tissue from the hound's attack marred the skin. His foot twisted to one side, the muscles no longer responding when he tried to straighten it. He probed at the bandage around his knee. The result argued the leg was best left alone. Gritting his teeth, he managed to lift it high enough to slip a cushion beneath the knee before falling back into his pillows once more.

Alone, he let bitterness rise in his throat, twisting his mouth into a resentful line. That day in the courtyard had ruined his life. He did not regret saving the prince, but he was no saint—he could not help but begrudge the cost.

And now the leg was damaged further. If it would no longer bear his weight, what would he do?

With a sigh, he picked up the book the girl had handed him, hoping to take his mind off his leg. He flipped through the pages, scanning lines here and there. A phrase caught his eye, and he frowned, stopping to read the entire ballad carefully.

The song was written in an ancient style, and the notation featured unusual chord structures. His fingers itched for a lute to play it. Having none, he sang the lyrics aloud, sounding out the tune as he tried to recreate the archaic rhythms:

An elven lay there was of old,
Of Sunstone bound in setting gold,
Of Moonstone wondrous to behold,
And Bloodstone foretelling tomorrow—

The reference to an elven ballad sent a frission of excitement through him; he wished he could see the original. This song seemed more a retelling of an old story than a translation

In ancient days when elves were king—

The legends tell of a wondrous thing.
In elven hands, together bring—
And see an end to all sorrow.
But Bloodstone was to humans tossed,
While Moonstone's healing gifts held cost,
And Sunstone's mystic powers, lost,
Lie hidden until the morrow.

A whisper of sound outside the curtained entrance drew his attention from the book. Stefan slipped the volume beneath his pillow, blinking away the familiar rush of vertigo as he strove to sit up straighter. As best he could from the awkward angle, he pulled together the remnants of his leggings to hide the knee—pride made him keep his scars hidden as much as possible.

The curtain drew aside, and an elf entered the room, coming to attention next to the opening. Stefan shrank back against the headboard, tensed for whatever might be happening.

The newcomer stared straight ahead as he intoned, "His Majesty, King Andundal Etheraborae." Sweeping the curtain completely open, he bowed as an imposing figure in green and silver strode in.

Stefan clutched the edges of the couch in white-knuckled desperation. The stern visage of the king terrified him, and he braced for the punishment he had dreaded since awaking in this strange place.

King Andundal came to tower above the frightened squire, and Stefan cowered. An inscrutable expression flickered across the king's face. Then he went down on one knee beside the couch, a gentle smile transforming his austere features.

"Twuae liami vieindi, Steavil? How are you feeling?"

he murmured, reaching for Stefan's hand.

"M–my name is Stefan," whispered the boy, pulling back farther. "I do not understand you. Please, I must see my prince."

The light died in the king's eyes.

"Of course. I will arrange for Prince Roland to come to you at once. Do you require anything else?"

Stefan shook his head, too numb with fear to reply.

"Very well." The king rose to his feet. "You remember nothing?" he beseeched.

"I do not understand you, my lord!" Stefan repeated, fear becoming panic.

"I see. I had so hoped…" The king sighed and returned to the doorway. "I will send the prince to you. Rest easy. *Ithneimi endi, ethiae thuathae.*"

"I will. *Euae veisthli,* Noile," Stefan replied without conscious thought—then wondered where the elven words came from.

Andundal's smile brought the light back to the king's eyes.

"You do remember something, my son. You may not be conscious of it yet, but it is there. Perhaps, in time, we shall have you fully with us once more." He swept from the room as grandly as he had come.

Stefan stared after him.

What did he mean? And what did I say to him? Where did I learn it? But he had no answers, and he felt like a lost child again, alone, and terrified of the dark.

Chapter 14

Norfulk stood before a large wrought iron cage suspended beside his ebony throne. He was careful not to touch the iron—detrimental to those versed in magic. He toyed with Stefan's silver amulet.

"Tell me, little friend, what news?"

The raven that had dogged the boys throughout their journey clung to a perch within the cage. It spoke to the sorcerer in a harsh parody of speech.

"He lives, my lord. I have seen him."

"And where is he?" Norfulk purred.

"He entered the Forest of Night. The elves will have him now."

"No!" Norfulk spun on his heel, stalking across the room. "I have worked too hard for this. I thought I had destroyed that arrogant Roland at last. This time, I must make sure to do so personally." His fingers tightened convulsively, crushing the small silver disk in his hand. The fragments fell through his fingers like stardust.

Surprise made him pause, and he stared down at the bits of silver clinging to his glove.

"Hold on a minute..."

"How will you get him free from the elves?" croaked the raven, flapping his wings to distract the sorcerer. "They will not relinquish him willingly. They have their own disputes to settle with the prince."

Norfulk shook his head as if to clear it, but answered smoothly, "Surely you can deal with the pitiful handful of elves skulking amid their dark trees, little wizard. Your powers have come a long way since our first meeting.

"Tell me, what was it that sent you fleeing to the world of men in the first place? I would think you were the type of good little elf who bowed to king and crown above all others."

"That is none of your concern," muttered the raven.

"Come, come, we are friends here," prodded Norfulk. "I know you hail from Dark Wood, and not the Forest of Night. You have said as much. But leaving both for the environs of men seems...foolish at best."

"Curiosity drove me as much as anything else." The air around the raven shimmered as its shape shifted. Where the bird had swung now slumped the figure of the Woodwatch Ferry jewelry peddler. He looked at Norfulk with hatred in his sea-green eyes, a lock of ebony hair falling across his forehead.

"Ah...that's better. Now we can speak as colleagues instead of master and man—or bird, as it were. You were hardly inconspicuous in Fangspur Cove with that combination of hair and eyes, now, were you?" Norfulk waved a languid hand at the elf's clothing. "Especially in that flamboyant costume, Eeonathor Ravenwing. A cape? In a fishing town? Dear me." He laughed derisively. "You should have expected the beating you got."

"I suppose so." Ravenwing shrugged his slim shoulders. "But I was young—and, yes, foolish."

"And there I found you, peering up through one slitted eye, the other already swollen shut. What was it I said to you?"

"You said—" began Ravenwing in a tortured whisper.

"—I am your salvation," Norfulk interrupted him.

"And I, being foolish, believed you."

"Remember that. And remember the prize we work towards. I am sure you can take care of things with the elves—after all, we both know you have claws." Norfulk absently fingered a set of thin parallel scars on his cheek. "Pity you are so reluctant to use them." With a wicked laugh, he strode from the room.

"The day I met you, I desperately needed to believe in something," Ravenwing murmured to the empty hall, "so I trusted you. But now I know you, I am certainly not telling you why I came to be outside that tavern."

That I had been driven out.

"I may be powerless within this iron cage, but the time is nearing when I will break these chains. The day when I will have my revenge at last."

***

The chamber to which he and Roland were taken proved surprisingly comfortable for a dungeon. The room measured ten paces square, with two bunks on one wall and a small wooden table with two stools against the opposite. In one corner, a spring fed into and out of a natural stone basin and a tiny alcove housed privy facilities. If not for the barred door, Collyn could almost have convinced himself it was a guest suite in a poorer inn, but he knew better.

Sinking down on the farther bunk, he fought to remain alert, but the strain of two sleepless nights caught up with him. Exhausted, he let his head fall back against the wall with a sigh.

Roland dropped onto one of the stools, his chin resting on his hand.

"This is some kettle of fish we find ourselves in. What does the king mean when he speaks so cryptically of honor and betrayal?"

Collyn rubbed a hand across his face.

"It's a long story, my lord."

"It looks as if we have plenty of time."

Collyn sighed once more. "Despite appearances, a cell is a cell, and the king has good reason to be angry with me. I have earned his displeasure. We all have demons that haunt us. You spoke to me of yours, I'll tell you now of mine.

"I was scarcely older than you are when I found myself in the Forest of Night, hunched over a tiny fire that barely dented the cold. My leaky coracle was drawn up on the shore—"

"Why were you in the Forest, Collyn? Everyone knows the dangers."

Collyn could see his younger self in his mind's eye, staring moodily into the flames.

"I had been traveling for so long, and I was weary beyond measure. I think, in a way, I was looking for danger. It had been a long, lonely year since I'd had a home."

He closed his eyes, swallowing hard. Behind his lids, a cabin burned, the night shattered by phantom screams. Those screams were never far from him, even after all this time. They had faded to mere whispers unless he gave in to them, but they were never truly gone.

"I held my dagger, watching the play of the firelight along its blade as I tried to summon the courage to kill myself."

Roland gasped. "You were going to take your own life?"

"As I said, my prince, we all have our demons—some are more difficult to live with than others. It doesn't matter, though, because, as I hesitated, there was a soft step behind me, and I turned.

"Before me stood an archer with a great horn bow drawn back to his ear."

"An archer?" Roland breathed. "Elven, I assume?"

Collyn nodded. "Though I didn't realize it at the time. He was taller than I, dressed in green leathers that made him hard to see against the trees. And the crystal-tipped arrow in his bow was trained right on my heart."

"What did you do?"

Collyn's hand crept unconsciously to massage his shoulder.

"I dove to one side, and the arrow struck high in my shoulder. I rolled onto my back beside the fire, staring up at the archer as the blood seeped through my fingers. I expected to die—I wanted to die—and yet..." He shook his head in bemusement.

"But, Collyn..." the prince protested, his face wreathed in incredulity.

"The stranger quickly nocked a second arrow, and I remember saying 'Go ahead. Do it!' That surprised him. He hesitated, a puzzled frown replacing his anger." Collyn rose and began to pace, still massaging his shoulder. "The archer lowered his bow, keeping the arrow nocked. 'You are young and strong,' he said. 'Why do you wish to die?'"

"What did you say to him?" whispered Roland.

"I told him my home, my family, my honor— everything had been taken from me. My life was little enough to have left."

The prince leaned forward, a frown creasing his brow. "What do you mean?"

Collyn raised a hand to forestall any further questions. "I can only tell this if I do it in my own way, my lord.

"The archer continued, 'And yet, you dove to avoid my arrow. It seems you are less willing to die than you think.' He laid the bow down. 'Let me see your wound.'

"I pulled away from him and growled, 'Let it bleed.' I was a surly pup in those days." He chuckled. "'A coward's way out,' the elf replied softly, and I protested that I was no coward."

"I can attest to that. Did he believe you?"

Collyn nodded. "Or so he said. He warned me the wood was haunted. 'By demons and elves, they say. All one and the same, if you ask me,' I answered him as he probed at the wound. It hurt like the Blazes. 'Hold still,' he warned. 'This will hurt.' He shoved against the arrow until the tip exited the back of my shoulder."

Roland shuddered.

"It was long ago," Collyn said. "It no longer aches unless there's a change in the weather coming." He shrugged and continued. "'I am sorry,' the stranger said. 'This is necessary.' He picked up a brand from the fire and lit the end of the arrow. The feathers burst into flame. I could feel the heat on my face. 'Take a deep breath—this will be worse.' He grabbed hold of the arrowhead and jerked the burning shaft through the wound to cauterize it."

"How did you stand it?" Collyn didn't need to see Roland flinch—he heard it in the prince's voice. *He's a sheltered lad...I must remember.*

"I fainted dead away," he admitted with a rueful smile. "I have never felt such pain, before or since. When I came to, I found myself propped against a pack with my shoulder bandaged. The fire had been built up, and the stranger sat on the other side of it, calmly tending his bow."

"Andundal?" guessed Roland.

Collyn nodded, a half-smile crooking his lips. "My first glimpse of an elf. And it was the king. 'What did you expect to find in an elven glade?' he asked me. 'Am I truly the demon you feared?'

"'What will you do to me?' I asked him. 'For someone who wishes to die, what does it matter?' he answered.

"I didn't know how to reply to that question," Collyn murmured, running his fingers through his hair. He continued, "The elf shook his head, and said 'When it comes down to it, again you choose life. Tell me, what drove you to my wood?'"

He sank down on the other stool with a heavy sigh. "That one I could answer." The cabin burned again in his mind as he stared down at his hands. "There was a fire. Eliesa...my...my wife...I couldn't save her." His voice caught in his throat.

Roland stared at him. "By the Fla—" He realized what he was saying and broke off the oath.

Collyn gulped and continued. "I heard a sigh

whisper across the fire, and glanced up. Andundal had buried his own face in his hands. 'What is it?' I asked him. His hands came down slowly, shaking, knotting themselves in his lap. 'I, too, had a wife. Human marauders murdered her and my son at the place men call the Lake of Sighs. Is it any wonder we distrust you humans?'"

Roland gasped. "So, Stefan was supposed to have been murdered all those years ago? Father brought him home from a mountain hunting trip. It must have been almost immediately after this happened."

Collyn nodded. "That's what I believe."

"I can't even begin to imagine such loss," murmured Roland, his face ashen.

"And I hope you never do," Collyn replied vehemently. He returned to the story. "'I, too, toyed with the thought of death,' the king sighed, 'but to what purpose? It would not return my wife and son—and as long as I have breath, there is a chance of avenging them.'

"I felt a flicker of hope spark deep in my soul at his words. If I could give Eliesa peace, perhaps I could find some of my own. I vowed to try."

Roland shifted on the hard seat, stifling a yawn. "I'm sorry, my friend. It's not your tale. It's just been a very long day."

"My story is almost done," Collyn answered with a shadowed smile. "The king rose to his feet, waving me down when I started to rise. 'Rest here tonight, with my blessing,' he said. 'If you are disturbed in the night, show them that.' He nodded at the arrowhead he had pulled from my shoulder. 'My men will not shoot before you have a chance to explain. You have the word of Andundal, King of the Starlit Elves.' He held out his hand, and I clasped it, giving him my own name.

"'Fare thee well, Collyn Silverbrook. Tomorrow, take your boat and leave the forest. The river is the only safe passage for a human. You must swear on your honor never to stray from that path again, on penalty of death.'"

"Ah," Roland breathed.

"Now do you see, Your Highness? I gave my oath, and I have broken it, knowing full well the consequences." Collyn's hand strayed to the crystal arrowhead hanging by its thong about his neck. It still bore Andundal's rune. "Now will come the reckoning."

***

Roland stared as the trader clutched the amulet about his neck. In the short time of their acquaintance, the prince had learned to value the man's advice.

Collyn stifled a yawn of his own.

"How long have you gone without sleep for us?" Roland asked. "It's been...by the Flames, Collyn! You sat guard two nights in a row. And it must be near dawn of another—I should have noticed sooner."

The prince rose and moved to one of the bunks, stretching out with his head pillowed on his bent arm.

"Look at me, Collyn." He sighed. "Crown prince of Irthlan, and here I am, imprisoned in a subterranean cavern by a people I never even knew existed outside of children's stories and ancient history lessons. What a fool's venture this has turned out to be. By now, news of the raft's loss will surely have arrived in Crown Keep.

Father will be beside himself with worry.

"And what if Stefan's dream truly was one of his visions? What if Father is ill? By the Flames, I have made such a mess of things! If only I hadn't tried to cut short my journey."

Collyn sank down on the unoccupied bunk.

"It's all behind us now, my lord. We must try to move forward." His face split in a jaw-cracking yawn.

"Get some rest, Collyn. You must be exhausted."

He nodded and turned toward the wall. His breathing deepened almost immediately.

Roland shook his head with a smile, shifting to fling an arm across his eyes. He was drifting off himself when he heard a noise outside and sprang to his feet, facing the door.

The heavy oak panel swung open, and Dèodar appeared in the doorway.

"My lord, the king has sent for you. Would you come with me, please?"

"Of course." Roland glanced uneasily at the sleeping Collyn.

Dèodar followed his eye. "I give you my personal bond he shall be unharmed," he vowed, one hand to his breast.

Roland hesitated a moment longer then nodded.

"That's the best assurance I'll get, isn't it?"

"I tend to think so." Dèodar grinned.

Roland followed the warder back to the throne room. The king sat deep in thought when they entered the chamber, chin propped on one elegant hand while he stared into the far corner of the now-empty space. Without the scattered groups of elves, the room had an air of bleak loneliness despite the wealth of its furnishings.

The crystal lamps were extinguished, and only guttering torches provided light. The walls faded into obscurity beyond them, and the vaulted ceiling was a roof of darkness overhead. Only the dais glowed with light.

More than darkness shadowed Andundal's face as he gazed beyond the room at whatever he saw in his mind. Roland was struck by a sudden sense of familiarity.

"He reminds me of my father," he whispered to Dèodar. "Is it the weight of the crown that brings lines of care to their faces and silver to their hair? Both look years beyond their age—I am not eager to be king."

Dèodar nodded. "Better you than me," he whispered back.

Andundal sighed, covering his eyes with one hand.

"My son...what new game are the gods playing now?" he murmured.

It was obvious the words were not meant for Roland, and he felt uncomfortable overhearing them.

"My Lord King," announced Dèodar, stepping in to cover the awkwardness. "His Highness, Prince Roland."

Andundal started out of his reverie. "Yes, of course. Leave us, Dèodar."

"As you command." He bowed and obeyed.

As the door slid closed behind the young guard, the king turned to Roland with a sigh.

"My son is asking for you. He holds you his master— not equal, as is his birthright—and cares more for your safety than his own."

He rose to his feet, descending the dais to stand before Roland, with hands clasped behind his back. Roland met his gaze without trembling.

"While he has been my squire, he has also been my friend. He has been treated with nothing but kindness. Stefan has been the brother I do not have by blood."

"Stefan—even the name is so close. Why did you choose it?"

"When he was found by my father's hunting party in the mountains near the Lake of Sighs, he was but a tot. No one could understand what he was saying, or even recreate the sounds, and the closest anyone could come to what seemed to be his name was 'Stefan.' Soon, he spoke our language. We always assumed the other a child's babbling, my lord. We never recognized it for another tongue—I doubt anyone at court has ever heard the elven language spoken aloud."

"They found him near Desolation Lake?" The king's voice died to a whisper. "What cruel irony."

Having heard Collyn's story, Roland could imagine the thoughts running through the king's mind, and felt a surge of sympathy.

Andundal's face grew shadowed, and he turned away, sinking onto his throne.

"We are but a handful of people, the remnants of a once-proud race—this keep is our last outpost. But once, elves flourished in all the woodlands. My queen, Deveiria, came from the royal house of Moonrise Wood, known to you as Dark Wood. After Steavil was born, she wanted to visit her father. I...I was too occupied to attend her. She postponed her journey several times.

"Finally, when the boy was five, she received word

her father was ill, and decided to go alone. She felt she could no longer wait—"

"Excuse me, my lord. When Father found Stefan, he could have been no more than three."

A brief smile crossed Andundal's face, as if the prince had said something witty.

"You forget, my boy, Steavil is not human. He was always small for his age, and quick to adapt. Does he look the fifteen you have thought him to be? Our rate of aging differs from yours. Although he may look but thirteen, he is nearly twenty."

Roland was at a loss for words. His relationship with Stefan had always been that of a slightly patronizing older brother. To find the squire might be the elder disconcerted him.

"But...twenty! That's impossible!"

The king nodded. "It is true. My queen set off with a twenty-man escort," Andundal continued. "Mendana took ill, and chose to remain home at the last moment. Somewhere between my borders and Moonrise Wood, the party was ambushed. We found the bodies in the mountains ringing Desolation Lake. We never discovered the responsible party. My wife... my wife was murdered, the escort butchered. No trace was found of the boy, but then, it was very...difficult... to be sure.

"The shock hastened the death of Deveiria's father, and the Moonrise elves were leaderless. Their numbers were few, their kingdom dying. They came to join us here in Starlit Wood, abandoning their homes. I spoke truth when I told you this is our only stronghold. I have a handful of subjects here. No more than fifty remain of a race that once roamed the entire land.

"And my son, who was—and shall again be—my heir, asks only for 'my prince,' as if he were a common servant. He has lost all memory of his heritage, although deep inside, I feel, he does remember. He is a prince! How can he not think like one?"

"My Lord King," replied Roland, his voice thoughtful, "if you are truly seeking an answer to the question, I can only venture a guess. For three-quarters of his life, Stefan has been my squire. He was a prince for a very short time in comparison, and those years were very long ago. He needs to adjust to the change of fortune. Shall I speak to him?"

"And say what? What can you say to make him the king he should be?"

Roland stood in stunned silence, suddenly realizing something that would never have struck him before this ill-fated journey began.

"He will be a great king, Lord Andundal. Much better than I. He has lived among the people of Irthlan like an equal. He understands their problems in a way I can never hope to do."

"He will not be king of Irthlan. His subjects will not be human."

"But the problems will be the same. Our peoples are not so very different."

Andundal glanced at him, his expression speculative.

"Perhaps you are right, young prince. But you are forgetting a most important fact. To rule his kingdom, Steavil must leave yours." He got to his feet once more. "Dèodar will show you to my son."

He called out to the young guard waiting in the

hallway. Dèodar stepped into the throne room, once more bowing to his king.

"*Alianiae, deastia threami oth ionavo an ethiae thuathae.* Please take the prince to my son."

"*On twiae stimarimi.* As you command." The warder nodded, gesturing Roland to go before him.

Roland started from the chamber, his thoughts churning. Andundal had given him something serious to think about. Whenever he'd thought about life after he ascended the throne, Stefan had always been at his shoulder to counsel and advise him.

"Is something wrong, Lord Roland?" asked the young guard.

"Things *will* be different now, won't they? The king is right. For Stefan to fulfill his own destiny, we will have to separate." Knowing the separation would be for life cut him to the quick.

"But it must be so. Do you not wish him to fulfill his destiny?" The elf's voice was puzzled. "His heritage is to be a king, my lord, just as your own, not to serve at the stirrup of another."

Roland felt ashamed of the servitude he had placed on Stefan, albeit unwittingly.

"You're right," he agreed. For the first time, he put the squire's needs before his own. "The only way to make it up to Stefan for the way he's been treated is to convince him to take his rightful throne. I must make him see reason." With the decision came a lightness of heart that told he'd made the right choice. "It is not like we'll never see each other again," he continued. "This can only serve to unite the two kingdoms!"

"It may be as you say," replied the elf, "but there

are centuries of distrust to overcome. Fortunate as this happenstance may be, do not expect that mistrust to melt away like the snow overnight."

"But think on it! The uneasy truce between our peoples can end in a true peace. Why, the elves will be able to return to Dark Wood if they desire. In time, perhaps our peoples will live and work side-by-side without fear or mistrust."

Roland's boot heels clicked faster against the stone as he got caught up in the momentum of his thoughts. He registered only dimly the indulgent smile on Dèodar's lips as the elf lengthened his stride to keep up.

"There is so much we could teach each other, Dèodar! How those lovely crystal lamps would intrigue my father—an apparently perpetual light source like that!"

"Kitchen magic," shrugged the elf. "They are simply convenient."

"They would be marvels indeed at Crown Keep. And if our weavers could but learn the art of weaving your beautiful silks, my kingdom would become the envy of the world with such wares to sell." He ticked the points off on his fingers while he hurried down the corridor.

Dèodar's laugh rang out. "Slow down, my lord! Do not get ahead of yourself, lest the fall come hard."

"But what can we offer you in turn, Dèodar? What skills are lacking here in your kingdom?"

The elf frowned thoughtfully. "Well, your husbandry with animals is something we could stand to learn— though I have been trying to convince my uncle of that with no success. Hunting is scarce feeding the court these days, and if we could raise our own meat supply that would be Eostivil's blessing. And your horses are much stronger mounts than the skittish stock we breed."

"I am sure that can be arranged."

"And your architecture—if elves come out into the sunlight once more, we will need to learn a completely different style of building." Dèodar seemed to be warming to the subject.

"And your fascinating elven tongue—Father loves languages. He will be so interested to hear you speak. Just wait until I tell him about—"

Suddenly, Roland's excitement vanished like a wayward breath of smoke, and he stopped dead. For a moment, he had forgotten he was still a prisoner, and the choice of what was to come not his.

"Even if I am freed to return home, what will I find there?" His heart sank when he realized he might never see his father alive again.

"Are you all right, my lord?"

"I must return to Crown Keep! My father's life may be in danger. Still...the thought of the elves and the humans working in concert, sharing, and learning from each other—it is a beautiful dream, is it not?"

"Indeed, Your Highness." The elf smiled. "Here is the chamber, my lord. I am sure the prince will be glad to see you."

Roland nodded and took a deep breath. Calling out a soft greeting from the hallway, he waited for an answer.

"Come in," replied a quiet voice.

Roland edged back the curtain, poking his head

around the drapery.

"Prince Roland!" Stefan exclaimed, stretching out his hands. "Please, come in!"

"How are you, my friend?"

"Much better, my lord. Lady Mendana is a powerful healer. My head throbs little now. I think 'tis nearly mended. If not for my knee, I would be fit to attend you—"

"You shall not attend me any longer, Stefan," Roland murmured. He smiled as he perched on the edge of the bed, careful not to jar the elevated knee.

Stefan's eyes grew huge in his pale face. "Have I done something wrong, my prince? Or is it my knee? I'll not slow you any more than usual, I swear it! 'Tis the ruined leg that was broken."

"No, my friend. You've done nothing wrong." Roland met his eye squarely. "You cannot serve me because your first duty is to your own people."

"But, my prince—"

"And I am not your prince. The heir of one kingdom does not bow to that of another. You are your own prince, Stefan, and you need to get used to the fact."

"What are you saying, my lord?"

"You need no longer call me 'lord,' for one thing." He flashed a dazzling smile. "Your father has told me much about your past we did not know."

"My father?"

"Yes, Stefan, your father—the elven king."

Chapter 15

Stefan leaned against the headboard, staring at the ceiling. Emotions warred within him, and he fought to regain his control. Having had years of practice, he soon calmed himself

"It is true, then?" he asked Roland. "Everyone calls me 'lord' and 'your highness.' And memories keep surfacing from somewhere. Especially one of a beautiful lady—much like Mendana, but older."

"Your mother, I expect."

"Mother..." The word was like a prayer. "Where is she?"

Roland bit his lip then murmured, "She's dead, Stefan. She was murdered near the Lake of Sighs when you were a child."

A scene flashed through Stefan's memory like lightning—a party of travelers resting under the stars, talking quietly. Then, with the piercing shrieks of carrion birds, a pack of raiders descending out of the night. A struggle...death all around him...a woman's scream...silence. Calling out desperately for his mother. The sensation of overwhelming terror as he ran. Darkness falling in a seamless shroud.

He remembered awakening an infinite time later in a nest of brambles, scratched and bruised, his mother's final gift clenched tightly in one small fist. He had held on to that little silver disk through everything that happened to him—until the night on the raft, so hauntingly similar to that long-ago massacre.

"No!" He ground the heels of his palms into his eyes to crush the memories now bubbling over inside his head.

"What is it? Should I call someone?"

"No. I–I will be fine." Stefan felt he had aged ten years in as many seconds. "I...remember," he said, his voice a hollow whisper.

***

Roland watched the war of emotions range over Stefan's face. He still looked scarcely thirteen, yet all at once, as if he had shed a long-worn disguise, ageless wisdom lurked in the depths of his eyes, revealing a spirit far older. Thinking on it, he realized that wisdom had always been there—shining out whenever he needed Stefan most. He had come to rely on it to keep him in line, trusting Stefan to be his conscience.

Though, to his shame, he had not always listened.

"What do you remember?"

"Who I am, where I came from, Father, Mendana, my language...Mother. It all rushed back to me like a dike giving way."

"Would it ease your mind to share some of those memories?" Roland asked gently.

"They are not all painful." Stefan's face lit with a smile. "I remember many things from my childhood I thought were lost forever. Little things...not earth-shattering... but they have given me back what was mine."

Roland leaned against the footboard, one knee cocked on the mattress to make himself more comfortable.

"Was it much different from Crown Keep? I mean—"

He felt his face heat, realizing that the life of a prince was, of course, different from that of a servant, even a favored one. "Was it different living here in the wood?"

Stefan settled himself more comfortably among the pillows. "Let's see...I remember lying flat on my stomach in a forest glade one day watching a line of insects bustling through the bracken...then someone called my name, and I looked up to see Mother and Father standing arm-in-arm under a towering oak.

"I ran to meet them, and Father scooped me up off the ground and swept me around in a circle until I felt as if I were flying. We were so happy then...and Father's hair was jet-black, without a trace of silver."

"I remember my father doing the same thing." Roland laughed. "I guess it's one of those things fathers know to do for their children. I wonder how they learn?"

"From their own fathers?" Stefan guessed.

"What else do you remember?" Roland leaned forward, chin on hand.

"Mother was so beautiful, with hair like midnight— where your mother was sunlight, mine was moonlight. I remember her sitting before a stone hearth, my head on her lap while she stroked my hair and sang to me. Her gown rustled like autumn leaves. Mendana sat cross-legged on the floor beside us, writing on a piece of parchment with a goose quill pen while the firelight reflected from her shining braids. She's always been so serious..."

"Do you remember how my father came to find you?"

Stefan nodded, his eyes brimming with unshed tears.

"Yes," he whispered. "I remember." He sounded weary, as if he bore the weight of the lost years on his slender shoulders. "And now that I do remember, I wish to the gods I did not."

"What happened, Stef—Steavil?"

Roland stumbled over the pronunciation of the unfamiliar name. Stefan gave him a crooked ghost of his normal smile.

"Please, Roland, I have become accustomed to 'Stefan.' I would prefer to keep it."

"As you wish, my friend. Can you tell me, or would you rather not speak of it?"

"No, it is time to tell the story. Will you bring my father and Mendana? I...I do not think I could face it twice."

"Of course, at once." Roland rose from the bed. "Will you be all right?"

Stefan seemed preternaturally pale, all color leached from his cheeks by his memories. The eyes he turned toward the prince were dead black.

"I will be fine. It will just...take some time to accept it all." He favored Roland with another wan imitation of his usual grin. "Unlike you, I am unused to being a prince."

"I will bring your father," Roland murmured, reaching out to squeeze his shoulder. "I'm here for you, if you need me."

Stefan laid a hand on his arm. "I thank you, my friend. I am sure I shall, in the days to come."

With a nod, Roland left the room. Dèodar waited in the hallway, a discreet distance from the doorway.

"I must return to the king," Roland told him. "The

prince is asking for his father."

"The prince?" Hope bloomed on the elf's face, and Roland nodded.

"He has regained his memory."

"Eostivil be praised," breathed Dèodar. "I shall take you to the king at once."

***

Mendana sat before her mirror, running a brush through the unbound river of her hair with thoughtful, even strokes. Something about the repetition soothed her jangled nerves, and they definitely needed soothing.

Her gaze wandered from the reflection in the glass to roam about the familiar room. The same bright tapestries gracing Stefan's room hung on her walls, but hers bore images not of trees and dragons but of the sea. Blues and greens dominated, the frame of the mirror and the bedstead were great gilt seashells, and the bed was spread with shimmering blue velvet, which brought to mind a still tidal pool.

Beside the mirror stood a small silver-and-gold flask, and Mendana set the brush on the table to pick it up. She removed the stopper and took a deep breath. The scent of lavender wafted up, and she closed her eyes. The perfume had been her mother's. It gave Mendana comfort whenever she needed it. She dabbed it now on her wrists and temples, massaging away the beginnings of a headache.

She picked up the brush again and renewed her steady strokes. A ghost from her past had come back to life tonight. She had long ago resigned herself to the thought she would never see her beloved little brother again.

"Now, from nowhere, he has returned," she confided to her reflection—a habit bred from sparse companionship among her dwindling clan. "The return is not unwelcome, but it is a shock. Particularly considering the wretched condition Steavil is in."

She felt her face harden like marble. His injuries tore her heart. She had done what she could, but his leg would never fully recover; and a split skull such as he had suffered would have killed Prince Roland had the human been struck instead.

At the thought of Roland, her hand froze in mid-stroke.

"The human prince intrigues me, he is so altogether different from my kin. The fire of his hair shines like the sunset, and the green glitter of his eyes when he looked to me for help..."

Blood rushed to her cheeks. There was something special about the man. It set her pulse racing just to think of him...but some things she would not speak aloud, even to her mirror.

Sighing impatiently at her foolishness, Mendana quickly rebraided her hair into its practical plaits and smoothed the soft green folds of her gown.

"There is work to do. No time to sit and daydream."

She picked up a covered wicker basket and went to check her medical supplies. She called out to the court messenger as she passed his chamber, "Leithan, bring your pen and tablet—my brother needs healing, and I may need you to fetch some things."

Leithan scrambled to obey—he was a young elf,

perhaps four or five years younger than Stefan but six inches taller, with the sea-green eyes of the Dark Wood elves.

"Your brother, Lady? I thought he was..."

"He has returned to us," she informed him happily.

"Eostivil be praised!" Leithan breathed. "A miraculous return, indeed."

"Aye." Her smile evaporated. "But he has been grievously hurt. I may need you to make a trip above to collect herbs."

As she stood before the supply cabinet moments later, Mendana stared into the lavender oil bottle.

"How could I have allowed this to get so depleted? It's not just for perfume."

Leithan nodded solemnly and made a note in his careful script.

She peeked into a low wooden box and noticed it, too, was almost empty.

"That clout on the head is going to leave him with some terrible headaches. He'll require a deal of tonic."

"So, you will need a fresh supply of birch leaves?" he asked as he jotted down another note.

"You are a quick study. Have you considered becoming a healer? It worries me to be the only one for the entire clan."

"I will think about it, my lady, but I do so love the travel...and there are few enough to need such ministrations now."

"That is all too true." She lifted the lid from a basket. "He's been bleeding quite profusely, so we will need horsetails. Be careful not to crush them this time. They lose a lot of their potency prematurely that way."

"Aye, my lady."

"While you are searching, if you see any foxglove and witch hazel, bring them, too." She sighed, pushing back the tendrils of hair at her temples too short to catch up in her braids. "I should have done an inventory weeks ago."

She pulled down a large basket and counted her stock of bandages. She had gone through several strips caring for Steavil's injuries, but there should be more than this. With a frown, Mendana recounted the rolls of spider-silk one more time.

"Where haves all my bandages gone?"

"Captain Aerlann's patrol ran afoul of a ghostcat—fortunately, it was a small one, barely fifteen stone..."

"*Ruathia.*"

She turned at the sound of Andundal's voice. "Yes, *Noile?*"

"Steavil is calling for us. Prince Roland says he has regained his memory."

For the first time, she noticed the human standing behind her father, and her heart leapt. She fought to keep her composure.

"Wonderful, Father. Shall we go to him?"

She glanced at Leithan, and he nodded and stowed the list in his pouch. He bowed to the king and slipped quickly away.

Andundal led the way out of the room. Roland stepped aside and gestured her ahead.

"Thank you," she murmured, taking care to keep her voice formal when she brushed past him.

He fell into step beside her.

"I'm glad he has regained his memory, Your

Highness. He deserves to know his heritage."

"Please, call me Mendana, my lord." Her voice was husky with her unspoken feelings, and she inwardly cursed her transparency.

"Only if you will call me Roland, Lady."

"As you wish."

"Your home is beautiful, Mendana."

The sound of her name from his lips sent a thrill through her, and she had to force herself to concentrate on his next words.

"The crystals are spectacular. I've never seen anything like them. How do they glow?"

"Magic," she returned, unwittingly echoing Dèodar's answer as she risked an impish glance at him and smiled.

Before he could reply, they reached Stefan's room, and she gratefully ducked past the curtain, Roland at her heels.

***

Isolated images kept popping into Stefan's head—playing with his sister at the feet of the thrones, hearing his mother laugh, looking up to find her watching them in fond amusement; riding double with his father and learning to handle a horse almost before he could walk.

Now the gates had opened, the memories came in a rushing torrent. He remembered Dèodar kneeling beside him and fitting an arrow to a bowstring, patiently showing him how to aim and shoot.

I felt such a...a thrill hitting the target for the first time.

He sat up, burying head in hands. So many memories...

The image of a quiet elf with laughing eyes and a ready smile adjusting his fingering on the neck of a lute made him catch his breath with a gasp.

"I was taught to play! I remember now...but something happened..."

The rest of the memory would still not surface.

The curtain swept open without a hail, and Andundal strode in, closely followed by Mendana. Roland hung back beside the doorway.

"My son...?" whispered the king.

Stefan held out his hands. "*Noile.*"

Andundal's stern face transformed to a gentle smile, and he was beside the couch instantly, enfolding Stefan in his arms. The prince returned the embrace eagerly.

"Father," he repeated, his voice a mere whisper.

"I never thought I would see you again, my dearest son."

The king stroked Stefan's hair, and Stefan clung to him with all his might. For as long as he could recall, he had envied Roland Frederick's love. He had been starved for a family of his own.

"I cannot believe Fate has brought me back to you," he mumbled, comforted by his father's strength. "Oh, Noile..." He felt tears gathering, and buried his face in Andundal's velvet robe.

"Shh, *euae thuathae*," the king soothed. "We are here now, my son. We will not fail you again."

Mendana stepped to the far side of the couch, and Stefan gulped, brushing the back of his hand across his eyes with a shaky laugh. He reached out to take his sister's hand, unwilling to let go of his father completely. She sank onto a stool beside the bed, never breaking their connection.

Roland edged toward the doorway, but Stefan called out to him.

"Please, Roland, come closer. I would like for you to hear this as well."

The human prince settled on the floor near the bed.

Looking around at his family, both natural and adopted, Stefan took a deep breath.

"This will be hard—for me to tell and for you to hear—but it must be told. You have a right to know what happened that night, Father."

"Go on, *thuathae*, I am ready to hear, my son. I have waited so long to know."

"We rode toward Moonrise Wood," continued Stefan. "It was the night of the full moon, and Mother grew impatient. She feared she would not be in time to say goodbye. We rode until well past sunset before we finally stopped for the night beside Desolation Lake. We had supper around the campfire, and Raethan began to play.

"I remember drowsing on and off while I sat at Mother's side. I awoke past midnight—the moon just beginning to fall—to the sound of harsh cries as we were beset by a band of riders. They were dressed in solid black and rode black horses, almost impossible to see in the darkness, even with night-sight. There must have been powerful sorcery at work for them to come so close to the camp undetected.

"The raiders were armed with crossbows and swords. Before our archers could bring their own weapons into play, they were slaughtered. Mother hid me in a cave, then she...

"I...I still can't remember what happened then. The next thing I remember is running. It seemed like forever. Then I tripped and fell.

"That is all I know until I awoke sometime later." He trembled violently, reliving the terror, and his father tightened his grip on the hand he held.

"I was alone. It was cold and dark. I didn't know how I got to where I was or where I had come from. All I knew was I felt tired and hungry. I wandered for hours. I suppose I must have partially circled the lake. That would explain why Frederick's party found me and not the bodies. I had fallen asleep again, and his men awakened me with their horseplay.

"I remembered nothing of what I had witnessed, only my name and a few words for necessities. Even those words soon faded as I learned new ones. That is all I remember of that night, even now. I'm sorry I cannot tell you more, Father."

Andundal's head hung low, and Stefan felt a hot tear splash on his hand. He squeezed his father's hand in turn, and the king smiled up at him gratefully.

"Thank you for what you have given me, my son. She died bravely, as I knew in my heart." He drew a shuddering breath. "I must ask you one thing more. What of the Sunstone talisman? Do you recall anything about it?"

Something stirred in Stefan's memory, and an image flashed across his mind.

"Yes—at least, I believe so. One of the first things I do remember is lying in a velvet-lined cradle and reaching up for a spinning golden bauble. I laughed when it caught the light—it flung reflections around the walls like stars..."

His hand reached out at the memory, as if to catch the spinning bauble. Something important about the pendant lay just beyond his grasp.

"I found it pretty. I liked to look through it at the light. It was like looking into the heart of a golden fire. And the gryphon looked so proud and free. I remember gazing at the fire through it after supper. But I don't know what became of it."

"I think I do." Roland reached behind his head, undoing the clasp of the chain hanging inside his jerkin. "Is this the talisman you mean?" he asked, pulling the gryphon pendant from around his neck and rising to his feet in one fluid motion. He held out the chain to the king.

"Where did you get that?" demanded Andundal, his voice grating with unspoken accusation.

"I purchased it in the market at Woodwatch Ferry. It appealed to me, so I bought it." He fell to one knee, handing the chain to the king. "Take it if it belongs to you. I knew nothing of its importance."

The king lifted it from his hand with a reverent sigh, murmuring, "It is the symbol of our house. When a male heir is born, he is given the gryphon." He placed the chain around his son's neck. "I return it to its rightful place." He smiled. Then his face fell, haunted by a shadow. "Once it had a companion, which Deveiria wore, but we will never reclaim her amulet. It would be too much to hope."

"What was it?" asked Roland, his tone curious.

"A second pendant—more delicate—bearing the device of Moonrise Wood. A scribed silver disk depicting a half-moon with a moonstone held between the horns of the crescent to complete the circle. It was said to endow its possessor with great powers of healing, and it is true Deveiria was a master healer. Legend also says it brings naught but pain to anyone of dishonorable character who touches it. Whoever murdered my queen will have found little joy in it. But, I fear, it is lost to us forever."

"Perhaps not," murmured Roland thoughtfully, "if, as you say, the thief will have had no joy from the theft, it may be easier than you think to find the amulet. Give me leave to search for the Moonstone."

"Why would you want to do something like that?"

Roland flushed, and Stefan saw his glance dart swiftly to the princess and back to Andundal.

"I would like to repay Stefan in some measure for the debt I owe him, Lord, and to gain back favor in your eyes for the sons of men. We are not all villains."

"But what of your father, Lord Roland?" Stefan protested. "You must tell him you are alive."

"That is up to *your* father, Stefan. Perhaps I can earn my freedom by this venture and still somehow get word to Crown Keep."

Stefan questioned whether that was Roland's true motive but kept silent.

"Where would you begin?" asked the king with a frown.

"Perhaps there is a clue at the lake."

Stefan's heart fell. Their parting would come much sooner than he had expected. He had hoped for time to become accustomed to the idea, but if Roland left on a quest, he could not follow. Not with his ruined knee.

Such an injury was known to incapacitate a stronger man than he for a year, if not permanently. There was a good possibility this new damage would render his leg totally useless.

"You have my permission to leave the keep," Andundal consented at last, nodding in acquiescence. "Though I fear your quest is a fool's errand. It has been too long. If it lay amid the carnage, it was lost long ago." He sighed. "'Twas once said the Sunstone and Moonstone were joined, as were the elven houses. That the one could be used to find the other if need arose. But I never saw any evidence this was true. 'Tis likely just another story for children."

"I crave one further boon, my lord," requested Roland hesitantly, bowing his head.

"What more do you require?"

"May I plead for Collyn Silverbrook? He is a good man, my lord. Give him leave to return to Crown Keep and protect my father—he must know the full story of the treachery at the raft."

Stefan reached out to touch his father's sleeve.

"Roland speaks true, *Noile*. Collyn has offered far more aid than hurt. I forced him to help me follow the prince when I should have listened to him and stayed abed. He did not want to enter the Forest but would not allow me to go into danger alone. Please do not let King Frederick be endangered merely to punish Collyn for my foolishness."

Andundal's mouth set in a hard line.

"We had an old bargain, Master Silverbrook and I. It is a private matter. He made me a promise, and he has broken it. If I do not exact the punishment expected, how can my word be taken seriously in the future?"

"I have heard some about that bargain," answered Roland slowly. "I understand the need for a king to stand behind his word. But are there never circumstances that shift the tide of Fate? Surely, no monarch should be a stranger to mercy—no matter how stern his laws."

"Perhaps there is wisdom in what you say, young prince, but..." Andundal's brow furrowed.

"Perhaps I may offer an alternative solution, *Noile*," Mendana suggested. "Send our own messenger to warn the prince's father—you know Leithan can be trusted—and let Master Silverbrook have this chance to redeem himself. You have just said that a man without honor cannot touch the Moonstone. The quest itself will prove his mettle. It is my birthright which is to be sought, and I request Collyn Silverbrook as my champion."

"An acceptable compromise," Roland agreed. "I would welcome him on the journey."

"There is truth in what you say, Mendana. Very well," Andundal conceded with a scowl. "He may go with you. But Dèodar shall go as well, to keep an eye on both of you."

"I accept your condition, my king. I'll draft a message for your messenger to give my father and make preparations to leave at once." Roland stood and bowed, exiting the room.

Stefan let his head fall back, jaw grinding in impotent disgust.

"Some king I will make—the Lame Monarch, unable to walk his own kingdom," he muttered.

"You are tired, my son. You must rest." Andundal's

quiet voice brooked no argument as he rose to his feet. "We will leave you now. Come, *Ruathia.*" He held out his hand to Mendana.

She bent to kiss Stefan's cheek, whispering, "All will be well, *inithi thiuveia.* Do not worry, little brother."

Stefan looked up at her with a grateful smile. "As you say, *ethiae riuveia.* Thank you, my sister." He squeezed her hand. "*Noile,* please, don't forget to send Roland's warning to King Frederick. He will be frantic about the prince's disappearance. And don't let the others leave without saying goodbye."

"Do not worry," Andundal replied, unknowingly echoing Mendana's words. He smiled. "I doubt Roland would do so under direct orders. He is very headstrong, your young prince."

Stefan felt his cheeks flush. "It is his greatest fault. I try to curb it, but..."

"It is no longer your concern," murmured the king. "*Ithneimi endi.*" With a nod, he led Mendana from the chamber.

Stefan stared after them, his heart bleak when he contemplated the truth of Andundal's words. How well he knew the prince was no longer his charge.

I have found a kingdom and a family, but have I lost the only friends I have ever known? Is it a worthy trade?

Chapter 16

Dèodar led Roland back toward the humans' cell, words spilling over each other like those of a wide-eyed child in his excitement.

"I can't believe it! A quest...an adventure...I have dreamed about such things but never expected to be sent on one by the king. Except for the night journey when we came across the mountains from Moonrise Wood, I rarely venture outside this forest. Is it true there are vast tracts of land where no trees grow?"

The prince hid a smile. "You'll see soon enough. Be patient." He glanced at the other speculatively. Though the guard appeared little older than he, he now realized elven appearances could prove deceptive. "How did you become a warder, Dèodar?"

"My father served as Chief Warder in Moonrise Wood." His head lifted, and his voice filled with pride. "When we fled that sanctuary to come to Starlit Wood, I was seventeen. He petitioned the king, and my lord Andundal allowed me to join the warders—the youngest ever to be granted the privilege. Most posts go to men of at least fifty." His hands moved in eloquent counterpoint to his words. Dèodar rarely remained still for more than a breath.

"If you were seventeen when the exodus occurred," mused Roland, "then you must be..." He stopped, turning to the warder in astonishment.

"Thirty-two as you count years," answered the other with a laugh. "You will grow accustomed to such surprises."

Roland shook his head, continuing down the hallway.

"Our peoples seem so similar, and yet are so vastly different. For example, how can you stand to live beneath the ground, away from the sunlight?"

"I can't. None of us relish our exile under the earth, but some of us adapt better than others. I can't stand more than a few hours at a time within these walls. That's why I'm a warder. We're here, my lord."

The elf turned the key in the lock and swung the door wide. Collyn sat up as the panel creaked open. An expression of calm resignation shadowed his face as he turned toward the doorway.

"Get up, Collyn!" called the prince. "We must ready ourselves for a journey. We leave at sunset."

"Leave?" For once, Collyn's stoicism deserted him, hope lighting his face. "Stefan?"

"Is well. His head proved just as hard as ever," Roland replied with a fond smile. "But he broke his leg when he fell." The smile faded into a frown. "'Twas his left. It will likely finish the leg."

"If the Princess Mendana tends him," broke in Dèodar, "there is a good chance it will be no worse. She has the healing gift. She may even be able to correct the old damage to some extent."

Roland studied him. "You seem to know a great deal about the running of this palace for a mere warder, Dèodar."

"My father was Queen Deveiria's elder brother," answered the elf with a shrug. "Steavil and Mendana are my cousins. The princess has confided in me since childhood."

"I don't understand. If your father was the heir to Moonrise Wood..."

"I never claimed he was the heir. I merely said he was a prince. He didn't become king on Grandfather's death because Moonrise Wood has a female line of succession, complementary to the Starlit kings. Deveiria would have become queen. With her death, Mendana was next in line. Technically, she *is* queen of Moonrise Wood, but no kingdom remains to rule."

Roland dropped onto his bunk, leaning back against the wall.

"I don't understand."

Dèodar perched comfortably on the edge of the table, arms wrapped about a bent knee.

"For centuries, the kingdoms of Starlit and Moonrise Woods have intertwined. Control of Starlit falls to the eldest male heir, control of Moonrise to the female. My grandfather became king because he had no sisters. It is not so complicated. Are things that much different in your kingdoms?"

"The mainland has been united into one kingdom, Irthlan, for the last fifty years, and there is only one royal house. I am sole heir in the direct line. If I die or disappear, my cousin Norfulk becomes king at Father's death as the next in the blood lineage."

"Would he prove a good king?"

"No!" answered Collyn vehemently.

Roland and Dèodar both stared at him in surprise.

"What makes you so sure?" asked the prince. Roland could not remember ever seeing the big man display such strong emotion, not even when he spoke of his wife's death.

Collyn's eyes turned stormy as he responded in a voice harsh with bitterness.

"I have traveled to many places in my lifetime—few of them by choice. Once I fished out of Fangspur Cove, barely out of my teens and but six moons married. Eliesa was expecting our first child. Norfulk the Ravager took all I loved away from me. He was fifteen when his father died suddenly—some whisper mysteriously—and he inherited the castle men now call Crypticia Keep."

He stood and began to pace, as if he could remove the pain of his past through action. The click of his heels in the confined chamber sounded like the snapping of restless fingers.

Roland had heard bits of this story before, but not all of it.

"I don't understand. Norfulk was responsible...?"

"The land below the Lake of Sighs languishes in Norfulk's iron fist, and his influence creeps outward daily. The plain around his castle lies barren and desolate, and little grows there. They say this results from Norfulk's sorcery. You may think there exists but one kingdom, my liege, but no one in Fangspur Cove would have the courage to agree with you."

"He is Father's regent in the southern regions, but surely..."

The big man whirled to face Roland, jabbing his finger at the prince for emphasis.

"Believe me, my lord, no one in those lands dares acknowledge allegiance to any but the Black Lion." He swept his hand before him in a gesture of negation.

Roland was struck again by the vehemence of Collyn's emotions as the trader continued.

"But I was young and foolish at the time, and he a

mere boy. I refused to give him the lion's share of my catch. I told him my loyalty belonged to King Frederick, and I would tithe to no other monarch."

"As it should be. How can Father allow such arrogance? I know he mistrusts Norfulk. I cannot believe he ignores such behavior."

"I told you, my lord—your father leaves much to his ministers, of late, and not all of them are as loyal as they should be, I wager. Someone within that council must be in Norfulk's camp. And your cousin is a master of showing a fair face to those he wishes to impress."

"What has this man done to you?" asked Dèodar curiously.

Collyn's hand rose to his lips, as if to stop the words to come. He gave a ragged cough and wiped a line of sweat from his lip before resuming his story.

"One day, with my boat far out to sea, his men torched my cabin. The fire could be seen from the fishing grounds, and I raced for home, but it was too late. My neighbors didn't dare put out the flames." His voice sank to a grating whisper. "Even though the doors and windows were boarded shut before the fire began—with Eliesa inside."

The final words were almost a moan.

Roland's heart contracted in his chest. "How can you possibly go on from day to day with such tragedy in your past?" he whispered, picturing the scene in his mind's eye. "Collyn, I don't know what to say."

"It was a long time ago," mumbled the big man, sinking down on his bunk and staring at his hands. "I picked up where I could and moved on." A wan smile flickered across his face as he told Dèodar, "I wandered your Moonrise Wood once. It was a beautiful place, though silent now beneath those trees. It helped me to heal the wounds on my soul, and taught me a great deal about myself.

"I scaled the mountains surrounding the Lake of Sighs and rafted from the mountains to the sea along the Great River. I tended a tavern in Stormhaven and sailed along the outer coast to Sailor's Wood. But no matter where I traveled, the Black Lion's men ferreted out my steps. He does not take kindly to defiance."

Roland wondered if Collyn's assessment was correct. Did Norfulk really care so much about the comings and goings of a lowly fisherman, or was it something else? Either way, Collyn obviously believed what he was saying. And the portrait he was painting was of darkest black.

Collyn leapt to his feet again, resuming his pacing as if afraid to stay long in one place, even within the shelter of the elven stronghold.

"For a time, I considered myself safe within the anonymity of Overlake, but four moons ago, I saw Norfulk's dogs sniffing about the streets." He slammed the flat of his hand against the rock wall. Roland could see the frustration in every line of the big man's body. "I moved on yet again, cashing in what little I owned, and started over."

Dèodar listened in solemn silence, his expressive features mirroring the trader's pain. His sympathy seemed all the more eloquent for its lack of platitudes.

Collyn murmured, "I found a small farm outside of Crown Keep, but the land had gone fallow and I could not plant this season. The taxes proved more than I anticipated—even being the king's honest portion, which I was more than glad to pay. It drove me into the town itself, looking for work."

"I cannot believe there has been no word of this within the castle. Are all the ministers corrupt?" Roland asked.

"Someone is keeping the king informed of only what the Lion wishes him to hear. I believe to the bottom of my heart His Majesty is a good man, my prince, but I fear for his future. Especially in light of recent events."

Dèodar cocked his head in a strangely familiar gesture.

"Human politics seem much more complicated than our own," he commented.

"The rest you know, my prince. I hired on with Captain Jarome for the season, hoping to raise the tax money before true winter fell. My life has been unremarkable, save for the destruction caused by the Lion." Collyn shrugged. "But can you see why I stand so strongly against Norfulk's rule?"

"How could I not?" Roland answered, deeply disturbed by the trader's story. "And don't worry about the taxes, Collyn," he continued, his voice soft as he rose to lay a tentative hand on the farmer's broad shoulder. "I waive their payment. You have more than earned the exemption."

"When we return home, my prince, I'll remind you of that promise. Where do we go at sunset?"

The trader seemed eager to change the subject, and the prince respected the wish.

"On a quest, my friend!" Roland cried, crossing to

the table to include Dèodar in his sweeping gesture. "To search out an artifact lost near where Father found Stefan as a boy."

Collyn's face grew still as death. "Where was the child found again?"

"On the shores of Desolation Lake..." Dèodar faltered, his youthful face registering the same shock that struck Roland even as Collyn completed the thought.

"The maw of the Black Lion."

"Surely, his influence doesn't range so far!" Roland protested. "Crypticia lies at least two days travel through the mountains from the Lake of Sighs."

"Norfulk's spies roam everywhere, my prince," Collyn warned. "Even at Crown Keep itself."

"I refuse to accept that!" Roland exploded, feeling the hot blood rush to his head. The thought of spies within his very home infuriated him.

"You can't afford to be so naïve, my lord. Why do you think the attack on the raft occurred? Why on *this* trip? Do you seriously think it a coincidence?"

The riverman's implacable logic only angered Roland further, because it made such chilling sense.

"Someone knew you journeyed on the river," Collyn continued, "and good men lost their lives because of it. Do not make the mistake of underestimating your enemy, my lord, as I fear your father has of late. Norfulk Roderickson is the most dangerous man in the kingdom, and he wants you dead. There is no way he believes that attack was successful. Not after our stay in Woodwatch Ferry."

Roland cupped his hands under the rivulet of water

in the corner of the cell. The liquid cooled his flushed face as he bathed his burning cheeks. It tasted faintly of minerals, although not unpleasantly so, when he sipped from his cupped hands to calm his frazzled nerves. Collyn's words had shaken him to the depths of his soul.

"Is Norfulk's influence truly so pervasive?" he said softly. The idea sobered him.

"That is one of the reasons Jarome traveled to Stormhaven—your father's spies are more subtle than some. There were rumors of trouble in the city. Jarome was to investigate while he was there. He was your father's most trusted agent. His loss is doubly great—"

"Jarome was a *spy?*"

Collyn shrugged. "He was the king's man, whatever title you wish to give him."

"Come, my friends," Dèodar murmured, slipping down from the table with the unconscious grace of the elves. "This is fascinating, but we have committed to a journey, and there is much to prepare before sundown."

Roland accepted the distraction gratefully. "Lead on, Sir Elf."

"After you, *inithio ionavo,*" replied Dèodar, with a grand gesture toward the door.

"What did you just say?" asked Roland, instantly suspicious.

The elf's laughter rang against the stone walls of the hallway.

"Do not worry. It was not derogatory. I merely called you 'little prince' in my tongue."

"I see. So, I could greet Stefan in his own language!" exclaimed Roland, delighted by the prospect.

"In his case, the correct form would be *inithi ionavae*," replied his teacher.

"Why the difference?" asked the prince, his curiosity aroused.

"Because he is an elf. And the princess would be *inithia ionavia*, in case you are interested," continued Dèodar with a wicked grin, "because she is an elven female. Although I would not advise the 'little' in her case unless you wish to feel the sharp edge of her tongue." He walked backwards before his companions with an easy confidence Roland envied.

"It is all so confusing," sighed Roland.

"Not really," the elf replied, his tone merry. "Once many of your people spoke with us in our own tongue, but whereas we remembered the language they taught us, the humans forgot what they learned. I will gladly teach you if you care to learn."

Roland thought of the princess and how her lovely eyes would sparkle if he could complement her in her own beautiful language.

"Could you really teach me?"

"Even an addlepate like you should be able to learn something." The warder shrugged.

Roland felt a spark of anger, and then realized the elf merely teased him. He flashed a grin.

"'Tis a good thing I need not be wise to study, with a jester for a tutor."

Dèodar threw back his head and again filled the corridor with laughter.

"Well said, *entheiro*—friend." He clapped Roland on the shoulder as he led his companions through a doorway and into a room filled with the savory smells of roasting meats and drying herbs.

Roland's mouth watered, and, to his chagrin, his stomach grumbled protest over recent neglect. He studied the room with keen interest, comparing its compact proportions to the cavernous kitchens of his own castle. The cooking staff at Crown Keep fed more than two hundred servants and guardsmen daily. The size of the elven chamber underscored yet again their dwindled numbers.

Dèodar winked at them and threaded his way across the kitchen to a tall woman with coal-black hair coiled an elaborate pattern of braids atop her head.

"Sylvania, my sweeting," he wheedled, "have you anything for hungry men who go to seek adventure at sunset?"

Sylvania laughed, a low throaty chuckle, and swatted the hand Dèodar reached toward a platter of cakes.

"Go along with you, Master Warder!" she scolded.

Roland sensed a strong affection between the two, and it sent a deeper thrill of envy through him.

"Don't I have enough to do without your nonsense?" she continued.

"Won't you make us up a pack? It will be a long quest, and hungry work."

Sylvania sighed gustily. "Come back in an hour."

He hugged her from behind, laying his cheek against hers.

"And do you have something that can take away the edge of our guests' hunger while we wait? We can't have such rumbling from so noble a stomach."

She rolled her eyes. "Here, take these meat pies

and get out of my kitchen. And let go of me, you fool!"

Dèodar scooped up a handful of the small pies from the platter she offered and planted a smacking kiss on her cheek. The lady blushed as scarlet as her dress as she clouted him on the head with a spoon, and the warder danced out of range.

Back in the corridor, Collyn commented with a dry drawl, "Have a care, my friend, such a wench may prove more than a match for the likes of you."

Dèodar passed them each a pair of the pies.

"A fine woman, without a doubt," he agreed. "Too fine for the likes of me, indeed." He took a hearty bite of a pie, but Roland thought he detected a note of wistful regret in the denial.

Roland bit into his own pie, and his mouth filled with the flavor of smoked venison and sweet onions. He tasted delicate hints of herbs he didn't recognize, but the resultant combination assuaged his hunger like nothing since he and Stefan began their journey.

"Excellent," he breathed, then applied himself to making his pies disappear with all feasible haste.

Dèodar turned to Collyn, his hands on his hips.

"What sort of guardian are you, Master Silverbrook? You starve your charge, and lead him to consort with elves..."

The unintended meaning in Dèodar's last statement brought another rush of heat to Roland's cheeks as he thought of Mendana. Then the wink he caught passing between Dèodar and Collyn argued perhaps the meaning was not so unintentional after all.

Collyn grinned, and his face lost years of care with the expression.

"Aye. 'Tis a pity I didn't have your sobering guidance to see me through."

Roland felt the tug of a smile at his lips as his companions burst into gales of laughter. Remaining angry at the merry elf was impossible, and it was good to see Collyn's solemnity lighten. He could ask for no better comrades on his journey, and wished only that Stefan could join the fun. If all of the elves were as personable as those he had met so far, the distrust between their peoples could surely be overcome.

Chapter 17

Stefan toyed with the gryphon pendant. He longed for his beloved lute—his music could at least have offered him comfort during this enforced bed rest.

"What troubles you, Steavil?" asked Mendana, rolling a bandage with deft fingers.

"It's just...I just wish I hadn't had to smash my lute. If I must lie caged, at least I could sing." He smiled, a little sheepish to appear so ungrateful in light of all she had done for him.

"Perhaps I can solve that particular problem. I will see what I can find for you."

She turned back to her basket of healing supplies, dropping the neat roll on top. Picking up another length of spider-silk, she began to wind it about her finger, careful not to tear the fragile fabric. Stefan watched her work, curious about the spun silk but still not comfortable enough to bombard her with questions.

After mere hours, his head felt completely healed, and his knee already seemed much better. He would have thought it impossible, but now it felt no different than usual. However, feeling better only made his frustration worse, and he sighed, restless and bored.

"Mendi..."

"Yes, *inithi thiuveae?*"

Little Brother. The endearment lifted his heart.

"Will I walk again?"

His sister bit her lip against a heavy sigh, setting down the filmy bandage and coming to perch on the edge of the bed beside him. She smoothed the coverlet with a thoughtful frown then took his hand in hers.

"I will not lie to you, Stefan. The old damage will never fully heal. Your doctor set the original break badly. The new injury snapped the bone cleanly, but it is in another spot. There still may be some correction of the previous problem, but not as much as if it had broken in the same place."

"Could you not break it again then?" he asked eagerly. "To fix the former damage?"

"That might or might not work, little one. As your healer, I do not think it worth the chance at this time. Perhaps later, if you still wish it, we can discuss that option.

"Yes, I believe you will walk again. But will you run? I don't know. At least you should limp no worse than before. Does that answer your question?" A gentle smile illuminated her face.

"Yes. *Itheamia.*" The elven expression conveyed his gratitude far better than a mere 'thank you' could.

"*Enirmae, inithi thiuveae.*"

Her reply warmed him inside. His memory was beginning to fill in most of the gaps in his past. The language was returning fastest of all.

"Mendana, are you sorry you will no longer become queen?"

"No, foolish one," she laughed, returning to her basket. "If I wished to, I could reclaim my own kingdom tomorrow. I am happy here, and your homecoming but adds to that happiness."

She went back to her task, humming under her breath.

It struck Stefan that the soft music was the only sound he heard. Used to the ceaseless bustle of Crown Keep, he found the silence rather disconcerting. He turned on the couch to face her, his good leg dangling over the side.

"One more question?"

"What is that?"

"How long before I may get out of this bed?"

She shook her head with an indulgent giggle. It made her seem much younger, and more accessible.

"An impatient one, aren't you? I tell you what. I will find you something to occupy your time. If you promise me to lie there and behave for the night, in the morning, we'll see how you fare. By then, the leg may well hold your weight, with care."

"That's impossible. When the dog attacked, I lay abed for months."

"Perhaps because a human doctor treated you as if you were a human patient." Mendana finished packing her basket and turned to him once more. "You are not human, you are an elf. If treated correctly, our healing rate far outstrips that of the humans. A fractured skull such as you suffered would have taken much longer to heal for someone like Prince Roland, for example."

Her cheeks colored prettily, and Stefan noted the fact with interest, although the rapidity with which she regained her composure made him wonder if it had been an illusion of the light.

"That head wound might have taken much longer to mend, even for you, but it received proper treatment before I ever saw it. Who was the doctor?" she asked, her voice tinged with professional curiosity. "If I didn't know better, I would swear he was elven."

"An old man named Ravenwing, they tell me."

"Ravenwing! That explains a great deal."

"Do you know him?"

"We have crossed paths before. He is a rogue and a scoundrel, but he is a good healer when he wishes to be. I must remember to thank him when next we meet. Though, if the Raven's hand works here, there are strange forces afoot, indeed."

A polite cough sounded outside the curtain, and Roland stuck his head into the room.

"May we come in?"

"Of course," Mendana answered, lowering her gaze, and fiddling with the bandages and bottles within her basket. Her fingers plucked a bunch of herbs from the tangle, and just as quickly replaced them.

Stefan was struck again by her manner. Mendana seemed flustered by Roland's presence.

"Excuse me, my lord," she murmured, slipping past the prince with her eyes still downcast. She ran straight into Collyn, and dropped her basket. All three of them bent to retrieve the scattered supplies, and Roland and Mendana reached for the same roll of bandages. Their hands brushed together, and the princess pulled away as if burned, blushing furiously.

"Thank you, my lord," she mumbled, collecting the last of her things.

Stefan caught Dèodar's eye where his cousin lounged against the wall, and both grinned with amusement.

Everiar, he mouthed.

Dèodar nodded in agreement, turning to Collyn to explain in a stage whisper, "Love."

"For both, I'd wager," replied the riverman in the same tone.

Dèodar laughed aloud. Mendana glanced from one kinsman to the other with a sharp glare. Stefan put on his best innocent air while she gathered her skirts to stand.

"I don't know what you two play at," she remarked, her voice haughty, "but I have work to do. I cannot lollygag about here all evening. Remember what I said, Stefan." She stepped to the curtain.

"My lady..." Roland called after her.

"Yes, my lord Roland?"

"I shall bring you back your birthright."

"It would be worth nothing if you died," she replied, her soft voice charged with emotion. "Return safely. That is all I truly require."

He swept her a low bow. "As you command, my lady."

Stefan and Dèodar looked at each other again and caroled in unison, "*Everiar!*"

***

Feeling her face catch fire, Mendana flashed both her kinsmen a killing look, and fled, spurred on by the puzzled expression in Roland's eyes. She cursed under her breath as she stalked away from the chamber.

"Maybe I am *not* so glad to have my little brother home again!" She shook her head. "No, that isn't true... but he *is* irritating."

She wondered if she should tell her father that Ravenwing's hand had dabbled in this business. It had been years since she last saw him, and the circumstances of that parting were less than amicable. Still, they owed him a debt of honor now, it seemed. Better to shield them from each other. If Andundal knew Ravenwing had strayed anywhere near the wood—even if no closer than Woodwatch Ferry— Eostival alone knew what the outcome would be.

The teasing echo of the exchange in Stefan's room reverberated in her head once more. Mendana sighed. It did no good to deny the truth.

She shook herself out of her daydreams and hurried toward the kitchen. At least she could keep her promise to Stefan.

"Sylvania," she called, scanning the room for the cook.

"Here, Lady." Sylvania rose from a crouch beside the hearth and dusted her skirts.

"I need a favor. My brother feels restless but is confined to his bed. I need something to distract him. I wondered..."

"If I might still have some of Raethan's instruments around the nest?" Sylvania's smile was sad. "Aye, I believe I have the very lute he taught the lad to play on. Not a high quality instrument, to be sure, but maybe it will comfort the prince to have something familiar in hand."

Mendana laid a gentle hand on the other's arm. "He told us what happened...on that night. He said Raethan saved his life twice over. You can be proud of him, cousin."

Sylvania swiped her hand across her eyes. "I have always been proud of him. But I would rather have him here to help raise our son than pride and an empty grave."

"May I ask you something?" Mendana said tentatively as Sylvania led the way toward her quarters.

A sad, little smile quirked the other's full lips. "Of course, my lady. Whatever you like."

Mendana acknowledged the hurt in that brittle tone.

"You've suffered so much—do you ever feel it would have been better never to have met him than to lose him so?"

"You're wrong, my lady. I haven't lost him. That is what it is like to love. The days I had with him are a treasure that will never fade—to have never had our time together would have been far bleaker, indeed. Is it safer to keep your heart for your own and never give it away? Aye...but it's too late for you, isn't it, my dear?"

A vision of Roland flashed through Mendana's mind.

"Is it that obvious?"

"I have known you too long, Mendana. Practically raised you since that night. 'Tis doubtful your father will notice." She smiled more brightly.

"May I ask you something else?"

"Of course."

"Is it difficult...being a human here among us?"

"To be honest, I seldom think of it. It has been so long since I came to the wood."

"How did you learn to fit in?"

"Raethan smoothed all rough ways. He was the most wonderful, loving being I ever met."

Sylvania swept the curtain from the doorway of her chamber, gesturing the princess in before her. Mendana glanced around the familiar chamber, seeing details that reminded her of the cousin she barely remembered—a half-carved animal leaping out of the branch that still hid its hindquarters; a stand with a sheaf of music on it; a set of pipes hanging from a peg on the wall.

"Does Leithan play?"

"No. I fear he shares my tin ear, not his father's ability." Sylvania bent down before a curtained cabinet and began to rummage inside.

"Does he...does he know you are not elven?"

Sylvania straightened quickly, spinning to face the princess.

"No!" She drew her breath with a ragged sigh. "Please, do not tell him. Raethan thought it best he never know. The king agreed to keep our secret, and it was so decreed. There has been no cause to divulge the truth." She turned to another chest and fumbled inside it, coming up with a battered lute. "Here you are, my lady."

Mendana accepted the instrument gratefully then stood twisting the neck of it in her hand.

"I've never asked you...how did you come to be among the elves?"

Sylvania moved to a softly cushioned bench and patted the seat beside her

"Sit with me, and I will tell you all you want to know."

Mendana followed the other to the couch and sat beside her. It was easy to see why Leithan did not know his true parentage. Sylvania was taller than Stefan, and her hair was black as Mendana's own. Her eyes were a clear, steady gray—without the green of the Dark Wood elves but close enough to be unremarkable.

Yet as Mendana studied her companion closely, she

noticed subtle differences that had never struck her before—highlights in the cook's hair, a warm blush to her skin, a slight imperfection to her beauty that was the result of time's hand.

"As a girl of nineteen, I was traveling north with my family from Stormhaven to Overlake. One night, there was a great storm. I was frightened by the lightning and thunder—I know it was foolish for a girl of my age, but I have never liked storms. We were camped near the trees, and I ran under them for protection.

"Raethan was on patrol. His orders were to let no human out of the wood should they enter it—and he was a very literal man for an artist." She smiled in fond remembrance. "He clapped a hand over my mouth as my family called for me. I almost bit down on it so I could escape...and then I looked up at him.

"He was the most beautiful creature I had ever seen. I decided then and there I never wanted to leave his side again. A year later, Leithan was born.

"When Andundal chose Raethan to ride with Deveiria's honor guard, it was the proudest moment of his life. He promised to come back to me—it was the only promise he ever broke."

"Will Leithan not learn the truth...in time?" Mendana asked gently.

Sylvania nodded, her face grave but resigned.

"It is inevitable, especially now he has seen the humans. I am already beginning to feel old among your ageless people. Oh, I know that you do age—none of us are truly immortal—but I was no more than nineteen when Raethan found me. You were already nine. Look at the two of us. I look every one of my years, if not more, and you look not yet twenty." She shook her dark head with a rueful smile. "I doubt I can keep it from him much longer."

"The world is changing for us all, Sylvania. It is time he knew the truth—and faced the future."

"What has turned your thoughts to this path, my dear? You've never seem interested in such things before."

Mendana felt her cheeks grow hot. "Just something my brother said."

"Has he been teasing you?"

She plucked idly at the strings of the lute.

"I just wish he were not so perceptive. *Dèodar*, however, I could cheerfully strangle."

"And what has that scamp done now?" asked Sylvania in mock severity. "Sometimes he makes me want to take him over my knee!"

Mendana giggled at the image. Sylvania sighed and leaned forward confidingly, one hand on the princess's knee.

"And other times, I feel that perhaps I, too, could love again," she whispered. "Now, what is troubling your heart?"

Idly plucked a lutestring, Mendana mumbled, "It's just...it's just that life has suddenly become so complicated, all at the sight of Prince Roland's russet hair and emerald eyes. I am too old to fall in love at first sight. That is a game for children. But neither can I lie to myself. He has stolen my heart."

Sylvania patted her knee. "My child, in this world there are far stranger things. I fell in love with your cousin the instant I saw him. Perhaps it is the magic of the wood." She smiled.

Mendana returned the smile, albeit a bit crookedly. "Perhaps you are right, cousin, for I am definitely falling in love."

***

Stefan and Dèodar finally managed to control their laughter. The elven prince shook his head.

"I wish I could go with you," he murmured with a wistful sigh.

Collyn came to Stefan's side.

"How are your injuries, my lord?"

"Please, Collyn," Stefan reached out to touch his hand. "To my friends, I am still Stefan. There shouldn't be any titles between us."

"As you wish, Stefan. And the answer to my question?"

"Mendana says I may try to stand tomorrow."

"On a broken leg?" asked Roland in astonishment.

"I told you, she works miracles," Dèodar said with a grin and a casual shrug.

"But you are leaving tonight, and I cannot go with you..." Stefan's voice trailed into silence.

"I'm sorry, Stefan, but we must take advantage of the darkness," Roland explained, coming to sit on the edge of the mattress. "Since your father promised to send his messenger to Crown Keep at first light, we decided to start under the cover of night, when we are less likely to be observed."

"You will need this." Stefan slipped the gryphon pendant from around his neck and handed it to Roland. "If the stories are true, it may help you on your quest and bring you back more swiftly."

"I will return it to you soon," Roland promised, slipping the chain over his head, and once more settling the amulet inside his jerkin. "Here—in exchange, you shall keep this in trust for me." He pulled the heavy signet ring from his finger, handing it to Stefan. "Wear my grandfather's ring for me. There is a legend connected with this stone as well. They call the jewel the Blood Stone."

Stefan felt a shiver run through him. The ballad he'd read in Roland's book told of the Blood stone as well as the Sun and Moon stones. All the legends were converging in one intricate knot, and he hoped he could unravel it if—or when—need arose.

Roland continued his explanation, clearly unaware of the effect it was having.

"They say the stone clears like a diamond if its owner dies—as if the blood has run out of it." His quick grin flashed. "I expect it back as dark a crimson as it is now."

Stefan took the ring with great reluctance and placed it on his finger. A disquieting flash of premonition gripped him as the color seemed to drain from the polished stone, leaving only a tinge of pink deep in its heart.

His mind reeled, and he fought to hide it.

"'Tis beautiful, Roland. I...I did not know the legend."

"What's wrong, Stefan?" asked Collyn, the perceptive edge to his voice warning not all Stefan's visitors were as preoccupied as Roland.

"I am just a little tired," he lied.

"Of course," replied Roland. "And we must go. Be well, Stefan. We shall return before you know it." He gripped the hand wearing the ring in farewell, and Stefan felt an echo of his vision.

"Take care, Roland," he pleaded, clutching the prince's sleeve.

"I will, my friend." Roland moved aside to allow the others their goodbyes.

"I'll take care of him, little one," Collyn murmured, too softly for Roland to hear. "I swear it on my life."

"I pray it will not come to that," Stefan answered with equal softness, his heart troubled.

Collyn nodded, moving back to flank Roland.

"If I could speak to Dèodar alone, please?"

Ducking his head in acknowledgement, Roland led Collyn from the room.

"You had a vision, didn't you?" asked his cousin, his mobile features grave as he perched on the edge of the couch. "Your mother had the Sight, as did my father. I know that burden weighs heavily—will you share it with me? Please, tell me what you saw. Perhaps I can help."

Stefan stared down at the ring on his hand.

"If Roland's legend is true, he goes to great danger. Collyn alone may not be able to protect him. After all, he is only human." Stefan's mouth twisted at the irony of his words. Yesterday, he had thought himself the same. "You must watch them both, my kinsman," he charged Dèodar. "The prince cannot die. It is for my honor, and for the sake of Mendana's heart."

"Aye," Dèodar replied. "She never found true love before, though long ago I hoped to one day win her hand."

"I am sorry for that pain, but think what could come of this."

"We could be standing on the brink of a new time," Dèodar agreed.

"But only if he survives," Stefan reminded his cousin. "Only if he survives."

"Then I better get him back his sword," remarked the warder with a grin. He gripped Stefan's shoulder in farewell. "I will keep him safe, cousin. Rest now. The king needs you."

Chapter 18

Norfulk Roderickson pored over a large map of Irthlan. It was a twin to the parchment Roland had studied in his lessons, but there were subtle differences. Woodlands merely outlined on the official map were meticulously detailed on Norfulk's, and the elven names were written under the human designations. He thoughtfully traced the outlines of Moonrise Wood with his finger. Moonrise—Mendana's kingdom.

He had seen the elven princess from afar, and observed her in his crystal. It didn't matter that they had never actually met—she was the key to his plans.

Mendana was officially a queen already, although the kingdom of Moonrise was no longer of any real importance. It was a tiny crescent of diseased land, disintegrating daily into waste as his magic exacted its toll. But if he were to wed the wench, he would legitimately be her consort, and when she succeeded her father, he would have all the elven lands in his full control. Of course, for her to do so, the throne must be vacant—but that was a trifling detail.

It didn't hurt that she was a comely lass. He would take pleasure from their union.

His smile was that of a complacent cat with a bird in its claws.

***

Stefan tried to rest, but every time he closed his eyes, he would see the color leaching from Roland's ring.

His visions never proved false.

As a boy, he had feared there was something odd about him, and he kept his premonitions to himself far more often than not, acting upon them in private. However, sometimes he would slip, so Roland and the king had come to know about them.

Now that he remembered his true heritage, he no longer considered the visions strange—he had heard whispers about elven mystics all his life. Something in their nature made the race sensitive to currents humans could not feel. Now, those currents swirled around him, and they would not let him rest.

With a heartfelt sigh, he lay back on the bed, arms folded behind his head, and stared at the rough ceiling. He hated this enforced inactivity.

Finally, unable to stand it any longer, he sat up and took a deep breath. Swinging his good leg to the floor, he placed a hand on either side of his injured knee and lifted gently.

Before he could continue, a sharp voice called out from the doorway, "Hold it right there, *inithi iothinae!* Do you want to be bedridden for life, you little fool?"

Stefan dropped his hands. "Why does everyone insist on calling me that?" he sighed. "Now I can be called 'fool' in *two* languages."

"Perhaps if you stopped acting like one!" She visibly harnessed her temper. "You made me a promise."

"I'm sorry, Mendi. I just can't take this any longer. I am going mad lying here while the others..." He trailed off, not wanting to worry her.

She bustled to his side, settling him back against the pillows. "While the others what?"

"Go on without me," he mumbled, face hot at the lameness of his excuse.

"You must to get used to it," she reminded him, her voice gentle. "When he returns, Roland will go home to Crown Keep..." Her voice died off in turn, but she pulled herself together. "And you will stay here. That is the way it must be."

He could hear how hard she was trying to convince them both as she continued, her tone brisk.

"The two of you will both be kings, and a king must rule his kingdom." She busied herself examining his knee.

"Then why aren't you ruling *your* kingdom? Is not a queen governed by the same edicts?"

"I've told you, *inithi thiuveae*. There's no one in my kingdom to rule. Myself, Dèodar, a scattered handful of others—these are all the Dark elves left." She finished her examination with a trace of a frown.

"Please, tell me you're not going to keep me chained to this bed any longer," he pleaded.

"Until morning, young man! I told you that is the minimum time I must enforce. However, I brought you something that may ease the wait a bit."

She stepped to the doorway, and returned with a battered lute. Despite the instrument's worn appearance, she held it as if it were sheathed in gold.

Stefan sat up straighter, holding out his hands eagerly. Mendana placed the lute in his lap.

"Do you recognize it?" she asked, sitting beside him.

His fingers automatically searching for the proper chords, Stefan felt a teasing brush of memory.

"I..." *A flash of a dark head bent over his own, adjusting his fingers on the frets. A gentle voice telling him the names of the strings, how to hold his hand just so...* "Yes," he breathed. "I do. Raethan taught me to play on this lute. He promised me it would be mine when I was old enough..."

"Now you are old enough. Keep it safe in his memory."

Stefan tried to hand it back. "I can't keep this."

"Sylvania wishes for you to have it. Her son has no desire to play, and there is no one else. Make Raethan proud once more."

He swallowed hard.

"Now," Mendana said firmly, rising to her feet, "you stay in that bed for the rest of the evening. I will return in the morning, and we will see what we will see."

"Yes, *riuveia.*"

"That's a good boy."

Stefan made a face at her.

Mendana laughed. "I will return at first light. I know you grow impatient to be up and about, but you really must stay in bed until I come."

He nodded absently, absorbed in the music he coaxed from the battered instrument.

Mendana laid the book of ballads on the bed beside him and ruffled his dark hair. He jerked his head away in annoyance, and her laugh rang out.

"Sleep well, *inithi thiuveae.*"

"Yes, Mendi. And...thank you."

She flashed him a bright smile and was gone.

***

Roland and his companions walked through the night, staying under the fringes of Starlit Wood for as long as possible. The air carried a hint of coming frost; winter was nearly upon them, and Roland could smell decay as the forest shed its leaves to blanket the feet of the trees. The prince was grateful the keen-eyed elf journeyed with them, for Dèodar eased their way countless times.

Little light leaked through the canopy of tightly interwoven branches, despite the fact the moon had waned only a day or two since the night the raiders attacked the raft. Roland stumbled over upthrust roots and snare-like vines at first, but soon he heard Dèodar singing under his breath—and the undergrowth seemed to melt away from the path. He clapped the elf on the back to show his gratitude, and Dèodar grinned.

They stole like shadows past the outskirts of Woodwatch Ferry, coming to the Great River in the gray of false dawn.

"I advise you to remove your clothing," Collyn whispered, proceeding to strip. "You'll thank me on the other side."

"Are you mad?" blustered the prince.

Dèodar skinned out of his own clothing and bundled it in his cloak.

"Think about it, *entheiro*. Would you rather risk your dignity for a few minutes, or freeze in wet clothes?"

"When you put it that way..." Roland replied, with a heavy sigh. He sat down to pull his boots off. "I wish Stefan were here."

"So he could help you dress?" Dèodar teased.

Roland scowled up at the elf.

"No. So he could enjoy the adventure with us." He pulled his tunic over his head, bundling his clothes together in imitation of the others.

Stepping into the water felt like wading into a snowbank, and Roland shivered as they hurried across. They used their cloaks to dry themselves as best they could on the far bank, and the prince was grateful for Collyn's foresight as he pulled on his dry breeches and boots.

As they pushed on into the growing dawn, Collyn commented, "We should look for a place to wait out the sun. It'll be full day soon, and we'll be vulnerable on this open plain."

"But we're nowhere near the lake."

"And we wouldn't be if we walked all day and through the next night."

"We have to move faster!"

"Perhaps we can grow wings," Dèodar scoffed, pointing at a wheeling bird. "That's the only way to travel to Desolation Lake in less than two days."

"I may have an idea," Collyn murmured. "Wait here." The big man faded into the semidarkness.

Roland shivered, rubbing his arms for warmth.

"Winter is truly on the wind."

"Aye. I hope we have enough stores for the season. The hunting has been poor this year, and we have no space for crops beneath the Forest's canopy."

"How have the elves survived?"

"Wits and woodcraft."

Before Roland could pursue the matter, there was a rumble of wheels and the soft whicker of a horse. Collyn appeared, perched on the seat of a hay wagon piled high with harvest.

"You owe a debt to yet another local farmer, my

lord. I 'borrowed' this cart with only that raider's sword for collateral. At least we can travel more quickly this way. If we take turns on the reins, we may reach the mountains by mid-morning. I'll take first shift. You two climb up into the hay and get warm. Sleep if you can."

Roland nodded, scrambling into the sweet-smelling hay, and burrowing into its relative warmth. Soon after Collyn had clucked the horses into motion, the prince was fast asleep, lulled by the rocking of the cart and the rhythmic clopping of hooves.

Chapter 19

Stefan woke with an uncomfortable heaviness in his bladder. He felt sure he could make it to the privy facilities at the rear of the room, and started to stand. Mendana strode across the room to intercept him, her eyes flashing with fury.

"You really do want to be bedridden for life, don't you? You think it will be a colossal joke for me to wait on you hand and foot. What, as recompense for not being with you at the lake?"

Her vehemence took Stefan aback.

"You said I might get up this morning. I needed to... to..." He gestured helplessly toward the privy.

Her gaze followed his, and the anger evaporated as she hid a smile behind her hand.

"Oh. I see. Well, I can hardly fault you for that."

"I really must..."

"I probably should bring you a chamber pot instead!" she scolded, but her face softened. "However, I did promise we'd try to get you up this morning, but you must again promise me something in return." Her expression turned solemn. "Your knee is not completely healed, Steavil. You mustn't overextend. If I say rest, you must do as I say, when I say. Otherwise, you may permanently destroy it."

He nodded. For her to use his elven name, he knew she must be serious.

"I promise, *evleeia*. I will do as you say, beloved."

"Good. First, swing your leg around. Now, put

your left arm over my shoulder." She leaned over him. "Stand up with all your weight on the right leg. Put a little weight on your left foot, and gradually increase it. Stop the instant you feel pain. Do you understand me?"

The pressure in his bladder was momentarily forgotten. A flutter of excitement built inside him.

"I understand."

He swung his bad leg off the couch, and she slipped a supporting arm around his waist. Taking a deep breath, he put all his weight on his right leg and slowly rose to his feet. Carefully, he shifted his center of balance until he felt a twinge of pain.

"Let's take care of your little problem first." She helped him to the privy and stepped away while he relieved himself. "Now, shall we show Father your progress?" She offered him her shoulder once more.

"Yes, please," he murmured, feeling as if he could float to the throne room.

Leaning heavily against his sister, Stefan hobbled the short distance to the great hall. Outside it, he stopped.

"From here, I must walk alone, *ethiae riuveia*," he whispered.

"I don't think that is a good idea."

"*Deastia*, Mendana...please!"

With a heavy sigh, she helped him get his balance then stepped away.

"*Opieviami*," he called out, and the door slid open. Taking a deep breath, he limped forward.

Andundal glanced up from the scroll he was reading, and the parchment slipped from his fingers unheeded. Stefan bit his lip to counteract the white-hot needles pricking the nerves in his left leg.

"It is no worse than before," he lied to himself in a whisper. "You have withstood greater. Don't be such a baby. You can do this. You must."

Wiping a bead of sweat from his upper lip, he found traces of blood and realized he had bitten through his lower lip.

"My son." The king rose to his feet and descended the dais steps. Stefan felt grateful when Andundal came no closer. It was important for him to do this alone. It meant all the difference between regaining his freedom and being a slave to his infirmity.

The strain on the knee began to tell on him, and he paused to gather his concentration. *Just a few feet farther.*

Out of the corner of his eye, he glimpsed Mendana hovering in disapproval, ready to jump to his aid if necessary. He shook his head, waving her away with an impatient gesture, and limped on, practically falling into his father's arms.

The silk brocade of Andundal's robe felt rough under his cheek, and he smelled a comforting blend of pipe-smoke and soap.

"Oh, my son."

Stefan's arms tightened around his father's waist.

"You've had your way," Mendana ordered impatiently. "Now get the weight off that knee before I tie you to your couch for the rest of your life!"

"Come and sit," the king urged. His hand trembled as he brushed the sweat-dampened hair out of Stefan's face with a loving caress, laughing with delight. "Oh, my precious *thuathae*, my dearest son. I thought I would never see you again." He helped Stefan up the steps towards the thrones, careful not to let it show how much support he gave.

Stefan noticed, though, and smiled up at his father. Then a thought struck him.

"Mendana…" He gestured toward his sister.

She laughed. "I do not mind relinquishing my seat for you, little brother. Now, sit, before I *make* you do so."

He fell onto the soft-padded throne, running a wondering finger along the intricately carved arm of the chair. The velvet cushions cradled him in a luxurious embrace, and he sighed. They were like billowing clouds beneath his strained muscles.

"Here, put your foot up on this," ordered Mendana, placing a thickly cushioned stool before him.

For once, he obeyed without a murmur, his knee throbbing with more than usual violence. Mendana's warning of more permanent damage echoed in the back of his mind. He had pushed the leg almost beyond the limit. The pain was much worse than usual, and he could see the muscles trembling, even though the leg no longer bore weight.

His sister sank with lissome grace onto a cushion between the thrones then curled her arms around the armrest of his chair and rested her head against it. He reached down, laying a hand on her shoulder.

Andundal resumed his own seat. "I was just about to send the promised dispatch to King Frederick. Have you anything of your own to add to Prince Roland's message?" he asked Stefan.

"Only that the prince fares well, Father, and the king must take care."

Andundal nodded.

Leithan entered the chamber, dressed in solid brown jerkin and leggings, a dark-green cloak fastened over one shoulder. Soft leather boots came up to his knees.

Mendana's face brightened with a delighted smile. "I suppose I'll have to go and collect those herbs myself, won't I, Leithan?" she teased.

"I left them in the cabinet, my queen," he answered with a bow and grin of his own. "I gathered them this morning."

She clapped her hands.

"Thank you! You are a treasure. I will be sure and tell your mother how helpful you have been." She winked, and the messenger blushed scarlet, ducking his head.

"Leithan," Andundal said, "it falls to you to take this news to King Frederick's court. I know you have been training to pass among the humans. Do you feel ready for this mission? You are still a child—"

"I'm nearly sixteen!" protested Leithan, and Stefan felt hard-pressed not to laugh. He knew that frustration well.

"Not *too* young, I see," Andundal continued in wry amusement. "Speak directly to King Frederick. You're to give him the message his son is alive and well." He held out a rolled parchment. "Give this note from Roland to his father. Trust your message to none save the king."

The youth nodded, stepping forward to take it.

"The warders will provide you with a horse when you reach the edge of the forest. It will take you several hours to get that far, so I advise you to leave at once."

Leithan bowed again, and strode from the throne room.

Stefan noted Mendana's fond smile as she watched him go, and the way the smile wavered into a frown as the door closed behind him.

"He's the youngest of our subjects, Father. I hope the decision to send him proves wise." She sighed then smoothed the soft green wool of her dress with a visible effort to compose herself and changed the subject. "What were you reading when we came in, Father?"

Andundal bent to retrieve the scroll he had dropped. His long fingers spread out the parchment as a thoughtful frown creased his brow.

"The news is not good, *ruathia*. 'Tis a report from the scouts in Moonrise Wood. You know we watch your borders closely, in case one day you wish to return, Mendana. The report says there is a great deal of movement underway in the region. Parties of cutthroats and brigands roam the plain. Strange ships anchor in Perilous Harbor. The assessment is that Crypticia Keep masses for war. I included a note of my own with Roland's, warning the king of this danger. We may find ourselves allied with the humans whether we wish to be or not. Though I do not know if he will trust a message from a stranger when his own council sees no threat."

Stefan felt Mendana stiffen beneath his hand as he tightened his grip on her shoulder.

"Roland has gone into the middle of that danger," he whispered.

"Yes," the king agreed with a grave nod.

"We must warn them!" Mendana cried

Stefan could feel her trembling. For the first time, it was clear how much Roland had come to mean to his sister, and he regretted the teasing of the day before.

He stifled a sigh as Andundal continued, "How do you propose to do so, my daughter? We just sent our best messenger to the human court, and we don't even know for certain where they are going."

"Ravenwing will know," she murmured.

The king's eyes grew cold, and his frown deepened. "He is forbidden here."

"Then I shall go to Moonrise and find him. He is my subject, Father. I'll speak to him if I choose."

"Enough, Mendana," Andundal commanded. "He causes nothing but trouble—"

"Apparently he saved my life, Noile, if it is the same Ravenwing. Mendana says his skill as a doctor is why my skull has healed so quickly."

"Shouldn't you rest, Steavil?" Andundal said brusquely. "I must send an answer to this report."

The clipped dismissal confused Stefan. The rejection stung. Mendana stood, and he could feel tension radiating from her. The smooth column of her throat rippled as she gulped back whatever response had leapt to her mind.

She slipped an arm beneath his and helped him to stand. He felt the tremors continue to shake her slim frame, but her voice was cool.

"Come, my brother."

Again, Stefan sensed currents swirling in the room he couldn't interpret, and he was grateful to leave before he drowned in them.

***

Mendana's thoughts raced.

"Why is Father so angry, Mendana?" asked Stefan.

"It is because of something that happened long ago."

"Forbidding a healer of Ravenwing's skill from being a part of the community seems rather...foolish... to me, with so few elves left."

"He has his reasons."

"What happened?"

She shrugged. "It was my fault. When I was younger, I thought I was in love with Ravenwing—he was so handsome and charming..."

"Where was I?" His face creased with a frown. "His name means nothing to me."

"Do you remember hearing of Eeonathor?"

"That sounds vaguely familiar. Wasn't he Dèodar's brother?"

"Yes. That is Ravenwing's true name. He did not visit here often. His home was in Dark Wood at Grandfather's court."

"So, he is also a cousin?"

She nodded. "Anyway, one day when the brothers were visiting, Ravenwing...kissed me. It wasn't supposed to happen—I certainly hadn't planned for it to happen—but it did, and I was...I enjoyed it. But I..." She threw her hands up in exasperation. "I realized it was improper. I was confused. I was upset...but I wasn't. I protested, as any refined young lady should do. I pushed him from me, and then..."

"Father?" Stefan guessed.

She nodded, remembered misery bringing a blush to her complexion.

"Father was livid," she whispered. "And Dèodar stood behind him with his bow drawn—he looked ready to kill Eeonathor. Dèodar fancied he was in love with me himself. I never meant to hurt him—to hurt either of them."

"Dèodar told me as much," Stefan said, tactfully concentrating on placing his feet. "But if I read him correctly, his love has matured to that of a brother for a sister."

She was glad he kept his eyes on the floor. Her face felt like it was on fire—she was surprised the walls did not glow a reflected crimson.

"I think you are right, and I am glad of it. In many ways, he has filled that hole your loss left in my life."

"Am I so easily replaced?" Stefan asked in mock protest, but the smile on his face was mirrored in his voice.

She stopped, staring down at her little brother.

"Some things about you will never change, Steavil," she said with a laugh. "You teased me as a child as well!"

He squeezed her shoulder. "I am happy to hear you laugh, Mendi. It was a sound I did not know my heart missed until I heard it again." He looked away, hiding shy embarrassment by focusing on the floor again as he hobbled forward once more. "So that was why Father sent him away?"

"Yes."

"Is Father always so...?" He hesitated.

"Harsh?" she finished for him. She shook her head. "He wasn't like this while Mother lived. Her death changed him. He has become so...inflexible. It is as if he fears any attempt to bend will break him instead. In truth, I think he fears that...brittleness...far more than he worries about appearing weak to the rest of us if he changes his mind.

"That fear colored his reaction to your friend Master Silverbrook as well. Once, no law or judgment—either his or any other's—would have stopped him from welcoming your rescuer as the hero he is."

"Do you think he will allow Collyn to live when they return?"

"I hope so. He is not a monster, Stefan. You are home again, safe with us. I do not believe Father could bring himself to execute the man who brought you back to us, no matter the past circumstances."

They walked in silence for a while, and then Stefan cleared his throat.

"Mendi, may I ask you one more question?"

"Of course."

"Was that kiss really such a surprise? Was it truly unwelcome...in any way?"

She sighed heavily. "No...and yes...but no. I really did think I was in love with him. I half-hoped he would make such a move—I knew I certainly couldn't be the one to kiss *him*! But, Andailia's Mercy, Steavil, it was—it is—all so complicated. I thought I would never...that one stolen kiss would be all the romance I would have to cherish till the end of my days. I never dreamed I might..."

This time he completed her sentence. "Find love from such an unexpected source?" he asked softly, face wreathed in a smile.

She nodded. "But now Roland has gone into who knows what danger? Will I lose him, too?"

Chapter 20

As the first rosy tint of sunrise lit the sky the morning of the second day, the prince led his party into the foothills of the Ring of Tears, the unbroken mountains circling the shores of the Lake of Sighs. They had left the cart and horse in a deserted barn a short distance away, planning to retrieve it on their way back.

A light wind soughed through the towering rocks like a mournful spirit, bringing with it the stench of dead fish. Roland wrinkled his nose at the unpleasant taint.

He glanced at his companions. Dèodar appeared tireless, but Roland could see fatigue shadowing Collyn's eyes, and he had to admit he felt a bit done in himself despite the wagon ride.

"Let's find somewhere to rest a bit before we start our search," he suggested. "Somewhere out of sight. I feel odd here in the open."

"I agree with you," murmured Collyn. "We're too close to the Lion's den for my comfort."

"Here's a cleft in the rocks," called Dèodar from the other side of the formation Roland leaned against. "There's a space at the end of the split large enough for a day's shelter, and it has a natural chimney if you want a fire."

"Right now, I'll settle for a place to throw myself down and sleep for a few hours." Collyn yawned.

"After you." The prince grinned, clapping the riverman on the shoulder as they joined Dèodar. Collyn lay down in the rear of the shelter. Within seconds, he was asleep.

"I wish I could fall asleep as easily," Roland whispered with a shake of his head. He stifled a yawn of his own.

"Go ahead and rest—I'll stand guard."

Roland sank down on the rocks just outside the entrance of the cleft.

"I'm too keyed up to sleep yet." He leaned his head back against the stone. "How do you do it, Dèodar?" he asked, curious to know more about this newfound ally.

"What, my lord?" The elf lounged against the cliff face, one foot propped behind him.

"You act as if you could go on forever."

"We don't tire as quickly as humans, my friend, just as we do not physically age at the same rate. Many differences exist between our peoples, but I believe you will find there are many similarities as well."

"Tell me." Roland smiled up at the tall elf.

"I'm sure you've run across several of the differences, even if you didn't realize it. My cousin has been beside you for many years now. What struck you as odd about him?"

"Well, he has the most beautiful voice in the kingdom. Any instrument he touches, he can play. I suppose those things aren't terribly exceptional, but they've always struck us as a little unusual, since he's had no formal training."

"Well, now you know that he did have a teacher— and Raethan was a very gifted musician. Still, since he didn't remember any of those lessons consciously, I suppose that counts." Dèodar grinned.

"And he sometimes sees things before they happen. It's always been a trifle upsetting," Roland admitted with a rueful chuckle.

The elf laughed. "It's also upsetting to those who bear the gift. Not all of us do, thank the gods, though it runs strong in our House. Anything else?"

"He speaks to the animals, and they seem to listen to him, especially his little mare, Astreal."

"He named her 'Star,'" Dèodar commented, with a fond smile. "Even when he couldn't remember his own name, he used the elven word for *star.*"

"And there's Mendana's healing. I've never seen anything like what she did for Stefan."

"It runs in her mother's family. *My* family, I suppose I should say. Strongest in the women. It makes them particularly good queens. But it is not exclusively a female trait—my brother is a decent healer."

"You have a brother?"

"Yes. His name is Eeonathor. He is several years older than I."

"Is he at court?"

The elf hesitated. "No. He and Andundal do not see eye to eye."

Roland sensed some evasion in the answer, but let it go. He had no right—or reason—to pry further.

"Now, what else?" mused Dèodar, sinking to the ground beside the prince. "Our senses are sharper than those of humans. We tire less easily—as I said earlier. I've been told we withstand pain to an exceptional level, a claim that I, by the grace of Eostivil, have had no reason to gainsay."

"I've seen Stefan almost paralyzed by pain."

"Then think how much worse the pain would have been for you to bear," Dèodar replied, his tone full of sober pride. "Our prince is strong, and very brave. He'll prove a mighty king."

"I don't doubt you there, my friend." Roland yawned again.

"Get some sleep. I'll wake you at midday."

"All right. It'll be a long day."

"Rest easy, my friend. In my tongue, *ithneimi endio, ethiae entheiro*."

"Thank you. *Itheamia, ethiae entheirae*," replied Roland, his tongue tripping over the lilting words. "Correct?"

A broad grin split Dèodar's handsome face.

"Very good, my friend! I knew you could do it if you tried. You have a fine ear for the language. More lessons later. When you are awake. Right now, your brain is asleep."

Roland nodded, sheepishly admitting the truth of the observation. He stretched out beside Collyn. As he started to turn over, he noticed Dèodar staring up into the hazy morning sky, and followed the elf's line of sight. Just within the limits of his vision, a lone bird circled, dipping, and soaring.

The archer took an arrow from his quiver and stood fingering his bow with a frown. Roland started to call out, but his eyes drifted shut before he could open his mouth. He tried to force them open again, but they refused to obey.

Despite his fatigue, however, thoughts buzzed like angry bees within his brain, and he tossed and turned, trying to find a comfortable position. It was many long minutes before worry unwound enough to let his body find peace and slide into the depths of slumber.

***

Ravenwing soared above the Ring of Tears, circling the makeshift campsite. His sharp eyes saw Dèodar fingering his arrow, and he decided a retreat might be the wisest course. Being skewered by his own brother would hardly move events in the right direction.

He banked to his left and flew back to the abandoned farm where he had left his companion. He cawed sharply as he descended into the yard. The little cutpurse stepped out of the barn, yawning in the early morning light to hold up one arm like a falconer. Ravenwing landed on the outstretched wrist.

Cocking his head to one side, he croaked, "Did they see you when they left the cart? Is the horse cared for?"

"Aye, Master," Daerci answered. "Do ye want me to take it back to that other farm?"

The raven hopped to the ground, transforming as he did so. He shook back his cloak and smoothed his hair.

"Not necessary. I will need you here before you could go and return. Do you remember what I told you?"

"Aye," the urchin replied, grinning broadly. "I been collecting rocks for the last hour. Me pouch is full, and I found some sacking and made another. I'll be ready."

"Excellent." Ravenwing threw an arm around his companion's slim shoulders. "Let's go see if we can find something to eat around here. I'm starving. We can waste one or two of your rocks on a leaper."

A well-worn sling materialized in Daerci's hand as if by magic.

"Just show me where to hunt."

***

"Roland, 'tis noon. Wake up." He felt a light hand on his shoulder, shaking him to consciousness. With a reluctant groan, he left dreams of sea-green eyes and long black braids to find Dèodar grinning down at him. The elf's earlier concern seemed to have been set aside.

"Wake up, sleepyhead. Here, inside the Ring, we should be safe, unless we have already been spotted, and if that is the case..." Dèodar shrugged with wordless eloquence before rising to his feet.

Roland had already noted the mercurial nature of the warder's temperament. One moment he was utterly serious and the next jesting at every turn. But the prince had also seen that the elf's moments of gravity were worthy of attention. If Dèodar was unconcerned with their current safety, they were out of harm's way— at least for the moment.

He got up and moving much more slowly, and noticed Collyn was already out and about. The sun shone hot on the barren rocks, reflecting in blinding flashes from the crystals embedded in the towering formations. Roland squinted against the glare, shading his eyes with his hand.

However, where sunbeams should have danced on the waters of a great lake, there was nothing but a dark, sullen-looking liquid hole. No greenery grew on the margins of that inky pool. Roland shuddered.

"Where should we start to look, *entheiro*?" asked Dèodar. "This was your idea."

Roland's head felt fuzzy, and he shook it to clear his thoughts.

"Perhaps we should begin with the site where the bodies were found..." He trailed off at the pain shadowing Dèodar's eyes. "I'm sorry. I wasn't thinking."

"No," replied the elf, his voice soft, "you're right. It is the logical place to start. Perhaps, even after all this time, there may still be a clue. We've no other starting place. Come, it was near here that my father discovered the bodies."

"Your father?"

"He was Chief Warder of Moonrise Wood, remember. Our stronghold lay closer than Andundal's, and the queen was his sister. Besides, he shared Steavil's gift of visions. He had a dream that something was amiss and rode in hopes of saving her, but we arrived too late. A smoking campfire and a slaughter were all we found. The bodies were so hideously mangled it was hard to recognize even the queen. I always secretly hoped Steavil had survived somehow. I searched everywhere but could find no trace of him."

"*You* searched?"

Dèodar smiled faintly. "My first ride with the warders. I was still not an official guard, but I begged my father to let me come. When I saw the carnage, I cried. I was barely seventeen." He shrugged. "They lay here." He pointed to the faint soot traces of a large bonfire partially sheltered by an overhanging formation. A tall stone cairn rose nearby. "We raised a mound for our dead. The raiders, we burned." His handsome features grew hard and cold. "I would have left them to rot, but I was outvoted."

Not knowing what to say, Roland pulled the gryphon pendant from inside his jerkin. He squinted idly through the stone at the sun—and gasped with amazement. A series of light scratches marred the rear of the gem. As he turned the stone slightly, the lines became razor-sharp.

"Dèodar, look at this." He passed the amulet to the elf. "What do you see?"

"Well, I see several marks etched into the gem." The warder frowned, studying the configuration of the lines. "It looks like one of the mountains." He turned in a slow circle, the pendant to his eye. Several times, he adjusted position, finally halting to point across the broad lake to a distant peak. "They match up exactly with the contours of that far mountain. Someone went to a deal of trouble to etch a map on the stone..." He turned the pendant over in his hand. "I wonder who did so, and when?"

Collyn joined them, tossing an oily black creature at their feet. It was covered with thick viscous slime.

"So much for fishing," he commented. "The lake is dead. Some inhabitants still swim its waters, but only those that don't know they should be dead." He shook his head, his face sad as he stared at something only he could see. "Once this lake sparkled like a jewel. In those days, the 'sighs' were those of beauty and awe. Now they are of outrage and despair."

"We may have found the place to begin our search," Roland told Collyn. "Shall we go exploring?"

The trader dusted his hands and squinted across the lake.

"Might as well. We don't want to be caught out in the open after dark."

"There must be a cavern somewhere in that peak," Dèodar observed, bending to collect his pack. "I doubt we'll find the Moonstone dangling from a rock. If its hiding place is indeed what these marks are meant to convey."

"Well said. Collyn, can we eat that thing?" The prince pointed at the misshapen fish.

"You might, but I wouldn't care to join you."

"Then I suppose I'll leave it be as well, and tighten my belt. Pity...I'm starving."

"This should help," called Dèodar, tossing him a hide flask. He seemed to have recovered his spirits, letting the memories wash away from him with characteristic speed. "Sylvania packed enough of this for us to get by for a few days at least."

"What is it?" asked Roland doubtfully, eyeing the flask.

"Her secret recipe. She's been perfecting it for decades. Try some—it will assuage hunger better than any food I know."

Roland uncorked the flask and took a tentative sip. Its flavor was more delicate than the wines he was used to—slightly spicy, with a hint of honey beneath a mix of fruits. His hunger melted away.

"You're right. This is exceptional. What do you call it?"

"She calls it *Eostivil's Veisthi*—Luck's Promise." He tossed Roland a wrapped meat pie as well. "That should finish off the rest of the immediate need. Save the Veisthi for later when we have nothing else."

Roland recorked the flask with a sigh. The drink was delicious—he could finish the entire thing in one sitting—but he realized the wisdom of Dèodar's caution. They had no idea how long this quest would take, or where their next rations might come from.

He gathered his own pack, chewing absently on the meat pie as they started the long trek around the lake. He noticed Collyn gazing about him with the same sad, wistful expression as they hiked.

"What is it, Collyn?"

"When I was a child, we would come to the shores of this lake every summer. There were always other families camping nearby, and the air rang with the laughter of children. They called the mountains 'the Ring of Tears' because of the sparkle of sunlight on the crystals. We held contests to see who could find the largest ones. We strung them together, and the little girls would drip with 'diamonds' like they could never hope to possess outside their imaginations. Looking at this place now, you'd never believe it once held such gaiety."

"What happened to it?"

"I give you three guesses, *ethiae entheiro*, but I think you need only one." Dèodar slipped his longbow from his back then ran a questing hand along each section of the curved frame with a restless distraction.

"Trouble?" Roland frowned.

"Probably nothing, My Lord Prince," the rangy elf replied, managing only a trace of his usual insouciant grin. "Just a little itchy. For one thing, where did those scratches come from? And how did the Sunstone conveniently wind up in that market stall when you would be handy to buy it? Steavil doesn't remember where he lost it, but it certainly wasn't in Woodwatch Ferry. It's too convenient...but I'm probably starting at shadows."

"It's more than that," Collyn murmured, casting about, and finding a sturdy branch beside a long-abandoned fire. He swung it experimentally then nodded to himself before continuing. "Something wicked taints the air." He gazed around him with a frown.

Beside him, Roland glanced upward instinctively, but the sky was clear.

"What do you mean?"

"A feeling of evil haunts this place, growing ever stronger as we circle the lake. There may well be eyes upon us. I fear it may not be as simple as you hoped to retrieve the Moonstone. I suggest we make a cache of any possessions not essential to our search. In the first place, it'll lighten our loads if we must fight; and in the second place, if we do run into trouble, we will have provisions for an escape."

Dèodar nodded approval. "'Tis good counsel, Roland. I see a niche in a rock over there that should serve our purpose." He pointed to a formation fifty paces to their right.

"Your eyes are as sharp as a hawk's!" growled Roland. "All right, what should we keep with us?"

"Here," Dèodar handed Collyn another flask of Veisthi from his pack, slinging a third over his own neck.

"Sylvania must brew this by the barrel," teased Roland.

"And how do your vinters make wine?" answered Dèodar with a cocked eyebrow.

They arrived at the feet of the rock he had indicated. Dèodar wedged his pack securely into the back of the tiny recess.

"The Veisthi will keep you from starving for many days if necessary, but ration it. Don't let the taste seduce you. It will get you drunk if you aren't careful."

"And I don't wish to carry either of you," added Collyn dryly.

Dèodar continued. "I'll keep my bow and quiver, but I leave my dagger here, and advise you to do the same, Roland." He slipped a beautifully wrought stiletto from its sheath inside his boot and carefully hid it in the folds of his pack. "We may well lose our weapons if we run into trouble, and at least we'll know where others can be found."

"I didn't even know you carried that," Roland commented with an absent frown as he stripped off his own pack and hesitated between his sword and his dagger. The longer blade offered a certain comfort, but it would be difficult to conceal.

The elf looked up from his crouch beside the rock with the sparkle of his characteristic grin.

"There is a very great deal you don't know about me, young one—and most of it you probably will never learn." He glanced over at Roland, standing with sword in one hand and dagger in the other. "Keep your sword. If we must fight, we'll need every advantage we can get." Lifting his head, he scented the air then froze. "There *is* a taint of something in the wind not belonging on these shores. We need to be prepared for anything."

Collyn nodded. "He's right, Your Highness. That sword holds an edge over our other weapons we can ill afford to lose."

"Collyn, will that cudgel be enough?" asked Dèodar.

"Aye, my friend," replied the burly riverman, swinging his pack to the ground. "It's what I'm best with, and it suits me well."

"Good enough," cried the ranger, stowing the last of the baggage and leaping to his feet. "Shall we go?"

Roland took one last glance around them, noting the slanting position of the sun in the afternoon sky. "Aye. We can't afford to waste any more time. I fear we've tarried too long as it is."

Chapter 21

Stefan tossed uneasily. Mendana had forced him back to bed and given him a sleeping draught after their audience with the king, but she could not turn off his dreams.

He stood high on a cliff above Desolation Lake, looking down at the lifeless water. He saw Roland's party far below and tried to join to them. His left leg refused to move, and he discovered it was encased in stone to just above the knee, pinning him to the spot. He could only watch in helpless horror as brigands emerged from among the rocks and attacked, outnumbering the trio four to one.

Dèodar dropped, his great bow, snapped in two, beneath him, and Collyn went down under a press of attackers. Roland stood alone, sword flashing, desperately trying to defend himself.

Finally, one man managed to get behind the prince and brought down a heavy rock on the back of his head with a victorious whoop. Roland crumpled and lay still.

"No!" Stefan bolted upright, sweat plastering his hair to his face. "Oh, by the gods, no," he whispered, raising shaky hands to sweep it back. "It cannot be. Please, gods, let it not be too late to prevent this!"

He lay back for a moment, struggling to organize his thoughts.

I must go to Roland and the others. But how?

From the morning's trip to the throne room, he knew his leg would support him, but his limp was much worse; and Mendana's warning of permanent damage continued to clang in his head with the urgency of a fire bell.

But which is the greater loss—being able to walk, or my friends?

He set his teeth and threw his legs over the side of the couch. *I must go and damned be the consequences.* Gripping the headboard, he hauled himself to his feet, biting back a cry as he put too much weight on his damaged leg. He held his breath until the flare of agony subsided to its usual dull throb. Concentrating grimly, he lurched about the chamber, collecting his belongings. As he did, he caught a glimpse of the ring on his finger, and his heart filled with hope. The stone was still deep crimson. What he had seen must still lie in the future. Perhaps he had time.

He was fastening his cloak, when a sharp voice from the door behind him froze him in mid-gesture.

"Steavil, *twuae inithi iothinae!*" Mendana cried, the laden dinner tray she'd held crashing to the floor as she ran to catch him when he wheeled and almost fell. "What are you doing?"

"No. No, I'm all right. I'm fine. Let me go."

"Go? Go where? You look as if you've seen...oh, my goddess!" Mendana's face reflected his terror as she forced him to sit on the edge of the bed. "What *have* you seen?"

He closed his eyes, taking a deep shuddering breath.

"They're in trouble, Mendi. They'll be hurt, maybe killed. I must warn them!"

"Stefan, you can't. Your leg isn't strong enough for such a journey. It would damage it beyond all skills of healing. We'll tell Father. He can send men."

"Father has no men, Mendana! There is no one to go but me, and go I shall. You cannot stop me."

"He can spare a patrol. Aerlann and his men are itching to redeem themselves for bringing you to court as a prisoner. We will tell Father—"

"There's no time!" His heart pounded in his chest, threatening to choke him with urgency. "I must go. I am the only one who knows where they will be."

"Be quiet. I must think." She began to pace.

"Mendi..."

"I will go to Father and convince him to send Aerlann's patrol to the lake by the swiftest road possible. You can give them general coordinates, surely."

"But..."

"While they move overland, you and I will go under. I can tell by your stubbornness you will not stay here quietly and rest until they report back. We can find the prince and the others and warn them, then guide the warders to where they are. I will go with you—"

"No."

"You cannot stop me," she repeated back at him. "They journey on this quest because of me. Dèodar is my subject as well as my kinsman. The prince..." Her voice failed, and she cleared her throat as color rose in her cheeks. "The prince is an honored guest. I'll not see them hurt while seeking some bauble for my jewel casket."

"The Moonstone is more than a mere bauble, and you know it."

"Even so, the situation remains the same. It isn't worth their deaths, no matter what its value."

"It will be dangerous."

"I'm fully capable of handling danger, my foolish brother. I can shoot a sparrow at a hundred yards with my bow, a handy skill when ambushing brigands, don't you agree? And I may at least be able to keep your pain tolerable," she added, her voice soft with sympathy, "because this will cause you agonies beyond any you have ever known."

He took a deep breath and met her eye, accepting the cost

"I have dealt with pain before. It is a small thing compared to Roland's life."

"All right. Wait here until I return. I will see Father at once about sending Aerlann. Then I must change, and arrange for mounts."

He frowned. "Mounts? But how...?"

"There are still a few surprises hidden in our caverns. With the animals, we can ride underground beneath the river and be swifter in arriving. They don't move as quickly as Aerlann's men will be able to, but the way is shorter, and at least they will save you some walking."

"If it is a shorter journey, why not tell the warders to take that path?"

"We no longer have enough *istionthi* to mount a full patrol."

"Enough what?"

Mendana laughed as she stood and started for the door. "You will see."

"I pray we are not too late," he sighed.

"As do I, little brother," she whispered without turning around, clutching the curtain in a white-knuckled grip.

Then she was gone.

***

Roland and his companions reached their destination just before sundown. Angling rays of sunlight revealed the forbidding face to be honeycombed with openings ranging from hand-sized holes to man-high caverns.

"We could search for days," complained the prince, heart sinking into his boots at the prospect.

"Cheer up, *inithi ionavo*," laughed Dèodar, clapping him on the back and almost flattening him, "we should be done before you're fifty."

"Thank you for your confidence, *entheirae*," replied Roland dryly.

"What does the jewel say?" asked Collyn, with a reprimanding glance at the elf. Sitting on a rock, he began smoothing a rough place on his cudgel with a sharp bit of crystal.

"Of course," Roland groaned, pulling the pendant out of his jerkin. "Whoever put these marks on the stone did it for a reason. If it *is* a map, he would not want to search all day to retrieve his prize."

"Ah, yes, but he would also know where he left it." Dèodar tested the string on his bow, drawing it back empty to his chin then removing the string and stowing the bow on his back.

"It can't hurt to try." Roland studied the scratches on the stone with a careful eye. "There is a tiny mark all by itself about two-thirds of the way down the outline of the mountain. Shall we start our search up there?" He pointed to a cave in approximately the correct location.

"Might as well," Dèodar shrugged. "It's the only clue we have. Besides..." He squinted from sun to cave mouth. "...it looks like a good spot to make camp tonight."

"Camp," Roland snorted. "No bedrolls, no food, no fire. A poor camp if you ask me."

"Good thing no one asked you, then," quipped the elf, examining the base of the mountain.

"You've lived too soft a life, my prince," Collyn said with a grin. "I've known many nights where I dreamed of a nice, dry cave in which to camp. Sleep hungry under the stars in the shirt on your back after two days travel, with rain before dawn then see if you complain about a cave to sleep in."

Roland felt his face grow hot

"Let's get moving. If we're planning to scale the cliff, we'd better get started. It will be dark soon."

"Aye." Collyn stepped up to the towering rock face and searched for a handhold. Finding an outcropping, he started up. "Too bad we brought no rope."

"Will this do?" Dèodar tossed him the end of a thin coil of plaited cord.

Collyn caught it in one hand and pulled it up.

"What will this hold, Master Warder? One of your Veisthi flasks?"

"Tie it around your waist and see."

Collyn did as instructed before shrugging down at the prince.

"I think the sun has scrambled what little brains he had."

"Just keep climbing. At the first cavern mouth, step inside, and we shall see whose brains are scrambled, Master Silverbrook."

Roland grinned at the byplay. He watched with

interest as Dèodar fed out the rope until Collyn reached the cave. When the trader waved, the elf tied the rope around his own waist and climbed nimbly up the face of the rock as Collyn braced to take his weight. He slapped Collyn on the back and tossed his end of the rope to Roland.

"Now you, *entheiro*."

As he looped the slim cord securely around his waist, Roland smiled to himself. Elf and human working together side by side. There was no reason why the two cultures couldn't coexist in peace. With Stefan king of the elves, and himself on the Irthlan throne at Crown Keep, the dream might so easily become a reality.

***

Mendana returned with Captain Aerlann and a pair of his warders. Her scowl did not bode well.

"Your Highness," the captain murmured, bowing before Stefan. "I have come to ask the location of the ambush you have seen so that we may prevent it."

Stefan shook his head in confusion.

"I...I don't know where it will be. Just amongst the rocks of the Ring of Tears."

"Were there any discernible landmarks? Was any formation particularly notable?"

Stefan felt again the dream-panic that had paralyzed him.

"No, I just saw rocks. They were threading through other rocks and were attacked by men hiding among different rocks. I don't know anything else to tell you!"

Mendana rested a comforting hand upon his shoulder.

"He cannot help you further, Captain. Shouldn't you set out? The situation calls for haste."

Aerlann raised an eyebrow.

"We will do what we can, milady, but with these directions, I fear it will be of little use." He bowed again and hurried away.

He left his warders behind.

Stefan glanced from the stoic elves flanking the doorway to his sister.

"Mendi...?"

She glowered at the guards and sank down on the couch beside him

"Father wishes to make sure you rest, Stefan," she murmured. "He has requested I stay here with you 'in case you need something.' These...gentlemen...are here to run errands for us." She leaned toward him and hissed in his ear, "And to make sure we stay in this room. But we have a plan."

"Who—"

"Trust me."

Stefan nodded.

"Always."

Mendana rose to her feet and began fussing about the bed, plumping pillows, and straightening the coverlet.

"Lie back, and I will get your tonic," she told him.

Stefan settled into the pillows.

"I am a bit tired," he answered, making sure his voice would carry to the doorway.

The princess made as if to leave, and one of the warders stepped into her path with a polite throat-clearing.

"May I help you, milady?"

"I need to fetch the ingredients for a tincture for my brother."

"Tell me what you need, and I will be happy to retrieve them for you."

"Come with me, then," she ordered. "It would be too difficult to describe to you what I require."

With a pointed look at his companion, the warder followed Mendana from the chamber.

Stefan eyed his remaining guard. The elf was older than any he had seen so far, his hair fully silver. The warder smiled at him.

"It is good to have you home, Lord Steavil. I remember when you were just a tot."

Before Stefan could ask for details, Mendana swept back into the room with her basket of supplies and a pitcher of water. She set them on the table and began to mix a potion, pointedly ignoring the guards. Stefan was confused. What was she playing at?

He took the potion when she handed it to him and drank it dutifully, grimacing at the medicinal taste.

"I know it isn't pleasant, Stefan, but it will sooth the pain and let you sleep."

There was a soft hail from beyond the curtain, and then it was swept aside by a woman in an apron. She carried a large tray of food, a carafe of wine and several goblets.

"I brought the meal you requested, milady," she murmured.

"Thank you, Sylvania," Mendana answered with a smile. She turned to the warders. "Something to eat, gentlemen? Perhaps some wine? Since you are stuck watching us for the day, at least we can offer you a meal."

Sylvania poured each of the warders a goblet of wine, offering it to them with a smile. The guards exchanged a glance then shrugged and accepted the drinks. The elder one winked at her.

"I never turn down your wine, Sylvania. It's the best in the kingdom."

The guards drained the goblets as if they held water. As Stefan watched, a foolish grin spread over each face, and they slumped down the wall to the floor.

"What...?"

"Don't ask," Mendana ordered. "Thank you, Sylvania. I hoped you would get my message."

"They won't be out for long, milady, and they will know I helped you. You had best be off as soon as you can." She reached outside the curtain and retrieved a bundle of clothing. "Here are your tunic and trousers. Dress quickly. I have packed food and Veisthi for the trail. Your bow is at the stable, along with two score arrows. It was all I could arrange so quickly."

Mendana took the bundle and gave the woman a quick hug

"You are a lifesaver." She stepped into the alcove at the rear of the room to change, calling out to Stefan, "Get yourself ready to travel. You are the only one who knows exactly where to look. Father wouldn't let us ride with the warders—might be too dangerous. So we will follow my original plan and go through the tunnels. We'll try to catch up to the patrol in time for you to help them find the spot." She came out, fastening her cloak. "Let's go."

Stefan's head whirled at the speed of events.

"What about...?" He gestured at Sylvania.

Mendana bit her lip

"I *do* hate to leave you to deal with the consequences, Sylvania."

"Don't worry about me, I'll be fine. Now, get moving before those two wake up."

Mendana helped Stefan to his feet.

"Come. It isn't far to the stables."

Chapter 22

Roland stared into the flickering heart of the campfire. His thoughts shifted like the flames. Before they reached the marked cavern it had gotten so dark the ascent became too risky, so they had taken shelter in another cave about two hundred feet below it.

Now, as he watched the dancing firelight, thoughts of Mendana flowed into worry for his father.

"I should never have broken my journey home for this quest," he muttered. "Father may be ill. He needs me...but so does the princess. She deserves her heritage...doesn't she? Oh, this is madness!" He threw a handful of tinder onto the fire with a sigh. "This is all so complicated. I should return home at once."

The thoughts kept circling in his head—on the one hand, his duty to his father; on the other...

In the end, the thought he could brighten those beautiful eyes overcame his fear for the king.

"I know I should not let my heart get in the way of duty...but it's more than mere infatuation—Father would understand."

Roland massaged his temples, as if he could rub away the turmoil. He had forced Dèodar to get some sleep, knowing the elf had been pushing himself far harder than he let on. Collyn had volunteered for the watch, but Roland waved him off to bed as well.

He twisted Stefan's pendant between his fingers, watching the way the firelight reflected off the polished stone. The talisman brought other thoughts to the fore, overriding his fears for both his father and Mendana. Was it actually possible Norfulk's influence in this section of the kingdom was as strong as Collyn had intimated? What was his cousin playing at? Did he really intend to usurp the throne? Would Norfulk try again to kill him?

"By the Flames, what will he do to us?" he whispered aloud. "What can *we* do to *him*?"

There was a flutter of sound above him, and he reached for his sword, staying his hand when he saw its cause. A sleep-fuddled raven had blundered into the cave, perching on a ledge well above the fire and tucking its head beneath its wing.

"Just a silly bird." He yawned. He suddenly felt abysmally tired. He must get some sleep. On the ledge above, the raven shifted, looking down with a cock of its head and the unaccountable trace of what could only be called a smirk to its beak. Roland started to wake Collyn to take the watch, but crumpled beside the fire instead, asleep before his head hit his crossed arms.

***

Stefan and Mendana rode through the night. The broad tunnels were lit only with widely spaced crystal lanterns, and the dim light made their progress almost dream-like.

The mounts she had arranged for them—albino beasts the size of ponies with pale violet eyes and large, padded feet—picked their way surely through the dimly lit caverns, born and bred to darkness. The graceful creatures fascinated Stefan; he had never seen anything like them in the world above ground. They reminded him of great long-legged cats with their soft, shaggy coats that gave off a faint odor of cinnamon and allspice.

He leaned forward in his saddle and took a deep breath of the soothing aroma rising from the male he rode. Its perfume lifted his heart, despite the urgency of their quest.

"What gives them that scent, Mendi? Why do they not smell more like...well, animals?"

Mendana's laughter spilled like tinkling music to fill the dim cavern.

"It is part of the magic of their creation, *thiuveae*. They were created and bred long ago when the elves had much greater power. In that time, our magic forged many such beings. But now..." She sighed. "There are only ten pair left in the stables."

"What about the warders?" he asked her, curious to know more about the ways of his people. "Father mentioned that they had horses. Surely, they don't use these mounts on the surface."

"There is some equine stock bred in Moonrise Wood. We keep small corrals in both forests with a few head for riding. The warders and our messengers—like Leithan, for example—use those horses for riding above, but within the caverns, our *istionthi* are the best possible mounts. Is that not right, my beauty?" she crooned, reaching down, and stroking the neck of her skittish female with a fond caress.

"Can he be trusted?"

"Who?" Mendana asked, puzzlement on her face.

"Leithan."

She laughed. "Of course. Do you not remember

him? He has been in the castle since he was a babe. He is Raethan's son—not yet a year old when the exodus occurred. And there have been no children born since." The amusement died in her face, replaced by a wistful sadness.

"No children in over fifteen years?"

"Our race is dying, Steavil. There are so very few of us left. Most of the women are past bearing age." Her face darkened as she blushed. "Dèodar and Leithan are the only unattached young men in the clan, and they are my kin."

"And Ravenwing?"

The blush deepened. "He hardly counts—and is also kin. If things remain as they are, I...I will never marry."

"Then perhaps a change *is* needed..." he suggested with a gentle smile. They rode in silence for a while longer; then he ventured a hushed query. "Mendi, will I be a good king?"

She glanced at him, her face reflecting surprise at the question. "Why do you ask? How could you not be? You were born to be king."

"But that doesn't mean I'll be a good one. I often listened to Roland's lessons. Many times the masters would speak of princes who proved to be cruel or incompetent kings. I've had no training to wear the crown. What if I fail?"

"It isn't something you need be concerned with for many years, *inithi thiuveae*. Father will be here to teach you. There may be few of us left, but we are a long-lived race. He's not yet ready to relinquish his seat."

"Yes, of course, you're right." He favored her with a wan smile, wincing as he did so.

"Is it your knee?" she asked, her voice anxious.

"'Tis a bit of a strain, that's all." He shrugged, trying to minimize her worry. "I will be fine."

They passed under one of the crystalline lamps, and Stefan glanced at the crimson stone in Roland's ring. It remained blood-red, and he breathed a little prayer of thanksgiving.

"We're under the river now," Mendana remarked some time later. "Look."

She pointed to a ribbon of water cascading from the ceiling in a miniature waterfall. It pooled then flowed into a rippling stream that intersected their path. "There is beauty here in our caverns, Stefan, as much beauty as above, if more subdued."

He looked where she pointed, but even his sharp eyes had difficulty making out details. He felt as if the walls were moving in on him.

"How do you stand this shadow world?"

"You will grow accustomed to the dark," Mendana promised.

"But how can you stand never seeing the daylight, Mendi? Or gazing at the stars? I've spent countless hours simply watching cloud shadows on Golden Heath. I'm not so sure I can give it all up."

"I often go above to the portal clearings and sit in the forest to feel the sunlight, or hear the wind. Our life isn't as awful as you fear, I swear to you."

"It will just take some getting used to, as you say." He glanced at the ring once more.

"What is it, Stefan? Has it changed?"

"Not yet," he replied, a frown creasing his brow, "but I fear it will soon." He kicked his mount up to a canter. "We must hurry, Mendana. We must be in time. King Frederick entrusted me with Roland's keeping. Now the prince is in danger. I've failed Frederick's trust. I failed again. Failed..."

Her face was grim in the shadows as she rode up beside him.

"Stop berating yourself, Steavil. You have done your best. No one could have expected you to do more."

He sighed, but said nothing more. The istionthi's pounding feet echoed the refrain of failure in his heart until his head whirled with it.

The loping animals ran through the night, but his thoughts were too chaotic for further conversation. Hours flowed into a featureless blur, punctuated with bitter self-recrimination and the throbbing of his knee.

"Are you all right?"

Mendana's voice cut through the fog of exhaustion and pain that had him clinging to his mount with desperate determination. He shook his head to clear it and managed a weak smile.

"I'm fine. Just a little tired. Are we nearly to the exit?"

"Almost. Would you like to rest?"

Stefan shook his head again, uneasily checking the ring. "No. It's getting late. Time is running out. I can feel it." He kicked the animal to a gallop.

"Stefan!" Mendana called after him. "Be careful! The floor is not as smooth as you think."

"We have no time to waste!" he shouted back over his shoulder.

The feeling of unease was growing stronger, goading him ever forward. He heard Mendana's mount behind him and forced himself to rein in as he came to a crossroads where the tunnel branched in several directions.

"Which way?" he cried, hearing the impatience in his voice but powerless to prevent it.

"To the left. We should come up just outside the Ring of Tears. The istionthi are much faster and require fewer rest periods than horses. We should have beaten the warders to the mountains. That will give you time to rest."

"I am fine, Mendana. We need to warn the prince as soon as possible."

"I strongly advise you rest, Stefan. If that knee stiffens up and you are exhausted, it will be difficult for you to climb, perhaps impossible."

Reluctantly, he had to admit the validity of her warning. Already his knee felt permanently bent to the saddle.

"We will rest for an hour. By then, the sun will have risen, and we will be able to see to climb."

She nodded. "It's just a little farther along this corridor. Then we can tether the mounts."

She kicked her animal ahead and led the way to a comfortable chamber carved out of the cavern. Along one wall was a long straw-filled bin with water troughs at either end. Mendana slipped gracefully from her mount then looped her reins over the rail before the bin. She stroked its neck.

"*Itheamia, entheiria.* You have served well."

Stefan tried to free his left leg from the stirrup to dismount, but his knee would not cooperate. Searing pain raced through him, and he choked back a cry.

"Steavil...?"

"I...I'm all right. Just give me a minute." He took a deep breath, concentrating all his will on his knee. Clutching the saddle horn, he gritted his teeth and forced his leg free. He swung it over the animal's back, and as he touched the ground, only his grip on the saddle kept him upright when the leg buckled beneath him.

Mendana ran to his side and caught him around the waist.

"You've overdone it, haven't you? I warned you!"

He drew himself upright, trying to stand on his own.

"Do I have a choice, Mendana? He is my brother—maybe not by blood, but my brother just the same. And I swore to his father on my honor I would protect him."

"At least sit down and let me look at your knee."

He nodded, clenching his teeth against the pain. She helped him limp over to a flight of stairs that ascended into darkness. He sank onto the rock step with a grateful sigh, leaning back against the risers and clutched the edge of his seat with desperate tension.

Mendana knelt on the floor beside him, lifting his leg in gentle hands and propping it on her bent knee—it was obvious his knee was swollen to twice normal size. Carefully, she undid his legging to expose it; the flesh was tight and waxy, mottled with angry bruises.

She bit her lip at the sight.

"I should never have let you come. Now you will never walk properly."

"It will be worth it," he grunted, "if we can save them." He let his head fall back and stared up at the ceiling. "Can you make the pain stop? Damn the consequences, can you just make it stop? I need to be able to move without feeling it."

"Do you realize what you are asking me to do?" Her eyes were bright with unshed tears.

"Yes. But I have no choice. I have tried to stand it, but I cannot. I have to find them before it is too late. If you can block the feeling in the leg, fine. If not, I will somehow go on anyway. *Deastia, evleeia.* If you can, please make the pain go away."

"I will do all I can, *inithi thiuveae,*" promised his sister, her face grave and still. She placed gentle hands on either side of the knee. "I'm sorry," Mendana whispered, and twisted the leg sharply.

The pain that knifed through him sent his senses skittering to the edge of oblivion. The world spiraled in around him like a bud closing on itself. Everything went gray, then like sand running through an hourglass, the world faded to black as Stefan fainted.

Chapter 23

Roland's party had awakened at dawn and continued their climb. Now they stood inside the cavern where they hoped to find the Moonstone. Thousands of glorious crystalline structures sparkled like frozen fire in the early morning sunlight. The cave was musty after the clean, crisp air outside, and Roland sneezed as they kicked up the dust covering the bedrock. He blinked against the dazzle of the dancing reflections, gazing around in despair.

"The Moonstone could be anywhere in this confusion." Dèodar shrugged.

"We better start looking, then, hadn't we?" He pointed Collyn toward the rear of the cave. "I'll take the left. Roland, you take the right. We'll work our way back to meet Collyn."

"Sounds good." Roland began to search. There were hundreds of little nooks and crannies among the pillars, the crystals were sharp as knife blades, and before he could finish the first pillar, he had sliced his finger. He hissed in pain and stuck the finger in his mouth, tasting salt blood as he sucked it until the sting dissipated.

"This is ridiculous," he said with a sigh.

As he continued slowly toward the rear of the cave, he felt a seed of warmth against his chest. It was very faint at first—he almost didn't notice it—but as he moved farther from the entrance, the sensation grew stronger.

Less than a third of the way around the cavern, the heat became intense. It burned like a coal, and he tore at the lacing of his jerkin. As he ripped open the shirt beneath to expose the pendant, he gasped with wonder. The Sunstone glowed with inner fire.

"Dèodar, look at this."

The elf strolled over and rested an elbow on Roland's shoulder.

"It's glowing."

Roland forced himself to count to ten.

"I know it's glowing. Do you know why?"

Collyn joined them.

"Perhaps it's seeking its companion. Or its companion is calling to it."

"It's possible," remarked Dèodar. "Certainly worth consideration. Andundal spoke of legends they were linked. Follow its lead and see where it takes you."

Remembering how the ring had led him to the pendant in the first place, Roland nodded, slipping the chain from his neck, and placing the pendant in the center of his palm. He stepped toward the rear of the cavern, and the glow became brighter, the heat almost unbearable.

Just when he felt he must drop the stone before it seared his flesh, the glow began to diminish. He backtracked to the point where the heat was greatest and turned in a slow circle until all at once the stone flew from his hand to cling to the side of a stalagmite.

Dèodar let out a low whistle

"Well, what do you know about that?" He plucked free the Sunstone pendant, which was once more cool and dark. Handing it back to Roland, he hunkered down beside the crystal formation. "Let's see what we have here. There's a cavity here at the bottom," he announced, feeling deep inside it. "And here, unless I miss my guess, is what you seek."

He pulled out a small object wrapped in soft cloth and peeled back the fabric with care. In his hand lay the Moonstone, its silver untarnished despite fifteen years of neglect and the stone glowing with lambent radiance.

"The Moonrise heritage," he breathed, all flippancy banished from his voice. "It is the symbol of my people, and it has been absent far too long."

"Will you keep it until it can be returned to its rightful owner?" asked Roland softly.

"Oh, no, *entheiro*. I leave that in your hands," Dèodar answered, giving it to him with a little bow, his easy grin back in place. "I seem to recall you made a promise to a very beautiful lady."

"I would suggest we return it to Her Majesty with all possible haste," murmured Collyn. "An inheritance this precious should be with its owner."

"Aye," agreed Roland, slipping the Sunstone around his neck once more. Now they had found the object of their quest, he remembered the doubts that had assailed him the night before, when he wrestled with whether or not he should follow his head or his heart.

"We best be getting back—I'll return the amulet to Mendana then leave for home. Stefan said Father is in danger. My first duty is to him—and I have an uneasy feeling about the state of things in Crown Keep myself." He glanced at the mouth of the cave. The angle of light showed their search had taken longer than he'd realized. "Time is running out."

Collyn nodded. "I fear you're right to worry, My Lord Prince. The Black Lion will move while there is doubt as to your whereabouts. Even if Andundal's messenger has arrived to confirm your safety, if you aren't at the palace soon, Norfulk will find the kingdom easy pickings."

"Let's start now." Roland's voice was grim as he rewrapped the Moonstone and stowed it deep inside his shirt. "Before it is too late."

***

Mendana worked another miracle with her healing touch. When Stefan returned to his senses, the pain was gone, along with all mobility in the knee. The joint was locked, and he had to drag the leg behind him as he crawled up the stairway.

They came out of the cavern scant yards from the foothills, and took cover among the rocks with all possible speed. From the angle of the sun, it had been clear they had lost several hours.

Now, as they scaled the cliffs surrounding the lake, Stefan had to fight for every inch of progress. Worse, he sensed they were being watched, and it made him uneasy. With grim determination, he scrabbled for finger holds, pulling himself upward by sheer strength of will. He dared not let Mendana know he grew weary, because she would insist they stop and they could not afford to rest. His fear for the others was growing. Every moment of delay was potentially disastrous.

He glanced at his sister. With a graceful economy in her movements, she climbed steadily, nimble as a goat despite the longbow she carried. He felt a stab of envy at the ease of her movements then reminded himself his own choices had brought him to this pass.

"We will be too late!" he gasped, breath ragged in his throat as he tried to make himself move faster. "We must hurry!"

"I know that, little brother," Mendana replied through gritted teeth. "I may not have the Sight as strongly as you do, but I feel it as well. The danger is near."

He felt terribly vulnerable scaling the mountain face. A chill breeze fanned the sweat from his face, and he shivered, licking salt from his lip as he paused and scanned his surroundings for a hidden watcher. Only a single bird wheeling high overhead moved in the desolate landscape.

He reached out for a handhold and missed. His right foot slipped, and all his weight was thrown onto his bad leg. The world grayed out.

He swayed, and his soft boots slid against the rock. Terror welled. His heart slammed in his chest as he flailed for a hold. His fingers could find no purchase as his feet continued to slip.

There was the stink of fear-charged sweat in his nostrils, and the taste of sour bile in his throat. Time seemed to stand still, frozen in an endless moment as he teetered for balance. He choked on the scream bubbling up his throat.

And then he felt a strong hand grab his wrist.

"I have you, Steavil," Mendana reassured him, drawing him toward her with a firm and steady grip. "There is a little outcropping just a foot or two above you. We will rest there."

Stefan nodded, too exhausted to argue. He had nothing left to give.

Mendana hauled him up to the ledge with little aid on his part, and he slumped down onto a fallen rock, panting. He spat the taste of fear from his throat then drew the rough edge of his sleeve across his mouth

"Put your foot on this," she ordered, propping his leg up with her pack. "I will get our bearings."

"Is there any sign of the warders?"

She raised a hand to shield her eyes, scanning the area surrounding the lake.

"Not yet. We'll rest here."

Grateful to sit still for a few moments despite his driving urgency, Stefan shook the hair out of his eyes and let his gaze wander. A flash of recognition hit him, and he pushed to his feet, feeling a fresh surge of panic.

"Mendi—" His throat tightened with fear.

"Shh!" she ordered, crouching behind a boulder. "Someone's coming."

He lurched to her side.

"*They* are coming," he grated, clutching her sleeve. "Roland and the others. They are coming, and they will be taken!"

"How do you know?" She seized him by the shoulders, giving him a rough shake. "Tell me! How do you know?"

His teeth clicked together with the force of her shake, and he swallowed hard.

"My vision. I was there—here—when they were taken. This is the spot. I have to warn them."

"What exactly did you see? Tell me!"

Stefan moaned low in his throat, fighting to keep control.

"Many men, perhaps as many as a dozen, hiding in the rocks. Roland and the others walked into an ambush there." He pointed to a scatter of rocks just beneath them.

"Well, I doubt the gods will let us change the vision so greatly as to cancel the encounter, but at least we may even the odds. I wish you could have given Aerlann better directions—they are probably halfway around the Ring." She grabbed her bow, strung it, and began scanning the rocks, looking for the ambushers.

Stefan stepped back, panic mounting. Weaponless as he was, he could no more influence the outcome now than in his dream. He could almost feel the stone oozing upward like molten lead to encase his leg. The ambush was coming. The vision was about to become reality, and there was nothing he could do to stop it.

He saw Mendana stiffen and stepped toward her.

A hand clapped over his mouth, and his arms were pinned behind him. He struggled like a mad thing, and his hands were twisted sharply, bringing a gasp of pain.

"Stand still and be quiet," ordered a soft voice in his ear.

He froze.

"Good boy. I'm going to let you go now. If you make a sound, the consequences will be on your head."

The hands released him, and he saw a handsome Dark elf, a hair's breadth taller than Mendana, standing beside him. He opened his mouth, and the stranger shook his head with a warning frown and a finger to his lips.

Somehow, Stefan knew it would be wiser to do as the stranger said.

Where did he come from? We are halfway up the mountainside, and I heard no sound of his approach.

He soon saw why as the stranger crept forward, noiseless in thigh-high leather boots. He opened his mouth to warn Mendana, but the newcomer spun, gesturing toward him. Suddenly, Stefan felt his throat begin to constrict, and he fought to breathe.

The stranger stepped behind Mendana and pulled her from the edge of the outcropping with a hand to her mouth, preventing her from crying out. She dropped her bow with a clatter and fought against her captor.

He turned the princess towards Stefan. "One word," he murmured close to her ear, "and I finish the job."

Stefan shook his head, despite the pressure building in his lungs, but Mendana's face paled as she nodded.

The elf released her, and she spun to slap his face. He caught her hand before it could connect.

"Now, now, Mendana Andundalia, is that any way to greet an old friend?"

Chapter 24

Despite the chill in the air, Roland regretted his cloak as they worked their way back down the mountain. His shirt clung to his skin beneath the jerkin, and his hair was lank with sweat.

He followed behind the elf as the Collyn led the way, Dèodar's elven magic of no use for moving lifeless rock. The merry elf tried to keep up their spirits, but mostly he failed. Roland was too hot, and too hungry, to be jollied out of his mood.

He thought about stopping for luncheon—little as that might be—but contented himself with a slug of Veisthi. There was no time to spare. They must hurry back to the Forest, so he could return home.

He felt the packet with the Moonstone shift position inside his shirt and admitted to himself it was not food he craved, but Mendana's reaction to the return of her amulet.

Suddenly, Dèodar stopped abruptly, scanning the cliffs around them. He halted Collyn with a hand on his shoulder. Roland's hand flew to the hilt of his sword. Before he could clear the scabbard, a ragged band of cutthroats descended on them.

Dèodar pulled an arrow from his quiver, but before he could nock it, he let out a wordless cry and crumpled to the dirt, hit by a sling-stone in the temple. His bow snapped beneath him as he fell.

Roland's sword sang free of its scabbard as he stepped toward the elf. He had no time to reach his fallen companion before he found himself surrounded by a group of four men, all armed with short swords or long daggers.

The prince gulped. He risked a glance at the ground to make sure of his footing. It was one of the earliest things he had been taught. His mind raced as he tried to remember all of Fortenbraes' drills, but even so his training had been for the battlefield, not gang attacks. He was a stranger to street fighting, which his assailants clearly were not. Their weapons and tactics were unfamiliar.

One of the men leered and swung his sword in a short arc aimed at Roland's midsection. Roland caught it against his blade with a ring of steel. His confidence soared.

Then they all attacked at once. The sharp taste of fear surged into his throat. He was hard-pressed to keep them at bay, pivoting from one breath to the next to parry blow after blow. His arm ached from the slamming impact of the weapons. He had no time to think. He was fighting by instinct alone.

His heart pounded as he twisted and spun. A lucky flick of an attacker's dagger traced a line of fire across his right arm, and the copper scent of blood brought a rush of nausea to his throat. He felt hot liquid flowing from the wound, and it made him all the more desperate. The sword became harder to wield as his hand became slick with blood.

Out of the corner of his eye, he saw Collyn forced to his knees by another foursome, all punching and kicking with savage fury as the big man laid about him with the cudgel.

A thought flashed through his mind. If any one of them had a blade, Collyn should have been dead by now. *Why are they holding back?*

The riverman fought to his feet, but was knocked down again almost at once. After that, Roland lost all track of his companions as he fought for his life.

His sword flashed in the sunlight as he thrust and parried with desperate urgency. He wounded one of the men in front of him, losing sight for an instant of his danger in a flush of triumph. It caused him to lower his guard...and the world exploded from behind.

Through a red haze of pain, he sank to his knees, fighting for consciousness and losing the battle. He felt the sword slip from his numbed fingers as he fell into darkness.

***

"And there we have it!" cried Ravenwing, leaping gracefully to stand atop a boulder. He gave a lilting, wordless cry. The attacking ruffians began to drop where they stood from slung stones placed with uncanny accuracy. The swish of the stones as they flew was counterpointed by grunts and cries of pain as the brigands crumpled.

Ravenwing chanted a brief spell, sketching a figure in the air, and several more of the villains dropped.

"Yes!" he crowed, with a negligent wave.

Stefan felt the invisible bonds holding him vanish. He stumbled forward to crouch awkwardly at the edge of the cliff, studying the scene below. A single tear broke free and rolled down his cheek.

Gods! I have proven useless to Roland yet again.

He heard Mendana running behind him, and as he turned to look at her, Ravenwing stepped off his rock into midair. Stefan stared in open-mouthed astonishment as the wizard spread his cape and shifted, shrinking into a small bright-eyed raven that swooped toward the ground.

"*Oluvi ilianae!*" Mendana spat after him, her voice ringing harshly in the unnatural silence.

Numbed by the sight below him, Stefan glanced down at the ring. Its color had faded only slightly, and his heart eased somewhat. At least Roland did not appear to be seriously hurt.

Yet.

"I will kill you, *ilianae!*" Mendana shouted, scooping up a rock and launching it at Ravenwing.

"We must get down there, Mendi," Stefan murmured, his voice grim. He struggled to his feet. "I must help them."

"Yes, we must, and quickly."

"Look." Stefan pointed.

Down from the rocks came a boy, tucking a sling into his belt. A cap was pulled low about his ears, and on his shoulder perched the raven. Slipping silently among the fallen, he collected purses from the cutthroats. He stooped over Dèodar, carefully removing the warder's quiver, and slipping a silver band from the elf's little finger.

"That does it!" Mendana growled, her eyes snapping as she fitted an arrow to her bow. She drew back the string, and Stefan lunged forward, jarring her aim as she released it.

"Mendi, no!"

She glared at him but released the tension on the string and thrust the bow at him.

"Fine! I will go down *there* and deal with them." Before he could protest, she was scrambling down the cliff toward the thief.

Stefan watched while the pickpocket rifled Collyn's pouch, apparently finding nothing of interest. By the time Mendana reached the ground, the cutpurse was hunkered beside Roland, head cocked as if listening to the raven.

Ravenwing cawed harshly, and the boy shifted Roland onto his back. The little thief raised an eyebrow and ripped open the prince's jerkin with a small dagger, baring his chest. The Sunstone pendant glowed.

Mendana leapt on the lad when he reached for the ornament, and the raven took to the air. She pounded the thief around the head and shoulders. The cutpurse merely raised his arms to protect his face.

Stefan chewed his lip in indecision. Should he try the descent, or wait as Mendana had ordered?

"Call her off!" ordered a harsh voice in his ear as a silk-clad arm curled around his throat and a sharp blade pricked his side through his tunic.

"No."

The blade pressed harder, and Stefan felt a tremor of fear. He gulped.

"Do it, *iothinae*! She'll ruin everything. I don't have time to convince you politely." There was a note of desperation in the wizard's voice, and the blade broke the skin of Stefan's side.

"Mendana!"

She looked up, eyes narrowed against the sun as

she held the thief in a secure grip.

"Stop hammering on my companion, My Queen, and I promise not to skewer your unfortunate brother," Ravenwing shouted down at her.

"Let him go, Eeonathor!"

"I think not."

Stefan swallowed hard against the arm around his throat. He felt a moment of disorientation and dizziness and closed his eyes. When he opened them again, he and his captor stood on the ground beside Mendana and her captive.

"Impasse, My Queen. Shall we trade?"

"I should have let them kill you when I had the chance," Mendana hissed.

"Look, you stubborn *iothinia*, we have little time. My spell will not hold those brigands forever. I need the pendant of Starlit Wood. It is my ticket into Crypticia Keep. There is but one prayer to stop the madman living there, and I am it. Now let me have the Sunstone, and release my subordinate."

"As you say, wizard, impasse. I will release your boy when you release my brother."

Despite his current danger, Stefan found his curiosity drawn to the quiet little thief. He stood in sullen silence, strands of lank blond hair straying from under his cap. His eyes were a startling, vibrant green, the only spark of color in his pale face.

Stefan felt a twinge of sympathy.

"Let him go, Mendi. I doubt it was his idea to come."

"Well spoken, My Prince," murmured the wizard. With a heavy sigh, Ravenwing released him. "'Tis no use, is it, *evleeia*?" he asked Mendana, his voice a soft caress. "You will never forgive, and I cannot forget."

Deliberately, Ravenwing turned his back on the princess, squatting down beside Dèodar and gently examining the slight gash on the warder's forehead. He murmured some inaudible words and passed a hand over the wound. "Sleep now, *thiuveae*. All will be well, little brother."

His hand lingered on the warder's shoulder.

"Daerci, give me the ring," he ordered sternly, holding out his hand. "It wasn't part of the deal."

The thief reached into a side pouch and pulled out the silver ring he had taken from Dèodar. Jaw thrust out defiantly, he slapped the ring into Ravenwing's palm. With a cool stare of disapproval, Ravenwing slid it back onto Dèodar's finger.

"How could you do this to Dèodar?" Mendana snarled. "You let your own brother walk into an ambush. This is on your head!" She swept a hand over the scene while still keeping a firm hold on Daerci's arm.

"Dèodar will survive. I would never hurt him, and you know it." Ravenwing's handsome face was dark with rage. "Someone else was not so kind once, I recall. And remember, it was he who held the bow that day. Don't worry. None of your friends have suffered grievous harm. I merely needed them unconscious. Some of these cutthroats were not so lucky.

"Now, will you release Daerci and give me the pendant freely, or must I force you? It is your choice, My Queen." From his lips the title sounded like an epithet.

Stefan had listened to the heated conversation in silence. Finally, limping over to Roland, he undid the clasp holding the pendant. He coiled the chain into his palm with thoughtful deliberation and slowly returned to Ravenwing's side.

"Here." He held it out to the wizard.

"Stefan! You don't know what you're doing!" Mendana cried.

He turned to her, head held proudly.

"It is my birthright. I may do with it as I please. I choose to trust this man. He saved my life. I owe him that trust."

Ravenwing dropped to one knee, extending an elegant hand to Stefan with dark head bowed.

"Stefan!" Mendana protested again, as he laid the pendant on the outstretched palm.

The long fingers curled around the golden stone. The wizard's voice was a soft, reverent whisper. "*Itheamia, ethiae ionavi*. It is the only way."

There was a weak groan from Roland, and Mendana shoved Daerci toward Ravenwing. The boy stumbled into his master, who leapt to steady him.

"Take your thief, *ilianae*," Mendana spat, her voice harsh with hatred. "You deserve each other." She ran to kneel at Roland's side, cradling his head in her lap as he started to regain consciousness.

Stefan was now all but alone with Ravenwing. The wizard came closer, looking down at him.

"Your trust in me will not prove groundless, *inithi ionavi*. This I swear to you."

"I do not remember you."

"That is not surprising, *eathinae*. I did not often visit Starlit Wood, though my heart once rested there. I was curious after you disappeared. Something told me you were not dead, but I could not track you for some time—I think I now know why.

"However, since the fiasco on the raft, I have kept an eye on you." He laid a hand on Stefan's shoulder and gave it a gentle squeeze. "You are a strong man, Steavil Andundalae, and wise for one so young. Listen to your heart."

He slipped the chain of the amulet around his neck, settling the gryphon pendant inside the open throat of his flowing white shirt. It glowed against his smooth tan skin.

"What do you plan to do next?" Stefan asked his newfound kinsman.

"I plan to claim your kingdom."

Chapter 25

Roland lay with his eyes shut, contemplating the strange and wonderful dream he'd just had. He felt a hand on his shoulder, and mumbled for Stefan to give him a few more minutes.

"I want to set this memory in my head so I can daydream about it later. It was the most amazing—ow, my head! How much wine did I drink last night, Stefan? Must be why the dream was so vivid. Get me that brown doublet—I can't miss my fencing lesson again. Master Fortenbraes will not go easy on me this time."

His eyes fluttered open—to find Mendana gazing down at him, an anxious frown marring the smooth beauty of her brow.

"By the Flames, it was no dream..." he breathed.

She slipped an arm under his shoulders, and he realized with a flush of embarrassment that he was lying with his head in her lap. He struggled to sit, and she guided him upright.

"Are you all right, my lord?"

He stared around at the fallen bodies of companion and enemy alike.

"What happened? I don't remember...and the others were already down..."

Suddenly, he became aware of a cool breeze on his chest and looked down to find his jerkin open and the pendant gone.

"The amulet!" he cried. "What happened to it?" He tried to stand, but Mendana laid a restraining hand on his arm. He hissed with pain, and she dropped her hand with a cry.

"You are hurt! Let me see." She ripped away the jagged remnants of his sleeve and examined the wound then heaved a sigh of relief. "It is not deep. It will heal clean." Dampening the rag with water from her pack, she bathed the wounded arm.

"Mendana, I must find that pendant." He struggled to rise, but she shook her head.

"Don't trouble yourself. Stefan took it." The deep bitterness in her tone was unlike anything he had ever heard her use when speaking of her brother.

"It *is* his by right."

"He's a fool!" she spat, confusing him more than ever while she bound his arm with a strip ripped from the hem of her tunic that was cleaner than anything else available. He winced as she jerked the bandage tight but said nothing.

Following her line of sight as she glared past his shoulder, he saw Stefan engaged in quiet conversation with a strange elf who loomed over Dèodar's sprawled form. Even from where he sat, he could see the gleam of the golden Sunstone around the stranger's neck.

As he watched, the two clasped hands. Then the tall elf vanished, and a bird soared upward and arrowed away from the lake.

"Who was that, Mendana? I don't understand."

"That was the infamous Ravenwing everyone is so enamoured of," she growled. "I don't want to talk about him. Can you stand? Many of these men are only sleeping. We must get far away from here before they wake. See to Collyn. I must tend to Dèodar."

Feeling a little dizzy, and very lost, Roland nodded. As he gingerly rose to his feet, he watched Mendana cross the gully to her cousin's side, ignoring Stefan as she passed him. An expression of infinite, wistful sorrow crossed her brother's face; then Stefan turned away to lean against a nearby cliff. The elven prince's limp was worse than ever—it looked as if he could no longer bend the knee.

A slight, slender figure in rough homespun and ragged cap went to stand beside Stefan. With a start, Roland recognized the little thief from the Woodwatch Ferry market.

"Where did that one come from?" he wondered aloud. He had certainly missed a great deal while he was unconscious. He winced at the memory, raising a hand to the back of his head. His fingers came away bloody, but as he explored the damage, he decided the slight gash at the base of his skull wasn't terribly serious.

He staggered to Collyn's side. The riverman lay facedown on top of one of his attackers. His hands circled the man's throat, and the villain's head was twisted at an awkward angle. Roland whistled. *Collyn* gave good account of himself, he thought in admiration. There is certainly much to be learned about Collyn Silverbrook.

Prying loose the big man's fingers, he gently turned Collyn onto his back. His face was battered almost beyond recognition. His nose appeared broken, and both eyes were already starting to blacken. Collyn's breathing appeared labored, and Roland gently cleaned away some of the blood clogging his nose to ease it.

A cursory examination for further injuries located

a bruised or broken rib, but no other serious damage the prince could discover.

"Collyn," he murmured. "Collyn, wake up, my friend. We need you."

With a muffled groan, Collyn blinked and gradually regained his senses. "Where am I?"

"We're still near the lake. Wheels are turning, and I don't know where they'll take us, but one thing is for sure—we must hurry and get out of here. Most of these villains will be ready to fight again soon."

Collyn sat up, moving with extreme caution. His hand went to his throat, checking to make sure his arrowhead was still in place around his neck.

"Aye." He glanced around him. "Where's Dèodar?"

"Over there. Mendana's examining him."

"The queen? What's she doing here?"

"I haven't a clue, but she and Stefan came after us. I'll get her to wrap that rib for you."

Collyn shook his head. "You can do it. I'll explain how. I've had plenty of practice," he added ruefully, removing his shirt, and handing it to the prince. "Tear this into strips and wrap it as tightly as you can. Don't worry, you can't make it too tight."

Roland followed his instructions and bound the rib in place.

"Can you stand now? We must get moving."

"I believe so." Leaning heavily on Roland's arm, Collyn rose to his feet. The prince glanced over at Stefan as they passed him on their way to Mendana and Dèodar.

Stefan stood against the cliff, his weight balanced on his good leg while he chewed pensively on his lip, an expression Roland had seen many times in their years together. Stefan was off in his own world, his thoughts far from the reality of the moment.

I wonder what he's gotten into his head now? Roland mused.

When he and Collyn joined the others, he look one look at Mendana's flushed cheeks and grim frown, and asked, "What's wrong?"

"Stefan gave his birthright to Ravenwing," muttered Mendana, her voice choked with anger. "It is his heritage, and he handed it over without a murmur."

"He must have a reason, Princess," replied Roland. "Stefan has never been thoughtless. Headstrong, maybe. Stubborn, surely. But never thoughtless."

"Speaking of heritages, my prince," Collyn reminded him, "don't you have something for the lady?"

"Ah, yes!" The prince reached deep inside his shirt and pulled out the Moonrise pendant, still wrapped in the scrap of folded fabric. "That much at least went well." He handed the packet to Mendana with a bow. "The Moonstone, My Queen."

She caught her breath with a reverent sigh as she unfolded the soft cloth.

"It is just as I remembered it," she said, her voice hushed.

"May I?" Roland reached for the amulet, but she shook her head.

"No." She turned to Collyn, her sea-green eyes grave as she studied the trader's face. "Master Silverbrook, will you fasten it for me?"

Roland scowled as a deep flush suffused Collyn's tan cheek. He had forgotten that aspect of their quest.

Andundal's distrust of the riverman was unjustified, and it rankled to see Collyn humiliated this way. But the legend of the Moonstone, and the inability of the wicked to handle its purity, would settle the matter beyond further question.

"A test, my lady?"

"It will answer the question, once and for all, Master Silverbrook," replied Mendana. She laid a gentle hand on the big man's arm. "Before these witnesses."

"The test will only prove what I already know—that Collyn Silverbrook is a good and loyal man."

"I am sure you are correct, Roland," Mendana soothed. "Please, Master Silverbrook." She swept her hair aside.

"As you command." Collyn reached for the Moonstone then carefully lifted it from its bed of cloth. He held it flat on his palm for a long moment, eyes locked with Mendana's. Finally, he moved behind her, fastened the chain around her throat and stepped away. The stone in the pendant glowed like reflected moonlight.

"Thank you, Master Silverbrook."

"My lady." Collyn bowed low.

"The stone appears content," Roland said with a crooked grin.

"Aye," Mendana replied, turning to him, and stroking the stone with a tentative finger. "*Itheamia, ethia ionavo*. Thank you for returning it to me."

"You are welcome, my lady. *Enirmae*." The word was still unfamiliar to him, but her eyes shone in appreciation.

I could get lost in those eyes and drown...

***

Stefan didn't notice the exchange, lost in contemplation of his conversation with Ravenwing. The wizard's plan was a noble one but doomed to fail. It would almost certainly lead to his death—and yet, none of the rest of them had even a whisper of a prayer of carrying it off.

"Least of all me," he murmured with a sigh.

His gaze followed the path Ravenwing had taken in his flight. Ah, to have the freedom to soar the skies—it was a wondrous dream. With a smile, he shook his head at his foolishness. He had chosen his path and now ran along it at full speed. There was no turning back.

"Milord," whispered a tentative voice at his elbow.

He turned, surprised to find Ravenwing's boy at his side.

"Milord, them what the master put a spell on will be waking soon. 'Tis dangerous to stay here. We had best go quickly, and them others, too."

"Why are you still here? Why didn't you go with Ravenwing?"

The cutpurse snorted with derision. "D'ya see feathers on me back? I'm no shape-shifter. Besides, he asked me to keep an eye on you, he did. He's terrible worried about you, you know."

"No, I didn't know. Your name is...?"

"Daerci, milord." The little thief tugged off the ragged cap and swept him an awkward bow. Fine blond hair spilled halfway to his waist

Stefan gaped at the grimy figure in surprise. "You're a girl!"

"Aye, milord. Never said as I weren't."

He laughed. "No, I don't suppose you did. Of course, you never said you were, either. It might've saved you some rough treatment from my sister. Where did you learn to handle a sling like that?"

"A scrap o' leather and a bag o' rocks are practically free, milord—even I could afford that." She grinned at him. "All they need to master 'em is a lot o' practice. I've had plenty o' practice—and plenty cause as well. Rats taste fine when ye ain't had better for a week, milord."

"Please." He smiled down at her, topping her height by several inches. "Don't call me 'milord.' I am far too set in my ways, and will have far too many people do so later, to allow my friends to do so now. My name is Stefan."

"Am I yer friend?"

Stefan detected a familiar note of hunger in her voice. "We might be unlikely allies, Daerci, but any port is haven in a storm. You shall be my friend, and I yours, if you will have me. We both could use one right now. I fear I have just lost most of my old ones."

She grinned up at him, her face radiant.

"I'm proud to be yer friend, mi—Stefan."

He looked over at the others, now clustered around Dèodar. The light-hearted elf looked pale but composed. Stefan felt much better about his decision.

"Daerci," he whispered with soft urgency, "I need your help."

The little thief leapt to his side. "What can I do, mi—Stefan?"

"I must get away from here while they are all distracted, and I can't make it alone. I need your help. Lend me your shoulder."

"Aye." She slipped an arm around his waist, and he draped his over her shoulders.

"Quietly now," he murmured. "If we're careful, they'll never notice we're gone until it's too late."

"I don't understand, milord," she whispered back, taking great pains to place her feet so as not to jar his knee. "Where're we going, and why alone?"

"To follow Ravenwing, because no one else will."

"Why didn't ya say so! I know where the horses be. We can be off after the master before anyone be the wiser."

"Let's hope so," Stefan replied, his voice grim with resolve. If the others saw him leaving, they would only try to stop him. And he knew no one else would help the wizard.

Whatever Ravenwing had done in the past to merit Mendana's displeasure, he had earned Stefan's trust, and the prince refused to let the shape-shifter go into this battle alone.

He bit his lip as they skirted a large outcropping of rock and came upon a small group of horses. His knee was throbbing with greater than usual violence.

"You must help me mount, Daerci, and then we'll drive off the spare horses. The others mustn't follow us."

"As you command, milord."

Stefan allowed himself a faint smile of exasperation. *It will take a while to break her of that habit, I fear...*

They managed to get him onto one of the horses, then Daerci vaulted into the saddle of her own mount with supple ease, gathered up the reins of the extra animals, and nodded to Stefan. They stole away from the Ring of Tears at a walk.

When they were clear of the rock formations, Daerci set the extra mounts free, with a loud whooping yell to scatter them.

"Let's go!" Stefan cried, slapping his horse into a gallop.

Daerci rode at his heels.

***

"What was that?" Dèodar cocked his head in a gesture eerily reminiscent of Ravenwing.

"I didn't hear anything," Roland replied, frowning.

"It sounded like a shout."

Mendana glanced around the gully.

"Where is Stefan? And that thieving brat is gone as well. If Ravenwing hurts my brother…"

"Eeonathor was here?" cried Dèodar in disbelief.

"And you have him to thank for that lump on your head, *eathinae*. Remember what he has done to us."

"And you remember that he is my brother, Mendana Andundalia. Whatever he has done in the past, he will always be my brother."

"Please forgive me if I speak out of turn, My Queen," murmured Collyn, "but there is no time to argue the point now. Whether or not Stefan left to seek out Ravenwing or merely started home alone, he is not here. You say the men who attacked us will be awakening soon, and the odds are not enhanced by your presence, my lady. If we don't leave now, we'll soon experience the proof of that firsthand."

"Aye," Roland agreed. "We'll find Stefan, but first we must get away from here."

"How about now?" broke in Dèodar. "I believe I saw

someone stirring over there."

"Yes, let's hurry," Roland affirmed, flexing his right hand, and wincing at the resultant pain. "I don't want to fight again if I can avoid it." He flinched as he explored the wound on the back of his head with his fingers.

Mendana nodded.

"We should leave as quickly as we can. Father sent Captain Aerlann's patrol to the rescue, and they should be here any moment. They cannot find me here. They will deal with any of these bandits who remain."

"Shall we go find our errant brothers?" Dèodar grinned, "or shall we be sensible and return to the palace?"

Roland felt a surge of indecision. "My first duty is to my father—I must return to Crown Keep if the king will grant me permission. But I hate to leave you in trouble, Mendana."

"Father will not be pleased that Steavil has vanished again after running off to save you," she replied. "I fear returning to his court would not be your wisest choice, Roland."

"Why does Stefan always have to be difficult?" the prince groaned. His indecision was replaced by a familiar surge of anger. He felt it pounding in his temples as his teeth ground together. "He can be so selfish!"

"Come, now," chided Collyn. "Is that the truth?"

Roland had a flash of memory—Stefan's white face as the terrified child thought first of his master and shoved Roland into the branches of the tree as the savage hound rushed toward them. His anger ebbed as suddenly as it had flowed.

The prince sighed. "No, it's not. Stefan never gives his own needs or safety a second thought if someone else is in trouble. But what's he thinking, disappearing like this?"

"He's gone after Eeonathor, I wager," Dèodar said, "hoping to help." He shook his head. "He is an amazing man, my cousin."

"Well, I can do nothing more for Stefan," Roland decided, although he hated to abandon his oldest friend. "I love him like my own brother, but I must return to my own kingdom." He sighed. "My father and my own responsibilities must come first. I should never have delayed this long."

Mendana nodded, biting her lip to stop its trembling. He longed to brush away the tears he saw threatening like summer rain.

"Please understand, my lady. Stefan chose his own road, and I must leave him to it."

Mendana laid a hand on his.

"I understand, *entheiro,* and I know Steavil would as well. I have to." She buried her face in her hands, while her slender shoulders shook with sobs.

Roland took her into his arms without stopping to weigh the consequences. She leaned into him, and he stroked her soft hair.

"How can I leave without him, Roland? He was lost for so long. All alone..."

Roland inhaled deeply the light lavender scent perfuming her hair.

"My lady, we must trust him to Fate. We don't even know where to begin to look."

He lifted her chin, gazing down into the brimming

pools of her tear-filled eyes. Mendana searched his face, as if memorizing its every line.

"You are right," she gulped. "Come, we have *istionthi* in the caverns. They should be rested enough to carry double."

They eased around the rocks with extreme caution as the cutthroats yet breathing began to sit up. Besides the man Collyn had dispatched, three others lay crumpled and silent.

Hoofbeats in the distance resolved the debate.

"Here come the warders," Dèodar murmured. "I'd rather not be caught by Aerlann's patrol, either."

"Over here." Mendana led the way into the caverns.

Roland looked around with undisguised awe. It was his first glimpse of the elven gardens, and the crystalline flowers surrounding the stairway stopped his breath. Their delicate stone petals glimmered in the light of the magical lamps, and the soft tinkling murmur of falling water played a constant musical accompaniment.

He circled to take in the whole cavern. The pair of *istionthi* lying at rest beside the trough caught his eye. The animals panted, blinking their big eyes in the gloom. He moved to pat the neck of one, which scrambled to its feet and shied from his touch.

"They are highstrung beauties," Dèodar murmured fondly, soothing the animal with a caress. "Aren't you, *entheirae*?"

The animal butted his hand with a noise halfway between purr and whinny then lifted its head and licked the elf's chin. Dèodar laughed.

"We'd best be leaving, my prince," Collyn reminded Roland. "I've an uneasy feeling about home."

"Aye." Roland looked only at Mendana, his heart thudding in his chest. "If my Father was not in such danger..."

"I know," she whispered. And those two words spoke volumes.

"Time is short, my lord," Collyn reminded Roland.

The prince turned to the animals and tried to catch the reins of the male.

"Let me help with that," the ranger said with a smile, soothing the beast. "You'll have to be gentle. Collyn, I suggest you mount first."

With a nod, the big man eased into the saddle as Dèodar held the animal steady.

"Now you, *entheiro*."

Collyn offered a hand, and Roland settled in front of him.

Dèodar leapt to the back of the other *istionthi*. He reached down and helped Mendana into the saddle in front of him.

"The caverns go all the way to the far edge of the forest," he said. "You'll have to leave the *istionthi* underground, but you'll be at the verge of the plain you call the Golden Heath. You should be back to Crown Keep by tomorrow sunset if you ride all night." His mobile features grew still and solemn. "I envy you the journey. We must face the king. I do not relish explaining how we lost his son—again."

"We did not lose Steavil!" Mendana retorted, her voice hot as she flushed crimson.

"Ah, then, you know where he is?" Dèodar kicked his mount into motion.

"I'll find him," she vowed.

They came to a fork in the path, and Dèodar pointed down the left branch.

"There lies your way. Good fortune, my friends."

Roland gazed one more time into Mendana's eyes, suddenly realizing they had come to what might be a final parting of their ways. He could read something indefinable in their gentle sea-green depths and impulsively reached out—to find her hand in his.

"*Euae astreal,*" he murmured. "My star..."

"My prince...*ethia ionavo*. Rest easy, all will be well. *Ithneimi endo, evleeo,*" Mendana whispered as Dèodar urged the animal along their road and her hand was pulled away.

Roland stared after the retreating pair. His Elven was sketchy, but he thought he understood what she had said. He just wasn't sure he dared to believe it.

***

Stefan and Daerci galloped away from the Ring of Tears then slowed to thread through a range of descending foothills toward the nearby outskirts of Mendana's Dark Wood. He looked around as they rode. There was a slim band of plain between them and the forest, and it was a barren wasteland, the grass dead and brown.

He understood the wisdom of planning his next move, but his head was a whirl of confusion.

"Somehow, I must follow Ravenwing, but is jumping down the Lion's throat the best way to do it?" he mused out loud.

"If that's where he be going, do we have a choice?"

The sun had begun to set by the time they reached the wood, and the slanting beams drew an answering flash of fire from the stone on his finger.

"By the gods, I forgot to return Roland's ring! I must get it back to him."

Daerci reached over and grabbed his arm.

"Please, Milord Stefan, kin it not wait? Me master is alone. He thinks he's invincible, but he's not. We must help him. We're his only chance."

"Poor chance at that," he sighed, frowning down at the ring. "But this stone is Roland's birthright."

"As the Sunstone pendant is yours, but didn't he give it you as freely as you gave the other? Please, milord. You kin return the ring to Prince Roland when Master Ravenwing is safe."

"I suppose you are right, but what use can we be to my cousin? If his magic cannot save him, how can I?" He pounded his fist on his left leg in impotent frustration. "What good am I to anyone with this?"

"As long as you sit that horse, you're as good a man as any, Steavil Andundalae. What comes after, we'll worry about then."

Stefan looked at her in astonishment.

"How do you know my true name?"

Daerci blushed, and the color rising in her cheeks lent a becoming sparkle to her green eyes.

"The master told me. He told me a lot about you—and your sister," she added hastily.

"I wish I could say the same. No one has told me much of anything. I don't know where to turn, or who to trust. My life was much simpler when I was just Stefan, Roland's squire, instead of Steavil, Andundal's son."

"I swear, milord, you certainly are a one fer feeling sorry fer yerself! By the Flames, but yer enough to drive one mad. Fate deals the deck, milord, and sometimes deals dirty, but ya kin only play the cards She gives ya. Moaning to yerself will never change that. So, let's get busy with a plan that relies on our strengths rather than bellyaching about our weaknesses."

Stefan stared at the little thief then burst into peals of laughter.

"Well said, little one. You must've been sent to be my voice of reason—I have been Roland's for so long my own has grown rusty from lack of use. Shall we make camp and start in the morning rested?"

He swung down off his horse, barely catching himself as his bad leg took more of his weight than he anticipated. His breath hissed between his teeth.

Mendana's handiwork was beginning to wear off. The pain was flooding back into his knee as if it had missed his company.

"A comfortless camp 'twill be," Daerci grumbled, sliding from her own mount with graceful ease. "I weren't thinking, not to snag the packhorse as well."

"Such is fortune. Don't fret. I've a flask of Veisthi and a flint in my pouch. We may not share a sumptuous meal or silken tent tonight, but at least we'll have a fire."

He glanced about him with a frown. The trees were stunted, twisted shadows in the fading sunlight. The forest might once have been a place of beauty, but there was something foreboding about it in the twilight.

"I'm sure Mendana will not begrudge us a few fallen branches from her woodland."

"I hope not, milord." Daerci murmured, making a sign against evil. "Elves can be terrible cruel."

"I cannot blame you for your attitude," Stefan

sighed. "I was raised on the same stories myself, but it still pains my heart. Especially since I have found the opposite to be true. All the elves I've met are wise and gracious. Has my name smoothed my way, or are the stories as false as I am beginning to believe?"

Daerci merely shrugged and scowled.

"She *is* my sister," he said at last, his defense mirroring Dèodar's of Ravenwing. Eyes downcast, he busied himself collecting scattered twigs for tinder to start a fire.

"I am sorry, Yer Highness.I forgot meself."

He sensed a wall rising between them and sighed. He had hoped for an ally, but he feared the differences between their peoples would prove too much for the girl to ignore.

"Would it make you feel easier to leave the wood, Daerci? It is dusk now, but we could probably find shelter somewhere on the plain before full dark."

"Where the eyes of the night could spot us a hundred leagues away? No, milord prince, here we shall stay."

He winced at the cold formality of her tone, remembering her spirited attack minutes before in defense of Ravenwing.

"I'll start the fire then move off under the trees. I... don't wish to cause you any discomfort."

"Don't be a fool. Share the fire. I could use the company."

"But you so obviously dislike us."

"I dislike elves."

"I am an elf, and so is Ravenwing."

"Aye, but yer different, and so's the master."

"What makes you so loyal to Ravenwing when you

bear so obvious a grudge against elves in general? You risk everything to help him, and you aren't even his kin."

As he talked, Stefan piled the gathered twigs and a double handful of leaves in order to make a small fire. He had often lit one in Roland's chambers, but those controlled circumstances little prepared him for such a task in the open wilderness. He would no sooner strike a spark from the flint than the wayward breeze snuffed it out. The sharp, white-hot scent of the sparks refused to soften into the comforting smell of woodsmoke.

His heart sank. He wanted to prove something to Daerci, and to himself, but the fire would not cooperate.

"Why won't the Flames-damned thing light?"

"Let me do it," Daerci grunted, taking the flint and steel from him. She added a handful of dead grass and sparked it into flame with a deft twist of her wrist. She blew gently on the tiny fire, feeding it into a crackling blaze. Warm gold flames licked upward, against the night, filling the air with their perfume. "I'll get some bigger sticks to keep it going."

Stefan sighed. *I am beginning to feel that incompetence is my strong point.*

He stared into the flames, as she moved quickly around the clearing, gathering firewood. He found some measure of solace in their warm depths. Slumping beside the fire, his bad knee stretched out stiff before him, he idly tossed twigs into it. Pain throbbed in time to the beating of his heart.

Daerci returned and piled a few of the branches on the fire then sat back on the far side, her knees drawn up under her chin.

"I'm sorry, Stefan," she murmured, her voice nearly inaudible over the crackle of the flames. "I didn't mean to hurt yer feelings."

He raked the hair out of his eyes with another heavy sigh.

"It's just...I grew up with those same fears. How will I ever be able to combat such prejudices when I become king? I may be elven by birth, but I was raised human, same as you. I only want to unite both my peoples."

"Perhaps you will. With Prince Roland for yer ally, there's a true chance of it. But as long as that devil sits in Crypticia Keep, there's no hope. That's why the master went to confront him."

"Why do you call Ravenwing 'master?'"

"Because he *is* my master. He taught me everything I know."

"How did you come to travel with him?"

"He saved me from slavers in Fangspur Cove. I was about to be shipped south across the sea."

"No one lives across the Southern Sea," Stefan scoffed, plucking at something growing in the needles carpeting the forest floor. He threw it down with a grimace of disgust when he realized it was a slimy, mutated mockery of a mushroom. "No one."

"Tell that to the strange crews putting into Dangerous Harbor. They're wicked creatures, more animal than man, and they like their females young."

"How old are you, Daerci?"

Stefan took a swig from the Veisthi flask and passed it to her. She raised it and took a swallow, wiping her mouth with her sleeve as she passed it back.

"Sixteen."

"Are you Ravenwing's slave?"

"Were you Roland's?"

Stefan opened his mouth to protest then stopped in stunned realization.

"I suppose, when it comes down to it, some people might say I was. But I never thought of myself that way. I always thought of myself as a brake to his coach." He laughed self-consciously. "Foolish, isn't it?"

"Not in the least. And what you feel for Roland, I feel for Eeonathor Ravenwing. If it weren't for him, I'd likely have died on that sea voyage," she continued, her voice soft and pensive as she stared into the heart of the flames. "I'd have leapt overboard rather than submit to the beasts. I owe him me life."

"So do I. That's why I came. I just hope I can help rather than hinder."

"Stefan, 'tis a wise man who knows when to doubt himself, but a fool who cannot trust himself," Daerci scolded, her voice exasperated. She stretched out beside the fire. "Brood if ye like. I'm going to sleep. Tomorrow brings hard choices."

"I'll keep watch."

Her breathing soon leveled out in slumber, but he sat, staring into the fire, for hours, trying to calm the chaos of his thoughts.

***

Mendana allowed herself the luxury of leaning against Dèodar's sturdy shoulder as they rode. She was very tired. And frustrated. Events had taken a decidedly unwelcome turn, thanks to Ravenwing's interference, and her loyalty was torn to shreds. She wanted to follow and protect Stefan, but her heart rode with Roland, and her duty was to her father.

"*Ionavia*," murmured Dèodar, his breath stirring her hair. "May I ask you something?"

"Yes?" She stifled a yawn with the back of her hand. After the sleepless night and the stresses of the day, the motion of the *istionthi* was lulling her into drowsiness. "What is it?"

"That day in the clearing, was Eeonathor's embrace an unwelcome one?"

She turned to look up at him. There was an unaccustomed sadness deep in his eyes. She longed to wipe it away but felt she owed him the truth.

"No. I won't lie to you, *entheirae*. I thought I loved your brother once. He was dashing and so..." She searched for the word she wanted. "...different," she finished, dissatisfied with the description but lost for anything better.

Dèodar smiled a crooked grin.

"Aye. 'Different' he's always been. And now?"

Her face hardened.

"He betrayed us."

"Did he?"

"He bragged that he was being paid to ambush you!"

"He didn't do too thorough a job for his gold, did he? Somehow, I doubt the Lion just wanted his rival knocked out for a few minutes."

"You might all have been killed."

"But instead, none of us was seriously hurt. And his minions weren't trying very hard to injure—clubs against Collyn? Why not swords? Besides, Stefan seems to trust him—"

"Stefan is a fool!"

"So everyone keeps saying, often to his face. Good for building a nervous boy's self-confidence."

"He is not a boy! He is a grown man."

"Who was treated as a child until three days ago. Think how confused he must be. And no one helps him, only chides him for a fool."

"Dèodar, may I ask you something?"

"It's your turn," he said with a chuckle.

"Why do you defend Eeonathor so hotly? That day in the clearing...I saw your face. You would have killed him at a word."

"That day in the clearing, I was angry and hurt. I did love you so, Mendana. I do still, in a different way. Eeonathor was boldly claiming what I had been denied. I would indeed have killed him at that moment. And I have often wished since for a chance to apologize.

"Whatever else he is, whatever he has done, he is my brother, *evleeia*. I love him. And I haven't seen him since that day, more than fifteen years gone.

"I realize your separation from Stefan was hard, but at least you thought him dead. I've known all along that Eeonathor lived, and yet never got to tell him I'm sorry. To know he was so close, and I missed this opportunity is not an easy thing." He looked down at the silver band on his little finger. "All I have left of him is this ring."

"Dèodar, I would like to offer you an apology."

"Why, Princess?" he asked, his voice tinged with astonishment.

"Because I hurt you. I truly am sorry."

"Don't worry, *ionavia*. My heart healed of those

bruises long since. Besides, I think you are destined for another."

"But will I ever see him again?" She sighed.

"Undoubtedly. If he lives."

***

Roland and Collyn rode on in silence; he was grateful to Collyn for keeping his own counsel. The prince was in no mood for idle conversation.

Suddenly he reined in with a little cry of shock.

"What is it, my lord?" Collyn asked.

"The little fool! Stefan didn't go *with* Ravenwing, he went *after* him, and Ravenwing—"

"Was traveling to Crypticia. To beard the Lion."

Roland's heart sank. Stefan was ill-equipped for such a venture

"We must go back. We have to stop that idiot before he kills himself." He started to turn the animal.

Collyn reached out a hand to stop him.

"Roland, you never spoke truer than when you told the queen that Stefan chose his own path. Your first duty, painful though it may seem, is to your people, and *your* kingdom. I know he is your friend, but his is but one life."

"But..."

"Norfulk could easily have destroyed your father and subjugated your people in the length of time we have been away from Crown Keep. Andundal's messenger will have met with suspicion at best, even if your father believes him. If he even made it to your father, which I fear is too unlikely to hope. Only your physical presence can hope to mend any breach the

Lion's insinuations have caused."

Roland sighed, kicking the creature forward.

"You're right, as always. And in view of your uncanny logic, Collyn Silverbrook, I hereby appoint you high advisor of my kingdom...if I ever get one."

He felt the man stiffen behind him.

"Do not mock me, Lord. It ill suits you."

"I'm not mocking you." Roland protested, twisting around. "I'll need an advisor I can trust. I always assumed I'd have Stefan as a sounding board, but he'll have his own troubles, among his own subjects, and no time for mine. Please, Collyn, I ask you now. Will you be my high advisor?"

The riverman frowned.

"You're serious?"

Roland nodded.

"Aye, my lord prince. You do me great honor."

The *istionthi* skittered to a stop inside another large cavern, dancing nervously at the foot of a flight of stone steps.

"We must've arrived," commented the prince, sliding to the ground. "I would have liked to go back for our horses, but I suppose we wouldn't have gotten through the forest on them anyway. I'll have to send someone for them later. If we push ourselves, perhaps we can reach Crown Keep earlier than Dèodar predicted."

Collyn nodded. He dismounted and slapped the animal on its flank.

"Go home, my beauty. Tell that scoundrel Dèodar that we have safely returned above." He turned to Roland. "I wonder if I shall ever see that rogue again?"

"Only time will tell, my friend." Roland started up

the staircase. Then, struck by a thought, he turned back to Collyn. "Besides, we might've had some trouble had we shown up at the inn. After all, I'm dead."

Collyn laughed. "An undead king might prove immensely popular, my lord. Perhaps it can be arranged."

Roland sobered as quickly as he had laughed.

"I only pray I am not yet any kind of king. My father has many years left to rule. If Norfulk has murdered him..." The statement remained unfinished, but his eyes grew cold.

"I will gladly kill the Lion for you," Collyn replied, his tone grim.

"Let's hope it won't come to that. Though I know in my heart there will inevitably be bloodshed." With a heavy sigh, the prince continued up the stairs and examined the face of the rock covering the exit. "I can find no mechanism. It must be voice commanded. Let's see just how good my Elven has become."

Frowning in concentration, he repeated Captain Aerlann's command in a halting murmur. "*Andundal sti...stimariali.*" There was a reluctant groan of protest, but the rock slid open, revealing a small clearing near the edge of the forest.

Collyn gestured Roland aside and stepped cautiously through the doorway.

"Clear, my lord." he whispered, and Roland followed him out into the slanting rays of the setting sun.

A gentle breeze played among the trees, and the prince took a deep breath of fresh air.

"I know the forest is the same, but it feels so much more...human on this side."

"Aye, but we're still on Andundal's land, and he'll not be pleased with the queen's report. I suggest we hurry, my lord."

"Wise counsel, High Advisor. I knew you would be a worthy choice. Come on, it'll be far too dark to see our way out of here before much longer."

Roland led the way out of the wood with all possible speed, but by the time they reached its outermost fringes, they were stumbling through darkness. The moon sent down shafts of liquid pearl that occasionally managed to pierce the trees, but, as they stepped out of the forest, turned the plain to a deeply shadowed woodcut.

They started forward, the plain stretching before them in silver splendor. Suddenly, there was a soft whicker behind them. Roland whirled. Noble and Astreal were tied at the edge of the wood.

"It seems we were anticipated, my lord." Collyn led the way to the horses then ran a sure hand across the gelding's flank. "They seem to be well."

Roland examined the dainty mare.

"Look, there's a note here, and full saddlebags."

"What does the note say?"

Puzzling out the flowery letters by the light of the moon, Roland read aloud.

"'Thought you might need a little help, my friends. Ride like the wind. Your father needs you—Ravenwing.'" He stared at Collyn, eyes wide. "How...?"

"'Tis better not to look a gift horse in the mouth, they say," said Collyn with a grin. "The point is, he's done it." He stroked Astreal's soft nose. The mare danced skittishly at the end of her reins, avoiding his touch.

Roland stepped forward to calm her, and Collyn looked over at him.

"I'm sorry, my lord, but the mare could never hold my weight, even if she were willing. You'll have to get her to carry you, or ride double on the gelding."

"Astreal has never borne anyone but Stefan. He raised her from a foal."

"You must convince her otherwise. 'Tis a long walk to Crown Keep."

Roland whispered soothingly to the high-spirited mare in his broken Elven, and gradually she quieted, rolling her eyes as he eased into the saddle. Without a word, he turned her head toward home and clicked his tongue, knowing better than to kick such a high-strung animal into action.

She bounded forward, and he leaned into her gallop. Pounding hooves beat an urgent tattoo on the hard-packed earth of the plain as the high grasses swished past his thighs with the sting of countless lashes, whipping him to greater speed.

His heart told him there was no time left to waste.

Chapter 26

Mendana and Dèodar reached the Elven stronghold near sundown. He leapt lightly down from the istion-thi's back, slipping a hand under her elbow as she slid from the animal with a weary sigh.

"You should rest," the warder counseled. "You are in no condition to face the king's wrath tonight."

"It won't get any easier. I'd rather get it over with."

"Then I'll come with you. Perhaps I can bear the brunt of the blame."

"But you didn't do anything!"

"I'd rather he blamed me than lay the burden on Roland."

Mendana sighed. *If only all my people were as willing to trust the humans as Dèodar. I fear he is right to worry about Father's reaction.*

"Dèodar, the fault belongs to Steavil alone. His own rash foolishness drove him to this fate."

"Or his rare act of courage. The prince is brave, if inexperienced. He goes into certain danger to save a man he never met before today yet trusted with his birthright. Nevertheless, the king will need a scapegoat. Shall we go?"

She nodded reluctantly. Logic warned that Dèodar might come to regret saving her from Andundal's wrath. She could see no way to avoid the coming confrontation. Her father had been so overjoyed to regain his son—and now Stefan had rushed headlong into who-knew-what danger alone in aid of someone their father had banished.

She felt so helpless. Andundal would never let her go after Steavil—she would be lucky to ever leave her room unescorted again. And knowing Roland must save his own kingdom had not made that parting any easier.

She was torn between her brother and the man she loved, yet trapped at home, unable to aid either one.

***

Ravenwing fluttered to a stop on the inside sill of a small barred window at Crown Keep just as the sun set in a sullen blaze of fire. A guttering torch beside the heavy door opposite the window provided the only light in the chamber. In the corner, his quarry slumped against the wall, arm draped across one bent knee. The prisoner's forehead rested on the propped arm.

Cocking his head, the wizard stepped off the windowsill, transformed by the time he reached the floor.

"Leithan," Eeonathor called softly. "Leithan, I have come to help."

The young messenger looked up, and Ravenwing drew in his breath with a hiss. Leithan's eye was blackened, and his lip swollen to twice its normal size—injuries with which he was all too familiar.

"Who are you? How did you get in here?"

"A friend. That is all that is important at the moment. Who did this?" Ravenwing hunkered down beside the boy.

"Does it matter?"

"Did you see King Frederick?"

"They never let me get that far—you'd think no human ever sported dark hair and green eyes. When I said my message was for the king alone—"

"I can imagine." He lifted the boy's chin with a gentle hand. "Let me look at that eye. I can heal at least some of the damage for you."

Leithan jerked away. "What good would it do to heal it? They plan to execute me."

"Frederick would allow that?" Ravenwing's heart contracted in his chest. Would the human king really go so far? Was there any true hope for reconciliation?

"The king is ill, many whisper dying. I doubt he even knows I've come." Leithan shifted position with an involuntary wince of pain. "Everything they say about humans is true. They didn't even give me a chance."

"Do not judge them too harshly, lad." He daubed a bit of salve from the pouch of medicines he always carried on the blackened eye, chanting a healing phrase. "Their king is ill, and their prince is missing. They are frightened. But don't give up hope—Roland is on his way home. He will see you freed."

"If it's not too late."

Ravenwing laid a hand on the youth's shoulder. "All will be well, *inithi entheirae*. After all, you are the youngest—the best and brightest hope of the entire Elven race." He grinned. "What do you think my uncle would do to me, if I stood idly by and let the humans put you to death?"

"Your uncle...?" Leithan peered more closely at the wizard. "Are you the one they call Ravenwing?"

"Some call me by that name."

"Why don't you just spirit me away, my lord?" asked

Leithan, his face lighting with eagerness. "The whole kingdom whispers tales of your powers. Even if the king forbids your name."

"Whisking you away would just bring the wrath of the humans down on the Forest. You are their prisoner, and if you escape, they'll start remembering that they consider elves their enemies. As it stands, they are willing to treat us as mere children's stories—dismiss us as harmless. It is not yet time for that impression to change."

"But..."

"You must wait for Roland. He will see you freed, I promise you."

Eeonathor murmured the words of a spell, and Leithan went rigid under his hand with a little gasp. Then the boy's eyes drifted closed

"Sleep, little one," murmured the wizard. "The spell will help the pain. I wish a spell could heal the rift between the races with such ease."

For now, he must return to Crypticia before Norfulk grew suspicious of his absence. It was not yet time to reveal his hand. It was a dagger's edge he danced on, and he could not afford to slip.

***

Stefan woke with a start, jarred awake as his chin hit his chest. He groaned, rubbing at a kink in his neck.

Some sentry I proved to be. He gazed around him, trying to gather his scattered wits.

Daerci lay fast asleep on the other side of the dying embers, her face tranquil. She seemed much more vulnerable in repose. Stefan's lips crooked in a lopsided smile

What an odd pair Fate has thrown together, and yet we seek to take on the world alone.

He sighed, staggering to his feet to stretch cramped muscles. How long had he slept sitting up? Fatigue fogged his thoughts. From the tightness in his back, it felt like hours. Stepping away from the camp to the fringe of trees, he relieved himself.

Restless, he moved around the campfire in an expanding circle. The fire gave off fitful light, being now more coals than flame. The scent of woodsmoke would normally be comforting but now only intensified the underlying stench of decay permeating the forest. The hiss and pop of the dying fire was the only sound, except for the soft rustle and drag of his steps in the dessicated fallen leaves.

Something about the trees made him uneasy. It was more than just the stink of corruption. Everything seemed...tainted. Some evil had invaded Mendana's kingdom, and he felt a compulsion to know what.

He was ten yards from the fire when they attacked.

Creatures the size of house cats swept down from the trees on strong leathery wings. They circled just beyond his reach, chittering and snarling, horrid mockeries of the plump flying squirrels he and Roland had chased as children. These perversions had sharp claws curved like talons and glistening fangs that would pierce flesh like needles.

One of the beasts darted at him. Lightning-fast, it struck at his face. He threw up his hand to protect himself and cried out as the razor-sharp teeth sank deep into muscle. The creature wrapped all four legs around his arm and began sucking like a greedy infant.

Loathing welled up inside him. He bashed the abomination against the solid trunk of the nearest tree until the beast went limp. Even then, its fangs stayed embedded in his flesh.

With a shudder, Stefan wrenched the dead monstrosity loose, tearing a sizable chunk of meat from his palm. The curving talons scratched deep rents in his arm. He threw the thing from him as he stumbled toward the fire.

"Daerci! Daerci, wake up!" He practically fell into the coals, tossing frantic handfuls of tinder onto the embers to revive the flames, and following them with a couple of larger branches, lucky not to smother it completely.

The—things—circled just outside the firelight, swirling horrors of leather and fur. The situation would have felt ludicrous if not for the fierce throbbing in Stefan's hand and the dripping blood, which argued for their deadly intent.

Daerci woke with the full control of one used to sudden rousing, one hand already reaching for the sling at her hip. She needed no explanation, just began launching her sling stones with cool efficiency.

The rodents dropped with sullen thumps like rotten fruit. As they fell, Stefan thrust a burning brand onto each, and they burst into blue-green flame. A noxious reek filled the air as the creatures burned. But for every creature felled, another two took its place. They were making no headway against the onslaught.

After what seemed like hours of fighting a losing battle, Daerci panted, "I'm running out of stones." Her voice was grim. "What do we do then?"

Stefan shook his head, too weary to speak. His right hand felt as if it had been plunged into a snowbank, numb and cold.

One of the creatures emitted a high, imperious cry, and, as abruptly as they had appeared, all of the survivors soared into the air.

"Thank the gods," Stefan croaked, pointing toward the east. "Dawn."

The creatures wheeled for a moment, shifting, and scuffling to establish pack order, and then flew off toward the heart of the wood.

Stefan sank to the ground, wracked by violent shudders.

"Let me see yer hand." She reached for his hand.

He pulled it back with an impatient shake of his head. "I'll be all right. Just let me...sit here a moment..."

She swung her loaded sling with studied casualness.

"Will you let me tend to yer hand, or shall I knock ye out first?"

"Oh, all right." Too exhausted to fight with her, he thrust out the bloodied, swollen hand.

Daerci clicked her tongue over the mess and doused the wound with water, rinsing away dried blood with patient care.

"I'll say this fer you, milord—pain seems to have made you its personal manservant."

Stefan managed a weak grin.

"I fear you're only too right," he murmured, wincing as she sponged away the last of the blood and exposed the raw flesh. A jagged hole about half an inch in diameter was torn deep into the meat of his hand. The edges of the wound showed a vivid discoloration, and the deadening cold now radiated upward along his arm.

"Those were nasty little beasties, and I don't like the looks of that wound. I'm afraid they might be venomous, Lord Stefan. Best let me bleed it more."

"What makes you so sure?"

"Me master's the finest healer I ever knew. D'ya think he's taught me nothing these long years?"

"How long could you possibly have traveled with him?"

"Four years now—five, come winter proper."

"Then you were..."

"Very young to be a concubine. Aye. But not all men are fine gentlemen like you, milord," she said with dry irony, dragging the point of her dagger across the wound to reopen it.

Stefan bit back a hiss of pain. He ground his teeth when she began to squeeze out the bad blood.

"That should help, Lord Stefan," she announced at last. She tipped the Veisthi flask over his hand, and liquid fire rippled through his arm to counteract the deadening chill of the poison.

He moaned.

"I'm sorry for the pain, but 'tis necessary."

"I understand," he murmured. "Don't worry. I've had worse."

"That I don't doubt." She tsked, ripping a length of fabric from the hem of her shirt to bind up the wound. "How does it feel?"

He flexed his fingers. He had full movement in them, though they felt a bit stiff.

"I'll live." He managed a crooked smile. "We should

go, but I feel so very tired." He yawned, fighting fatigue.

"Sleep for a bit, milord. We've a long journey ahead of us come full daylight."

"Even an hour would help."

"You'll have that, milord. Though little else, I fear."

Stefan stretched out beside the dying fire and was instantly asleep.

***

Roland pushed hard through the night, dismounting to walk the horses for a bit when necessary, but restless until they could ride again. Collyn kept silent, for which Roland felt an eternal gratitude. His feeling of disquiet grew in direct proportion to their proximity to Crown Keep. He dreaded what they would find at the castle, and that made him urge Astreal to even greater speed.

Some miles out from the castle, Collyn broke his silence at last.

"My lord, these horses are too well known. Even disguised, we will draw attention. I suggest we hide them and proceed on foot."

"Wise counsel, though I dread the delay. Where shall we hide them?"

"I have just the place. Follow me."

Just before dawn, they cantered into an abandoned farmyard. Although rundown, the buildings were otherwise neat. A small corral stood empty beside the sagging barn, and the fields grew only weeds.

"Welcome to my humble home."

Collyn slid off Noble's back and led the gelding toward the barn. Roland dismounted and followed, studying the farm with a thoughtful eye. An atmosphere of palpable hopelessness hung in the air, despite Collyn's dreams of making it work.

"I took so much for granted," he murmured.

"You are still very young, my lord."

"When I return home, things will change. I swear it."

"I'm sure you will do your best, Roland."

The prince led the little mare into a stall. Collyn forked down some hay for her while Roland hurriedly wiped her down—despite the urgency, he refused to let the horse suffer. The riverman did the same for Noble. Finished, he followed Collyn outside, plucking a spear of grass in the dooryard and chewing thoughtfully on the stem. The sharp tangy sap tingled in the back of his throat.

The first blush of dawn glowed in the east; then rose and gold replaced the mauve dominating the sky. Roland paused for a moment to admire the still beauty it lent the farm. The ramshackle buildings showed neat patches of lighter boards where Collyn had repaired them against the coming winter. The lines of the corral fence were spare and clean, and showed no breaks. A cord of wood made a neat windbreak beside the cabin door.

Roland took a deep breath of the clear, cold air. It smelled of wild hay in fallow fields and the musty haven of the barn at his back. Wind rustling leaves beside the farmhouse counterpointed the contented munching of the horses.

The tranquility of it, even in its present sadness, caught at his throat. Seeing it like this, he could begin to understand why Collyn felt so willing to fight for it.

Hearing a step, he spun to find the riverman beside him.

"'Tis the best I have to offer, my lord. Most of my stores have fallen into decay, but here is some dried meat and a bit of cheese. I also have some of Dèodar's magical Veisthi here—just a swallow or two, but it should be enough to wash down the meat. Eat a little. You'll need your strength. I fear what we find in the castle won't be to your liking."

Roland nodded, accepting the food with a word of thanks. He took a bite of the jerky, suddenly realizing how long it had been since his last meal. Ravenous, he wolfed down the scant repast with gusto.

"We should have a plan, my lord. We can't just stroll up to the castle. Even if our misgivings are unfounded, it would be foolhardy to ignore them."

Roland narrowed his eyes in concentration as he envisioned the castle compound and the surrounding town.

"I don't know which guards we can trust, so I don't want to approach the patrols. There *is* one weakness we might be able to take advantage of. There's a drainage ditch running out under the wall in the back of the town, behind the orchard. It's small and easily overlooked. It's the only entryway that's any distance from a patrolled gate, and there's only a simple grate covering it. Stefan and I used to crawl out through that pipe to play on the Heath. We should be able to uncover it without too much difficulty, though it's been several years since I've gone that way. At least, it's worth a try."

"One other suggestion, my lord," Collyn commented with a thoughtful frown. He stroked his chin. "Once we enter town, our problems are just beginning. To reach the castle, we must pass unnoticed. As you say—we don't know who to trust. That hair of yours is a flame that'll draw moths."

"What do you suggest?"

"I know a tincture that will darken your hair. A few other minor alterations, and your own father won't recognize you."

"Let's hope we have a chance to test that theory," replied Roland, mouth set in a grim line. "What must I do?"

Chapter 27

"Noile."

Andundal glanced up at the sound of her voice. He sat on his throne with his great horn bow across his lap, examining the bowstring. He had cast aside his robes of state for a practical leather tunic and dark green leggings. Rising to his full height as they entered, he set aside the weapon.

"Where have you been? When the guards reported your behavior, I—Where is your brother?"

Mendana took his arm and sat him back down. Dèodar remained standing at attention just inside the doorway.

"Noile," she began, her voice hesitant, "I...I have bad news."

She could see him die a little. Damn Stefan's stubbornness!

"Where is your brother?" he repeated in a hollow whisper.

"He has vanished."

"Vanished? What do you mean, vanished?"

Dèodar spoke for the first time. "They came after us as the result of the prince's vision."

"Mendana told me of the vision. I sent Captain Aerlann and his men." Andundal turned to his daughter. "Why did you follow? I told you to let the warders deal with the problem."

"Stefan couldn't give Aerlann any details of where the attack would occur..."

Dèodar continued his report. "An ambush had been laid. The prince and princess arrived before the warders. After the skirmish, Steavil followed Eeonathor from the battle." He hung his head. "We think he rides to Crypticia."

"And you didn't stop him! Where are the humans? They were your charge, Dèodar."

"When Prince Steavil disappeared, my wits were addled by a blow to the head, Your Majesty. I didn't see him go. 'Tis no excuse, but 'tis the truth. As for Prince Roland and his companion, they fulfilled their quest and returned to Crown Keep."

"By whose authority?" breathed Andundal with deceptive calm. His eyes narrowed into slits as his hands clutched the arms of his throne in a crushing grip.

Mendana could see the fury mounting and swiftly wracked her brain for some way to divert it.

"Mine," she murmured.

It proved the wrong choice.

"You are not queen in *this* realm, daughter. They rode under my sentence. How dare you release them!"

"Noile, please. If King Frederick held Steavil or me prisoner while we worried for your safety, would you be displeased if he released us? They were honorable men who fulfilled their charge. Let them go in peace."

"And what of your brother, Mendana? Shall I let him go in peace as well?"

"He made his choice, Father. He told no one when he left. We only guess he follows Ravenwing."

"Then I 'guess' someone will have to follow him." He glared at his nephew, his jaw tight with fury.

"As you command," murmured Dèodar, bowing.

"Father, no! It would be suicide. What chance has a lone elf against the Lion of Crypticia? At least Steavil has his size and relationship to Roland on his side. Norfulk will no doubt keep him alive as a hostage. It is not possible for him to know the truth about Stefan. We may yet have time to plan."

"What, then, do you propose, my daughter?"

"Time to think. Without a solid plan, everyone in the clan will die, not just Steavil." She met Andundal's glare and took a deep breath. "After all, he was dead to us for so long. If it will save the kingdom—"

"I should let him go back to being dead? This time irrevocably?"

She gave a miserable nod. "If it saves the kingdom, we have no choice."

***

With great reluctance, Stefan allowed Daerci's gentle shaking to bring him fully awake. It felt like he had just closed his eyes, but the sun already peeked over the tops of the trees. Several hours must have passed instead of the one she had promised.

"I'm sorry, milord. I couldn't bear to wake you sooner. You looked as if you really needed the rest."

"Thank you. I did." He stretched, testing the flexibility of his wounded hand. Although his fingers still felt stiff, they responded to his wishes. He prodded the bandage, finding a slight soreness, but nothing like the pain he expected. "You are a good healer, Mistress Daerci. You've learned your lessons well."

"I had an excellent teacher in yer cousin." She cocked her head, a habit he had observed in Ravenwing.

"May I ask ye something, milord? What caused the rift between yer House and me master? He don't realize how wistful he speaks of home."

"I wish I knew, but I'm as ignorant of it as you are. He told me only that he left home when I was a babe and seldom returned to either Wood. No one else will speak of it at all." He stirred the ashes of the fire to make sure it was completely extinguished then rose to his feet, dusting his hands. "It's time we moved on."

"Have we a plan, Lord Stefan?"

He flashed her a crooked grin. "Not exactly. As I see it, either two boys foolish enough to travel alone into the Lion's Den will be escorted into his presence, or Eeonathor will hear a rumor about them and come to intercept us. Personally, I'd rather face the Lion. As for you, I fear you'd do better without that mane of yours."

"I'll gladly cut me hair," she replied, pointing to his left hand, "if you'll remove that lodestone round yer finger. Any thief within ten miles will try and relieve ye of that ring if they catch even a glimpse of it."

Stefan slipped Roland's ring from his finger. "What shall I do with it?"

"Take off your tunic and shirt and I'll show ye."

He stared at her. "I beg your pardon?"

"Just do it, milord," she replied, her voice dry with amusement. "I promise not to ravish ye. I haven't the time."

Blushing furiously, Stefan did as she bade him. He watched with interest as she picked loose a piece of the hem in his shirt with the point of her dagger then drew a bodkin from her pouch.

"Give me the ring."

He handed it to her, and she slipped it inside the fold of the hem. She stitched up the sides of the little pocket with deft fingers then closed the top, securing the ring in place. "There you are. Now, wear yer shirt tucked in yer leggings at all times, with the tunic pulled over. 'Twill be safe unless ye're searched. In that case, nothing will hide it anyway."

She handed Stefan back his clothes, and he slipped into them with a grateful nod. The air carried a hint of frost, the strongest sign to date that winter fast approached.

As soon as he was dressed, she gave him her dagger.

"My turn." Turning her back to him, she flipped her hair over her shoulders so that it rained down in a soft golden cloud. "Have at it."

Stefan hesitated before reaching out and taking hold of the shimmering waves. It felt like raw cornsilk between his fingers, and his hand trembled at the touch.

"Please, Stefan," Daerci murmured, her voice hushed, "just get it over."

Taking a deep breath, he began hacking at the shining tresses with the sharp edge of the dagger. Soon, he had reduced it to a ragged mass ending just below her ears. He spirited a twist of the cuttings into his pouch, unsure why he did so. The rest of the fallen hair he swept into the remains of the campfire, spreading the entire circle with a thin layer of earth, and scattering a covering of twigs and leaves over the whole.

Together, they cleared the rest of the campsite to obliterate their presence in the glade. They worked in efficient silence, wrapped up in their own thoughts.

Stefan found his emotions in turmoil, and had to force himself to concentrate on the task at hand.

He tightened the girth on his saddle with a jerk. The horse stamped his foot, and Stefan mumbled an apology. The animal shook its head with a snort then bowed its great neck. He laughed and stroked its soft hide.

"You're right. I shouldn't take out my frustrations on you," he soothed.

"Are ye ready, milord?" Daerci asked as she swung into her saddle.

Stefan mounted the big roan with difficulty. "What I wouldn't give for Astreal right now," he said with a sigh.

"A sure way to be recognized fer yerself. That horse of yers is well known throughout the kingdom. Perhaps Prince Roland ain't traveled much, but stories of him have, and 'tis only natural that ye have played yer part in those tales."

"Really? And what do they say?"

"Merely tell of a serving boy brave enough to risk his life fer his prince instead of running fer safety, a boy who charms the birds off the trees and sings like a nightingale, a boy who, 'tis rumored, sees beyond time's veil and whispers of tomorrow. And many a maid there is who envies yer coal-black hair and lily skin, milord," she continued. "You ain't disguised because ye ride a different horse."

"Then 'tis a good thing we go to be caught."

"Do you really think this is a good idea, Lord Stefan?"

He could hear her doubt and turned to her with a wide smile reflecting the fact that he knew their quest was foolish—but was glad they were sharing the folly. "Not really. Do you have a better? I'm quite willing to discuss any option."

"Perhaps there's someone ye could go to fer help."

"Who? My family ostracized Eeonathor, and Roland has his own kingdom to consider. No, my friend, I fear there is no one else who can help. I must go forward. I would be glad of your companionship, but, if necessary, I shall go alone."

"That would be more than me life is worth. I best be alongside ye if we do find the master."

"Then let's ride."

He twitched the roan's head around and slapped it into motion, galloping away from the shadows of Dark Wood toward the heart of the wasteland.

***

Collyn's mixture did its work. When Roland examined the results in the water barrel beside the front door, his russet waves now hung in lank strands of dull muddy brown.

Inside the house, the riverman stuffed an old grain sack with straw and tied it across Roland's shoulders to create a hunch then covered it with one of his own loose shirts. It hung about the prince's knees like a smock, and Collyn jammed a wide-brimmed hat down over Roland's eyes.

He studied the results with a critical eye. "It'll have to do."

The battering he had taken in Ravenwing's ambush served to disguise his own features from the few in town who might recognize him.

Roland laughed. "What a sight we present. Even Father won't know me."

"Let's just hope you fool the townsfolk we meet. If you've ever trusted my counsel, Your Highness, trust it now. Let me lead in this venture. Play along with whatever I say. It's our only hope of getting the information you seek."

"I bow to your judgment, my friend. But we should go. I'm more and more anxious as to what we'll discover in town."

Collyn nodded, picking up a heavy quarterstaff leaning against the wall and tossing it to Roland, who caught the sturdy staff in one hand.

"Are you well versed with that, my prince?"

"I've had a few lessons."

"Well, keep them in mind. That is the weapon of the farmer, and will not arouse suspicion. Your sword you must lay by for now."

Roland undid his sword belt with reluctant fingers and handed it over with a rueful grimace.

"I feel rather lost without it."

Collyn climbed into the sleeping loft and tucked the sword securely into the thatch of the roof. He pulled handfuls over it to cover the scabbard.

"It should be safe—probably more so than we'll be," he promised, swinging down from the loft without bothering with the ladder. He secured a stout cudgel to the belt of his tunic. "Now, let's be off."

He retrieved a second staff from a neat stack of farm implements and led Roland out into the fallow fields.

"Cross-country to Crown Keep, even on foot, should take us less than half a day. We'll be there by nightfall.

Remember, follow my lead at all times."

Roland nodded, hefting the quarterstaff, and giving it an experimental swing.

"Let's go."

"Even before we encountered the elves, whispers ran rampant in Woodwatch Ferry. It was common talk at the inn," murmured Collyn in a grave voice as they walked. "Rumors abounded that the king had fallen ill in your absence—and those who knew you to be in town wondered why you still were. Others whispered darker thoughts. Any and all of the rumors could be true. If so, you must trust me and control your desire to rush in and rescue him. You must remember that you're no longer the prince. You're a serf."

"I understand," Roland murmured.

"If a better speaks harshly to you—and all are betters to a serf, my lord—nod and smile. If a courtier cuffs you, accept the blow. I'll not be with you at all times, so please remember what I've told you. Our lives may depend upon it. If you don't control your temper, Irthlan could very well become Norfulk's by right, not theft."

"But, Collyn, if my father is ill—"

"Trust me. You won't be able to save him if you rush in like a fool. Besides, we aren't even sure the rumors are true. Your father may be well and whole, for all we know. Let's at least verify our concerns before we panic."

He watched Roland bite back a hot reply and nodded to himself. He knew how difficult it would be for the willful prince to pretend servitude within his own capital. Roland's acceptance of the necessity was a good sign, the first stirrings of the king within the boy.

They walked for several hours before sighting the rough stones of the town wall. The prince pointed around back, and they worked their way to the rear. They halted behind a small rise about twenty yards from the orchard wall.

"There," Roland murmured. "The mouth of the ditch is just within those bushes. I can't tell from here if the grate has been reinforced or not."

"We'll have to risk it. If the king is really ill, strangers won't prove popular at the main gate. Now is our best opportunity, my lord, while the guard is at the other end of the wall."

"Aye. Wait for me here." Roland bounded to his feet then dashed the short distance to the cover of the bushes, sliding feet first into the trench. He found the grate just as he remembered it, and struggled to remove it. It had taken both of them to shift it when he and Stefan came this way as children, but he had expected to move it with ease now.

He sensed someone behind him, and spun—staff ready to attack. Collyn stood at his back. The riverman reached over with one hand and lifted the grate.

"Go," he ordered, and Roland dove through the opening.

Rotten leaves, brackish water, and substances he didn't want to think about, half-filled the drainage ditch; Roland sank to his knees in the pungent muck. Wrinkling his nose in distaste, he started forward, only to lose his footing in the uneven slime and fall headlong into the ditch. He came up sputtering, coughing, and covered with filth.

Collyn waded up to give him a hand.

"Clever touch to enhance your disguise." He grinned. "'Tis sure no one would mistake you for Roland the Vain now."

Roland pulled away from him, stung by the teasing, and started forward again. This time, he sat hard when he fell backward. Glaring daggers, he accepted Collyn's proffered hand with ill grace but made it out of the ditch without further mishap. They were standing behind the king's orchards inside the town proper.

Collyn looked up and down Roland's bedraggled costume and raised an eyebrow.

"Even for a peasant, my lord, I think you've overdone it. Do you know of a place where we can clean you up a bit?"

Putting aside his ill humor as best he could, Roland thought hard.

"It won't be easy to get anywhere from here without being seen. There's no building near the orchards we could be coming from." He pointed across the orchard. "The guards' favorite tavern is a rather seedy place where no questions are asked, but going into the lair of the guard doesn't seem our most intelligent option."

"I agree, my lord. We certainly don't want to be tossed into the dungeons as thieves."

"The nearest buildings beyond the orchard are the forge and the stock pens."

"If we can get to the stock tank, we might be able to wash the majority of that filth from you before we go any farther. But if we're seen, remember—let me do all the talking."

Roland nodded. "Let's just get on with it."

***

Mendana tossed on her couch, lost in the throes of a dream. She had left the audience with her father more confused and disheartened than ever. Nothing had been decided, even Andundal seeing her fatigue and Dèodar's pain. The warder hid his injury well, but Eeonathor's ministrations had been cursory at best, and her merry cousin had been unconscious for several minutes. At Mendana's urging, the king had dismissed them both until the next day. She had welcomed the chance to snatch some rest.

Now, as she slept, one hand clutching the Moonstone, visions chased through her head.

She stood on the edge of a cliff overlooking a pearl-gray sea. The color appeared to be natural rather than a trick of the light. Waves broke against the jagged rocks at her feet with savage force.

In the choppy harbor, a black ship rode at anchor, her sails ragged and the wood of her hull pitted. The wind sang in the rigging, and slapped loose ropes against the canvas with whip-crack snaps. Her crew shouted to each other in a guttural language Mendana had never heard before.

One of the sailors looked in her direction, and she stifled a gasp. His face was bestial, with sharp teeth protruding from lower jaw to curl over upper lip. His brow hung low, shadowing eyes that held a glint of red.

A commotion began onshore, and she looked toward the bleached sand. Several of the creatures scuttled toward a longboat pulled up onto the beach. One jerked on a rope, pulling a pair of stumbling captives toward the boat. The lead prisoner, slight and dark, fought desperately to keep his feet beneath him; the other, a slim, fair-haired boy, ran beside him as if to compensate.

Stefan, and Ravenwing's little thief!

Mendana moaned, trying to awaken...

Her brother fell to the sand. His captor dragged him several yards without noticing. Daerci yanked on the rope, trying to give him slack enough to stand, but the prince lay still. She saw a sparkle of tears in the little cutpurse's eyes as he sat hard on the sand to draw the attention of their captors.

One of the creatures turned and cuffed the boy across the mouth. Blood flowered from a split lip as he fell over Stefan's motionless body, sobbing bitterly.

Mendana bolted upright, wracked with violent shudders.

***

The earth spread out beneath his wings like a vast map. Only the sigh of the wind broke the silence, and he allowed himself a moment to revel in the peace.

Eeonathor Ravenwing pretended he did not care what the world thought of him, but in truth, the banishment from Starlit Wood had destroyed part of his soul. It drove him to the lands of the humans, where he'd met Norfulk. At first, the young sorcerer had fed his ego, pretending to learn from him, although Ravenwing now knew the boy's skills had already far outstripped his own even then.

When he was first banished, Eeonathor had wanted nothing more than he wanted to hurt his imperious uncle. Norfulk had little trouble convincing him to aid in the theft of the Moonstone and Sunstone pendants from his aunt and young cousin. He had flown with the raiders that night, masking the attack until it was too late.

Then Norfulk murdered Deveiria. Only then did he realize just how far down the wrong path he had strayed. His feeble attempt to stop the human was fruitless—though Norfulk bore the scars of the raven's talons on his cheek to remember it by.

When the raiders stormed off, unable to find the treasures they sought, he had stayed behind. He found the Moonstone concealed inside his cousin Raethan's jerkin, but the pain when he touched it, the proof of his dishonor, drove him to his knees. He knelt on the rough ground beside the bodies of his slain kindred, nursing his hand, and wept for the innocence he had lost.

Pulling himself together after a time, he slipped the pendant over his head, steeling himself against the pain, then flew up to hide it in the cave where the searchers had found it.

With the queen's death was born inside him a thirst for revenge so strong it had driven him for more than fifteen years. He continued to pretend servitude to Norfulk, bearing his near-fatal punishment for attacking the other in stoic silence, and he waited. So far, he had managed to convince Norfulk of his loyalty, but he was beginning to wonder if the ruse was wearing thin. He had noticed several calculating stares from the sorcerer lately.

In time, he managed to return to the scene of the raid, and there he found the Sunstone, buried in the cold ashes of the elven campfire. He scratched the map on its surface and kept it hidden against the day it would prove useful.

When Prince Roland had reached Woodwatch Ferry, that day arrived at last.

He banked and wheeled, soaring high above the wasteland near Crypticia Keep. Suddenly, the sight of two horses plodding across the empty plain caught and held his sharp eye.

Gods, what are those foolish children doing?

He swooped down to meet them.

Chapter 28

Roland washed in the stock tank, rinsed the muck out of his mean garments the best he could. He made a face at the feel of the sodden burlap against his skin then sneezed at the sharp, dank smell of it.

"I need to dry off a little before I venture into public," he muttered.

Slogging from the edge of the tank, he led the way to a spot under the globefruit trees, reached up, and plucked two of the ripe red fruit. He tossed one to Collyn then sat beneath a tree.

"We also need to plan our next move." He took a bite, savoring the tart crispness.

Collyn nodded, sinking down beside him.

"I think we should first test the truth of these rumors about the king. We must also discover if Andundal's messenger ever arrived. We'd best seek a tavern and nose about. You'll be my younger brother, and I feel we'll be safest if you don't speak. I suggest you be a mute, and it won't hurt our cause if you play halfwit as well. No one holds their tongue around an imbecile."

Roland chafed at the advice.

"I've agreed to all the other suggestions, but this is going too far! Why don't *you* play the fool? I dare say you can wear that disguise as well as I."

Collyn shook his head with a sigh.

"'Tis just what I was speaking of, my lord. You aren't thinking with the logic of a king. You act from your heart and not your head, and 'tis likely to get us into trouble. I've enough of that on my own." He tossed his half-eaten fruit into the grass and rose to his feet. "My counsel appears no longer required. I wish you good fortune, my prince."

"No, please, stay!" Roland bounded up. "I...I'm sorry. You're right, Collyn. I will try. I must learn to curb my tongue. Perhaps this will be a valuable exercise for me."

"Any lesson well learned is valuable. Are you still dripping?"

"No, merely damp."

"Then let's go. We need to gather our facts before nightfall. That will be the safest time for an attempt if we need to enter the castle in secret."

Roland felt a chill run through him at the thought of having to steal into his own home. He nodded.

"There's a tavern against the outer wall across the common. I've been in there once or twice, but I know no one will recognize me like this." He wrung a bit more water out of his shirt. "As you say, I don't merit the nickname 'Vain' in these rags."

"Lead on, little brother." Collyn clapped him on the shoulder.

They crossed the common to the ramshackle tavern. Roland dropped behind Collyn and tried to affect a doltish expression, pulling his hat lower as he watched the riverman's back.

"Good morrow t'ya, master," Collyn greeted the man behind the bar. "Two ales, if ya please." His voice had a peasant's burr it normally lacked, and he slumped against his staff, cutting six inches from his height. Roland pasted a vacuous grin on his face, pushing up to stand beside him.

"Are you new here?" asked the barman.

"Me and me brother 'ave a farm outside town. We don't get in much." Collyn gave Roland a light cuff on the shoulder. "Wyll 'ere's a might slow, but 'e's strong as a ox, 'e is."

The man set the pints before them.

"Good health t' King Frederick!" Collyn cried in a loud voice before quaffing half the pint in one pull. He wiped his mouth on his sleeve. "That's good ale, that is. Drink up, Wyll." He smacked Roland on the back, knocking him into the bar.

Roland glowered up at him from beneath the brim of his hat. Collyn was becoming all too free with his blows. But he held his tongue.

"'Tis not wise to toast the king too loud," warned the barman in a hushed tone.

"I shall toast my king any time," answered Collyn, his voice gruff. "Why should I not?"

"He has not been seen for days. There are rumors he has already followed the prince into death. The news that Roland had fallen proved a terrible blow to him." He leaned toward Collyn. "The dogs of Crypticia's Black Lion have been sniffing the streets," he whispered. "Take your brother home, where he'll be safe. That be my advice."

"What o' the King's Guard? What do they say about these sniffing dogs?"

The barman leaned even closer, his breath ripe with bitterroot as he whispered, "Those loyal to the king are biding their time. I think they wait to see which way the tree will fall. Either that...or they've slipped into hiding. The ranks are thinner these days—the captain is having trouble manning the wall with full shifts."

Roland clutched Collyn's sleeve. His thoughts roiled in a fever of anxiety. *If Father still believes me dead, the messenger never arrived—or his visit was kept so secret no word of it escaped the castle. Either way, Father remains in danger.*

The prince desperately wanted to go to Frederick, but Collyn, sensing his thoughts, frowned down at him with a barely perceptible shake of his head.

"We come t' town t' see the sights. I reckon we'll do tha' afore we go back. What do they say ails the king?"

"Most say 'tis a broken heart. That irresponsible cub of a prince! Whatever happened on that raft will have been his doing, I warrant. Roland the Vain never wasted a thought before he leapt in with both feet."

The prince ground his teeth, but the man spoke no more than the truth. He had never been one to think before acting. But the only way the disaster on the raft could have been avoided would have been for him never to have sailed at all.

If I hadn't gone downriver, none of this would have happened! But if I'd never gone downriver, I wouldn't have met Mendana either

"Be there a place we can get a room fer the night?" Collyn asked. He threw an arm around Roland's shoulders, supplying gratefully accepted comfort.

"We're full up. Many of the outlying farmers are coming inside the walls. There are odd men roaming the Heath, and some say they've seen even stranger things abroad. You might try The Three Bells across town. I hear they had some rooms yesterday. Or mebbe they'd let you sleep in the stables in exchange for sweeping out. If yer brother's as strong as you say, perhaps the two of you can find some work within the walls. You'd be safer if you stayed in the settlement."

"Ah, no, we don't need permanent work. We just be visiting. Being caged by walls would break me heart. But we'll check with the stables fer the night. Thank ye. Come on, Wyll."

He turned Roland toward the door and led him out with one hand under his arm to both support and propel him forward.

"Keep still," he murmured as they left the tavern and Roland opened his mouth. "We'll talk in the stables."

They crossed town, keeping to the less travelled streets. They caught bits of conversation from huddled groups of people as they walked, most of it echoing what they had already heard.

When they arrived at the Three Bells, they sought out the stablemaster. Collyn slipped back into character.

"We be looking for a place t' sleep the night, good sir, and we're willin' t' work fer it. The man at The Flying 'Orse said you might 'ave an empty stall fer us if we mucked out the stables."

"I might," the stablemaster said in a guarded tone. "You look fit enough, but what's wrong with the young one there?"

Roland stiffened then forced himself to remember his role. He gave the man an oafish grin.

"Oh, 'e's jest a mite teched. He canna speak, but 'e can pull 'is weight right enough."

"I suppose. Just fer tonight, mind. Tomorrow ya look for other accommodations."

"Thank ye, sir." Collyn pulled his forelock, and Roland ducked his head.

"Start over there." He handed them a pair of pitchforks and pointed to the far side of the barn. "I'm going for supper."

"Thank ye, sir," Collyn repeated. "Come on, Wyll." He took Roland's arm and pulled him along.

As soon as the stablemaster left, Roland threw his pitchfork across the stable to stick quivering in the side of a stall.

"Damn Norfulk to the Flames!" he shouted. "Collyn, my father—"

"Calm down, Roland," Collyn warned. "One incautious word, and Norfulk's dogs will tear you to pieces. We must try and contact those guards the barman spoke of—the ones loyal to your father. Do you have any idea where they might go?"

"Perhaps. I know General Teodore would give his life for my father, and he'll know which of his men he can trust."

"Where can we find him?"

"He should be in the castle, but will he be?" Roland began to pace. "If he isn't in his rooms there, Master Fortenbraes will know where he's gone."

"Is Fortenbraes loyal to your father?"

"Oh, yes. He was Father's tutor as he is mine. He's only a few years older than Father, so he was more a friend to him and Jarome—"

"If he's loyal to the king, he may have left the castle as well."

Roland groaned in frustration, running his hands through his hair.

"I can't think. I don't know where they might have gone if they've left the castle—but I can't see them abandoning my father." He stopped and faced Collyn. "I must see my father, Collyn. I have to know if he's alive."

"We must wait until dark. For now, you might as well muck out that stall."

Roland crossed to the stall and wrenched the fork free then attacked the soiled straw with angry thrusts.

"If my father is dead, Collyn, so is Norfulk. I swear it on my mother's grave."

***

Stefan and Daerci rode through the wasteland, with no clearer destination than "south." Since leaving the forest, they had seen nothing living to break the monotony; the barren plain offered only bald rock thrusting sharp teeth through withered stalks of leprous grass. The sun disappeared behind a growling bank of thunderclouds, and icy rain began to pummel the dead earth.

Stefan shivered, and stole a sideways glance at Daerci. Her hair hung in dripping strands about her thin face as the rain beat down on her. She slumped in her saddle with an expression of resignation. The thin shirt clinging to her in sodden folds provided her little protection, and his heart lurched in sympathy. He reined in his horse, forcing her to stop as well.

"Do ye need a rest, Stefan?"

"Hang on a minute."

Undoing the clasp of his cloak, he carefully gripped with his good leg and managed to slip it over her shoulders. She stared at him, shaking her head in protest.

"No, milord, you keep it." She started to remove the cloak, and her hand brushed his. A warm jolt ran through him, and he jerked back in confusion.

"I have my tunic, and my shirt is heavier than yours. Don't be foolish, Daerci. If you fall ill, I'm no healer to care for you."

She pulled the cloak closer about her with a timid smile, and he no longer minded the rain. He urged his horse into motion, not trusting himself to look at her. He'd had no experience with girls at Crown Keep, and he didn't know how to deal with the unfamiliar feelings coursing through him.

Rain continued to pound them, frigid pinpricks that needled through his shirt to burst against his skin. The air grew rank with the stench of decaying vegetation, and his stomach turned. The plain seemed to stretch forever, seared to a dull gray-brown on all sides. Was the desolation the result of natural causes or of Norfulk's dominion? He laid odds on the latter.

"Are you in pain, milord?" asked Daerci, her voice anxious.

"You have the eyes of a hawk," he replied, realizing he must have visibly reacted to his thoughts. "No more than usual. Do not worry so, little one."

"Or the eyes of a raven. Look!" She pointed high above them, and Stefan shielded his eyes with one hand.

"Aye, I see it. Do you think it is Ravenwing?"

"Most like, in this wasteland. Be prepared. He'll not be pleased."

"I fear you speak truth in that."

He reined in, waiting. Daerci's mount danced nervously beside him. The raven swept down like dropped shot. Within feet of the earth, the now-familiar change began, and by the time he touched the ground, Eeonathor strode toward them. He all but radiated sparks of anger as he stopped before Stefan.

"Why are you here, cousin?" His hands were clenched into fists on his hips, as if it were an effort to control them. The tightness of his voice showed the strain of his civility.

Stefan's heart sank. "I feared for your safety," he mumbled.

"I'm a big boy now. I can take care of myself. And you." He turned a withering glare on Daerci, who seemed to shrink into her saddle beneath Stefan's cloak. "I gave you a charge, you little fool, and you broke it."

Something in Stefan snapped at hearing Eeonathor brand Daerci with the name so often thrown at his own head.

"She is not a fool!" he exploded. "She came because I would not listen to her counsel and she did not wish to break her trust, exactly the opposite of what you accuse her of doing. Daerci and I are not children, either, Eeonathor Ravenwing. And I, for one, am tired of being called a fool every time I try to do what I know to be right. I imagine Daerci feels the same way!"

Eeonathor cocked his head at Stefan with a quizzical frown.

"You haven't gone and formed an attachment for our winsome little thief, have you, my prince?"

Stefan felt blood rush to his cheeks at Ravenwing's perception, then drain as quickly away that Daerci should hear it. It left him dizzy. Ravenwing spoke a truth he had not yet fully acknowledged to himself, much less to her. He hung his head, unable to face either of them.

"Ah, I see. Well, that explains quite a few things. But it doesn't tell me what I should do with the pair of you. Most probably I should turn you both to stone or something equally ornamental, but I suppose my uncle would definitely frown on that. So, I suppose I should tend your wound instead, cousin."

"What?" The abrupt change of subject threw Stefan.

"Your hand is bandaged. You've hurt it, haven't you?"

"Last night one of the flying rodents in the Dark Wood bit me, but 'tis nothing serious."

Eeonathor's face grew grave.

"One of those black creatures bit you?"

"Aye, but Daerci tended it well."

"Let me see it, boy. We may be in deeper trouble than I thought."

He took Stefan's hand and swiftly unwrapped the makeshift bandage. The flesh around the wound still showed slight swelling, but no discoloration radiated outward, and the prince could move his hand when asked.

Finally, Ravenwing nodded.

"You're right, she did tend it well. I think you averted tragedy, little one," he murmured, smiling up at Daerci. "Well done. The poison in those bites is enough to fell a stronger soul than you, my prince. Praise the gods Daerci is an apt pupil."

The girl blossomed under her master's praise, and once more sat tall in her saddle.

"But that still doesn't excuse the fact you two are here," Eeonathor continued. "This is no place for you. Steavil, your very existence is a thorn in Norfulk's side. If he guesses your true identity, death will be a welcome relief. Your only salvation is he thinks you long dead. But I fear he begins to suspect otherwise. I should bespell these horses and force you to return to your father—but I will not treat you as children, since you ask so nicely."

He gave them a mocking bow.

"Instead, I appeal to the wisdom of the adult you claim to be. My magic will protect me. The Lion does not suspect my plan—that I guarantee. Return to Starlit Wood and keep Daerci safe...please."

Stefan sighed. The request was the rational thing to do.

"As you say."

"And go at once. Andundal will be holding your actions against Mendana and Dèodar, I fear. Tell your father that his messenger was ill-received by Frederick's minions, but I do not think the human court is under the rule of its rightful king. Roland might have found a nest of vipers when he arrived home. If Andundal can send aid, that crisis may be averted, at least."

"Come, Daerci, we have been dismissed."

"Aye, milord." She looked a bit nervous.

"Don't worry, I'm sure the rest of the elves will find you equally charming," Ravenwing told her, with a wink at Stefan.

The prince felt the heat rise to his cheeks.

"We'd best be moving," he mumbled.

Stepping away, Ravenwing raised a hand in farewell then launched into flight. They watched the bird dwindle into the distance.

"Should we follow him anyway?"

"Not unless ye'd rather be a fish or sumpin," she replied with a wry smile. "I'd rather face yer elves."

"Well, come on, then."

They turned back they way they'd come and rode in silence, each wrapped in private thoughts. Ravenwing's words weighed heavy on both. Trying to do the right thing had gotten them sent home like wayward children.

"I'm sorry, Daerci. I seem to have gotten you in trouble with your master," Stefan said after a time.

She sighed.

"'Tain't yer fault, Stefan. I should've knowed he'd be like that. He's terrible worried that Norfulk will harm you. He's always had a soft spot for children—"

"I'm not a child!" he protested hotly.

"Compared to the master, most of us are children," she replied, her face wreathed in smiles. "When I wuz little—" She broke off, a blush stealing up her throat to paint her cheeks.

"What was it like, when you first met him?"

"Well...it wuz cold. I remember that. It had rained a lot, and the pen where the slavers kept us wuz a sea of mud. I wuz covered with it. Me shoes were lost marching from me village to the pen, and I couldn't keep me feet warm to save me soul."

He shivered in sympathy.

"There wuz a clanging at the gate, and someone

new wuz thrown in the pen."

"And that was Ravenwing?"

"Aye," she nodded. "When I asked if he were hurt, he said no—leastways no more than he could heal, though I think his arm were broke—and I thought me heart were going to leap out o' me chest. Me mum wuz sick, y'see, and I thought I'd found her someone who could help."

"Did he?"

"He would ha' done, but she wuz dead when he found her. He offered to take me away instead—if I could pick the lock on the gate." She laughed aloud, the sound brightening the dismal landscape.

"Why would you need to do that? If Raven-wing's magic—"

"You ain't had much to do with magic, have ye? There's rules to follow. Iron—like that lock on the pen—is sumpin magic-users cain't touch without pain. Now, he might've bin able to fly away from there...but like I say, I think they broke his arm when they threw him into the pen. Besides, I figger he wanted to see what I wuz made of right off."

"Did you pick the lock?"

"Eventually. Took me two days tryin', but luckily I got it afore they were ready to ship us out."

Stefan shook his head.

"And you were only eleven?"

"Aye. But I'm a right good thief now." She grinned.

Now it was his turn to laugh.

"A useful occupation, indeed."

The horses suddenly stopped, whinnying and dancing. He frowned.

"What's wrong with them?"

Daerci fought to get her mount under control.

"I dunno. I ain't never seen either o' them act like this afore."

Over the rise of a distant hill surged a band of men, somehow broken in both movement and stature. Guttural cries and whistles carried to Stefan's ears.

"Slavers!" cried Daerci, her terror communicating to her horse. It bolted before Stefan could grab the reins.

He slapped his own reins, urging his mount after hers. The runaway animal shrieked in terror, wheeling in huge circles that tore great clods of earth from the ravaged plain. Stefan's heart was in his mouth as he watched. He couldn't catch her.

The distant pursuers closed impossibly fast. As they got nearer, Stefan could see more details—hunched backs, misshapen limbs, curling tusks

"What are they?" he cried.

"I told ye! They come from over the sea," Daerci shouted back, hauling at her mount's reins with both hands in an attempt to manage it. "They ain't human—that much I know."

Stefan's own mount had caught their scent now and went mad with fear, eyes rolling in its head as it bucked and reared. By the time he regained a measure of control, the horde of monstrous creatures, a twisted hybrid of man and beast, filled the plain around them.

A cracking whip licked the flank of Stefan's horse, and it shot out from under him, spilling him to the ground. He fell on his bad leg, and the world went white with agony. A scream burst unbidden from his throat.

"Stefan!"

He dimly heard her through the haze of pain and gestured for her to escape while she could, but she turned her horse back and dismounted to kneel beside him.

"I told you to go on," he grated through clenched teeth, rocking against the pain as he clutched his bad knee.

"I'll never leave ye."

"Then help me up," he gasped, clinging to her shoulder. "I have to stand."

He bit his lip. His stomach clenched with the effort. Daerci braced her feet and pulled. Swearing under his breath, he exerted every ounce of will not to cry out again.

With her aid, he made it to his feet and stood swaying, leaning heavily on her slender shoulder. He gazed about them.

The creatures had them walled in.

Chapter 29

At full dark, Roland gave Collyn an impatient nudge in the ribs. With a glance at the stablemaster, who dozed in a chair near the door, the riverman nodded that he agreed. Roland traded his quarterstaff for the sharp tines of the pitchfork and tiptoed past the sleeping man into the dark night.

"We must hurry," he murmured once they were clear, his voice tight and urgent. "Father must be worried sick."

"That's what they're saying," Collyn reminded him. "Let's hope it's his only illness."

"What do you mean?"

"You told me about the kitchen wench you think betrayed you, and who did she betray you to if not the Lion? Unless she was incautious enough to arouse others' suspicions, Sara will still be employed at the castle. 'Tis a small matter to slip a pinch of something into the king's food.

"I wouldn't put it past Norfulk to poison your father. The people would think he pined away from grief. Your cousin is a villain, but he's not stupid. Remember, you're dead in the eyes of much of the world—and the few who know you live are unlikely to stand up to Norfulk. If Frederick's death appears natural, no one will dispute his claim without proof of his infamy, and only you can give that—if you live."

Roland nodded.

"What you say makes sense, but what do I do? If I'm

dead, what use will I be to my father? And if I reveal I live, how will I expose the plot?"

"Let's take it one step at a time, my lord. The first thing is to reassure your father."

They reached the outer wall of the castle and crept forward through the drainage ditch until they could scout the inner wall—this time Roland managed to keep his feet beneath him, and only his boots were wet. There were no guards to be seen, and Roland breathed a sigh of relief. Fighting his own guards was not a thought he relished.

"It looks clear," he told Collyn.

He jerked his head toward the side of the inner keep, and Collyn followed him to a sturdy rose trellis against the stone wall. It ended just beneath a window.

"That is my father's bedchamber," Roland whispered, pointing to the pale glow spilling from the casement. "I'm going up."

"I would advise—"

"Here I take no advice, counselor. I must see for myself." He laid down his pitchfork and set his boot into the first gap of the trellis. "Stand guard, my friend. I won't tarry long."

"By your command, my prince."

Roland started climbing, testing each crossbar before he trusted his weight to it. The perfume of blown roses filled the night air, their petals falling all about him. Thorns reached out to clutch at him, and his hands were torn and bleeding before he had gone ten feet. The icy air accentuated the sting of the cuts, as if he had plunged his hands into a snow-fed stream.

He reached the top, his head just below the window

frame, and raised up just enough to see into the room. The familiar furnishings gladdened his heart. Their solidity promised safety and comfort, as always.

The chamber was sumptuous, hung with velvet draperies and silk tapestries. Gilt ornaments adorned the oak mantelpiece, and jeweled trinkets littered the tops of occasional tables throughout the room. They were mostly keepsakes of his mother's—perfume bottles, boar's bristle brushes, and her jewel casket with a rope of pearls spilling from its mouth. Frederick kept all of Catianya's things intact, as if holding onto them made her more alive for him. Her portrait hung over the fireplace. Roland gulped at the sight of his mother's face in the flickering light of the dying flames.

The king lay asleep, the massive carved bedposts framing him like the portrait of an ancient sage on his deathbed. His wan cheeks were sunken, and the silver in his hair now dominated the chestnut. His hands lay outside the coverlet, still and limp. There was a taint of sickness to the air—stale scents of sweat and soiled linen.

A girl stood beside the bed. She set down the bowl she held on a table and leaned into the light of the single candle to check on the sleeping king. The light revealed Sara's plump features, and Roland caught his breath with a hiss.

What is she doing here? Where is his physician?

Seeing Frederick slept, her lips curved in a self-satisfied smile, and she gave a throaty chuckle. A gilded mirror on a nearby chest caught her eye, and she set the candle before it, brightening the room enough for her to study her reflection. She preened before its polished surface.

Suddenly, she spun round, and Roland ducked below the windowsill, his heart pounding in his throat. When he dared to raise his eyes again, Sara sat on the edge of the canopied bed, running her hand over the soft fabric of its heavy velvet spread. The mercenary speculation on her face turned Roland's stomach.

Then she sauntered to the jewel casket. She threw back the lid with a clatter, glancing over her shoulder at the king, but Frederick slept on. Licking her lips, Sara studied the jewels like sweetmeats then lifted the rope of pearls from the casket. She swung back to the mirror, examining the effect of the strand against her throat.

"You won't have need of these any longer, lord." she promised. With a smirk of pleasure, she slipped them into the pocket of her apron.

Roland felt white-hot fury roar through him, tempting him to leap through the window and confront the vixen where she stood, but he forced himself to hold still. The flare of temper subsided, leaving only ashes of his former feelings for the girl.

"Sleep well, my king," she murmured, contempt coloring her voice as she strolled back to the bed and retrieved the bowl from dinner. "Tomorrow will finish the job, and I shall be queen, as my lord Norfulk promised."

She spun about sharply once more, and Roland ducked below the level of the window again, his heart thundering in his chest.

"I am starting at shadows, my king," she murmured, her tone mocking. "I think I will leave you to your rest. In the morning, you will feel much better."

The candle went out, and Roland heard the chamber

door open then close behind her with a soft click.

He took hold of the windowsill and began to pull himself up—only to find the window was narrower than he had remembered. He might be able to squeeze through, but even if Collyn managed to climb the trellis without destroying it, he never could.

Roland clambered down the trellis. Things were worse than he had thought. He would need Collyn inside, so they would have to find another way. He leapt the last two feet to the ground.

"Your suspicions are confirmed. Sara is definitely Norfulk's."

"One of his spies, then," the trader answered. "There must be more."

"She's an idiot—Norfulk will never make a serving wench his queen. He will discard her with the same ruthlessness she now shows my father."

Collyn nodded.

"I assume the trellis is not a good way in?"

"The window's too narrow. We'll have to risk going through the secret door. It's directly off the kitchen, so we've got to be very quiet so as not to be caught."

He led the way to the secret door from the orchard into the keep. Easing it open, he stepped into the stone passageway. Emotions welled up inside him. He was home. For the moment, nothing else mattered.

Roland murmured words of caution as they eased their way past several closed doorways then through the secret ways of the castle to his father's bedchamber. As they stepped into the room, the door protested with a thin squeak of hinges.

"We'll need to take care of that," he whispered to Collyn.

Frederick called out in a weak voice, "Who is it? Who is there?"

Roland moved instantly to his side.

"Shh. Hush, Father," he soothed, kneeling beside the bed. "Don't try to speak."

"Roland?" Frederick raised a shaking hand to touch his son's face. "Have you come to me in another dream, or have I traveled at last to join you?"

"Neither, Father." Roland felt a tear slip down his cheek and dashed it away with an impatient gesture. "*I* have come to join *you*. All will be well, I promise."

"Are you really here, my son?" He clung to Roland's hand with desperate strength.

"Aye, Father, I'm safe. Did no message come? I was promised there would be a messenger sent, and I can't believe... No matter, I'm here now. I've been with the elves."

"With *whom*?"

"The elves of Starli—the Forest of Night. And, Father, you'll never believe it! Stefan is their prince. He was lost many years ago. Now he's found. And there are the most beautiful flowers of crystal. And lamps that glow without benefit of wick or oil. Oh, and the most wonderful girl in the world. But I'll tell you of it all in time. For now, we must make you well."

Frederick chuckled, the laugh a whisper of sound.

"Indeed you must. Oh, my son! I already feel stronger, just knowing that you live." And, indeed, his voice did sound closer to its old timbre, and his eyes held new brightness.

"It puzzles me that you didn't already know. Andundal swore a messenger would come to you, and I trusted that promise..." Roland frowned. "You must tell no one else I'm here, Father. I must remain an unknown in this game. Norfulk doesn't know where this particular piece may be, and he must remain in darkness. He is plotting to take the throne. Somehow, we must stop him."

"But how?" Frederick struggled to sit up. "You cannot do it alone, my boy. Let me send troops to Cryptica."

"Do you know who we can trust? Where is Teodore? I am surprised he has posted no guard on your door."

"He wanted to, but Marcell assured him there was no need. I had to agree, my son. Why should I need a guard in my own castle?"

"Norfulk's influence is strong, Father. The southern provinces are tithing to the Black Lion already."

"You must be mistaken, Roland. Marcell reports—"

"Marcell again. Do you trust *him*, Father?"

"He's been my chief advisor for many years now, my son. He was my brother's chancellor—"

"And came north at Norfulk's request, no doubt," Roland murmured. "Norfulk is too powerful for us to sit back and do nothing, and yet that very power makes it difficult to attack him. Perhaps Teodore and Fortenbraes will have some thoughts."

"I haven't seen either of them in days...only that kitchen girl and Marcell. Teodore has a cabin about a league upriver. They might have gone there. But I don't know how they will be able to help if they are no longer at court. And if I cannot trust Marcell, I don't know who among the guard are loyal. How could things have come to such a pass?"

Roland shook his head with a sigh. "We have been complacent, Father. Foolish indeed when you remember that Grandfather united Irthlan only decades ago. I should have listened to Marcell's lectures with a keener ear—even if they were biased."

"Go to Teodore, my son. I would trust him with my life. He will give you council. Knowing you are alive lightens my heart."

"And mine is glad to see that the rumors of your death are premature, Father. We must think on how to keep it that way. First, eat nothing more brought to you by Sara. I am sure she is in Norfulk's employ. I told no one else of my plans to leave the traders early. She has to be involved in the plot to have us ambushed on the river. If we hadn't found an ally on the raft, we wouldn't be holding this conversation."

"Then that man will be a trusted member of my court. But tell me—where is Stefan? I am surprised not to see him at your side."

"He chose to follow a different path, Father, and since he could no longer be my squire, I had to respect his choice."

"I still don't understand, Roland. You say he is... an elf?"

"Yes. Remember the gibberish he spoke as a child? It was really the Elven language—my friend Dèodar has begun to teach me some of it. We will learn it together."

"This is all so confusing, my son."

"I know. It's hard for me to grasp it all myself. Suffice to say—there are two kingdoms at stake here, Father, and the life of someone I love very dearly hangs in the balance." Roland smiled at the bemused look in his father's eyes. "I have lost my heart to the most beautiful woman in the land, and Norfulk seeks to claim that jewel as well. I would gladly trade my kingdom to save her and never think twice, but he wants both. I must stop him before he gets his claws on Mendana. Whatever the cost, he mustn't harm her."

"My son, who is this lady you speak of? Can you tell me nothing more?"

"Time is short, Father, but I'll try."

He sat down on the edge of the bed to begin.

***

Norfulk pursed his lips over the message that had just arrived by courier pigeon from Crown Keep—not as fast a communication method as the raven, perhaps, but easier to trust at the moment. Marcell's note was terse, but enlightening.

Roland had returned to the castle. The kitchen wench had witnessed it, and she was hardly likely to be mistaken, given her familiarity with the prince. He had a companion...but not the squire.

That was interesting. Where might Stefan be? He would never leave his master willingly, but since he had, perhaps he could be used as a pawn against the prince. If he could be found.

Norfulk snapped his fingers, and one of the beasts bowed and scraped its way into the room.

"Put out the word," he ordered. "Be on the lookout for a dark-haired boy with a limp. If he is seen, I want to know about it. No matter when or where."

"As you command, my lord."

He turned back to his message. The wheels were beginning to turn indeed, bearing him to ultimate triumph.

Chapter 30

Mendana longed to join Dèodar as he stood at attention before the dais and lend him her strength, but her father had made it clear he expected her to resume her throne. Andundal's pipe burned forgotten in its stand, sending a twist of gray smoke into the shadows. The aroma of the smoldering smoke-weed brought back memories of much happier times the three of them had spent in this chamber.

The broken halves of Dèodar's bow lay at the foot of the steps, along with the quiver of arrows and his badge of office. She could see the defeat in his eyes, despite his stiff carriage. Nothing in his life held more importance for him than that silver-trimmed badge of office and what it stood for. From the moment he'd first pinned it on his cloak, it was his glory to be the youngest elf ever to wear it, and he had never removed it from that day until this.

Now, he awaited his sentence, willing to accept punishment he did not deserve in order to prevent Andundal from looking further afield for a scapegoat.

She tried once more to make the king see reason.

"Father, this is not his blame to shoulder."

"Hush, daughter. I know what you would say, but it does not excuse Dèodar's actions. He failed in his charged duty. He let the humans go free without my consent, and he neglected to stop your brother from riding headlong into who-knows-what danger. That last I cannot forgive, even if I overlook the other."

Dèodar went down on one knee before his uncle, head bowed.

"I accept your judgment, my king, whatever it may be."

"As Mendana pointed out last evening, I have not the men to mount a search party. I must trust the gods to watch over Steavil. His fate is in their hands. But I cannot let your dereliction of duty go completely unpunished, Dèodar Eriaborae. You are stripped of your rank—I cannot have warders who defy my orders. Go to Moonrise Wood and report to the captain of the watchers there—perhaps, in time, you may return."

"I obey your command," Dèodar murmured.

"Father, no!" Mendana cried, springing to her feet. "Dèodar should not be faulted. He could barely see when Stefan rode off, and I chose to let Roland return home."

"I am aware of the situation, daughter. This may seem a harsh punishment to you, but I must spread my thinned resources even further with Crypticia's recent activity. I am sending Dèodar to Moonrise to supplement the men there. Under different circumstances, I would rather have him by my side, but now..."

"You cannot take away everything Dèodar loves because he followed my orders!"

Her cousin rose to his feet, chin lifted proudly.

"Nay, my queen. I received a fair sentence. I'll gather my things at once and go to Moonrise, to tend your borders there as I have willingly tended the king's. Maybe one day, you will be ready to reclaim your own throne. I'll try to make it ready for you."

He smiled, but his face was wreathed again in sadness as he bowed to the king.

"I regret having failed your trust, Your Majesty. Perhaps I can redeem myself in Moonrise." Turning on his heel, he strode toward the door of the throne room.

"Dèodar!" Mendana called after him.

He stopped and stood tensed, as if steeling himself not to look back at her, and then he hurried on.

"Father!" she began, whirling to confront Andundal. Her angry accusations died in her throat at the bleak expression in the depths of his black eyes.

"Now I have lost two sons," he whispered. He drew a shuddering breath and turned away.

***

Roland and Collyn stood beside the door of King Frederick's bedchamber, conferring in hushed voices so as not to disturb the sleeping king. An alcove opened off the main room where the riverman could hide if Sara returned, but they didn't expect her back until morning.

"I feel much better after speaking to my father, Collyn. As long as Sara's poison is intercepted, he should recover. His will is as strong as ever."

"Perhaps we should take the girl out of the game, my lord." Collyn's tone left no doubt as to his meaning.

"If we did that, Marcell would wonder where she'd gone. I'm not ready to let him know we've caught on to him. Let her continue as she has, but make sure the king is shielded from her. Once I have spoken to Teodore and Fortenbraes, and know who to trust, we'll deal with her."

"I'll make sure the wench doesn't give him anything more to eat, my lord, and he'll begin to regain his strength. Seeing you alive is the best medicine you could give him."

"I must find those loyal to the king. We may be able to marshall enough troops to launch a prepared attack."

"Good. To confront Norfulk without an armed escort is suicide. I'm glad to see you beginning to think more like a king."

"What choice have I been given?" Roland sighed. "But I don't wish to be king if this is the way of it."

Collyn laid a hand on his arm. "Whatever comes, you'll be a strong king one day, Roland. I've seen you grow before my eyes. But that requires survival, and your original plan carries no chance of that. Whatever the general might say, you must not confront Norfulk alone. Don't forget that."

Roland clapped him on the shoulder.

"Take care of my father. I leave him in your charge."

"I'll guard him with my life, my prince. May Eostivil go with you."

Roland cocked an eyebrow and grinned.

"We picked up a lot from the elves in the brief time of our acquaintance, didn't we?"

Collyn chuckled sheepishly.

"Everyone needs a little luck now and again. Perhaps the god can spare you a handful, even if you're not an elf."

"I hope so, my friend. I hope so." Roland shouldered a pack filled with food they had managed to steal from the kitchen storerooms. The food raid had almost proved their undoing. "I thought we were caught for sure when that spit boy came in looking for scraps to feed the dogs."

"Aye, my lord," Collyn replied. "'Twas Eostivil, indeed, guided that rat to run over his foot. I thought he would leap out of his skin."

Roland laughed, silencing at once when Frederick stirred.

"It feels good to laugh again. We'll get through this. By all the gods, I swear it. The bread and cheese we found should be untainted. It isn't as good as broth, but see if he will eat a little, Collyn. Now, I'll go to the farm for Noble—I must get to Teodore with all possible speed."

"Aye. Best be gone at once, before the dawn breaks. Do you know this cabin the king spoke of?"

"Teodore took me fishing there one summer. I believe I remember the way."

"Ride swiftly."

"Farewell." Roland turned to leave.

"Roland..."

The prince hurried to his father's side.

"Hush, Father. Save your strength."

"I know I cannot stop your going, my headstrong son, but give me your word that you will return."

"If it's in my power, I'll return to you, Father."

"That isn't good enough."

"It's all I can promise." He bent and kissed Frederick's wan cheek, a gesture he would never have had the courage to perform before his journey. "I love you, Father. Rest easy. *Ithneimi endo*, Noile." The elven words slipped out without conscious thought, and Frederick seemed comforted by them.

"I love you, too, my son. I never told you that enough."

Roland smiled, his heart soaring, then stepped to the door.

"Take care of him, Collyn—and grease this hinge." He slipped out of the chamber and was gone.

***

The obsidian walls of the chamber were dark, and the ebony and crimson velvet of the draperies proved useless against the chill. Dressed in elegant sable, Norfulk lounged in his throne-like chair, chin in hand.

Although his plans were proceeding according to schedule, something bespoke trouble ahead. A tremor in the cosmos defied even his skill at divination to interpret, and it made him nervous.

The throne of Irthlan lay almost within his grasp. According to his spies, Frederick would not last the week. Ravenwing's news that Roland had fallen in with the elves rather than perishing on the river was a minor setback, but that would be easily remedied on Frederick's death.

"Oh, yes," he murmured to the still room. "I'd almost forgotten. Dead tongues can't wag. As soon as Frederick is dead, Sara must follow."

A smile curved his lips at the thought of Mendana. He had waited a long time for that particular prize, and when he gained the human throne at last, he would declare war on the elves with the aid of his bestial allies from across the sea.

Then I will force the queen to marry me in return for peace. And I will see she becomes queen over Starlit Wood as well as Moonrise before the wedding. Andundal has been king long enough, and I made quite sure no male heir would challenge me.

The thought of the ambush brushed a phantom of unease across his memory, and he fingered the scars on his cheek with a frown. Something nagged at him. He should be able to divine its origin, but he could not.

Something had happened that night. He could not remember what it was, but somehow, he knew it was important. Lately, he had almost been able to catch the tail of that phantom and look it in the eye. Soon he would have it.

One of the beasts shambled into the room, his eyes lowered. Norfulk glanced up.

Good. The invaders know their place. I do not mind letting them run rampant—as long as they acknowledge me as their king.

"Yes? What is it?" he asked, his rich voice transforming even the guttural language of the beasts into a thing of beauty.

"Master, slaves taken on the plain. May interest you."

"Indeed. And why is that?"

"Two young boys traveling alone, heading toward the mountains."

The vague description was enough to pique Norfulk's curiosity—and potentially alleviate his boredom. "What about them?"

"One blond, almost a child. Other dark, lame, but brave—meets description you gave to look for. No value as slave." The beast shrugged. "Will kill if not one you want."

Norfulk's sense of cosmic disturbance grew.

"Bring me my crystal," he ordered, rising to pace.

The beast hurried out, bobbing his head in acknowledgment. The Lion prowled from one end of the chamber to the other, too agitated to stand still.

The room seemed to hold its breath, annoying him with its silence. He snapped his fingers, and the soft sound of strings filled the room, coming from no discernible source. He waved his hand, and torches flared into flame, the stone walls warming to life. The torches hissed, sending up aromatic curls of smoke. Norfulk muttered an incantation, and a censer sent up scented vapors to blend with the torch smoke. He inhaled deeply.

"Bah!" He clapped his hands, and the flames died, the music cut off in mid-note, and the perfume dissipated. "Better," he growled.

Striding over to a curtained niche in the curved wall, he swept back a crimson drapery with a rattle of ebony rings. Inside the niche stood a small black easel upon which rested a beautiful miniature of an elven woman with raven hair and eyes like haunted pools of night. She was a feminine version of Andundal. The artist had caught an expression of wistful longing on her face. Infinite pain shadowed her perfect brow.

"Well, Mother," he murmured, his voice making the endearment a mockery, "it seems we must wait a little longer for our kingdoms. But don't worry. Once my uncles are dead, I will claim both thrones in your name."

He flung the curtain closed once more and resumed his pacing, his hands clasped behind his back to stop them trembling.

"In light of recent events, I wonder...could I be

so lucky? Of course, there could be many lame dark-haired boys in the kingdom..."

He gnawed the tip of his thumb, focusing on the pain. Since childhood, pain had been a source of comfort. His hands were laced with self-inflicted scars. Pain had consistency. It never let him down. It never abandoned him. It never denied his existence.

After another circuit of the room, he threw himself down on the throne, a leg swung over the arm of the chair. He waited for the scrying crystal, one leather boot jiggling restlessly. Hearing the shambling step of the beast, Norfulk sat upright, once more cold and composed by the time the door swung open.

The beast set the stand holding the crystal before the throne with care and backed out of the room, its gaze fixed firmly on the floor. Norfulk waited until it had retreated then turned his attention to the globe. His hair swung forward in an unruly frame about his face as he bent his concentration on the depths of the crystal orb.

A dim shadow at first, and then, growing in clarity and detail, a scene unfolded before him as he stared into the crystal. Sounds drifted up, faint but clear on the sea air of the scene.

A battered slaver rode at anchor on the gray waters of Dangerous Harbor. Though much the worse for wear, it had a few voyages left—the beasts were not sticklers for comfort, and the slaves had no say in the matter. A longboat was drawn up onto the sand, and a raiding party made their way toward it. Looped together by a length of rope, two boys stumbled between their captors.

Even in miniature scale, Stefan was unmistakable. Norfulk had seen the brat holding station by his cousin's chair, and that limp was so pronounced only a miracle must be keeping him on his feet.

Something about the boy twisted in his mind, but he could not grasp it before it fled.

"Where is Roland?" he mused aloud. "Would Stefan abandon his charge? Or is it merely that his services are no longer required? Could the elves have dispatched my cousin for me? And that little blond one—I have seen that one before as well, haven't I? But where?"

The squire stumbled one last time and fell face-down on the ivory sand. He lay motionless. The slavers dragged him forward, until the blond boy pulled back on the rope and sat down beside his fallen comrade.

Norfulk nodded in grudging admiration.

That took courage. The beasts do not take kindly to defiance.

One of the creatures turned and cuffed the blond across the face, knocking him across his companion. The smaller lad lay weeping where he fell, as if to shield the squire's body. Blood from a split lip spattered onto Stefan's tunic, ominously prophetic.

Norfulk pulled back from the crystal.

"Well, well, well. I must get over there at once. The slavers will have to do without this particular pair of prizes. A little compensation should win them over easily enough. Until I know for certain Roland's fate is sealed, the squire may have information I need."

Rising to his feet, he chanted a brief spell. A shimmering curtain of light formed around him, and he disappeared from the ebony chamber.

***

Stefan could go no further. The agony in his knee was no longer isolated but seemed to engulf his whole body. He could no longer bend the leg at all. Sighing out Daerci's name, he collapsed on the blazing sand.

The jolt as his knee struck the hard ground kept him from completely slipping into unconsciousness, but he teetered on the brink. The slavers dragged him several yards before he felt the ropes around his wrists slacken. As he tried to muster the strength to open his eyes, he heard the smack of a blow, followed by Daerci's whimper of pain. He felt her fall across him, sobbing as if her heart were broken.

"*Neealimi, evleeia,*" he whispered, his voice rough with pain. "Don't cry."

Her arms tightened around him.

"Oh, Stefan, I feared you were dead!"

"Not yet, little one, just immobile. I doubt the slavers will bother to keep me long. I'm sorry it came to this. I wanted so badly to spare you pain..." He reached a trembling hand to dab away blood from her split lip.

She caught his hand and pressed it to her cheek, her eyes bright with tears.

"Shh, *evleeae.* We ain't neither of us dead yet. We'll get through this somehow."

Languid applause sounded behind her, and she whirled, coming up in a crouch, her hand flying to her belt for her missing sling. Stefan levered himself up on one shaky elbow, squinting into the sunlight.

Norfulk. Stefan's heart grew cold.

"What have we here?" mused the sorcerer, his beautiful voice hypnotic. "I believe we have the prodigal servant boy returned from the dead."

Daerci leapt to her feet, her fists balled aggressively.

"Just ye leave him be! He ain't done ye no harm."

"A feisty little companion you've found yourself, lad." The sorcerer sketched a symbol in the air, and Daerci froze in mid-gesture. "But a bit vocal for my tastes. Shall I kill her?"

"No!" Stefan cried, gritting his teeth as he tried once more to stand. "Leave her alone! She has nothing to do with this. Let her go." He braced his good knee beneath him and attempted to push up from the sand, but his bad leg would not cooperate.

"Here, let me help you." Norfulk waved a hand, and Stefan found himself balancing awkwardly on his right leg.

He lurched to Daerci and threw his arm around her shoulders for whatever slim protection he could offer. She was stiff as stone within his embrace.

He stared up at the sorcerer with his heart in his throat. He had never been a convincing liar, and now their lives might well depend on his skill, or lack of it.

"What do you want? Roland is dead. The king is sure to follow. You will have your throne. Why can't you leave us in peace?"

"But you are on your way to be sold as slaves. What peace is there in that? I am on your side, boy. I am saving you—or your loud little friend there, at least—from 'a fate worse than death,' as they say. And I am not so sure Roland is dead."

Stefan felt his shoulders tense and forced himself to relax.

"What do you mean?" he asked, with false casualness.

Norfulk strolled around him in a lazy circle, like a cat toying with a mouse.

"The report said both boys were killed, yet here you are alive. Then we hear of the prince throwing his weight around at a village inn. And whispers..." He raised a hand to his ear. "Whispers come from Crown Keep that there are curious strangers skulking about the castle. I don't think I will order a tombstone for my cousin just yet."

"I was struck in the head." Stefan swept back the thick thatch of hair covering his brow to reveal the jagged scar, livid against his fair skin. "I was left for dead. When I came to my senses, Roland lay slain beside me. I crawled off and hid until Daerci found me. She tended my wound, and we decided to travel together." He squared his shoulders and met Norfulk's eye, willing the wizard to accept the lie.

"I can almost believe you. It is something about those eyes..."

Then Norfulk's own copper eyes widened, and Stefan's heart sank to the soles of his boots.

"Those eyes! Why did I never see it before? So, Roland's pet slave is an elf. Well, well, well. This does put an interesting complexion on things. Where did you come from, little elf?" He tapped a well-shaped fingernail on his front teeth. "Let me see, how does the story go?"

Stefan bowed his head in resignation, sagging against Daerci. When Norfulk remembered where he had been found, it was inevitable the sorcerer would know his identity.

"So," Norfulk breathed, his voice a mere whisper, "a

prodigal, indeed. By the Flames, I should have guessed it long before. So, that is why you had an amulet of protection. Deveiria.

"Tell me, does your father know of your rebirth, Prince Steavil? You are a bigger prize than I thought. Much bigger. I thought myself free of you long ago. An oversight I must be sure to remedy." His voice caressed Stefan with velvet sweetness. "And to think the slavers were going to jettison you like so much excess baggage. That would have deprived me of all the pleasure I shall get from destroying you myself."

Lifting his head, Stefan stared at him.

"Let Daerci go, and I will go with you. I'll do anything you say. She has no part in this."

Norfulk laughed.

"How droll! He attempts to bargain with me. On the contrary, my young prince, I knew I recognized her. And now I know from where. She is your foolish cousin's pet human. I owe Eeonathor Ravenwing a thing or two as well," he murmured, fingering the scars on his cheek. "Perhaps she can help me repay him. Oh, yes, I think she will have a part to play before the end of the song.

"Besides, if I let her go, who will keep you company in my dungeon while you await your rescue? And Roland will come. If I let it be known you are languishing in my care, he will come."

A little smile flitted across Norfulk's face.

"Perhaps your sister will come as well. I doubt your father could be persuaded. A king does have his duties. However, perhaps Mendana will save me the trouble of fetching her. I do so want to make her my queen."

Stefan swung at the sorcerer. Norfulk sidestepped the clumsy attack with ease, and Stefan overbalanced, falling to the sand once more.

"You really must be more careful." Norfulk feigned a sigh. "Perhaps that knee of yours just needs a little therapy."

He raised his arms and chanted melodically. The beach around them dissolved in a curtain of light. When his vision cleared, Stefan was lying on the floor of a stone cell. Daerci stood before him, statue-still.

He tried to rise.

"Oh, how clumsy of me," Norfulk's voice murmured. "I hate a job done halfway."

Stefan was flung against the wall, chains snapping shut around his wrists and arms, his toes dangling several inches above the floor. An iron ring encircled his left ankle, placing agonizing tension on his knee.

He choked back a scream—unwilling to give Norfulk the satisfaction of hearing it.

Chapter 31

Collyn sank into a chair beside the king's bed. Frederick slept on, his face peaceful in the moonlight. The riverman watched him with a thoughtful frown.

What had become of Andundal's messenger? He toyed with the arrowhead around his neck out of unconscious habit.

It's not in Andundal's nature to lie, and he promised to send word. Somewhere, something went wrong.

He rose to his feet. Now, while the king slept, was a good time to see if he could learn what that something was. It was risky, he knew, but the fate of the messenger gnawed at him. He picked up a crust of bread from the king's tray.

Perhaps Andundal could find no one to send. Perhaps the courier had been lost on the road. Or perhaps, he had reached the castle and was prevented from seeing the king. If that were the case, he needed to find out what had happened to the elf.

Collyn slipped into the hallway. He didn't know much about the plan of the castle, but they seemed to follow a fairly standard set of rules, and it was safe to suppose if the messenger were here—and Frederick knew nothing of his arrival—he wasn't occupying a suite in the guest wing.

Wishing he had something a little more substantial, he broke off a bit of the bread and dropped it beside the doorway. There were enough cobwebs in corners and dust trails on the floor he expected the crumbs would lie undisturbed.

He slipped through the castle, taking any stairway leading down and leaving a trail of crumbs back to the king. He could not remember all the details of the route Roland had taken in their kitchen foray but managed to find it again without being seen. There was a moment's scare when he turned a corner and found himself back in the kitchen, but he drew up short in time to avoid discovery.

The kitchen bustled with activity. Pots rattled and banged with preparations for breakfast. The aroma of boiling porridge wafted from a cauldron suspended in one of the huge fireplaces, and fresh bread cooled on racks. Collyn's mouth watered, and he gulped hard— the fruit eaten in the orchard had been several hours earlier, and he hadn't wanted to eat any of the stores they had laid by for Frederick, not knowing how long they must last.

He forced himself not to think about it.

A large woman in a voluminous apron laid about her with a ladle as she berated the kitchen boys for their laziness, but he could hear fondness beneath her scolding tone. He scanned the kitchen again— and recognized Sara from Roland's description as she flirted with a potboy.

This was obviously a dead end. He would have to backtrack to the last hallway—

A tanned hand fell upon his shoulder with a grip of iron. Collyn spun, fist raised to strike. The tall stranger raised a finger to his lips and jerked his dark head back the way the trader had come then, without a word, melted up the steps until he was safe from any curious eyes among the kitchen staff. Collyn followed, equally soundless despite his size.

"We can talk in here," the newcomer murmured, stepping into an empty room.

"You must be Ravenwing." Collyn studied the distinctive black-and-white garb and unconscious arrogance of the slim elf before him.

Eeonathor grinned.

"And you are the inestimable Collyn Silverbrook. We met before, but I was older then."

"I hear I have you to thank for this." Collyn pointed to his battered face.

"Perhaps," replied the wizard, with a negligent shrug, "but you could well be dead instead."

"Why did you betray your master?"

"Norfulk Roderickson is not my master!" He paced away from Collyn as if distancing himself from the suggestion.

"You told the princess you were in his pay."

A scowl marred the elf's handsome features as he swung to face the riverman.

"That doesn't make him my master, human, and don't you forget it."

"It's the definition of master."

"We all have our parts to play in this game. I know mine."

"Why have you come here?" Collyn leaned back against the wall, arms folded across his broad chest.

"You are looking for the missing piece, are you not?"

"What do you mean?"

Ravenwing moved to his side, restless as the bird whose form he favored.

"The messenger. Andundal did send him as promised, you know. My uncle is an honorable man."

"I thought nothing less."

"Perhaps his choice was not the best, however. Leithan is young, with a quick tongue and a hot head. It has landed him in trouble. In fact..." The wizard cocked his head, studying Collyn with a thoughtful eye. "... you two could be brothers, from the look of your faces. Although his temper best matches that of your young prince. Leithan would like to take on the entire human race singlehanded for what they've done to him.

"But he needs your help, whether he wants it or not. He is scheduled for execution without ceremony in the morning, and no one will be the wiser."

"Frederick would not allow that!"

"If he knew of it. Did he not tell Roland no word arrived? Leithan never saw the king."

"How do you know so much?"

Ravenwing shrugged.

"There are a few advantages to magic."

"What can I do?"

"I can help somewhat, but Leithan must know his help comes from the humans as well. It will forge another link in the chain. I can get you inside his cell and weaken the stone around the bars of the window, but you must remove the iron. That I cannot do. There are also disadvantages to magic," he murmured, his expression rueful. Then he grinned. "It will appear as if Leithan managed to escape alone, and add a great deal to the elven mystique."

"We are all in deadly danger here. How can you be so lighthearted?" asked Collyn.

Ravenwing shrugged again.

"I suppose I share my younger brother's sense of humor."

"Is either of you ever completely serious? Although, I did see behind Dèodar's mask a time or two, and I sense neither of you is as foolish as you seem."

"Sometimes humor is the only light in the darkness."

"What will I do with the messenger after he is freed?" Collyn asked, trying to drag the conversation back to its point.

Ravenwing continued, eyes dark with the intensity of his emotion.

"Keep him beside you, Master Silverbrook," he said, his tone grave. "He may yet have a part to play. Show him not all humans are to be distrusted. He will have to get used to the idea sooner or later."

Collyn frowned. "What do you mean?"

Ravenwing favored him with an enigmatic smile.

"May Eostivil give you both good fortune."

The wizard gestured, and Collyn felt a tingling sensation as a curtain of shimmering light surrounded him. When the glow faded, he was standing in the center of a small dungeon cell. A slim elf lay stretched on the floor beneath the barred window, head pillowed on one arm. Moonlight streamed in, creating the only illumination in the chamber.

Collyn stole forward to lay a hand over the prisoner's mouth as he shook the messenger awake. The elf started up, biting down hard. The riverman hissed in pain.

"Stop that, *iothinae!*" he whispered, his voice sharp.

The messenger's eyes widened at the sound of the elven epithet.

"Now, I am going to take my hand away," Collyn continued. "I would advise you to stay silent!"

Leithan nodded, and Collyn removed his hand.

"Who are you?" the elf breathed.

"So much for silence." Collyn grinned, shaking his head. "Don't worry. Ravenwing sent me. We're going to get you out of here."

"How?"

"Leave that to me."

The big man stood on tiptoe, reaching up and taking hold of one of the window bars. His fingers just caught it, and his leverage was poor.

"I hope Ravenwing's confidence in me is not misplaced," he grunted, shoving against the bar as best he could. It grated loose from its moorings with a protesting whine.

Collyn tensed, throwing a glance over his shoulder at the door. He prayed it was solid enough to mask the noise. When no guard burst through it to investigate, he moved to the next bar. Soon, he had loosened all three.

"Come on," he ordered the young elf, his voice a mere breath, "get out of here." He made a stirrup of his hands to give Leithan a boost.

The messenger swarmed up the wall with the nimble grace of an accomplished climber and squeezed through the narrow window. Collyn leapt for the windowsill, but it proved too high to get a good grip.

"Leithan!" he called softly, "give me your hand."

There was no answer. The elf was gone.

Collyn felt his heart sink to his boots.

"Damn," he whispered. He slid down the wall. His head dropped into his hands as he contemplated the mess he'd made of things. "Now I have failed Roland as well, leaving the king unprotected. As usual, I chose the wrong path."

There was a soft noise outside the window, and his head snapped up. A slender length of elven rope snaked down the wall. Leithan's battered face peered over the windowsill.

"I'm sorry it took so long. I had to retrieve my pack. I knew I couldn't lift you alone." The messenger's voice was rain-soft, but clear enough to understand.

Collyn's spirits lifted as he took hold of the rope with murmured thanks to Eostivil. Bracing himself against the wall, he climbed to the opening. He grabbed the edges of the window and tried to crawl through. His heart skipped when his shoulders caught on the sides of the opening. Refusing to panic, he shoved hard, scraping off quite a bit of hide in the process.

"Come with me," he panted to Leithan as he rose to his feet. "It will soon be dawn."

He led the way back to the hidden doorway, grateful he wouldn't have to rely on the trail of crumbs after all.

They hurried through the hall as Collyn showed the messenger the way to Frederick's bedchamber. He jerked his head toward the alcove, and they stepped into the smaller room.

"We can talk here for a time. You should get some rest soon. The Lion's spies are trying to destroy the king. Roland has gone to contact some of Frederick's ministers he knows are loyal. Meanwhile, we must be vigilant. We will stand guard in turn." He lit a candle then turned to the elf.

He gasped when he caught his first clear glimpse

of the messenger. While Leithan was nearly six feet in height, his face was that of a young boy under its mass of bruises.

"You're only a child."

"I am sixteen!" protested the elf, his voice hot and his fists clenched.

A smile tugged at the riverman's mouth.

"'Tis sometimes a disadvantage to age more slowly, is it not? I heard Prince Roland voice the same complaint—and Steavil as well."

"You know Prince Steavil?" asked the youth in awe.

"We've met."

"Is he safe?"

"That, I can't say," Collyn replied, his voice grave as he considered what Stefan's present whereabouts might be. "We can only hope so."

**

Roland wasted no time returning to the farm but decided it would be foolish to ride Noble abroad in daylight. He spent the day checking and rechecking his gear and trying to rest. He begrudged the delay. However, when he took to the road at nightfall, he felt rested, despite having snatched only a fitful nap in the hayloft.

Dressed in his own tunic and leggings, he felt more comfortable, especially with his practice chain mail between his shirt and tunic. It was all he had been able to retrieve from his room at the castle; his other armor was sturdier, but it had been in the armory, too risky to go after.

The brown stain in his hair would not rinse out, and he decided it was for the best. At least it masked his most distinguishing feature.

The miles fell away under the gelding's pounding hooves. Before moonrise, he pulled the horse to a walk and began scanning the riverbank for vaguely remembered landmarks. A grove of trees surrounded a solitary cabin with a soft glow of candlelight streaming through oiled parchment windows. He slipped off Noble and led the gelding up to it. As he stepped onto the porch, a board creaked, and the door flew open.

A figure stood silhouetted in the door, a sword in hand.

"Who's there?" boomed the familiar voice of General Teodore.

Roland almost collapsed in relief. "It's me, General—Prince Roland."

Teodore stepped forward, sword raised. He peered at Roland in the dim light then tossed the sword away to clatter on the floorboards. With a whoop, he gathered Roland into a bearhug.

"I knew you weren't dead, you rascal! Come inside and have some wine."

Roland laughed breathlessly. "It's good to see you as well, General. Put me down."

Noble whinnied in agreement, tugging against the reins. Teodore let go, and Roland looped the reins around the post.

"I need your help, General."

"Of course. Whatever you need. Come inside. Fortenbraes is here as well."

"I hoped I might find him here."

Roland followed the soldier into the cabin, grateful for the warmth inside the cheery room. Fortenbraes looked up from a table beside the fire, a goblet of wine in his hand. His normally fastidious attire was crumpled, and his silver hair was mussed, as if he had been running his fingers through it. His eyes lit up at the sight of Roland.

"My lord!" he cried, pushing back his stool, and rising to his feet. "It is so good to see you."

Roland sank down across from the fencing teacher.

"It's good to see you, too, my friend." He took the mug Teodore thrust at him and drank the mulled wine. "That hits the spot."

Teodore, a giant bear of a man—even broader than Collyn—plopped down next to Fortenbraes. "Tell us everything."

"That's a tall order, my friend. I really would rather not take the time to tell you all, but in a nutshell, Jarome's raft was attacked by men sent by my cousin Norfulk. He has been poisoning the king. Father trusts you both. And I trust Father's judgment. So, I have come to you to see who else we can trust."

"I would once have said that all my men were loyal." Teodore sighed. "Now…"

"Why did you two leave the castle?"

"We were asked to. In no uncertain terms. Marcell told us the order came directly from the king." He took a gulp from his own goblet. Wine dribbled on his tunic unheeded. "I didn't believe it, but we had no choice. He had my own men 'escort' us from the keep."

"Some of the guard must still be loyal."

"Oh, aye. I hear there have been a rash of desertions lately." One massive finger tapped the side of his drink-reddened nose. "I do still hear things."

Fortenbraes pried the goblet from his companion's hand.

"We have been in contact with Tulley and Jamis—I trained them from pups, and trust both," he said. "They say there is a body of king's men assembling on the Heath a half-day's ride from the castle. I think the last numbers were three score or so. Another two score remain at the keep. You could trust Tulley to tell you who they are."

"So few amongst the entire guard?"

"The rest are mostly sheep. They will follow whoever makes the biggest promises. If Norfulk loses in this battle, they will become loyal to the king again." The swordsmaster shrugged. "It isn't pretty or noble, but it is life."

Roland stared at the rough ceiling, trying to make sense of it all.

"We have to do something, but Norfulk's influence is so pervasive. What strategy can we use against him?"

Teodore crossed his arms on the table, leaning forward.

"When a viper is in your midst, the only way to destroy it is to cut off its head." His eyes were sharp beneath a tangle of grizzled curls. "A company of men might be able to get to Crypticia if they rode hard and fast, but that demon spawn who rules there will see them coming halfway across the plain.

"There must be a diversion of some kind to hold his attention." He began to trace patterns in a puddle of spilled wine on the table. "If one squadron came straight through in plain sight, a second might be able to sweep behind the castle and come in close."

"How many men would we need?" Roland asked.

"Oh..." The general exhaled with a great gust of

wine-tainted breath. "More than we've got, lad. If you rallied every loyal man we know, you might get a slim company—less than five-score. We'd need another twenty at least to be sure."

"I might be able to get that many."

"From where, the moon?" growled Teodore.

"Not quite. The Forest of Night."

"No one lives in the wood, my lord," chided Fortenbraes. "This is no time to joke."

"There are allies to be had, but it will be a delicate matter. Teodore, I need you to go to the men on the Heath. Rally them to the cause. Fortenbraes, can you get back into the castle and speak to those who are loyal within?"

Fortenbraes nodded. "I still have a few tricks up my sleeve."

"I will go to the Forest, and speak to the king there—"

"What are you on about?" Teodore demanded.

"I'll explain it all later. For now, trust me. We will all meet at the Ring of Tears in two days. I know that isn't much time to prepare, but I fear we cannot spare any more."

"We'll do as you say, my prince," Fortenbraes promised. "Now, you should get some sleep. It's late."

Roland shook his head, pushing back from the table.

"I must be going. It will take some persuasion to convince Andundal to join us."

"One of us should come with you, my lord," Fortenbraes protested.

"No. I need you both to do as I have asked. I will meet you in two days."

He clasped hands with both men then stepped

back into the night. The air was keen with frost, and he drew this cloak closer. *Can I convince Andundal that destroying the Lion is in both our interests? By the Flames and Eostivil's luck combined, I hope so.*

He untied Noble and climbed back into the saddle. If he retraced the route he and Collyn had taken coming from the elven court, he should be there by morning. He turned the gelding's head toward the south.

Noble's pace ate up the miles as they rode through the night. The horse appeared tireless. As the moon sank behind the mountains, however, Roland sensed a falter to his gait, belying that impression. Noble would run until his great heart burst if his master commanded, but it was cruel to treat him so. He could not maintain this pace indefinitely.

He could hear the gelding's labored breath as the stumbles became more frequent. The horse's sweat turned to steam in the chill air, rising to tickle the prince's nostrils.

"That's enough, boy!" Roland laughed aloud, giving the horse's damp neck an affectionate slap. "I don't need to dive into trouble at your expense. Andundal will be just as angry tomorrow." He reined in and slipped from Noble's back before leading the animal forward through the dim starlight. "We'll find a sheltered spot to rest this side of the forest."

The night was clear and cold, and he could hear the crunch of frost beneath his boots. It was the first true frost of the winter. Snow would soon follow.

Just before dawn, he found a little copse of trees that supplied a sheltered spot from the wind. A gurgling stream ran through it, its bed already fringed with ice.

"What say you, friend? This looks like an ideal camping place to me. I can rest here for a few hours and let you graze. We'll seek out the elves in the sunlight."

It was comforting to tell his plans to the horse, even if it could not answer him. He thought wistfully of Stefan, and wished the other well.

Stifling a yawn, Roland unsaddled Noble and rubbed him down with a handful of grass. He hobbled the gelding then threw himself down on the soft ground to think, chewing on a tart stem of grass with his head pillowed against the saddle.

Somehow, I have to convince Andundal to join me in an alliance. For either side to go against Norfulk alone is certain death, but together we might prevail.

Without intending to, he drifted into a deep sleep.

Noble's indignant neigh snapped him awake. His hand fell to the sword at his side even before his eyes were fully open. He threw off the cloak he had been using as a blanket and drew the weapon as he leapt to his feet.

A man dressed in ragged homespun was trying to control the horse, which fought against his hold. Noble's struggles were hampered by the hobbles around his feet. A second man stood poised to strike at the prince, sword in hand. The weapon was far better than one would expect such a ruffian to own. The swiping attack he leveled at Roland showed he was no stranger to its use.

Roland parried the attack by sheer luck then found he was fighting for his life. The swordsman was not bound by the rules Roland had been taught at court, as the prince soon learned when his opponent threw a handful of grit into his face. Roland gasped when the stinging dirt flew into his eyes, temporarily blinding him. He stumbled out of range, rubbing his eyes with his fist. By the time he could see, the would-be horse thief had abandoned his prize and joined the swordsman.

Instinctively, Roland let his years of training take over. He thrust and riposted, parried, and lunged with cool efficiency, searching for an opening, forcing himself to remain unemotional and analytical as he fought. It was nothing like the fencing practice he had skipped so often, or even Eeonathor's false ambush. This was for real. He dared not let himself think beyond the next stroke. For the first time, he realized this battle would end in death, and he vowed it would not be his own.

The horse thief, not as skilled a swordsman as his companion, let his guard slip, and Roland thrust home, burying his blade in the man's chest. A look of surprise brushed the man's face; then it contorted in agony as a choked scream tore from his throat. There was a hideous gurgle, and blood-flecked spittle flew from the man's lips when he tried to call out to his comrade. The brigand crumpled forward over the prince's hand.

Roland gagged as hot gore splashed him. He jerked at his sword, but it was caught in the dead man's ribcage. He backed away in panic, tripping over his feet. He forgot about the second villain in his need to get away from the horror the first had become.

The dead man's companion felt no such compunction. He swung at Roland's head with his weapon, and the prince just managed to roll out of the way. His hand came down on the fallen sword of his victim, and he swept it upward, catching the second man across the throat. Blood flooded over him as the body collapsed on top of him.

Roland shoved the dead man aside with a wordless cry. The smell of blood enveloped him, and his gorge rose. Retching violently, he heaved up the scant contents of his stomach then dragged a hand across his mouth before remembering it was covered in gore.

He could taste it on his lips.

Stumbling to the icy stream coming down from the mountains, he scrubbed until his skin was raw to get the blood off. He dragged his tunic off and dunked it into the water, rinsing away the majority of the gore. His hands seemed to move of their own volition while he relived over and over the feeling of blade piercing flesh.

He crossed to the bodies, turning over the first man with his boot and grabbing the blood-caked hilt of his sword. Planting his foot on the dead man's chest, he braced himself and put all his weight behind it as he pulled. He had to rock the sword back and forth to get it free, and the bile rose into his throat once more. He gulped it back as the blade finally wrenched free, and he wiped it clean. Jamming the weapon home in its scabbard, he started toward Noble.

His legs gave out beneath him.

He sank to the thick grass, shudders wracking him as the adrenaline rush of the attack leeched out. He rocked back and forth, breath coming in quaking gasps. His tunic was soaking wet, and he shivered in the chill autumn air. He reached over and snagged the cloak he had flung aside at the beginning of the fight and pulled it around his shoulders. He huddled into it and stared at the bodies.

These men are dead. He kept reiterating that to himself in his head. *They will not get up in a few minutes and go to the tavern for ale.*

And I killed them.

Of course, they would cheerfully have done the same to him, but that was beside the point. He had never killed a man before. Some part of him had burned away when he thrust the sword into the villain's chest. The last shreds of his pampered childhood were torn free.

Roland felt hot tears welling up and buried his face in the cold frosted comfort of the grass, wrenched with bitter sobs. He could never take it back. He had killed these men, and life could never be the same again.

The prince got to his feet. There was no point in putting it off any longer. He had to move on. Turning his back on the dead men, he staggered across the copse of trees to corral Noble.

The horse was understandably edgy, and it took him several tries to catch the dangling reins, despite the hobbles. Roland soothed the gelding, crooning soft nonsense as he stroked the animal's flank to calm him. He bent to undo the restraints.

"Let's get out of here, old friend," he murmured, his voice weary.

Leaping onto the horse's bare back, he cantered away from the campsite, abandoning the blood-spattered saddle where it lay.

***

"Iothinae! May you rot in the Flames, you arrogant fool!"

Eeonathor cursed himself for his own stupidity. *A wizard of my class, and I did not foresee the folly of sending the children off on their own.*

He had wanted to make certain they would not fall into Norfulk's clutches. Instead, he had delivered them straight into the sorcerer's power.

The timetable has to be pushed forward. It is now or never.

He glanced around the tiny circular chamber. Everything he owned was contained in this thirty-foot sphere. It was the only home he had known since his banishment from Starlit Wood. He shook his head with a rueful smile.

"What does that say about my life?" he mused aloud.

Hidden deep in the mountains, the room was furnished for comfort and crowded with magical apparatus and bric-a-brac. His bed was built into the curve of the wall, a soft feather-filled couch piled with silk pillows and covered with a heavy velvet spread. Daerci refused a bed of her own. She slept on a pallet of furs behind a curtain in a nook decorated with her simple belongings.

The rest of the chamber was filled with cleverly arranged chests and tables heaped with scrolls, retorts, herbs, potions, candles, and spell books. Every possible inch of space was used to best advantage. The walls were covered with charts and memorabilia and the floor with fine carpets. A hole in the center of the ceiling was spell-warded to let smoke out but not let rain in. A circular hearth stood directly beneath it, with a fire-pit and spit.

His eye fell on Daerci's pallet, lying half-hidden in its curtained alcove, and the smile faded.

The last thing in the world I want is to see Stefan torn from Daerci like everyone else in her life. She deserves a chance to be happy at last. I only hope I am not too late to rectify my mistake.

He pulled the golden Sunstone out of his shirt and held it before him.

Thank the gods Steavil proved to be the man I expected him to be.

Ravenwing had kept the pendant safe for all those years, waiting for a sign. Only because Stefan had given it to him freely could he harness its powers for himself.

Closing his eyes, he chanted under his breath, channeling the spell through the stone. Norfulk had more natural power than he, but the Starlit heirloom was a focusing point that would increase his spell-casting ability in the inevitable showdown.

He just hoped it would prove to be enough.

The air shimmered, but Ravenwing did not need to see it. It was not until the temperature around him dropped several degrees and dankness assaulted his nostrils that he broke his concentration on the spell and opened his eyes. He bit back a gasp.

He stood in one of the windowless dungeon cells where Norfulk consigned his captives. Stefan hung by bloodied wrists from manacles attached to the wall. The boy's head lolled on his shoulder, and his long black hair hid his face. A weight attached to his left ankle pulled his body askew. Daerci stood before the wall, held in temporal stasis. Her fists were balled as if she were trying to defend herself. Or her prince.

Eeonathor felt something harden within him. He released Stefan from the wall, blasting the manacles loose with controlled fury, then laid his cousin on the stone floor before examining the boy with tender care. After rinsing off the raw skin of the prince's wrists with clean water from his pack, he salved them with an ointment from the kit at his waist. Loosening the legging around Stefan's lame knee, he ground his teeth in rage. The knee was swollen and discolored, and looked as if it were twisted out of line.

He undid the ankle fetter with a word and it flew across the cell. It clanged against the stone wall as Ravenwing salved the ankle and straightened the knee. Stefan moaned. Eeonathor placed a hand on the boy's forehead, murmuring a soft spell. The prince quieted but did not regain his senses.

"Perhaps that is for the best, my boy," Ravenwing sighed. He immobilized the knee as best he could then turned to Daerci.

"Ah, *inithia entheiria*, I let you down again," he whispered, running a finger down her frozen cheek. "I always seem to cause you pain."

Cupping the Sunstone in one hand, he murmured the words of another spell. Daerci's fist slammed out and caught him in the jaw as she completed the motion Norfulk had arrested. Ravenwing reeled back against the wall of the cell.

"I guess I deserved that," he sighed, working his jaw. "You throw quite a punch for someone your size."

"Master! I am so sorry!" The girl's face was horrorstricken.

He chuckled. "Don't concern yourself, little one. It

was an honest reaction."

Daerci was no longer listening. She knelt beside Stefan, brushing the ebony hair off his face with a gentle hand.

"Stefan, *ethia evleeae*. My beloved..."

Ravenwing hunkered down behind her, one hand on her shoulder.

"He needs the rest. Norfulk put him through the Flames. I did all I can."

"Thank you, Master," she answered, her tone distracted as she sank down beside the wall to sit cradling Stefan's head in her lap. There was a newfound maturity in the face framed by its uneven blond thatch.

"You are growing up, *ethiae ruathia*."

"Wonderful timing, ain't it?" She stroked Stefan's cheek with the back of her hand, smiling down at her prince. "Norfulk knows who he is—that spell didn't stop me ears. He's going to kill us, ain't he?"

"Not until he has no further use for him, and he will need you to control him, so the two of you are safe for a time. When you say Norfulk knows who he is, do you mean Stefan, or Steavil?"

"Norfulk knows he is the prince, and plans to let yer uncle know of his capture. He thinks perhaps the princess will come after him, and hopes to flush out Roland, if he lives."

Ravenwing nodded approval at her choice of words. She had learned her lessons well. If the cell were watched, there was nothing definite in the statement. Since she didn't know that Norfulk's arrogance was even greater than his own, and the sorcerer would never waste time monitoring prisoners, she knew better than to admit Roland lived.

Though I know Norfulk knows about Roland, since I told him myself. Damn it all to the Flames. Why did I think I could manage it all? Because I am an arrogant idiot!

Stefan stirred, and his eyes fluttered open. He glanced from one hovering face to the other.

"Daerci..." he whispered.

"I'm here, milord."

"I'm not your lord."

"He's fine, Master." She grinned, helping Stefan to sit up and resting his head against her shoulder.

"Eeonathor," murmured Stefan, "why are you here?"

Ravenwing saw Daerci tense, caught in the middle. His jaw set as he bowed his head.

"This is exactly what I was trying to avoid, *ethiae ionavae.* I wanted to get you far away from Norfulk's clutches. I should have known better."

"Indeed, little wizard," agreed a lazy voice.

Ravenwing spun to his feet in one fluid motion, standing to shield the pair on the floor. His hands came up, ready to cast if necessary.

"Oh, not yet, my friend. Our battle will come, but not just yet. I wait for other players. For now, stay here and tend your pet and her little lame prince." Norfulk murmured a phrase before Eeonathor could react, passing his hand before the iron bars of the cell door.

Ravenwing leapt for the bars, but the instant his fingers brushed them, he staggered back, wracked with pain, stunned by the force of the magic—it magnified the effect of the iron a hundredfold. Dazed, he fell to his hands and knees, and shook his head to clear it as the tearing agony slowly faded.

"Don't worry," Norfulk continued. "Your day will come, I promise you. I will enjoy destroying you, piece by piece."

As silently as he had come, the sorcerer was gone.

"What do we do now?" asked Stefan, leaning back against the wall. His arm circled Daerci's shoulders protectively as she leaned her head against his.

"We wait," the wizard answered, sinking down against the opposite wall. "And pray the rescue he's expecting never arrives."

***

Norfulk leaned back in his ebony throne, fingers steepled as he stared at the shadowed ceiling.

"How can we best get our message across?" he mused aloud.

The beast kneeling before him knew better than to answer the rhetorical question, and Norfulk allowed himself a wry smile.

"I doubt Andundal will be surprised to find his son lives. It is too much of a coincidence the cousin comes to the rescue. I knew I was right about that little cutpurse. Ravenwing's pet human is almost as well known as Roland's pet elf. Interesting, is it not? That juxtaposition of opposites?"

The beast nodded.

"You are so complacent it makes me sick."

He rose to his feet, planting one elegant boot against the beast's shoulder and kicking it off-balance. The beast backed up several feet and resumed its subservient posture. Norfulk sighed, circling behind the throne, and draping a casual arm over the back.

"Tell my spies to ride with all speed to the edge of the elven forest. I want them to be caught. They are to tell Andundal I have his son. Tell him I will trade the boy for Mendana. It is a lie, of course, but an anxious father will believe anything. He will not sanction the trade, but perhaps it will draw him out. Speaking of anxious fathers, how fares my uncle Frederick?"

The beast swallowed hard.

"He's not as sick, my lord."

"Improving? How is that possible?"

"I don't know. The girl says she gives him poison, but he seems better."

Norfulk came to attention, crackling with intensity "I want him dead! Tell the wench to double the dose."

"As you say, my lord."

"Of course 'as I say,' you idiot! I am Norfulk! I will be king!" He threw his arms up and lightning cracked in the chamber, filling it with an eerie blue-white glow.

The beast groveled.

"Oh, get out of here," Norfulk growled in disgust, throwing himself down on the padded throne with a wave of dismissal. The beast crawled backward out of the room. Norfulk rolled his eyes as the sounds of its shambling retreat faded in the distance.

Gnawing on his thumb until it was once more bloodied, he glanced over at an empty chair. A thoughtful frown quirked one brow, and he bit his lip. His free hand sketched a symbol, and an image of Mendana appeared in the chair. The sorcerer stood, moving to caress the smooth cheek of the simulacrum. It felt cold and waxen beneath his fingertips, beautiful but brainless. The creature sat motionless, staring at nothing.

"Well, well, well, my darling. You are here at last. What do you think of the place, my sweet?"

"It is as handsome as you are, my lord king," chirped the simulacrum in a vapid parody of Mendana.

"What a clever girl," he breathed, pleased despite himself. He bent and kissed the ivory cheek. There was no response.

A brief spasm of pain swept through him.

"Why is this not enough? I could people my castle with such soulless copies. They would fulfill my every desire, obey my every whim, yet they hold no charm for me." He sighed and straightened. "It is Mendana I want. Nothing less will do."

He stalked away from the chair and gestured again. Blue flame shot from his fingertips to engulf the creation, and it exploded.

Chapter 32

A single candle lit the darkened chamber, and an open casement framed a square only slightly lighter than the shadowed wall. The waning moon hung obscured by heavy clouds, threatening the first snow of the year. An older man slept in the bed, his face worn with care.

Collyn Silverbrook slept near the bed, head pillowed on his arms atop a table. A dagger rested under one hand.

The door cracked open, and a woman slipped into the room. She eased the dagger from Collyn's hand and, with a vicious downward sweep, she plunged the knife into his broad back.

He grunted in pain and slid to the floor, blood soaking into his shirt. The woman stepped over his fallen body and crossed to the bed. She picked up a pillow and held it above the sleeping man's face.

***

This is becoming a habit, Mendana thought bitterly, hugging her knees as shudders wracked her. She pushed sweat-soaked hair from her forehead. This time, the vision felt more like premonition than dream. Her thoughts raced. Had her ability to see visions lain dormant, now brought to life by the Moonstone's influence?

The dreams grew frequent and more detailed every night. However, this was the first without one of her loved ones present. What was she supposed to do about these events? Stop them? Tell someone?

She weighed her options. There were few. She had no idea where to find Roland and little time, even if she knew where to begin.

Why is Roland not at his father's side? Why does Collyn stand this vigil alone? If Roland...

She could not bear to finish the thought.

Perhaps I can get word to Dèodar that Collyn might be in danger. I know the two of them have become friends. But would he be able to do anything? She clutched her head, which was swimming. *By the time word reaches him, it could very well be too late. I must go myself.*

She could think of nothing else to do.

She rose and dressed in a thick wool tunic and heavy leggings; the air held a distinct chill these days. With deftness born of practice, she bound up her hair then swept a cloak about her shoulders and fastened it, lifting the hood to hide her face.

"Where are you going?" asked a quiet voice behind her.

Mendana whirled, breath catching in her throat. Her father stood in the shadows, dressed in his leathers, and leaning on his great horn bow.

"Noile!"

"I was coming to wake you. The warders have sent word the prince has returned."

"Steavil is home?"

A shadow crossed Andundal's face.

"No, Prince Roland. He is requesting an audience. I have granted him passage. Come, I think you should be present."

Mendana followed him silently. She would have a chance to warn Roland after all.

***

Roland composed his thoughts as he followed Captain Aerlann's ramrod back through the hallways of the elven palace. Andundal would listen. He must.

Captain Aerlann opened the throne room door and stood aside, gesturing Roland to enter. Nervously, the prince nodded and stepped inside. He knew Andundal had cause to be displeased with him but hoped the news he brought would override the king's anger.

He bowed low to the thrones, heart racing when he saw Mendana on the Moonrise chair.

"My lord and lady."

Andundal surveyed him coolly.

"You sent word of news and requested audience. What do you wish to say to us?"

"Your Majesty, the time has come to fight back against the Black Lion. As we speak, those men loyal to my father's throne are being gathered to march on Crypticia. Their numbers are limited, 'tis true, but my general believes we will have at least five-score men, and he hopes to gather more from the populace as we march. But we need allies—a squad of fighters with the skills of your warders to blend into their surroundings and rain death from afar with their bows might turn the tide. I come to ask that elves and men put aside their differences against a common foe."

"Your plea is most eloquent, young prince, but I fear your venture might be doomed from the start if you rely upon my elves to be able to slip in unnoticed. We captured a spy riding along the southern border not two hours ago. Norfulk sent him from Crypticia with a message. The sorcerer holds my son prisoner."

"What?" His mind reeled at the thought of gentle Stefan in Norfulk's clutches.

"Norfulk 'rescued' Steavil from slavers and took him to his dungeons. The Black Lion also claims to hold Eeonathor and his companion.

"Norfulk knows my son's capture is the one thing sure to rally my troops and force me into battle. The elves will not be able to move with stealth this time. Or remain in our fortress and do nothing, as we have far too often in the past."

"We must tell Dèodar," Mendana murmured.

"After all Eeonathor has done? I would think Dèodar likely to rejoice," retorted the king.

"That is his choice to make, Noile. He loves Eeonathor. His brother is as dear to him as Stefan is to me. He deserves to know."

"My men will assemble at the Ring of Tears by dawn two days hence," Roland explained. "We must wait for them if the plan is to work—and there is much to organize before it is safe to move forward anyway. Perhaps I could use that time to go to Moonrise and get word to Dèodar. If your men will join us, that is."

"The elves will join you, Roland Frederickson. I shall rally a company of my best archers."

"You banished your best archer to Moonrise Wood, and are too stubborn to call him back," argued Mendana. "If you take a full company with you, Norfulk will step in and pluck out the heart of our stronghold like a piece of ripe fruit. He is not a stupid man, Father. He'll count on you coming to Steavil's aid and destroy you at his leisure."

"What do you suggest?" Andundal's eyes were chips of obsidian ice.

Mendana gulped. She knew she trod perilously close to the limit of her father's indulgence, but she had to have her say.

"Let Roland go to Dèodar. He *is* your best archer. Take Aerlann's patrol—'tis less than a score but will not decimate the kingdom's watch. Norfulk..." Her voice caught. "...fancies me. I can distract him while you and your men rescue the prisoners." She turned to Roland. "I don't know if you should be away from your own kingdom, my lord. I...had a vision. Your father and Collyn are in grave danger."

"Your plan is too risky, Mendana," Andundal protested.

"Aye, my lady," Roland concurred, heartsick at the mere thought of it. "If we wait for the reinforcements, we can storm the castle and rescue the prisoners at the same time. Collyn watches over my father. I will trust him."

"I do not try to stop you from attacking that monster, because I know it would be pointless, but you will never win by direct assault," she argued. "Mine is the only way. And it was Collyn's back that took a knife at your father's bedside in my vision, Roland."

The thought made him feel a bit faint, but his plans were already in motion. Teodore and Fortenbraes would be on their way to the rallying point by now. If he returned to the castle to rescue his father and Collyn, he could not get word to them in time.

One of the few lessons he did remember from Marcell's droning history recitations was that indecision had been the downfall of many a campaign. But time was running out! Did they have the luxury of waiting for the troops to arrive, or was Mendana correct?

"We must wait for the troops," Roland said with a sigh. "It is the only viable course. But I will go and bring Dèodar home. His bow is an asset we can't afford to waste, King Andundal."

The king nodded. "Sometimes even the crown must bow to the inevitable," he answered with a tight smile. "And it will be good to have him beside us when we march."

"I'll go at once."

***

"Twuae liami vieindi, ethiae ionavae?" murmured Eeonathor, probing Stefan's knee with gentle fingers. "Do you feel any better?"

"I do feel better, cousin. *Euae vieindi, eathinae*," answered Stefan, the fatigue in his voice belying the brave words. "Is the knee worse?"

"Than yesterday...no. Than last week..." The wizard shrugged.

"Will it hold me this time?"

"To be honest, Norfulk's torture may have helped. I have heard of such things. But will you be given an opportunity to find out? It all depends on that madman—and I wouldn't count on it."

Stefan swallowed hard against the sudden lump in his throat.

"What will he do with us, Eeonathor?"

"There's no point in lying to ourselves. You stand in his way. Prophecy says you will destroy him, and he does not intend to give you the chance. He thought you dead many years ago and until you are, he cannot legally become king as he plans when he weds Mendana."

"But Father is king."

"That will not stop him long. He is being careful no one will be able to say he has stolen or forced his way onto the thrones, but he will have them both. Andundal is an obstacle to be removed, nothing more. Frederick is dying, and Roland will be next. He means to rule the entire land, and the beasts across the sea who think to save themselves by allying with him now will not have long to wait before he comes a-calling."

Ravenwing busied himself with the contents of his pouch, unwilling to meet Stefan's eyes.

"As for Daerci and I, the girl he may spare—send her to the slavers as a token of his favor—but he needs no other magic-users to muddy the waters. I have outlived my usefulness." A wry smile twisted his handsome features.

"Well, I ain't going to stand by and watch you both die!" Daerci declared, her voice hot as she jumped to her feet.

"What, precisely, are you going to do to prevent it, Flame-Cat?" asked Ravenwing, voice colored with laughter. "Turn into a newt and wriggle through the bars?" One dark eyebrow arched upward in amusement.

"I...I...I will think of something, I will!" she vowed, sitting hard, arms folded across her chest as a sulky pout settled over her plain features.

Stefan joined Eeonathor's laughter, the silvery peals incongruous in the dank dungeon.

"I have faith that you shall, *evleeia*." He gazed down into her flashing green eyes, brighter for the shine of tears.

Despite her upbringing, she was still just a girl—and very close to the edge of her endurance—but so determined to save the day. She was no beauty. Somehow, that only served to make her more precious to him. Suddenly, he wanted to protect her more than anything else in the whole world, and his heart sank as he realized he could not do it.

"I am feeling a bit weary, cousin." Ravenwing yawned. "I think I'll take a nap."

Stefan stared at him in bewilderment. They had just awoken from sleep not an hour before

Ravenwing rolled his eyes and drew his cloak around him, lying down against the far wall as he made a point of turning his back to them. He glanced over his shoulder, and Stefan flashed his cousin a sheepish grin when he finally grasped the wizard's intentions.

Thank you, eathinae, the prince mouthed.

Eeonathor winked then drew his hood over his head as he settled down for a needless nap.

Taking care not to jar his knee, Stefan slid over to the opposite side of the cell to lean against the wall. Daerci's face fell when he moved away from her, and she huddled into herself, accepting the rejection.

"Would you please come here?" he murmured in exasperation, holding his arms out to her. "It is hard enough to get a little privacy without you wasting the opportunity."

Her face lit up like the sun, and she flung herself to his side, her arms going about his neck in a stranglehold. Gently, he moved her grip to his waist, looking down at her upturned face with a crooked grin. His heart spasmed with love for her, and he began to sing, the soft words haunting in the dark prison.

I tried to write a song for you,
To tell you how I feel—
I tried to write a song for you,
But the words won't come out real.

I've loved you from the very start,

The first day that we met—
I've loved you from the very start,
And now I can't forget.

That to you I'm just another note

In an ever-changing theme—
And the hope I bear for love's return
Is only a passing dream.

He watched naked emotion chase across Daerci's expressive face. The infinite joy as she accepted he was serious delighted him no end. That reaction meant more than gold to him.

"Oh, Stefan! It ain't no dream," she whispered.

He hugged her to him. Every moment with her was a priceless treasure.

He knew Eeonathor spoke the truth. If the matter rested with Norfulk, his time was short. The thought chilled him, and his grip tightened with convulsive strength.

"What is it, my prince?" she asked, her voice a mere whisper as she raised a hand to touch his cheek.

The words caught in his throat.

"I...I am frightened, Daerci. I don't want to die. Especially not now."

She tilted her head back to look up at him, her emerald eyes two bottomless ponds.

"You shan't, Stefan. I ain't going to let you. All me life I wanted someone to love me. I'll be damned if I let ye go now."

"What about Eeonathor? He loves you."

She blushed crimson.

"That ain't what I meant," she muttered. Even his sharp ears almost missed it. "He don't love me—"

"Like I love you?"

She nodded. He caught one glimpse of her face, miserable at the revelation, before she hid her flaming cheeks against his tunic. He slipped a finger under her chin and raised her head so he could see her eyes. They glinted with tears still tenuously held in check.

"*Euae everiami twuia leietae oth astreales, evleeia...*I love you like the stars." He bent his head to kiss her. It was tentative and gentle, an exploration for them both, and for a little while, he managed to forget his fear.

Chapter 33

"My lord?" Collyn stood beside Frederick's bed, gazing down at the wan features of the sick man. The king's eyes fluttered open.

"What is it, Collyn? Has something happened?"

Frederick struggled to sit upright. Collyn helped him ease up in the bed.

"No. Nothing new. I just wanted to introduce you to someone." He gestured behind him, and a slight figure stepped hesitantly forward.

Frederick peered at the newcomer. "Who is it? Who is there?"

Collyn pulled the other into view. "I wanted you to meet our friend Leithan. This is the messenger who was sent to tell you Roland is well. He is the youngest member of King Andundal's court."

"You are an elf, my boy?" Frederick murmured.

"Aye."

Frederick patted the side of the bed.

"Sit. Tell me of your people."

Leithan perched on the edge of the mattress.

"What do you wish to know?"

"I have so many questions, I don't know where to begin." Frederick chuckled. "How have the elves remained hidden so long? We have thought them gone for centuries."

"No, my lord, there are still some of us here." The elf grinned shyly. "We keep to our forests—men do not venture there. Our home is below-ground, so that even if you were to travel through the wood and be allowed to exit it, you would never see any evidence of us."

Collyn took the chair beside the bed.

"Tell His Majesty about the crystal lamps. Roland thought you would be most interested in them, my king."

"We grow them like flowers—no, that isn't quite the way to put it. They form piece by piece, like...like your sea creatures sometimes do. And the light inside is a bit of magic that even the youngest child can do." He laughed. "I should know—I *am* the youngest."

"Can you show us?" asked Frederick eagerly.

"Of course. I will need something to...pin the light to. Something to glow."

"Look on that table over there, Collyn. I think there should be something that will do."

Collyn rose and stepped over to the indicated side table. The surface was covered with bric-a-brac and bits of jewelry.

"Am I looking for something in particular?"

"Something round that will fit in my hand will be best," answered Leithan.

Collyn found a globe of crystal.

"Here." He placed it in Leithan's hand.

Taking a deep breath, Leithan stared at the globe. He murmured softly in elven, and the heart of the crystal began to glow a soft blue. As he continued to chant, the glow grew brighter and brighter, until the light spilled over his fingers in visible rays.

Frederick clapped his hands in delight.

"How wonderful, my boy!"

Leithan gave the king the glowing ball with a shaking hand.

"A gift, my lord." His breathing was slightly labored.

"Are you alright?" Collyn asked, brow furrowed.

"Magic takes its toll. Some spells are harder than others, of course—and the larger the spell, the greater the cost. Like any craft, practice allows greater artistry. And some wizards can channel much greater magic without ill effect, or can turn the cost outward. Have you heard of the blight on the southern plain? It sounds like what would happen if great magic was performed and turned outwards."

"Hmmm," Frederick mused. "That is most strange. Magic is not something found in our family tree. If Norfulk is responsible, as the rumors say, where did he come by magic, and who trained him to use it?"

"Good questions," Collyn replied grimly. "I wish I could answer them."

Frederick laid the little globe on the night table, stifling a yawn.

"I think I would like to rest now."

"Of course, my lord," Collyn murmured, rising to his feet once more. "Come, Leithan. We need to grease that hinge."

Leithan rose as well. "*Ithneimi, ethiae linavao.*"

"What?" Frederick frowned.

"Rest, my king," the elf translated with a smile.

"I look forward to learning more about your race, my friend," replied the king as his eyes drifted closed.

Collyn jerked his head toward the alcove.

"I must get some grease on that door hinge," he murmured once they were out of earshot. "It wakes the king every time it opens."

"Isn't that a good thing? It warns us when someone is coming."

Collyn cocked his head. "You're right, young one. I never thought of that. I must be losing my touch."

Leithan grinned. "It is good to know I can still be of some use."

"More than you know, my friend." Collyn clapped him on the shoulder. "I haven't seen the king that animated since we arrived. You're a tonic better than any I could brew."

"Well, this tonic is beginning to weaken. Is there anything to eat?"

"Let's see what we can find."

***

After the supper hour, Sara received a summons to the high chancellor's study. She dried her hands on her apron and nervously smoothed her hair. She rapped on the door when she arrived, heart beating like a drum in her chest.

"Come in," came the sharp order.

"You wished to see me, milord?" She bobbed a quick curtsy.

Marcell looked up from a sheaf of papers.

"Yes...indeed." His gaze ran from the top of her head to her toes and back again. Naked lust slithered within his eyes.

She fought to keep from shuddering.

"What is it? I have chores."

He laid the papers on the edge of the table. There was nothing of the foppish minister Roland had so often dismissed in the man before her. He moved like a snake, flicking his tongue across his lips.

"I sent your message to the master as requested. He

knows the prince was back—and we know the prince is no longer in the castle. It has been searched from top to bottom."

"Did you search the king's room?"

He glided closer, circling her. "I looked there myself...and was distressed to note the king appeared to be growing in strength."

Sara stared at him.

"But...that's impossible! I have been dosing his meals as the master said. He should be nearly dead by now."

"Indeed." Marcell nodded, trailing a finger up her arm. "It is most puzzling."

Sarah gulped. "W–what do you wish for me to do?"

He brushed the back of his hand across her cheek. "Oh, I will think of something."

***

It was nearing midnight when Roland entered Moonrise Wood—the war council had taken longer than expected, but Andundal had given full blessing to fetch Dèodar. Noble's head hung low as they plodded into the forest, and he stumbled in the thick underbrush. His hooves rustled like an invading army in the silence of the dreary trees, and as they fought forward through the undergrowth, Roland had an uneasy sense there were eyes on them.

The prince slid from Noble's back and led the horse. The light from the waning moon scarcely penetrated the thick growth overhead, and Roland despaired of finding his way in the dark.

A welcoming flicker shone through the trees several yards ahead, along with the inviting odor of woodsmoke. Roland moved forward with caution, wondering if the fire belonged to friend or foe.

When he got close enough to tell, his heart leapt. In a day filled with bad luck, Eostivil had smiled at last. He chuckled to himself.

I am calling on the elven luck more and more often these days!

But to find Dèodar stretched out beside the crackling fire was definitely a gift from the god's—*or is that gods'?*—hands.

He stepped into the clearing—and froze as a blade flashed past his ear with a singing hiss.

"Glad to see you, too," he drawled.

"What do you expect, *iothino?*" complained the elf, rising fluidly to his feet. He came over and pulled the stiletto out of the tree. "You should know better than to sneak into a man's camp after dark." He clasped the prince's hand then glanced behind Roland. "Where's your strong arm?"

"I left Collyn with my father, *entheirae,* but he sends regards. How fare you?"

"I've been better." Dèodar sighed, sinking down beside the fire once more. "Come and sit, before you fall down."

Roland quickly hobbled the gelding, setting him free to graze near a dainty black mare.

"I'm glad I found you so easily. I was afraid I would have to search the entire wood."

A shadow settled in Dèodar's eyes.

"A lot of good it does to find me. I am banished from Starlit Wood." He busied himself with stoking the fire. "The king banished me to Moonrise for letting you return to Crown Keep. I was stripped of my rank and bow."

"Not anymore." Roland sank down beside him. "I know how great the sacrifice was for you, Dèodar Eriaborae—"

"Don't flatter yourself, princeling. I was merely trying to save my cousin the pain of seeing you in irons. She is so sensitive to that sort of thing." Dèodar shrugged, dusting his hands together as if to brush away the subject.

"Well, the king has seen reason. I have been sent to bring you home. The elves need your bow once more." Roland explained Norfulk's plot to kill the king, and why Collyn had remained behind. "We have a plan, and you are a key part of it," he concluded with a huge yawn.

"Well, you better get some sleep first. By the way, I like your hair. The color becomes you."

Roland threw the twig he was toying with at the elf then yawned again.

"I think I *will* get some sleep. Wake me for watch." He lay back with his head cradled on his arm. Things were looking up.

***

Stefan and Daerci huddled in one corner of the cell, whispering confidences. Every now and then one or the other would laugh softly over something the other said. The sound did Ravenwing's heart good.

It wasn't easy for Daerci, living a wanderer's life, more often than not pretending to be something she wasn't. She had never had a proper life. He was glad she had found some joy at last.

Ravenwing wracked his brains for some way out of this fiasco. If he could somehow play to Norfulk's ego, perhaps it could still be salvaged.

He glanced over at the children—no, they could no longer be called children. Somehow he must get them out of this dungeon. If Norfulk still thought of Stefan as merely Roland's squire, it might be possible, but Daerci had said that Norfulk knew Stefan's true identity.

He buried his face in his hands. What was he going to do?

***

Roland woke from a sound sleep to find weak sunlight filtering into the clearing. He rubbed a hand across his eyes to clear them.

"Morning, laze-abed," called Dèodar, stirring a pot on the fire. The thin trail of smoke wove into the mists blanketing the campsite. The elf chuckled, and Roland felt himself flush.

He sat up, shaking leaves out of his hair, and rubbing the chill out of his arms; his breath steamed. The forest was silent—even the birds were still, and it made him uneasy.

A savory aroma wafted on the frosty dawn.

"What is that smell?"

"Breakfast. You look like you could use some. Don't ask what's in it. You'd rather not know."

Roland clambered stiffly to his feet.

"Is there any water around here?" he mumbled, painfully aware how long it had been since his dousing in the stock tank—and that hadn't been a real bath. He grimaced with distaste.

"There's a stream just beyond those trees." Dèodar pointed across the clearing. "I'm surprised you didn't fall into it last night. Go wash up, then come and give me all the news."

Roland splashed his face and neck in the icy stream. The chill of the water shocked the last vestiges of sleep from him, and he felt refreshed and ready to fill Dèodar in on their plans.

Running damp fingers through his hair in a vain attempt to tame the unruly waves, he hunkered down beside Dèodar at the fire.

"Collyn sent me to find you. I'm going against Crypticia, and he suggested I shouldn't go alone."

"Wise counsel. What makes you think I'm stupid enough to go with you?"

"Past experience?" Roland shrugged. "Besides," he continued gravely, "your uncle says Norfulk has Stefan and Ravenwing captive."

Dèodar leaned forward, his face serious.

"It *is* stupid to go alone against the Lion. You know that. He is a powerful sorcerer, not some petty lord rebelling against the throne. He seems to know every move before it is made. You can't fight someone with his power."

"I don't really plan on going alone. Andundal is providing us with Aerlann's patrol to use as a distraction, and Father is sending a force of fivescore men. They'll meet us at the Ring of Tears at dawn tomorrow."

Dèodar tapped his finger on the side of his chin.

"Well, this is better than flitting about the countryside like some sort of flutterby. At least you have a plan this time. Now, you must stick to it."

"I intend to. For one thing, it's already in motion. It's too late to stop the troops now, even if I wanted to." Roland exhaled gustily.

Dèodar handed him a steaming bowl of stew.

"Eat up. We must douse the fire before the mists disperse."

Frowning thoughtfully, Roland blew on the food.

"What shall we do about your brother and Stefan?"

"If they're already in the Lion's clutches, do you think they'll be able to do us much good? Eeonathor always fancied himself a wizard, but I don't know how strong his powers really are. And Steavil is no warrior, he's a minstrel. I wouldn't count them in our army, my friend."

Roland dipped into the bowl Dèodar handed him. He wolfed down the thick stew, hardly tasting it in his haste to be on the road. Dèodar packed up his gear with quiet efficiency as Roland ate.

"You're sure my uncle has invited me home?"

Roland nodded. "I volunteered to come and fetch you with his blessing."

Dèodar threw his bags over his horse's back and leaping lightly after them.

"Have you no saddle?"

Roland's eyes clouded as he remembered where he had left it.

"Not anymore," he replied, pulling himself onto Noble's back. "Let's hurry. We must be back to the court by mid-afternoon if we're to make the dawn meeting."

The mare had no trouble keeping pace with Noble when they angled away from Moonrise toward Starlit Wood. Roland glanced about him as the daylight strengthened. He could not help but compare the stunted trees they were leaving with the beautiful growth he had seen in Starlit. Mendana's kingdom was touched with evil, and his heart was saddened by it.

"You should have seen it when I was a child," Dèodar murmured, as if he'd read Roland's mind. "The trees were tall and straight, mostly birch and ash. The leaves would whisper their music in the morning breeze. Moonrise Wood was an enchanted place then." His voice filled with pain. "Now, even the birds have deserted it." He sighed, shaking his dark head.

"I am sure it was a magical kingdom, *entheirae*," Roland replied, his voice soft.

"'Twas long ago, my prince." Dèodar changed the subject. "The most direct route back to the court will take us through the eastern corner of Starlit Wood. We'll need full daylight to negotiate that tangle."

They reached the edge of the trees before noon, but Roland had an uneasy feeling they were already much later than they should be.

Dèodar slid from his horse.

"There should be a warder path near here," he observed, his voice hushed. "The way will be easier once we strike it."

Roland dismounted. Taking the reins in his hand, he followed the ranger's lead. He could see the joy that touched Dèodar's face as he stepped once more beneath the canopy of Starlit's trees. The elf caressed the rough bark of the trees as he passed them, as if greeting friends he had been parted from. His head lifted, eyes closed to the feel of the breeze kissing his cheeks.

"Here is the path," he called soon after, his voice soft as the breeze. "We've a lot of distance to cover, and we'll have rough going, so let's hurry."

Roland nodded, leading Noble over to the vestiges of a path visible through the trees. It was barely a single man wide; the undergrowth stretched out eager tentacles on either side to trip the unwary. As Dèodar started forward, though, the vines drew back, and Roland hurried to follow before they snapped back into place.

They made fair time, and by mid-afternoon were far into the wood. The air warmed from the frost-laden morning, but it was still apparent winter was upon them. Roland shivered. It would be good to get back to the palace.

They arrived at one of the entry stones, and Dèodar opened the door while Roland tied the horses beside the rock

"Will they be alright here?" He frowned. "I hate to leave Noble unattended."

"We'll send someone back to take them to the corral—but I was under the impression you were in a hurry."

"True. This won't be a long stop, in any case. To be at the Ring by dawn, we'll need to ride hard and fast."

***

High in his tower, in an octagonal room with no windows, Norfulk sat cross-legged in the center of the floor. The walls were hung with the same black and crimson silks as the throne room, but this one contained no leisure furniture whatsoever, not even a chair. It held only the apparatus required by a master sorcerer.

An astrolabe sat atop a narrow table covered with charts, scrolls, and potion flasks. Against the opposite wall stood a small ebony cabinet filled with dusty volumes and various magical paraphernalia. A grinning skull topped the cabinet. Something in the size and shape of the macabre relic spoke of bestial origins.

The sorcerer sat before a shallow bowl-like depression in the floor and blew on the still surface of the dark liquid filling the basin. The fresh scent of herbs mingled with the vile stench of rotting flesh rose from the bowl. He murmured an elven phrase while feeding the basin a tidbit of bloody meat, which sank beneath the surface without a ripple. The liquid cleared to a brilliant crystalline blue.

As if a mirror shifted from the sky to the ground, the viewpoint of the vision altered, and the tops of trees appeared within the frame of the bowl's rim. He muttered a second phrase, and with stomach-wrenching speed, the vision zoomed down to focus on a clearing. Two horses were tied beside a large rock, and a man and an elf were disappearing into an opening in the rock.

Even with the fire of Roland's hair dulled, his cousin was unmistakable, and the elf with him bore a strong resemblance to Eeonathor—probably the younger brother he was always blathering about. A sardonic grin curved Norfulk's lips.

Well, well, well. This was a most interesting development. What were they up to? Did they plan to come calling? He must make sure the guest quarters were prepared.

Rising to his feet, he waved a hand over the basin, and the vision faded. In a better mood than he had been for days, he bounded down the tower stairs to the dungeon, bursting into it like a controlled whirlwind. Here, the walls of the keep were damp, and coated with traces of fetid slime. All the cages were windowless and separated from each other by thick stone walls. The stench of unwashed bodies and waste permeated the air. The fourth wall of each pen was the same heavy grill of iron bars he had ensorcelled against Ravenwing.

As he hurried along the corridor, there were piteous calls from some of the cells, and hands in various stages of emaciation reached toward him. Most of the prisoners were human, but there were one or two wasted elves, and a handful of the bestial slavers. Worse than the beggars were the cells that held creatures that could no longer be identified as to race, or even form, hideous remnants of Norfulk's experiments.

On a normal visit, the sorcerer strolled through his dungeon as other men walked in their gardens. Today, his glee drove him past his playthings as if they were not there. Events were moving at last—and he hadn't even had to kill anyone...yet.

He strode to the door of the cage holding Stefan and Ravenwing, taking in the scene within at a glance. Eeonathor napped against one wall, head resting on his crossed forearms. Against the far wall, Daerci lay nestled in the crook of Stefan's elbow, her head on his lap, her chest rising and falling in the even rhythm of sleep.

Stefan's head hung low as if he, too, slept. The sorcerer opened his mouth to call out, and the boy's head flashed up. His black eyes drilled into Norfulk's as he shook his head.

"Let them rest," he murmured.

Norfulk cocked his head at the prince.

"And if I don't?"

Stefan eased Daerci to the floor before pushing to his feet by bracing against the wall. He limped to the door of the cell, every halting step causing obvious pain. Reaching the grille, he put out his hands to support himself on the bars. Only a slight tightening of his jaw betrayed the effect of the charge that had sent Eeonathor stumbling across the room.

"Why should you punish them unnecessarily?" he asked softly. "Ravenwing is no match for your sorcery— he poses you no threat. And Daerci is merely a helpless child. Do not harm them. I am the only one standing in your way. Spare them. Send them away, and I care not what you do to me."

"How noble of you," replied Norfulk, not bothering to hide his sarcasm.

Stefan's eyes closed, and his shoulders sagged.

"I knew it was useless to reason with you, but I had to try. At least spare the girl, and I will do anything you say."

"Anything? Do not make that promise in haste, little prince." He thought for a moment, one finger to his pursed lips, then leaned forward. He whispered in a conspiratorial tone, "What if I ordered you to kill your cousin there to secure her release? Do you love your little thief that much?"

"I cannot." Stefan recoiled, face registering his horror at the suggestion.

"That is my price. Ravenwing is a nuisance. I wish to be rid of him. Kill him, and I will spare your concubine."

"He is my blood—"

"Oh, come, come. You were never close."

"Please, my lord…"

"Here." Norfulk slipped a thin dagger through the bars. "The choice is yours. Destroy the wizard, and I'll let the girl go. As for you, my boy, has life been so sweet death will be a punishment?"

"I never used to think so," replied Stefan, eyes on the floor.

"By the Flames, you really *do* love the wench."

A flash of envy disturbed him. His feelings for Mendana were based on expediency and lust. What would it be like to love something other than oneself with such passion?

***

Stefan huddled in the corner, his head resting on his bent right knee. He traced designs on the stone floor with the point of the dagger. Even if he fulfilled Norfulk's demand, what guarantee did he have Daerci would go free?

He touched the point of the dagger to the inside of his wrist, running it back and forth. Perhaps the direct solution would be best. At least he would be spared the pain of knowing when Norfulk betrayed his promise.

"Little boys shouldn't play with knives, *eathinae*."

Stefan jumped, pricking his arm with the dagger.

"Where did you get that little play toy?" Eeonathor continued, sitting up and leaning against the wall.

"Norfulk." Sighing, Stefan wedged the point between two flagstones.

"He came?" The wizard tensed. "What did he want?"

"For me to kill you."

"Oh?"

Stefan nodded, his eyes drawn to the sleeping girl. His heart twisted

"In exchange for Daerci's freedom," he murmured, voice miserable. "Or so he said."

"Then maybe you should do it."

"What?" He stared at his cousin, wondering if the jolt of the spell had addled his brain.

Ravenwing crossed the cell to kneel in front of him.

"Listen," he whispered. "I know a spell that counterfeits death. With a little blood, I will appear dead. A contingency spell to send my body home when it is searched, and I can continue to work against Norfulk. He will not be pleased, but it's a risk we have to take. I see no other option to escape him."

"Daerci will hate me."

Eeonathor did not try to lie to him, and Stefan was grateful.

"Aye, she probably will. She is going to be hurt and confused. But once I'm free, I can save her. Even when Norfulk betrays you—and you know in your heart he will—I swear I can resurrect her. Just make sure she has this." He slipped the golden pendant from his neck, murmuring the words of a spell over it. "If she dies or becomes unconscious, the amulet will take her home."

"Would you slip it into her pouch?" Stefan asked. "It is hard for me to move quietly. If she catches me, she will not take it."

"Surely, my lord." The wizard slipped across the

cell and carefully tucked the pendant inside the safety of the little thief's belt pouch. "I'm ready."

Stefan struggled to his feet, the dagger clutched in his hand.

"Will it work, Eeonathor?"

"I hope so. I promise you—I will save her if I can, *ethiae ionavae.*"

"I am very frightened."

"It is a brave man who can admit that, Steavil Andundalae."

"He will kill me, won't he?" The thought made Stefan's throat tighten until he found it difficult to breathe.

"He will try, but I hope it will not come to that, my prince."

Ravenwing opened the laces of his snow-white shirt to bare his chest and laid one hand on his cousin's shoulder.

"Strike here," he counseled, ssetting the tip of the dagger against his chest. He pressed two fingers on the blade and whispered a spell. Stefan searched the depths of his sea-green eyes for any sign of hesitation. "Deep enough to draw blood. Do not worry. It will not harm me, *eathinae*—the spell places a brake on the dagger. When the point breaks the skin, the feigned death will take effect. Strike now."

Stefan closed his eyes and put his weight behind the dagger. It slid penetrated with sickening ease. He felt the taller elf slump, and warm blood seeped down the blade to his hand. Gulping against a rush of nausea, he stumbled back from Eeonathor's body.

The wizard fell to the floor with a lifeless thud.

Stefan lurched away, wiping his bloody hand against the side of his leg. His mind spun in chaotic circles, and he felt the prick of tears behind his lashes. He tried to be strong, but his control broke with a strangled groan.

He collapsed to the floor, the dagger still clutched in one hand as he shook with wrenching sobs.

Chapter 34

Shortly after dawn, the allied troops set out from the Ring of Tears, riding toward Crypticia. Roland thrilled at the sight of the men ranked behind him.

There had been more loyal guard than Teodore expected, and nearly twelve score rode into battle. Some were in full armor, and these rode at the head of the line. Those in the rear were green boys and old men in patchwork leathers—but they were all here because they were loyal to Frederick and wanted to fight for him. Roland felt both awed and honored to lead them.

The warders rode on either side of him, bareback on their small, lithe mounts. The plan called for them to break off at the foot of the mountains to circle around and flank Crypticia Keep. Dèodar would ride with his comrades.

But for now, that parting lay in the future. Roland rode between Dèodar and Mendana. He had wanted her to stay behind, but she would have none of it; and Andundal had supported her decision, much to Roland's surprise.

"This is the final stand for the elven race," the king explained. "The few who are left behind will fight to the death, if it comes to that, but they are no match for the Black Lion. If Norfulk really does desire my daughter, she is safer with us than remaining home practically unguarded."

Finally giving in to the inevitable, Roland had to

admit he was glad of her company. If they lost the battle, at least they would have had these last few precious hours together.

They picked their way down from the final foothills to the level plain. The trees of Moonrise Wood were a smudge in the distance. It was time to put the next stage of the plan in motion. The king and Mendana would ride with the main force. Dèodar and Aerlann's patrol of warders would continue along the line of the mountains until they were in position.

"Here, take this," Mendana told her cousin, handing him her bow. "You are better than I—and it is better than that one." She pointed at the weapon Aerlann had loaned him.

Dèodar accepted with a nod.

"Thank you. I promise to return it unharmed."

Roland clasped hands with him.

"Good fortune, my friend," he murmured.

"And you, *entheiro*. I look forward to seeing your human city when this is over." The elf grinned. "I would like to taste this 'stout' Collyn prattled about."

"I'll buy," Roland promised with a laugh.

***

Norfulk sat once more focused on the liquid-filled basin. It provided an even clearer picture than his scrying crystal, and his heart beat a little faster at the sight of Mendana's beauty as she laughed at something the rider beside her had said. He hardly noticed the milling troops around her, enchanted by her smile.

His own smile turned to a snarl when he realized who it was riding beside the princess. And from the way the prince leaned in to take Mendana's hand in his, Roland was his rival in this as well.

"We shall see about that," he growled, passing a hand over the basin, and leaping to his feet. He kicked the now-black liquid, splattering it out onto the floor.

Striding to the thick wooden door, he wrenched it open with enough force to send it slamming against the wall and clattered down the steps of the tower. Fury lent wings to his feet as he burst into the throne room. He had not inherited the ruddy coloring his father and Roland shared, but he owned the fiery temper that went with it.

Calling out in the guttural language of the beasts, he paced, boot heels clicking an impatient tattoo. He gnawed the raw tip of his thumb until the pain began to restore some balance as he waited for a response. As soon as one of the creatures entered the room, he whirled on it.

"What took you so long? Where were you? I have a duty for you."

"I am sorry, my lord."

"Never mind. A company of troops is heading this way out of Starlit Wood. Ambush them. Kill them all if you wish. I care not. But bring me the elven girl and the human prince alive—you know the ones I mean. I want them here by dawn."

"But, my lord—"

"Here." He pulled a vial from the cuff of his sleeve. "Sprinkle a little of this on each of your party, and you will be transported to the plain near the forest. A second measure, and you will be returned to the throne room at once. Take your best men—take all your men, and the slavers, too, if you need them—but I will hold you personally responsible for the safety and return of those two prisoners. Destroy the others. All of them."

The beast took the vial and tucked it into his belt pouch.

"Aye, my lord."

"Go at once."

With a bow, the beast hurried to obey.

***

The attack was a rude awakening. One moment Mendana was laughing with Dèodar and Roland, and the next the plain before them erupted with a band of marauders. Grotesque beasts brandishing curved swords and spears swarmed them.

They had come from nowhere, dozens of them. They were fewer in number, but they were better armed than most of the humans. Ululating cries spooked the horses, and the seasoned guards fought for control while the citizen recruits were hard-pressed to stay on horseback at all. At least a dozen of the youngest were carried from the field by their bolting mounts.

The beasts slashed at the hocks of the remaining horses, unseating many of the armored humans. The dismounted warriors struggled to draw their swords, hampered by the dying animals and their heavy armor.

The elves had started away from the main force before the arrival of the invaders, and they turned back drew their bows, letting fly with deadly precision where they had a clear shot, but the melee hampered their aim. Dèodar and Andundal were caught in the main press, and had no room to use their own bows.

As his horse danced beneath him, Dèodar drew his stiletto from his boot and threw it, catching one of the beasts square in the throat. The creature dropped to its knees with a gurgling cry.

"Retreat to the trees!" Roland shouted. "There are too many of them."

"Aye," replied Dèodar, his face grim as his horse spun in a dancing circle. "Save the princess while you still can, entheiro. They will have us soon. Do not let them take her!"

Roland nodded. He grabbed Mendana's reins.

"I will return," he promised.

He turned Noble, kicking him hard to spur him forward. A group of the beasts split off to follow as their horses broke into a gallop. The creatures kept pace with them despite their speed.

***

Mendana twisted to look behind, straining to see what was happening to the others.

"Roland, we must help them!" Her breath caught in her throat. "Please!"

"I will do what I can, *evleeia*. You ride into the trees." His voice was merciless as he released her reins and wheeled to return to the fray.

She caught his arm.

"Roland, please—be careful!"

"The trees, Mendana!" His sword rang free of its scabbard. With a harsh cry, he thundered back into the fray, slashing about him.

Violent tremors shook her as she tried to distinguish the movements of the plunging horses amid the clumps of howling beasts. Her mount danced beneath her, and she bit her lip in indecision. Should she return, or follow Roland's orders? But what could she do? She had no weapon since she had given her cousin her bow.

Dèodar was knocked from his mount as one of the brutes landed a blow on his head with a heavy morning star. Andundal leapt down to stand over his nephew. He nocked an arrow and let it fly. One of the beasts went down. Her father drew another arrow from his quiver. Before he could nock it to the bow, an attacker struck him from behind. He fell forward over Dèodar's body.

"*Noile!*" Mendana charged, driven by reflex. Rough hands grabbed her legs and dragged her from the horse. She landed hard, the breath knocked from her by the fall. She struggled to breathe as strong arms wrapped around her, scooping her up and holding her tight.

She screamed her fury.

In the middle of the chaos, she saw Roland halt, sword raised. Noble danced first one way then the other as he wavered between choices. While he hesitated, a pair of the vile beasts descended on the gelding.

"No!" The denial burst from her throat.

A heavy blow landed on the side of her head, driving her to her knees. As darkness enfolded her in its suffocating embrace, she realized that all her worst nightmares were about to come true.

***

Roland watched in horror as one of the beasts threw Mendana across its shoulder. He urged the gelding toward it, but a pair of the creatures cut him off. He slashed one with his sword, hacking it nearly in two. The other swept a truncheon down on his wrist.

Pain exploded up his arm. The sword fell from his numbed hand. He fought to control the skittish horse with one hand while fending off the raining blows of the truncheon.

Noble reared, and Roland slid from his back with a wordless cry. The horse danced above him slashing at the attacking beasts with his iron-shod hooves; the prince threw his arms over his head. One of the flying hooves caught him in the side as Noble turned. He grunted with the impact. Sharp agony flared from a snapped rib.

A leathery hand reached down and dragged him to his feet by the throat, sending new pain through him. He struggled against the iron grip. His good fist flailed out, pounding down on the rigid arm attached to the hand around his throat. A blow across the face rocked his head. He tasted blood from a smashed lip. Panic swelled within his breast. He redoubled his efforts to break away.

He managed to wrench free at last and sprinted toward his fallen sword, which lay beneath Noble's dancing hooves. Pain from the grating ends of his rib slowed him, and he jammed a hand against his side as he ran. He could hear the beasts calling back and forth in their guttural voices. Teodore's bellow could be heard over the commotion, rallying his remaining troops to stand firm.

This was a real battle, and he didn't like it. Lunging for the sword, he rolled to his feet with it in his hand. His broken rib ground together again, sending a wave of agony shooting through him. He stood with teeth clenched, the point of the sword on the ground for support as he fought to sublimate the pain. He gazed around, searching for his companions.

Fortenbraes had managed to collect a dozen or so troops around him, and they fought grimly against twice their number. Teodore still roared orders—general to the last—but there were few left to answer him. Andundal still lay across Dèodar. Neither moved.

By the Flames, is the king dead? That will speed the end. Especially now Norfulk has Mendana in his grasp. For he had no doubt this bestial army had been sent by his enemy.

He heard rushing steps behind him, and whirled in time to receive a mailed fist in the mouth. His vision narrowed to a pinpoint, and he crashed to the ground.

Chapter 35

Stefan fell asleep, curled into a defensive ball in the corner of the cell, as far from Ravenwing's body as he could manage. His sleep was once more haunted by dreams...

He was very young, running down an orchard path after Roland. They laughed and played catch with a globefruit. It was long before the dog's attack, and he ran like the wind.

Roland sped up, turned a corner, and Stefan followed, skidding to a halt in horror. Norfulk loomed on the pathway, Roland dangling from a hand circling his windpipe in an iron grip as the prince kicked in a futile attempt to free himself. In the other hand, the Lion held the lifeless body of a raven, its head twisted at a grotesque angle.

"Did you really think you could fool me, little prince?" chided the sorcerer. He threw the bird down and twitched aside his cloak with an angry gesture, revealing Daerci's corpse, green eyes staring. Blood welled from her slit throat.

He screamed, and Norfulk threw back his head and laughed.

Stefan moaned deep in his chest. Eeonathor's trick would accomplish nothing. His cousin would still die, and Daerci as well.

"Master!"

The anguish in the cry snapped Stefan awake. He sat up, the dagger still clasped in his hand. Daerci crouched over Ravenwing's body. Her eyes met his, widening in horrified disbelief when she caught sight of the bloodied weapon.

"What have you done?"

He threw the dagger across the cell, but the damage was done. He saw hatred warring with the love in her eyes, and his heart turned to ash when the hatred won.

He lifted his chin proudly, swallowing hard.

"I made a deal."

She had to believe he had murdered Ravenwing. If she even suspected the trick, Norfulk would see it in her guileless eyes.

"He were yer blood! What kind of 'deal' is worth this price?"

He bowed his head, the last of his spirit melting away before the blaze of her anger.

"I did it to save you," he whispered.

"To save *me*?" She darted across the cell and retrieved the dagger, pressing the point to her breast. "I would rather die than stay here with you!"

"No!" Stefan struggled to his feet, lurching toward her then stumbling to a halt. "Please, Daerci. You are all I have left. Norfulk will not rest until he has my throne. I'll receive my reward for this. I doubt he will let me live the day out. Please! Don't make this sacrifice for nothing."

He hated the naked pleading in his voice but could not bear the thought of her carrying out her threat.

She sank to the floor, letting the dagger drop to the stone.

"I will wait, *ilianae*."

He winced at the virulent epithet.

"I only pray Norfulk will let me watch you die," she spat.

"That can be arranged," murmured a voice from the corridor.

They jerked their heads toward the door. Norfulk leaned against the far side of the corridor. He stepped forward, cocking an eyebrow at the body on the floor.

"So, my little prince. You fulfilled your part of the bargain, I see. You, girl, come here."

Daerci swept up the dagger again and circled the cell, ignoring Stefan.

"What do you want?"

"Examine the body. Is he truly dead?"

She dropped to one knee beside the motionless wizard, rolling him onto his back. She bit back a cry at the blood-soaked shirtfront.

Stefan's stomach clenched.

What if I miscalculated? The wound certainly looked fatal. Suppose Eeonathor was wrong. *Did I kill my own cousin?* He gulped.

Daerci threw one venomous glance in his direction and bent to Ravenwing. She reached to pull aside the bloody shirt, and a shimmering enveloped the body. Daerci rocked back on her heels as the corpse disappeared.

"This wasn't part of our deal!" Norfulk snarled, reaching through the bars, and grabbing her by the shoulders. He slammed her against the cell door, and Stefan saw panic engulf her. The dagger clattered to the floor as her hand jerked open.

"I know nothing about this!" Stefan cried, stepping forward in protest. "Please, let her go. I did what you asked."

"I think not. Whatever trick is involved here, it negates our bargain. Your pawn is forfeit." The sorcerer's hands moved to her throat then tightened around the slim column with crushing force. Daerci clawed at his fingers, struggling for air. "Say goodbye, little prince."

"No!" Stefan dove for the pair at the door, but his knee betrayed him; and he sprawled to the stones. He reached desperately for Daerci's hand, stretched toward him in appeal. Her eyes said she forgave him just before their light faded.

Norfulk let her drop. She crumpled to the floor in a graceless heap. Stefan groaned when the same shimmer that had enveloped Eeonathor surrounded Daerci. He sped a silent prayer to Eostivil his cousin knew what he was doing. When the glow dimmed, he lay alone on the cold stone floor.

"Whatever your pet wizard thinks, he will never defeat me," Norfulk snarled. "All you succeeded in doing is hastening your end, you little fool." The words were charged with cold fury, and Stefan shivered at the venom in the sorcerer's voice.

Norfulk spat out the words of a spell, gesturing at him. Stefan was slammed across the cell to land spread-eagled against the far wall. The manacles snapped shut over his wrists, and he hung helpless a foot above the floor.

"I should have known better than to leave the three of you together, but I am so soft-hearted."

Stefan closed his eyes in resignation. He had nothing left. It was all up to Ravenwing now. And he was so tired...

Norfulk passed a hand before the bars of the door, and the portal swung open. He stepped inside, coming to stand before Stefan. For the first time, the young prince realized the sorcerer's full height. They stared eye-to-eye, despite the distance Stefan hung above the floor. And that wasn't all. There was a haunting familiarity to the spellcaster's features.

Suddenly, he gasped as the resemblance sank in—Norfulk looked like Andundal.

"What's the matter, cousin?" the sorcerer snarled. "Didn't know about the black sheep of the family? I have a legitimate claim to your throne as well, little fool. My mother's blood would have insured I succeeded Andundal if my plans had gone unhindered.

"You and Mendana were both supposed to die with your mother that night at Desolation Lake. Then Mendana stayed behind at the last moment. And you—you slipped through my fingers like water. I tried to call you out, do you remember?"

Stefan stared at him, vague stirrings of memory rippling the surface of his consciousness. He was terrified they would break through.

"You would not come. Not when I beat your mother to the ground before your very eyes. Not even when I slit her throat with that same dagger you used to dispatch your meddling cousin."

"You're lying," Stefan groaned, the words more a plea than a statement. Pictures began to flash through his mind—Deveiria on her knees before a young man in black, his gloved fist smashing into her face as he screamed his fury that he could not find her son. It had been Norfulk, Stefan realized with a shock. It made things much clearer.

The pictures kept coming. His mother sliding to the ground as the attacker stove in her ribs with a vicious kick. The gush of blood engulfing Norfulk when he slit the queen's throat with a single stroke.

"No!" The denial was torn from his throat in a ragged shout.

"She died to save your scrawny neck, you pathetic little wretch. She was worth twelve of you, but she gave her life for you. And she gave you something else, didn't she? Something that postponed this meeting for far too long, my dear cousin."

"My amulet," Stefan murmured, his voice lifeless and dull.

"Yes. If it hadn't been for that blasted amulet of protection, I would have killed you that night and saved us both a great deal of trouble. You were a mere babe. It wouldn't have meant much to you one way or the other. To live, to die—they are equal adventures to a child.

"Instead, you suffered the agonies of injury, betrayal, love, and despair. Your mother did you no favors."

"You will pay for her death," Stefan vowed through gritted teeth, his hands clenching into fists. "I swear to the gods, you will pay."

"Perhaps." Norfulk shrugged. "But you will never see it." Before he could begin his spell, the guttural voice of one of the slaver beasts interrupted. He answered in the same harsh language. "Well, well, well. A brief reprieve after all. It seems I have other guests. Don't worry. I shall return."

Stefan didn't doubt it for an instant.

***

Eeonathor returned to consciousness through a thick haze of pain. His chest felt as if it were on fire—but he lived. He whispered a thank-you to Andailia for her help and gingerly sat up.

The familiar walls of his circular home greeted him. He looked down at the ruins of his favorite shirt with a rueful grimace. One of the hazards of wearing white, he mourned, staring at the crimson bloodstain.

The dried blood had stiffened the shirt, and he winced when he peeled it away from the shallow wound. Pulling it over his head, he moved to the washbasin to sponge away the gore then, laying two fingers over the gash, murmured a brief spell; the wound closed.

Stiff with pain, he bent to retrieve another shirt from his clothes chest. The cedar was silky under his hand, and its sharp scent brought a comforting rush of memory. His father had crafted it for his mother from a tree in Moonrise Wood. His fingers tightened on the edge of the chest as he drank in the comfort. It provided a brief moment of sanity in the chaos.

He returned to the matter at hand as he pulled the shirt over his head. Had the ruse worked? He closed his eyes and shook his head. Of course not. Norfulk was no fool. He would have seen through the trick in a heartbeat. But at least it had bought him a little time.

A shimmering above his sleeping couch caught his attention, and his breath hissed in his throat. Already? Norfulk had wasted no time.

He hurried to the velvet-draped lounge, kneeling beside it. He wanted to reassure her as soon as possible. She would be blaming her prince, he feared.

Daerci's slender frame materialized on the soft green couch. Her head hung limply to one side, livid bruises standing out against the tan of her throat. He swore a soft oath, grabbing her wrist and checking for a pulse. He felt more at ease when his fingertips found a slow, erratic beat. She would be all right.

He placed a hand on her forehead, murmuring the words of a healing charm. She moaned, breathing Stefan's name in a hoarse whisper. Ravenwing grinned to himself. *Yes, she will be fine.*

He slipped an arm under her shoulders as her eyelids fluttered open, lifting her up. She coughed against the constriction in her bruised throat.

"M-master?" she croaked in wonder. "I thought you were dead."

"You were supposed to, *ethiae ruathia*. Unless you believed it, Norfulk wouldn't have, either. Stefan must be a better actor than I gave him credit for." He helped her to sit.

"He said he killed you to save me. He had the dagger in his hand."

"Aye. He did, indeed, deliver the blow, and it nearly killed him, *evleeia*. He is a gentle soul. Norfulk will destroy him."

"We must save him, Master! We must."

Eeonathor sank down on the edge of the couch, studying his hands as he tried to frame the correct words.

"There is a larger picture here, *ruathia*. The most important thing we must do is to stop Norfulk. We fight to save the entire continent. If...if Steavil must die to accomplish that, we cannot change it. And he would not want us to."

"That ain't fair!"

"No. It isn't fair, but it is the truth. I hope it won't come to that, but you must be prepared for it, if it does. I know he is."

"Why are we just sitting here? We best be going." She jumped to her feet.

"Hold on, Flame-Cat. We need a plan. It will do us no good to rush into Norfulk's arms again. And we need to locate the others. The larger our force, the greater our chances.

"Roland will have spoken to his father. With luck, he will be leading an army against his cousin. Perhaps the elves can still play a part in this fight. Bring me my stone. I will try and find my brother."

Daerci nodded before retrieving the crystal globe. She carefully carried it to him, and he set it up on a low stand next to the couch. She sat cross-legged at his feet.

"Reach into your pouch and hand me that little trinket, will you?" he asked in an absent tone, holding out his hand.

She frowned, doing as he bid her. He grinned when her eyes widened at finding the chain and its topaz pendant.

"How did this get there?" she asked, pulling it out and placing it in his hand.

"I put it there. Now, be quiet and let me concentrate."

He slipped the chain over his head and took the pendant in his hand. He bent all his thoughts to his brother. He pictured Dèodar as he'd last seen him, looking up into the rocks before the ambush. He willed the crystal to show him the warder's whereabouts.

Gradually, a picture formed in the depths of the

globe. He saw the feet of the mountains spilling onto the blighted plain, and the distant edge of Moonrise Wood. Riders picked their way down from the foothills—a long column of armored men with a small party of elves at their head. Ravenwing recognized Dèodar in the lead, with their uncle behind him; and the wizard drew his breath with a hiss. *What can Andundal be thinking to leave the palace? It leaves the stronghold virtually defenseless!* He sensed a grim urgency in the riders. *They must have learned of Norfulk's captive.*

A tiny flare of jealousy ran through him when he recognized Mendana riding beside Roland. But, again, he could see the larger picture. Mendana and Roland could unite the kingdoms, and he wished his cousin well.

As he watched, a horde of the beasts beset the column, emerging out of thin air. The warriors fought with desperate courage but were hampered by their terrified horses—and then by their armor, in the case of the humans, and a lack of melee weapons, in the case of the elves.

Roland spurred his mount away from the fray, dragging Mendana's horse out of the fighting. Dèodar went down, knocked from his horse, and dispatched by a blow from a morning star. Andundal leapt from his own animal, visible even as the raiders circled. He nocked an arrow and fired. He reached for another arrow but fell, struck from behind.

As Roland spun his horse back into the fight, a slaver grabbed Mendana. The prince hesitated, and a pair of beasts cut him off from any escape.

Ravenwing watched the fight through to its bloody conclusion—broken warriors littering the field, human and elf alike. Mendana and Roland were carried from the field, but his brother and uncle were left where they had fallen. As if they were not worth troubling with.

Despite Mendana's ascendancy to the Moonrise throne—and my brother's lack of pretension—Dèodar is a prince in his own right. My uncle is a king. How dare this upstart pretender treat the royalty of my race so cavalierly? At times like these, I can understand what drove our ancestors to war with the humans.

"What do you see, Master?" asked Daerci with soft curiosity.

"Trouble. Get my things."

Daerci moved to collect their belongings with practiced efficiency. She asked no questions, for which he was grateful—he was in no mood to be civil. She could not be blamed for being human, but he could not help but hold it against her at this moment. He had no immediate family left other than his brother. If Dèodar were dead, Norfulk would rue the day. Somehow, someway, he would avenge that death.

Daerci came to stand beside him, his worn leather bag of healing supplies clutched to her chest. She remained silent, but her eyes spoke volumes. He threw an arm around her shoulders with a little squeeze of gratitude and grasped the pendant, murmuring the translocation spell. The shimmer engulfed them, and when it faded, they stood on a field torn by thundering hooves.

There were fallen slaver beasts sprawled in bloody heaps from the foot of the mountains halfway across the plain to the forest. But more of the dead were human—and Eeonathor caught sight of at least a dozen elves.

The dainty mare stood over Dèodar, as if protecting her master. Noble grazed nearby.

Eeonathor strode across the field and went down on one knee beside his fallen kin. He examined the bodies but could find no pulse on either. A bloody gash on the back of Andundal's skull appeared to be the cause of death. He moved him to one side with tender hands.

An anguished moan escaped him at sight of his brother's wound. The morning star had caught Dèodar in the temple, caving in the right side of his face. Even if he could restore life, the merry elf would never be the same.

He bowed his head, his jaw working violently as he struggled with the emotions surging through him. Daerci handed him his bag and left to round up the horses, sensitive enough to know he would rather be alone.

Working with swift expertise, he cleaned Andundal's wound, stitching the edges of the gash together and murmuring a spell as he worked. He levered the king's body up to rest on his bent knee and took a vial from his bag. Snapping the cork out of the potion with his thumb, he slipped the mouth of the vial between Andundal's lips then let his uncle's head drop back.

The liquid of the potion poured into the king's throat, and after a moment, Andundal let out a ragged gasp. Eeonathor whispered a prayer of thanks to Andailia and her brother Eostivil. *Healing and Luck both had a hand in this day, though I could wish the gods less capricious.*

"What happened?" asked Andundal, his voice hoarse.

"You were attacked, my lord."

The king struggled to sit up.

"Mendana?"

"Norfulk's minions took her and Prince Roland to Crypticia."

"Dèodar?"

Eeonathor's teeth ground together.

"There is nothing I can do for him. My healing skill is not great enough to heal so grave a wound." He met Andundal's eye with a bleak shrug. "And I only had one revivifying potion."

"What about your magic?"

"Some things even magic cannot do, my lord."

"I am sorry, Eeonathor. *Euae astami areistia, ethiae alianiae.*"

"*Itheamia.*" He sighed, sagging under a sudden weariness. "I thank you for that. I will bury him in Starlit Wood—with your permission. It is his home now."

"Of course. I lift your banishment, Eeonathor Eriaborae. You are welcome in Starlit Wood. I am sorry it has been so long coming."

Ravenwing nodded, fighting back the tears stinging behind closed lids. He could go home...but at what cost?

"Eeonathor," Andundal murmured, holding out a silver badge. "Bury this with him. I want him to be remembered as a full warder."

The wizard took it with a reverent sigh.

"Dèodar would be so proud." He pinned the badge above the warder's heart and bent to gather his brother in his arms. "I shall return for my companion, my lord. This I must do alone." Dèodar slumped against his chest like a sleeping child as the wizard struggled to his feet. "Norfulk will pay dearly for this."

Eeonathor Ravenwing translocated to the fringes of Starlit Wood and carried his brother's body into the shelter of the trees. He found a break in the underbrush that led into a tiny clearing.

A shaft of late-afternoon sunlight arrowed down through the canopy of leaves as Ravenwing laid Deodar on the ground. Letting his grief and anger channel through his fingertips in an arc of blue flame that blasted into the packed dirt, he cried out a spell. A crater appeared in the center of the clearing.

He placed Dèodar gently in the grave and folded the warder's hands on his breast then, bowing his head, murmured, "I am sorry for the pain I caused you, little brother. I never got a chance to tell you so. *Ithneili endi, inithi thiuveia*. Rest easy, Dèodar Eriaborae."

Passing a hand over the grave, he chanted a second spell, and a mound rose over the body. Vines twined over the bare dirt to create a soft green hillock. A single white blossom bloomed in the center of the shaft of soft sunlight. Saving his brother had been beyond his powers—but he could make sure Dèodar was remembered.

"A *rieathinarae* for you, my brother, the flower of remembrance," he whispered. "I swear to you—I shall never forget."

Chapter 36

Norfulk sat on his throne wearing a self-satisfied smirk. Mendana knelt before him, arms pinned behind her back by one of the beasts. A hand fisted in her thick braids forced her head up to meet his eye.

"Well, well, well. Happily met, my queen. You cannot know how long I have waited for this day."

She spat at him. He laughed with delight.

"Oh, I do so love a feisty wench. One thing I had in common with your unfortunate brother. Did I mention I knew your brother? Sad to say, our acquaintance proved a short one."

He could tell the shot hit home.

"By the way, I have another friend of yours as my guest." He gestured, and one of the bestial servants left the room to return dragging Roland. The beast kicked his legs out from under him, and the prince fell to his knees with a heavy thud.

"Look at what we have here," Norfulk purred, snapping his fingers.

The beast jerked Roland's head back, and Mendana gasped. The prince's lip was split, and one eye was swollen shut.

"Not so pretty now, is he, my pet?" Norfulk rose from the throne and circled Roland. "Just think. This is all that stands between me and the throne of Irthlan." He kicked Roland in the side, catching him square in the broken rib. His cousin groaned and doubled forward.

Mendana cried out, lunging toward Roland. The

hand in her hair yanked her back. Norfulk clicked his tongue in mock sorrow. He moved to tower over her.

"Still loyal to the wrong House I see, my beauty. Well, never let it be said I am ungenerous. I will give you time alone with your stalwart swain. You will soon see the wisdom of the more expedient choice." He ran a caressing finger down her jaw. "Oh, yes," he continued. "Let me express my deepest condolences on the loss of your father. This is, indeed, a sad day for you. To lose your entire family like that must be hard— father, brother, cousins. But just think—you found a bridegroom to take their place."

"I would rather die!" Mendana struggled against the beast holding her.

"You will change your mind, my love. You'll see." He returned to the throne and threw himself on it. "Take them away." Leaning into the soft cushions, he steepled his fingers as his orders were obeyed.

"Not a bad day's work at all," he purred to himself. "In one fell swoop, I have destroyed the ranks of the elven nobility. Only one loose end stands in the way of my throne, and that particular problem will not trouble me for long. But where, oh, where has my pet blackbird gone...a good question, indeed."

***

Stefan swam in and out of consciousness. A cold emptiness resided where his heart used to be. He whispered another prayer that Eeonathor's plan had worked.

"As long as Daerci is well and safe, I can die content."

He no longer entertained any illusions of rescue. A direct assault on the castle would never work, and there was no time for stealth. *I just hope I will not disgrace my family honor.*

He heard footsteps approaching and steeled himself for whatever might come.

"Please! Be careful. He is hurt!" a woman cried out. Catching his breath with a hiss, Stefan recognized Mendana's voice.

"By the gods, what is she doing here?" he whispered, closing his eyes.

"Are you all right, *evleeo*?" she continued, her tone strained and anxious.

"Yes, *ithneimi endia, ethiae ionavia*. Rest easy, my princess." Roland's voice, and he sounded exhausted, his voice thick with pain.

Stefan jerked against the manacles holding him to the wall. Norfulk had left them loose for greater damage, and his wrists were slick with blood; he pulled his left hand free with little trouble. Grabbing the chain above his right wrist, he dangled in mid-air, trying to force the other hand through the cuff. Years spent exercising it with the lute proved his undoing. He could not squeeze it through the iron band.

"Eostivil, be with me," he muttered, gritting his teeth, and he smashed his hand against the stones of the wall. Agony flared as bones shattered. He slammed it against the stone again, felt the bones in his wrist separate. He folded the hand in until it finally slipped through the cuff.

Dropping to the floor, he curled into a ball. Every day of his life for the past six years had been filled with pain. It did not take him long to sublimate the new torment.

Stuffing his broken hand into the front of his shirt to immobilize it, he staggered to the bars. The shock of the warding spell seemed trivial in the face of his other injuries.

"Mendana!" he shouted, his voice hoarse as he clutched a bar with his good hand. "Are you all right?"

"Stefan!" She craned her head back over her shoulder as her guards herded her past. "Thank the goddess you're alive!"

"You there! Get back," growled one of the beasts, flicking a whip in his direction. Stefan stumbled away from the door. He huddled in a corner and cradled his right arm.

Once the guards are gone, I will figure some way out of this cell. I have to rescue Mendana and Roland. I have to!

There was no one else who could.

***

Mendana's heart leapt at the sound of her brother's voice; she had feared never to hear it again. Roland stumbled, and she reached out to steady him. Her immediate concern was for the human prince. He must be suffering intense pain. She longed to hold him in her arms and ease away as much of it as possible.

The guards thrust them into a cell and locked the iron grate that served as a door.

"Rest well, pretty lady," one of the beasts snorted. "The master won't make you wait long."

Coarse laughter erupted from the creature's companions; then the party rambled off the way they had come. A pair of the burly creatures remained behind to guard the cell.

Mendana hurried to Roland. He lay huddled on his side, arms crossed protectively over his broken rib. Shock and exhaustion grayed his face.

"Let me do what I can," she murmured.

His features shone with sweat, and his good eye fought to focus on her face.

"Mendana," he croaked.

"Yes, my love?"

"Marry Norfulk."

"Are you insane?"

"If you marry him, he will let you live. Please, promise me."

She brushed the hair from his fevered forehead with a tender caress.

"Hush, Roland." She felt her cheeks grow crimson but plunged on. "Even if I believed that, I will marry no one but the man I love, *evleeo*."

"He will kill me, Mendana."

"Don't talk that way." She placed a finger across his lips. "He may try, but he'll not succeed if I can help it."

She clutched the Moonstone through her shirt. Breathing a prayer to Andailia, she concentrated all her power into healing the fractured rib. Roland cried out and fainted, but his breathing eased. Mendana slumped back against the bars, her power drained for the moment.

"I hope it is enough, my dearest. I fear there is worse to come."

***

As soon as the guards passed his cell, Stefan crawled to the bars. Norfulk's dagger still lay on the floor, forgotten. Swallowing hard as the sorcerer's description of his mother's death rang in his head, he swept up the blade in his left hand and thrust it through the bars. He slipped the point of the blade into the lock, holding his breath as he rocked it back and forth in the mechanism.

It was awkward attempting to manipulate the unseen lock, but he persisted.

"I wish Daerci were here...this would be child's play for her. I just hope I can—"

A faint click rewarded his patient efforts, and the bars snapped open. Stefan thanked Eostivil, and slipped into the corridor, dagger held ready. He headed in the direction they had taken his sister, peering into each cell he passed. His heart turned over at the sight of the creatures wasting away in Norfulk's prison.

He turned a corner then ducked back, heart hammering in his throat. Two of the beastial creatures stood halfway down the corridor. He had little doubt he had found Mendana and Roland.

But what do I do now? I'm no match for those creatures.

He wracked his brains for some way to distract the guards away from the cell. He had nothing to work with except the dagger and his wits—and those had been failing him regularly of late.

A shiver ran through him as a phantom touch brushed his hand. He glanced down and choked back a cry at sight of the skeletal fingers reaching through the bars of the cell behind him.

"Set me free..." whispered a voice like wind in trees. "Set me free."

Stefan turned to face the bars. The being within had

been rendered sexless by emaciation. Even whether it was elf or human was impossible to tell.

"There are guards around the corner," Stefan whispered back. "It would be no kindness."

The creature cocked its head, listening.

"The guards will be no matter. One is preparing to do a sweep patrol of the far corridors—and there are a great many corridors. The other is...regretting a bad choice of entrée at his last meal and in need of relief."

"How do you know?"

"Given enough time in these cells, you, too, would understand the beasts. Shh...the ill one is coming this way."

Stefan faded back down the corridor to his cell, stepping inside and holding the door closed just as the guard hurried by. The beast didn't even glance his way. As soon as it was out of sight around the corner, he headed for Mendana and Roland.

When he passed the cage containing his unknown adviser, the hand reached out.

"Do not forget me!"

"I will return for you, I promise."

"Hurry. There are many corridors, but even so..."

Stefan nodded and hobbled to where his sister and Roland were being held. The prince lay unconscious, his face battered almost beyond recognition. Mendana cradled his head in her lap. She looked up at Stefan's approach, prepared to fight, if necessary.

An almost comical relief swept over her face when she recognized him. She lowered Roland to the floor and came to clasp Stefan's wrist through the bars.

"Steavil, I thought I would never see you again."

"That would have seemed a fair bet."

He fit the point of the dagger in the lock with clumsy fingers. Her eyes widened at the sight of his makeshift sling.

"What happened to your hand?"

"It's nothing," he protested impatiently, jiggling the dagger in the lock. "I'll have you free as soon as I can. How fares the prince?"

"He has a broken rib, but it should mend now. His face looks worse than it is, I think. I just worry that something else is wrong. He seems so weak."

Finally, the lock clicked, and the door opened. Stefan stepped into the cell.

"Let's see if I can tell. Can you help me here?"

He lifted his right hand out of his shirt so he could pull the garment loose and get to the ring sewn in the hem. Mendana gasped when she caught sight of the bloody, swollen mess. She grasped it gently between her own.

"Steavil Andundalae! What have you done?"

"Norfulk had me in chains. The cuff was too small to slip my hand through, so I made my hand smaller." He shrugged.

"Oh, Steavil..."

"Don't worry, it's fine. We don't have much time. The guards may return at any moment. Help me get to the Bloodstone—it is sewn into the hem of my shirt."

She retrieved the ring for him and slipped it on his left hand. The stone paled to half its original blood-red color then held steady.

"He's not dying—yet. I think he will recover if we can get him out of the castle. Do you think he could walk?"

"We can try." She bent to Roland, her voice gentle as she placed a hand on his shoulder to awaken him. "*Ethia ionavo*...there's someone here to see you."

Roland's good eye blinked open to focus blearily on Stefan. A look of such joy flooded his battered face the elf gulped hard.

"Where have you been, *inithi iothinae*?" croaked Roland. "You're never around when I need you."

Stefan reached to help him stand.

"Come, my prince. We must get out of here as soon as we can. Norfulk's guards won't leave you alone for long."

"Aye. Lead the way, *entheirae*."

"Here, take this." Stefan handed Roland the dagger. "You will get more use from it than I."

Roland nodded, hefting the weapon in his hand.

"'Tis a good blade."

Stefan's eyes grew hard.

"It has served its purposes. The stairs are this way."

With cautious steps, he led the way to the dungeon stairs. However, once they reached the top he was at a loss. He had been translocated into his cell, and he had no idea of the castle's layout. He turned to Roland, his shoulders sagging.

"Do you know this keep?"

"I heard that my uncle Roderick patterned it after Crown Keep," Roland answered. His tone was thoughtful. "If so, there should be a way out down this corridor." He gestured with the point of the dagger. "It's worth a try."

They stole along the wide corridor, ears straining for any sound. They had gone only a few yards when the clumping of boots made them stare at each other in panic. Stefan threw open a door, and they piled into the room beyond.

"Oh, well done!" congratulated a melodious voice behind them. "You saved me the trouble of fetching you."

They spun—to find themselves in the throne room. Stefan groaned, sagging against the door at his back.

"Some leader I turned out to be."

Norfulk lounged on his throne, booted foot flung over the arm with customary abandon.

"Well, well, well. The final move is about to be played, my young princes. I shall marry the queen, and the kingdoms shall be mine. We will live happily ever after. Unfortunately, the same cannot be said for the two of you."

Roland stepped forward and threw the dagger. It landed quivering in the back of the throne, inches from Norfulk's head.

"That wasn't very nice," snapped the Lion, leaping to his feet and pointing in his cousin's direction.

Blue fire arced out to catch Roland in the chest, and the prince dropped to the floor like a stone. Mendana stepped in front of him as though to shield him.

"Now, as for you, little prince..." Norfulk snarled, whirling toward Stefan.

A golden shimmer filled the air, and Ravenwing appeared. He was flanked by Andundal and Daerci. The topaz pendant glowed around the wizard's neck.

Norfulk glared at him.

"I should have guessed your ruse, wizard. Wait your turn! First, I have business with our prince."

He raised his hand to cast at Stefan. Daerci threw herself in front of the elf just as the blue flame shot forth. The beam caught her squarely, and she crumpled in a heap at Stefan's feet.

"No!" He fell to his knees beside her, throwing up his uninjured hand. He would not lose her now. He would protect her to his last breath.

Norfulk threw back his head and laughed.

"Young and in love...isn't it sweet?" His face contorted in a snarl. "Too sweet to live. I will enjoy this." He raised his hand to cast again.

A golden bolt arced from the pendant around Eeonathor's neck. The wizard stared as the amber beam of light arrowed towards Stefan. An opalescent beam from the concealed Moonstone burned a smoking hole through Mendana's green shirt. The pearly light shone like moonlight itself as it converged on the elven prince.

The streams of light twined about the ring on Stefan's finger, and he felt power rush through him. He gasped, fighting to control it lest it shatter him to pieces.

His raised hand glowed with an inner fire. A blood-red beam shot from his palm and engulfed the blue of the sorcerer's flame then traveled along it to catch Norfulk full in its power. The sorcerer screamed.

The light grew in intensity until it became impossible to look at directly. Then, with a booming clap of thunder, the crimson light disappeared.

Norfulk had vanished. No trace of the sorcerer remained.

Stefan caught Daerci up in his arms, his heart in his

throat. She seemed nearly weightless.

"Let me see her," murmured Ravenwing, his voice gentle as he went down on one knee beside them. He examined the girl with quick skill; Stefan heard him praying softly to Andailia.

Daerci stirred. Her eyes opened, and she blinked up at the anxious prince.

"Ye almost got yerself killed again, *iothinae*," she chided him, her voice rough. "What am I going to do with ye?"

He stopped her complaining with a kiss.

***

Roland felt like a mule had kicked him in the chest. It hurt worse than when the horse had broken his rib. He groaned and reluctantly opened his eye—the one that still worked. He stared up at Mendana.

"You know, this is beginning to be a habit, *evleeia*," he murmured. "I could get used to this."

She smiled down at him. "Can you sit up?"

"I think so." Groaning, he managed it. He saw that he was still in the Crypticia throne room—but Norfulk was nowhere to be seen. "What happened?"

"No one is really sure."

"I am." Stefan limped over to them, his arm around Daerci's shoulders.

"Then tell the rest of us," urged Eeonathor.

A faraway look drifted over the elven prince's face, and his clear voice soared angelically as he sang the ballad he had found in Roland's book. He bowed his head when the echoes died away.

"The song is an old one, as it says. I saw the lyrics

first in Starlit Keep but didn't understand them. I forgot about it until today. I still do not completely understand the magics of it, but I believe that somehow, when we combined the powers of the three stones, the resultant energy turned Norfulk's spell against him."

He continued, "Until the three artifacts came together under just the right circumstances, they were merely focal points for the gifts of the gods they represent. Mendana's pendant focused her healing. It is under Andailia's sway. My pendant focused Eeonathor's magic because Eostivil rules it. Is not all magic merely luck?

"The ring combines the two yet serves neither. Its 'everyday' function is to show when the owner needs healing if he is lucky." Stefan chuckled self-consciously at the wordplay.

"Well, *ethiae entheirae.*" Roland clapped him on the shoulder. "You saved my kingdom. How can I ever repay you?"

"By following your heart and joining my family. If Father has no objections?" Stefan turned to Andundal as Mendana blushed scarlet.

"I fear I have no choice in the matter," the king mourned in mock dismay, throwing an arm around his son's shoulders. "Not that I would offer any resistance," he hastened to add when Roland's face fell. "I would be honored to link my House with yours, Roland Frederickson."

"And I with yours," Roland replied with all his heart. "If my lady will have me."

Mendana threw herself into his arms. "*Euia everiali muae, ethia ionavo.* I love you, my prince."

"Thank you, my princess. *Itheamia, ethiae ionavia.*"

"Well, then," cried Eeonathor, "it seems a celebration is in order." He took Mendana's hands. "Be happy, *evleeia*. It is all either Dèodar or I ever wanted for you."

"*Itheamia*, my cousin."

"Now I must head home," Roland announced, his face grim. "I'm anxious to make sure my father is safe." He slipped his arm around Mendana's shoulders. His expression softened as he gazed into her eyes. "Will you come to see my castle, beloved? It is not as spectacular as Starlit Keep, but it is lovely to me."

"Anywhere we are together is beautiful to me," she answered, her soft voice full of love.

His heart sang—until Andundal and Stefan caught his eye and brought him back to the present with a jolt.

"But I must go quickly now. My own father is still in grave danger. Beauty and happiness can wait until he is safe. I must return home at once and make sure of his health. There are also my troops to attend to—I don't know who survived the ambush, but I know we have much to do to restore peace to Irthlan."

He started for the door but moved too fast. The resulting stab of pain doubled him over. Mendana forced him to sit down.

"Mendana, I must return to my father," he protested, struggling to rise.

"You are not going anywhere until I say so, you stubborn, stubborn man!"

Roland gave in with a sigh.

Chapter 37

Ravenwing noticed the pallor on Daerci's face as she stood with her arm around Stefan's waist. He opened his mouth to say something, but Stefan turned to him before the words left his lips.

"Could you make sure Daerci is all right? That was no light spell Norfulk threw."

He sensed his cousin needed to speak to Andundal alone and nodded.

"Come, *ruathia*." He slipped an arm under hers and led her to a low stool in one corner. She sat without a word, and began running her replacement sling through her fingers abstractedly.

There was a telltale sparkle to her eyes, and she bit her lip.

"What's the matter, little one?" he asked gently, though his heart could guess.

She refused to meet his eye. "Stefan will return to his kingdom now, to learn to be king. He ain't going to need the likes of me tagging along."

"I think you gravely underestimate my cousin, *ruathia*. You are right, he must be taught to rule. He has not been groomed for the throne. He thinks differently than your stereotypical prince." He patted her hand. "I think a little thief, good with a sling, might be just the type of consort he needs to keep him out of trouble."

She stared up at him, her expression bleak. The maturity he had recently begun to notice hollowed her cheeks.

"It might be what he wants, Master, but it ain't what he needs. There's a difference."

"You are growing up, little one," he murmured, reaching out to stroke her cheek. His hand came away damp.

★★★

"Noile, I have a question for you," Stefan murmured as Andundal coaxed him to sit on the abandoned throne. "Norfulk told me many things, some of which I understood and others I did not."

His heart spasmed in his chest as he remembered the visions Norfulk had unleashed from his deepest subconscious.

"One thing puzzles me. He said his mother would have insured his claim to your throne if Mendana and I had been murdered as children. What did he mean?"

Andundal paled. "Arialaina," he breathed.

"Who?"

"I...had a sister as well, *ethiae thuathae*. She was a lovely creature, gentle as spring rain, and the soul of goodness. One day, she went to the river to collect herbs and flowers. She disappeared without a trace.

"A warder patrol reported later a boat went downriver shortly before we discovered her missing, and they thought they might have heard a cry. I never saw her again. Could the Lion's father have abducted her?"

"I would not consider it likely, Father. From what I have heard of Roderick Benedickson, he was an honorable man. We may never know how it came to be he was acquainted with your sister, but it is likely she was Norfulk's mother, from his resemblance to you."

"How could any child of my sweet sister grow to be so bitter?"

"If he felt he was denied both his birthrights," Stefan answered, "I could almost understand his reasons."

His father heaved a deep sigh.

"There has been too much bloodshed. Too many of our family have died. It is time to create instead of destroy, and I believe the future lies there." He smiled at Mendana, who sat cradling Roland in her arms.

"Aye. The elves are dying, Father. We will not last if we do not change. It is time we link our fortunes with the humans."

The king laid a gentle hand on his son's shoulder.

"It is true. Our world is changing. Perhaps the humans do have something to teach us."

"I believe they do, Noile...and I have found my own teacher as well." Stefan felt a blush rise to his cheeks. "Eeonathor's little thief has stolen my heart." Stefan met his father's eye. "Daerci makes me *feel* like a prince, Father—that is a miracle in itself."

"Then hold her close, my son."

"I shall. Let me..." He turned to call her so that he could introduce her to his father, but she was nowhere to be seen.

Stefan stared around the room in a panic. After all they had been through, he could not lose her now.

Finally, he saw her in a far corner of the chamber, huddled against the wall. He crossed the room and knelt awkwardly before her.

"What is it, *evleeia*? Are you in pain?"

She shook her head, not meeting his eye. "I...I couldn't bear to see ye so happy and know I weren't never going to share that again," she mumbled, her face miserable.

"What do you mean? I want you to share everything with me, Daerci. You are my life."

"No, yer kingdom must be yer life. Ye'll have a lot to do to rebuild it. The elves are dying, milord." She blushed crimson. "Ye needs must find yerself a nice elven wife who can bear ye fine sons."

"But I don't want an elven wife." He reached up and cupped her cheek. "I want you," he continued with soft urgency. "Besides, the only elven maiden available is my sister." He grinned a crooked grin. Then he grew serious once more. "You are right, dear one," he continued. "The days of the elves are done. It is time to combine the strengths of the races. Mendana and Roland will have a beautiful family, and we will visit them often, but the heirs to Starlit Wood will be half-elven as well, or there will be no heirs."

"Ye don't know what ye're saying, milord!"

"Oh, yes, I do. If you won't have me, Daerci, my line shall end with me. I could never love another as I love you. My fate is in your hands. Will you have me?"

Stefan swallowed hard and held out his hand to her. His breath caught in his throat. His future happiness hung on the next words out of her mouth.

Overwhelming joy transformed her plain face into a vision of ethereal beauty. Her eyes shone as she placed her hand in his.

"Oh, aye, Stefan. I will have ye."

He swept her into his arms, clasping her to him with all his strength. Stefan Andundalae, child of two worlds, had found his luck at last.

Dictionary of the Elvish Language

PRONOUNS

Person	First	Second	Third	Plural
Personal/Male	Euae	Twuae	Ruae	Ruaen
Personal/Female	Euia	Twuia	Ruia	Ruian
Possessive/Male	Ethiae	Twiae	Riae	Riaen
Possessive/Female	Ethia	Twia	Ria	Rian

VERB TENSE ENDINGS

Present	Past	Future
-mi	-ni	-li

GENDER ENDINGS

	Male	Female	Human
Nouns	-ae	-ia	-o
Adjectives	-ia	-ia	-io

Glossary

Aithar – to halt
Alianiae – nephew
An – to
Andailia – Elven goddess of healing
Areistia – sorry
Astar – to be
Astreal (es) – star (s)
Bostiea – fine
Deastia – please
Deimevia – forever
Ealir – to cry
Eathinae (ia; o) – cousin
Encrir – to do
Endi (ia; o) – easy
Enirmae – you're welcome
Entheirae (ia; o) – friend
Eostivil – Elven god of luck
Everiar – to love
Evleeae (ia; o) – beloved one
Ilianae (ia; o) – untranslatable epithet
Inithi (ia; io) – little
Inth – me
Ionavae (o) – prince
Ionavia – princess
Iothinae (ia; o) – fool
Itheamia – thank you
Ithneir – to rest
Istionthi – animals bred by elves for underground use

Liar – to feel
Linavae (o) – king
Linavia – queen
Leietae – like
Ne— prefix indicating negative state
Neve – no
Noile – father
Oluvi – treacherous
On – as
Opieviar – open
Oth – the
Re— prefix indicating positive state
Reve – yes
Rieathinarae – Elven name for a small, white star-shaped blossom
Riuveia – sister
Ruathia – daughter
Stear – to be certain
Stimariar – to command
Thieae – brother
Threar – to take
Thyesti – dungeon
Thuathae – son
Vieindi – better
Veisthi – promise
Veisthir – to promise
Yrethsti – enough

About the Author

Rie Sheridan Rose has been writing professionally for the last ten years or so as "Rie Sheridan." In that decade, she published four novels, one short story collection, two chapbooks of collected stories, and five poetry collections as well as contributing to several anthologies. Her stories have also been published in The Eternal Night, ShadowKeep and Verge ezines, as well as the EOTU and Planet Relish websites. Her poetry had appeared in the print magazines Mythic Circle, Dreams of Decadence, and Abandoned Towers as well as the Electric Wine and Tapestry ezines.

Her most popular stories to date are the adventures of Bruce and Roxanne, humorous horror shorts several of which have been collected into two print chapbooks. She has also written the lyrics to several songs for Marc Gunn.

Rie lives in Texas with her husband Newell and several cats, all spoiled rotten.

www.ingramcontent.com/pod-product-compliance
Lightning Source LLC
Chambersburg PA
CBHW020500020726
47493CB00001B/116